F
Sh 1   Shabtai, Yaakov.
b   Past perfect.

Temple Israel Library
Minneapolis, Minn.

Please sign your full name on the above card.

Return books promptly to the Library or Temple Office.

Fines will be charged for overdue books or for damage or loss of same.

PAST PERFECT

Books by Yaakov Shabtai available in English

PAST CONTINUOUS
PAST PERFECT

PAST PERFECT

Yaakov Shabtai

TRANSLATED BY
DALYA BILU

WITH AN AFTERWORD BY
EDNA SHABTAI

VIKING

VIKING
Viking Penguin Inc., 40 West 23rd Street,
New York, New York 10010, U.S.A.
Penguin Books Ltd, Harmondsworth,
Middlesex, England
Penguin Books Australia Ltd, Ringwood,
Victoria, Australia
Penguin Books Canada Limited, 2801 John Street,
Markham, Ontario, Canada L3R 1B4
Penguin Books (N.Z.) Ltd, 182–190 Wairau Road,
Auckland 10, New Zealand

First published in 1987 by Viking Penguin Inc.
Published simultaneously in Canada

First published in Hebrew under the title of *Sof Davar*
by Siman Kriah, Israel.
Copyright © 1984 by Edna Shabtai, Hamutal Shabtai
and Orly Shabtai.

LIBRARY OF CONGRESS CATALOGING IN PUBLICATION DATA
Shabtai, Yaakov.
  Past perfect.
  Translation of: Sof davar.
  I. Title.
PJ5054.S2643S613 1987   829.4'36   86-40493
ISBN 0-670-81308-7

Printed in the United States of America by
The Book Press, Brattleboro, Vermont
Set in Avanta

This book is Edna's

PART ONE

At the age of forty-two, shortly after Sukkoth, Meir was gripped by the fear of death—a fear that took hold of him as soon as he had acknowledged the fact that death was a real and integral part of his life, which had already passed its peak, that he was moving swiftly and surely toward it on a route that allowed for no digressions, and that the distance between them—which had seemed almost infinite during the Sukkoth holiday, let alone the summer, which now seemed no more than a distant dream—was growing shorter all the time, so that he could envisage it without difficulty and measure it out in ordinary, everyday terms, such as: how many pairs of shoes he would still buy, how many times he would go to the movies, and how many women he would still sleep with, apart from his wife. This realization, which filled him with panic and despair, invaded his life during the space of a perfectly ordinary week, without any particular reason of which he was aware, as if it were a slight, almost imperceptible ache stirring somewhere in the innermost tissues of his body, and then spreading and thickening until it was a canker gnawing at him without respite. And thus, from the minute he woke up in the morning, lying with his eyes still closed under the thin blanket next to his wife, Aviva, until he fell asleep at night—apart from occasional moments of mild distraction—he never stopped calculating the balance of his life and measuring the distance still remaining between himself and this death, which sometimes appeared in his imagination as a sunny spring day, with his wife and Pozner and a few other friends—usually the other man would suddenly appear and join them, too—strolling along the end of Dizengoff Street while he himself was absent in a final and permanent way. Sometimes he saw himself as an empty space cut out of the air between them, and sometimes as the dusty iron gate, decorated with the usual rosettes and fleurs-de-lis and set into the stone wall of the cemetery outside Nazareth, which he had seen when he accompanied his friend Gavrosh on a bird-watching expedition there at the end of winter a few years before. A path covered with gravel and pine needles and bordered by cypress and pine trees murmuring in the breeze led up to the gate, straight as a ruler and steeped in a silence saturated with the smell of the damp earth and the pungent scent of the pines, and something of this silence, together with the monotonous murmur of the trees out of which it had materialized, came fleetingly back to him as he lay listlessly on the soft sand with *The Bermuda Triangle* in his hand, gazing aimlessly at the calm sea and the horizon and from time to time, as his eyes roamed the beach, stealing a hopeful look at the girl tanning herself not far from him with her face lifted motionlessly to the sun, while at the same time he mentally followed its rays as they penetrated the cells of his skin and spread through them, awakening the tan that had been lying there dormant all these years. He imagined this tan rising to the surface and covering him like a thin layer of hot jelly and immediately remarked to himself, as a very light breeze sprang up and began blowing along the beach from the sea, how much he was enjoying lying on the beach and what a good thing it was that he had come down here and shaken off the panic and despair: if he persevered, and he was determined to persevere, his mental and physical condition was bound to improve, and he would feel refreshed and restored. He had no doubt that the sea had it in its power to bring this about—all he had to do was look at Pozner—and he turned his head and glanced hopefully at his body, but to his disappointment it was as embarrassingly pale as ever, only a little pinker than before, and he was sorry that he had waited till now, when the season was nearly over and winter was already at the door. If only he could turn the wheel of time back to the beginning of summer, or even to the previous summer, when Pozner had first suggested that he come with him to the beach! How he wished that he was at this very moment as deeply tanned as Pozner! He stole a quick glance at the sunbathing girl, who was as brown as freshly baked bread, and said to himself that everything was still ahead of him and he had to learn to look on life as a gift, for just as he had been born he could equally well not have been, just like a lot of other people. And he smiled.

The sun sank obliquely to the horizon as the first delicate threads of evening and approaching autumn made themselves felt within the summery warmth, and Meir measured the distance between the sun and the horizon, wishing devoutly that they would merge so that he could collect his things and go home, and made an effort to abandon himself to the pleasurable touch of the air and the sun on his hot, languid body, to the sight of the sea and the sky, and to that utter passivity which demanded the greatest effort of all. He envied Pozner's ability to abandon himself in this way almost as much as he envied his tan, and he said to himself that if he swam in the sea every day and played beach tennis and drank beer and began to spend a lot of time at the movies, just like Pozner, he would be saved from the distress in which he was trapped—which seemed, in fact, to be diminished even now—and he would be able to lead a bright, fresh life, too, without unnecessary worries and doubts and full of the same carefree physical and spiritual pleasures, since as far as he could remember he hadn't been so different from Pozner when they were at high school and in the army, or even on the kibbutz. The insouciance, the mockery even, with which Pozner regarded his own actions, and in fact life itself, aroused Meir's envy and admiration because they made life pleasant and gay and gave it a dimension of directness and boldness, and he sent a bolder look in the direction of the sunbathing girl and for a moment thought of taking advantage of the fact that she had changed her position in order to speak to her—he had no doubt that the other man would have done so—but he did nothing and went on lying and looking at the sea without moving, his hand digging listlessly into the soft sand, waiting for the sun to set, and then he leafed apathetically through his book, glancing from time to time at the sea, which was covered with soft shadows, and at the sun, which was approaching the horizon into which it would soon sink and disappear, at which point and not one moment before he would get up and take a dip in the shallow water and collect his belongings and go home.

Little by little, with a barely perceptible movement, the sun slid down and touched the surface of the water, and then dipped into it and sank into the sea, leaving a radiant orange glow that colored the water and suffused the air in its wake, and Meir lay on his side without moving as he watched the orange glow turning blue and merging with the shadows engulfing the sea and the shore, which was slowly being abandoned, and a feeling of relief and satisfaction spread through him, as if he had completed some essential task and a burden had been lifted from his shoulders. A cool breeze blew in light gusts from the sea, wrinkling its surface and banishing the remnants of warmth from the air, but still he went on lying there, digging in the sand, and looking expressionlessly at the sunbathing girl, who stood up and slowly collected her belongings and turned away, and for a moment he felt a desire to speak to her or at least do something, cough or stand up, to attract her attention and postpone her departure, but he shrank from doing so because the desire itself made him feel a kind of pain, and he went on gazing at the sea and the shore as they sank into the shadows—there was still a little murky white light lining the sky and everything was steeped in an inexpressible sweetness and calm and a tender, joyful melancholy—wishing with all his heart that Pozner could see him like this, and Aviva, too. It was clear to him that he had now recovered from his troubles, or at any rate that he was about to recover from them, and that he was standing at the beginning of

a new road in his life and everything depended only on him and his
determination to take it, and with a feeling of relaxation and reconciliation so complete that he was ready to resign himself not only to
death but even to that business of the other man, he put the book
down on his folded clothes and lingered a little while longer, feeling
a need to prolong his stay to the very limit and beyond it, and then,
after waiting a few minutes more, he rose to his feet and shook off
the sand and walked slowly into the darkening water of the sea, which
now looked like an endless desert of hardening lead, and took a quick
dip and came out and dried himself and collected his belongings and
walked along the empty beach to Frishman Street. He walked up
Frishman, and as he crossed Sirkin Street and passed the school, he
wondered whether to go on to Pozner's place and have a beer with
him on his balcony, but something urged him to go home, and he
turned and crossed the little square with the luxuriant ficus trees full
of the twittering of birds and went up to the apartment, where he
found a note from Aviva on the table saying that their son had gone
to the movies with friends and she had gone out to do some shopping
and then to go to a gym class, and his spirits immediately fell, but he
quickly reminded himself that he had just come back refreshed and
relaxed from the sea, and without putting on the lights he closed the
big window that was letting in a cold wind and went into the bedroom
and took off his clothes and then went to the bathroom to take a
shower. And when he was standing under the water enjoying the
feeling of his body, sunburned and pleasantly tired from the sea, he
said to himself that the moment he had finished his shower he would
call Drora and invite himself over. She was a single woman with a
lively air, who had come to work in their office as a draftswoman a
few months before, and from the first day he had courted her discreetly but persistently by means of little jokes and smiles, various
signs of intimacy and attention, sometimes buying her a doughnut or
pouring her a cup of coffee when he got one for himself—but when
he came out of the shower he postponed calling Drora until after he
had had a cup of coffee, and when he sat on the balcony drinking it,
glancing as he did so at *The Bermuda Triangle,* which he had bor-

rowed from Pozner, he felt the painful restlessness of the evening hour
—which up to now he had somehow managed to hold at bay—
creeping up on him again. As soon as he had finished his coffee, he
put the book on the table next to his bed and washed the cup and
went out into the street and turned into Bograshov and continued
along Ben Zion Boulevard until he reached the Habima plaza, where
he stopped for a moment and hesitated, and then he crossed the road
and went to the public telephone in Gan Yaakov and quickly dialed
Drora's number, but when he dialed the last number he left his finger
in the dial for a long time before letting it go, and then he quickly
put the telephone down, and he decided to go to Pozner's place and
have a beer with him on the balcony, or to go by himself to one of
the new places that had opened in the north of the city, and he went
on walking in the same aimless, drifting way until he came to the
square in front of the Mann Auditorium.

As he crossed the broad, almost deserted square in the direction
of Rothschild Boulevard, he noticed a couple sitting and talking in a
parked car, and although he could scarcely do more than guess because of the darkness and his angle of vision, it seemed to him that
they were facing each other and that the man's arm was lying along
the back of the seat. Without meaning to he slowed down slightly and
stared at them, and after walking on a little farther he turned his head
again, almost against his will, and could make out nothing but two
dim silhouettes in the car, which was shrouded in darkness and looked
very small to him, and the crowding and awkwardness made it all seem
more distressingly sordid than ever—but of course the thing had
actually happened in a big car, of that there could be no doubt at all.
Again his heart contracted in humiliation and pain—on no account
could he understand how and why such a thing could have happened
to him, and he immediately turned his head and went on walking
straight ahead as if he hadn't seen a thing, exhorting himself to let
it be since nothing could be done to mend matters, at least not in the
way he would have liked, and the pain and humiliation to which he
went on clinging so stubbornly were nothing but childish narcissism
and self-indulgence. He would do better to enjoy life as far as possible

and be grateful that he was healthy and had useful, interesting work to do and abandon himself to the pleasure of the fine, soft evening filling the air and the street with a sense of well-being, and thanks to these things, which he said to himself so firmly and persuasively, he felt the pain and insult retreating and a surge of happiness welling up inside him, together with a profound, uplifting feeling of sympathy for Aviva, even of admiration for the courage and independence she had shown, although it had hurt him so much, or perhaps precisely for that reason. But in the midst of his exaltation and the happy conviction that he had finally succeeded in overcoming his tormenting doubts and was about to create a new and deeper intimacy with Aviva and save himself in the process, he felt an insidious fear that this achievement, too, was only temporary and would soon disappear —he had been through it all before in the past few months—and indeed, when he reached Ibn Gvirol Street, which was crowded with cars and people and full of life, he felt all the old pain and confusion welling up in him again, and he was seized by the desire to do the same thing himself, at the same time and if possible in the same way too, and he decided to phone Drora from the first pay phone he came across. As soon as he reached the square in front of the municipality, he went up to a telephone and dialed her number, and after identifying himself, feeling extremely uncomfortable as he did so and trying to pretend that it was all a lark, he said that he hoped he wasn't disturbing her—the note of polite apology was a mistake, he had meant to take a different tone altogether—and Drora said, "No, no, it's quite all right," and rather taken aback at the lack of surprise and eagerness in her voice, he paused for a moment before asking her how she was, and Drora, who sounded indifferent, or at any rate not as enthusiastic as he had hoped, said, "If you really want to know, not so hot," and he asked her what she meant and she said, "I think I'm coming down with something," and Meir said, "It's the season. Everybody's sick now. What's wrong with you?" and Drora said, "There's something the matter with my throat and I feel a kind of heaviness and a slight burning sensation in my eyes," and Meir said, "Have you seen a doctor?" and Drora said, "Not yet, it's nothing serious," and Meir, still hoping for an invitation and already looking for a way of backing out, said, "You shouldn't neglect it; there can be all kinds of complications. You should take two aspirins right away," and Drora said, "I don't take pills," and Meir said, "Good for you" and asked in the same jocular tone if she was a vegetarian, and she giggled, but without enthusiasm, and said, "No, not yet. I just don't take pills," and it seemed to him that her voice was now reserved as well as tired, but nevertheless, in the middle of discussing her health and still preparing himself for a hasty retreat, he felt impelled to ask her if he could come up and see her, and Drora said, "If you like, but I'm afraid I won't be a very good hostess today," and Meir, who felt trapped, hemmed and hawed and in the end said, "I don't want to bother you when you're not feeling well. I'll come another time," and regretting having called her in the first place, he put the receiver down and crossed the square. He felt a disagreeable heaviness spreading through his body, or perhaps it was the chill in the air, but all he wanted now was to get away, and he walked along the wall of the zoo, sniffing the animal stench in the air, and continued along the boulevards with a gnawing feeling of bitterness and disappointment, especially at himself, for not being more demanding and even rude —he had no doubt that the other man, who kept on creeping back into his thoughts however hard he tried to keep him out of them, was plentifully endowed with this quality, which seemed to him a sign of vitality and the lust for life—and preoccupied by these gloomy thoughts, he crossed Dizengoff Street and turned into Emile Zola. And then, as he was walking slowly up the dark street, the knowledge came to him that if he turned into Dov Hos and crossed Gordon Street—there was something soothing and comforting in these familiar streets—his grandmother would appear on the corner of Smolenskin Street in her brown felt slippers and her gray housedress, with the big brown woolen shawl around her shoulders, and she would come toward him with a beaming smile full of intelligence and benevolence on her broad, beloved face, and all at once he felt the touch of her face on his as he hugged and kissed her and the touch of her hands, thick as a carpenter's, and the special, personal smell that enveloped her and her house until it had become identical with her, and in the same split second of thought he also saw the rich blue sky, the tender sky of spring or autumn, above the little balcony where the two of them had sat, he on the floor and she in her armchair, as the Italians bombed Tel Aviv, and the dense cypresses and the fig tree and the fresh green lawn in the yard, and without quickening his steps, with a feeling of heartrending happiness, as if it had all come true already and everything had returned to its original, good state before she died, he turned into Dov Hos Street, crossed Gordon, and continued walking along it until he arrived at his parents' house.

His mother opened the door with a vague smile on her face, which had been pale lately and whose natural brightness seemed overcast by a deep shadow of tiredness and resignation, and said, "I knew it was you by the footsteps," and Meir said, "I've only dropped in for a minute to see how you are," and went into the big room where his father was sitting watching television and said, "Hello, Dad," but his father, who did not hear him come in—the television was on full blast—did not respond, and Meir came a little closer and repeated, "Hello, Dad." His father started as if he had been sleeping, and a smile, which was welcoming but somehow lifeless, as if it were wrapped up in cobwebs, appeared on his aging face, and he said, "I didn't hear you come in. It's good you came. How are you?" and Meir said, "Fine," and glanced out of the corner of his eye at the newspaper lying on the couch while his father, whose smile had already disappeared into the weariness on his face, said, "How are Aviva and the children?" and Meir said, "They're fine," and picked up the newspaper with a casual air, and his father, his eyes already riveted to the screen, repeated, "It's good you came. Go into the kitchen, your mother will give you something to eat," and Meir lingered for a moment to skim through the headlines and then went into the kitchen, where his mother, who was in the middle of writing to her brother in Toronto, after which she intended writing to her daughter in Boston and filling in the questionnaire about her family tree that she had received over a month ago from some Jew in Houston, Texas, pushed the airmail cards and the pages of the questionnaire to the

edge of the table and asked him how he was and if he wanted
something to eat. All she wanted was to be left alone in the clean,
quiet kitchen now that the day full of countless duties and chores was
drawing to a close, to write her letters and perform this final duty of
the day, which she saw as an onerous and even intolerable imposition,
just as she saw all the other chores and duties of life that she nevertheless went on performing with boundless devotion and harried attention to detail, and she prayed that no one would come and rob her,
simply by being there, of her hard-earned peace and quiet and fragile
freedom, but she denied this wish with every word she uttered and
every gesture and expression, and Meir, who sat down in the place
that had been his since childhood, said, "No, no. I don't want anything; please don't bother." He said this emphatically but without
conviction, and his mother said, "There are a few pieces of gefilte fish
left over from Saturday; you should taste them," and with a practiced
movement she wiped the bit of table in front of him with a cloth, and
Meir said, "No, no. Sit down," but his mother had already placed the
plate and knife and fork before him and removed the fish from the
fridge together with a dish of peppers, which were a favorite of his,
and saying, "Here you are—the peppers didn't come out so well this
time," she put two pieces of fish on his plate, with a few spoonfuls
of the peppers in a separate little dish, and then she took a piece of
braided *challa* out of the bread bin and said, "I kept this for you
specially from Saturday." Meir tasted the gefilte fish and said, "The
fish is fantastic. I haven't tasted fish like this for ages," and his mother
said, "Your father said it was something special this time too," and
asked him if he wanted a piece of meat left over from the pot roast
and Meir said, "No. You've done enough today. Sit down," and he
watched her going to the fridge again and said, "The peppers are
terrific," and his mother said, "I don't want to force you," and placed
the glass dish with the meat on the table and put a large piece of meat
on a separate plate for him and returned the glass dish to the fridge
and filled a little square dish with homemade apple purée, and then
she said casually that she had intended writing to Rifka this evening,
glancing at the airmail cards on the edge of the table and at the same

time aimlessly pushing the plate of meat closer to him, and then very warily and reluctantly asked him if he had already written to his sister, and Meir said that he was very busy at the moment but that he hoped to do so the following week, and his mother nodded vaguely and said, "I'll put the kettle on to boil for tea," and she filled the kettle and lit the gas and then she said, "Write to her, write to her. It's important." She said this with touching timidity, and it was obvious from her gestures and the tone of her voice how much she would have liked to take the words back again, but how anxious she was, too, for him to take them to heart, and at the same time she removed the fish plate and took down the blue plastic cookie jar, and with a smile to which she tried to impart a roguish twinkle she said, "If only I could I would write for you," and she took a handful of butter cookies from the jar and put them on a plate in front of him, and Meir said, "Don't worry," and his mother said, "Don't put it off too long," and went to pour out the tea, already regretting this remark, which she knew was superfluous and annoying even before the words were out of her mouth, and she smiled in embarrassment and said that she didn't like writing letters or receiving them either, but there was no way of getting out of it. And she put the teacups on the table and asked him if he wanted anything else, and Meir said, "Sit down, already. You've done enough," and she sat down in her usual place and asked him again how he was, and Meir said that lately he had been tired because he had been working too hard, and his mother broke off a bit of a cookie and urged him to take care of himself and added, "You sound a little hoarse to me," and Meir said, "I think I've got something starting in my throat," and told her that he had been to the beach earlier in the day, and his mother, her face grave, said, "This is no time to go to the beach; it's winter already. There's a chill in the air," and Meir said, "Actually it was very nice," and his mother said, "After Sukkoth you don't go to the sea," and asked him to go to the doctor about his throat, and Meir said, "I'll wait another day or two," and his mother said, "It doesn't pay to neglect your health," and told him about some distant acquaintance, a landsleit apparently, who had caught a slight cold with a low fever, which as a result of negligence had developed into a heart condition, and Meir said, "Don't worry, I'll go," and drew the questionnaire toward him and asked her what it was. His mother took it from him and said that it was a questionnaire about her family that she had received a few weeks before with a polite letter from some Jew in Houston, Texas, probably an old-age pensioner with nothing better to do, whose family name was the same as her grandmother's maiden name, and who had decided to investigate his genealogy and accordingly sent out these questionnaires to people all over the world with detailed questions about all their relations and next of kin, their places of residence and dates of birth and death, promising that at the conclusion of his investigation he would send each and every member of the family a fully detailed family tree. After a short pause she added that according to this Jew from Texas the origins of the family were in Scandinavia, no less, and who knows —perhaps they were even related to one of the members of the Danish or Swedish aristocracy. The latter was evidently her own contribution, and she pushed the cup of tea and plate of cookies toward Meir with a faintly ironic smile, and he said, "I'm delighted to hear it," and took a cookie and put a spoon of sugar in his tea and stirred it, and his mother said, "So am I," and removed the empty plate of meat with the fork and knife and said, "The things people get up to," and stood up to put the dishes in the sink and suddenly, out of the blue, she said that she was sick of housework and visitors and her never-ending chores and duties and that she would like to leave everything and run away to the ends of the earth and live there by herself free of everything, all she needed was a little room and dry bread and a few olives, that was quite enough for her. Her face was overcast by weariness and bitter defeat and Meir took another cookie —he was crazy about his mother's crumbly butter cookies and could not resist the temptation, however hard he tried to restrain himself —and said, "Why don't you go for a trip somewhere?" And his mother said, "Where to?" and Meir said, "Why not go to Jerusalem? It's a wonderful city," and took another cookie, and she said, "By myself?" and Meir said, "Yes. Why not?" and his mother, who seemed momentarily bewildered or embarrassed, said, "I like being by myself," and Meir could not control himself and took another cookie and said, "Why don't you go to the movies occasionally or go and sit in a café?" and his mother absentmindedly took a teaspoon of the apple purée and said that it never worked out because either she had to worry about his father's supper or someone dropped in unexpectedly, or else she had to go and fix something up at the bank or the Sick Fund, and in a tone of resignation but with a trace of irony she added, "The longer you live the more things there are to fix up," and Meir said, "Yes, you're right," and drew the tea toward him, and after struggling with himself for a while, he took another cookie and said, "It was delicious," and his mother said, "It was only leftovers." A fragile, honeyed web of affectionate intimacy now surrounded the two of them as they sat in the clean, quiet kitchen, as if they were resting in a tranquil circle of warm, golden light, close to each other and separate from everyone else, and his mother said, "But I go out a lot. To the Weisses, or to Mrs. Krantz, or to Nahalat Benyamin or the optician," and she gathered a few cookie crumbs scattered on the table as she spoke and put them into her mouth, and then she added, "I never go anywhere in order to be somewhere but in order not to be somewhere else," and a full, tender smile illuminated her face and Meir smiled too and said, "Yes, I understand," and took one last cookie, listening unwillingly and with suppressed irritation to the shuffle of his father's slippers, and the next minute he was standing in the kitchen door smiling broadly and announcing loudly, "We're going to Gibraltar!" and brandishing his fist in the air like a victorious boxer, as he insensitively and instantaneously tore the web of intimacy and tenderness enclosing Meir and his mother. Meir was flooded by a bitter, if suppressed, wave of anger and resistance, and he knew instinctively, without a word or a hint from her, that the very same feeling was now flooding his mother, who nodded slightly at his father in confirmation, but under the thin layer of smiling affirmation there was something reserved, and perhaps even hostile, about her expression. His father brandished his fist again and said, "We're going in the summer. It's decided. We'll live it up—and to hell with the expense! We'll fly to London, and from London direct to Gibraltar.

Main Road. Scottish Corner. Africa Point. The Rock. Kings Yard Lane number 9. We'll eat and drink, we'll go up to the Rock. And then we'll tour a bit—La Linea, Algeciras, Cadiz, Seville. There's nothing like Seville." And as he held forth in this enthusiastic vein of jollity and devilishness, trying to approach and arouse Meir's mother, who remained withdrawn and unresponsive, the bell rang and he hurried to open the door, and they heard his voice saying, "Welcome, Mr. Gorman," and Bill's smiling voice saying, *"Shalom aleichem,"* and Meir said, "It's Bill," and took one final cookie before leaving, and his mother nodded her head with a reluctant expression on her face—not because she didn't like Bill, on the contrary, she was particularly fond of him, but because at that moment she knew that she had finally been deprived of her freedom for the rest of the evening. A moment later Bill appeared in the kitchen doorway together with Meir's father, both of them smiling happily, and in his heavy American accent he said, "Hello, how are you, lady?" and shook hands with Meir's mother, his flushed face wreathed in his perpetual, childish smile, and his mother said, "I'm fine. And you?" and Bill said, "Great," and then he turned to Meir and said, "Hello, Meir," and Meir gave him a friendly smile and said, "Hello, Bill," and Bill said, "How's your business?" and Meir said, "Fine. And yours?" and Bill said, "Very bad," and laughed hoarsely, and his mother smiled and said, *"Bist a millionaire. Was wilst du? Ganz America is deines,"* and in response to her suggestion they all went into the big room, except for Meir, who remained in the kitchen to finish his meal and took one more cookie while he was about it—by now there were only two left on the brown plate, and when his mother came back into the kitchen to fix a light supper for Bill, he said good-bye to everyone and went home.

Outside it was chillier than he had imagined, with a nip in the air that made him shiver slightly as he walked slowly along the empty streets, a disagreeable heaviness and fatigue spreading through his body and making his legs feel like lead. The minute he got home and opened the door, he knew that Aviva had already gone to bed, and overcome by a bitter feeling of disappointment, because he very much wanted her to welcome him and pamper him, he went into the bedroom, where he found her curled up in bed with *In Search of the Miraculous* beside her and the little lamp above her head shedding its light on her sleeping face, but when he approached the bed she opened her eyes a little with an effort and said, "I had a hard day. I waited for you until fifteen minutes ago." She said this in a slightly apologetic tone and shut her eyes again, and Meir, suppressing his anger and disappointment, said, "That's okay. Go back to sleep," and Aviva cuddled into the blanket and said "They phoned from the shop to say you should go and pick up the sideboard tomorrow," and Meir said, "We'll talk about it in the morning. Go to sleep," and went into the kitchen, where he automatically opened the fridge, still conscious of the heavy weakness spreading through his limbs, and thought for a moment of going into his son's room, from which a crack of light was visible under the closed door, and then he opened the kitchen cupboard and took out the aspirins and swallowed one with a little water and went back into the bedroom and began to get undressed. As he was taking off his clothes, still with the same debilitating sensation of heaviness and weakness, he felt a desire to make love to Aviva, and for a moment he even thought of waking her, but his anger and disappointment at the fact that she had not waited up got the better of him, and he abandoned the idea and put on his bedside lamp and got into bed feeling sullen and dejected and took up *The Bermuda Triangle* and said to himself that he didn't make love to her enough, much less than the average, at any rate according to what he had read in the report by Grace and Geoffrey Kaat—he couldn't remember the figures in the tables but only the definite impression that had remained with him after studying them and that was summed up in the words, which he did remember, "dreary sex"—and he glanced at Aviva, who was sleeping quietly with an attractive rosiness in her cheeks, and said to himself without moving his lips "dreary sex," and pulled the blanket over his shoulders, and trying to ignore the dull pains spreading through him and draining his strength, he opened *The Bermuda Triangle* and thought about all kinds of women he had been to bed with, and then, moving about to try to find a comfortable

and soothing position, he began to count them, looking darkly at
Aviva's soundly sleeping face as he did so. Even now, a year later, he
could not understand how this home-loving and honest woman had
done the thing that had astonished and dismayed him to such an
extent that he felt not only his confidence but his entire life collapsing, in addition to the painful insult and the growing jealousy that
accompanied him like a shadow without diminishing by one iota
despite the year—or to be more precise, the eleven months—that had
passed since then, and despite all his efforts to forget and all his
attempts to convince himself of the insignificance of what had happened. And he returned to the bitter consolation of counting all the
women he had ever been to bed with, this time trying to list them
methodically, beginning with the first and going through them one
by one, dragging in every girl he could think of from the furthermost
recesses of his memory, but the yield depressed him since it seemed
pathetically meager in comparison to the number of Pozner's con-
quests—he didn't know the exact number, but he could guess—
although it was definitely more than Gavrosh's, which wasn't much
of a consolation, considering that Gavrosh had been occupied for
years with a single love, but he felt somewhat encouraged nevertheless
and said to himself that if he made an effort he might still catch up
with Pozner, or at least come close to him. For a moment he was
satisfied, and he stretched out on his side and looked at the book and
read a sentence or two with heavy eyes. Unwillingly he remembered
the interview with Simenon he had read in a newspaper years before,
and which had been indelibly engraved on his memory ever since, in
which the French writer had confessed that he had slept with about
ten thousand women—this was the only thing he remembered from
the interview, and it had remained stuck in his memory like a thorn
—and once again he gave way to feelings of miserable failure and
defeat because he would never be able to reach a similar score, and
with the book still open in front of him he thought about Raya—the
way he had shrunk from doing all he wanted to then embittered his
thoughts and grew into something that was not only naive and ridiculous but worse than that—a missed opportunity that had ruined his

life and a sign of the meagerness of the life force pulsing inside him. For she had been so eager and willing to submit to him and respond to all his desires, and they were alone, with no one to disturb them, neither Aviva nor Bentz nor anyone else, in the long, narrow, dreary room with its high walls painted a drab beige color—if only he could turn the clock back to that point in time!—and his bitter regrets mingled with the depressing heaviness and weakness of his body, or perhaps they were nourished by them, as he remembered how in his panic he had shrunk from even looking at her naked body, and he closed his eyes and saw the two of them in that long, narrow, dingy room—it was only a moment or two since they had come in from outside, leaving the smell of the pines and the resin and the glaring sunlight behind them—with its high walls painted the drab beige color casting an air of dreariness and gloom and the barred window overlooking the yard with its few dusty pines, and the skimpy curtains and the rough bedspread made of coarse wool with its incredibly ugly greenish pattern, which filled him with disgust every time he lay down on it, and he saw them beginning to make love still standing up, while they were getting undressed, which is what he wished had happened, and continuing to make love standing up—if only he could turn the clock back, this, exactly this, is what he would have wanted to happen —and then separating while he went to lie down on the very wide bed and she went on standing and took the pins out of her hair and put them down on the table as he inspected her body at his leisure, and then, while she was still standing next to the bed, he slowly stroked her thighs and her belly down to her pubic hair, and then he asked her to turn her back to him—suspense and boundless pleasure spread through him and seeped into his flesh and mingled with the feeling of illness—and she did as he asked, for there was no one there and both of them were aroused and ready to enjoy themselves without restraint, and when she stood with her back to him he asked her to bend down a little, and she leaned over and rested her arms on the table, and after that he indicated with a touch of his hand that he wanted her to open her legs a little, and then he inclined his head slightly and looked, and then he put out his hand and very slowly, with a gentle but firm caress, he inserted it between her legs as she stood without moving, and he was filled with such tremendous excitement that he was afraid Aviva, sleeping soundly at his side, would sense the waves of emotion emanating from him and trembling in the air, and he got up quietly and went into the bathroom and stood in front of the bath and with all his being concentrated on this missed pleasure he ejaculated, and then he cleaned himself up and went back to bed and lay with his back to Aviva and took up *The Bermuda Triangle* again. Feeling the sensations of illness that he thought had already passed spreading through him again, he read a few more sentences, making a desperate effort to keep his eyes open, and then he closed the book and laid it on the bedside table and put out the light above his head and turned over and fell asleep.

He woke early after a heavy sleep, the feeling of illness still there, seemingly frozen inside his body, but although Aviva pleaded with him to stay at home, he got dressed and had a cup of coffee and went to the office, determined not to cancel his meeting with the architect of the Youth Center he was working on, since they were behind schedule anyway, and right after the meeting, after making a few notes and notifying the draftsman of the changes in the plans, he left the office and went home, but on the way, despite the ill feeling, which had intensified and filled him with heavy exhaustion, he went to arrange for the transportation of the new sideboard from the furniture shop. This was what he had planned to do this morning, and he felt that if he didn't do it now it would involve him in all kinds of hassles later, and accordingly he went to the bank to draw the cash he would need to pay the furniture mover and made a beeline for the Moroccan teller's counter, where a number of people were waiting impatiently, and joined the line, trying to catch her eye as he did so, and giving her a little wave as if they were friends, to which she responded with a nod and a slight smile, which immediately faded and deadened into the expression of boredom and resentment that never left her tanned young face, the face of a vulgar movie starlet, which somehow reminded him of Raquel Welch, but it was precisely this vulgarity that attracted him, and as he stood and waited his turn, scrutinizing her with pretended indifference—she had a wonderful neck and nice breasts, which were slightly exposed by the low neckline of the light blue blouse she was wearing—he decided that today he would ask her her name and perhaps invite her to have coffee with him or to go to the movies, and he wondered if he should come right out with it or hint, and then he decided to put the last part of this program off until he was feeling better, and while he was considering whether to ask her name directly or indirectly, one of the younger clerks approached and called, "Aliza, you're wanted on the phone," and she said, "I'm coming," and finished writing something in the customer's bankbook and gave it back to him and got up and walked away. After a few minutes, which seemed to Meir interminable, perhaps because he was feeling so ill, Aliza returned and resumed her work with the same sulky expression as usual, serving her customers with indolent movements full of demonstrative boredom and resentment, and when Meir's turn came he put his bankbook down on the counter with a winsome smile and said, "Hello Aliza," and Aliza said, "Good morning," and took the book with an expression of infinite boredom and weariness and a slight sigh, and Meir gave her a sympathetic, rather paternal, look and said, "You're not happy here," and Aliza said, "No, not at all." And Meir said good-humoredly, "Why not? This is a great place," and Aliza said, "What's so great about it? The faces of the customers, perhaps?" and Meir, embarrassed, said something about the air-conditioning and the salaries and benefits, trying to save the situation by imparting a humorous note to his words, and Aliza said, "You know what they can do with their air-conditioning and all their lousy benefits," and asked him how much money he wanted, and Meir said, "Nine hundred will be enough," and Aliza said, "This bank is driving me completely crazy," and took a bundle of bills out of the drawer, and in the meantime the previous customer returned because it seemed to him that she had made a mistake in his account, and with a curt apology he pushed in front of Meir and slapped his bankbook on the counter, very irritated and upset, and pointed to the place where in his opinion she had made a mistake and cheated him out of some money. Aliza, her face hard with anger and impatience, glanced at the bankbook, and in a tone of undisguised hostility, explained to him that there had been no mistake, and after he had thanked her meekly and gone away, she looked at Meir and said, "These old men, they really make me sick. As soon as I see one of them approaching in the line I feel as if I'm going to explode," and Meir, who had not taken his eyes off her, said, "Yes"—his desire to seduce her had now grown into an urgent lust, but he already knew that today he would not make any propositions or drop any hints either, which he attributed to the fact that he was feeling ill—and Aliza said, "In the army I had a great life. I'd go back tomorrow if I could," and counted out the money, and when she had finished she put the bills in front of him on the counter together with his bankbook, and he put them into his pocket and said, "Thank you," and gave her a big smile and left the bank and went to look for the Turkish furniture mover with the gray Peugeot who had been recommended to him by someone in his office. The Turkish moving man was standing with one foot on the mudguard of his gray Peugeot, a sandwich in one hand and a bottle of Coca-Cola in the other, and chatting easily with a tall girl with light red hair as he ate, and Meir, who did not want to interrupt their conversation, stopped a few paces away and waited until the man noticed him and asked if he was looking for him, and Meir said, "Yes," and asked if he was free to do a job, and the man asked when he wanted to move what from where —there was something about him, perhaps the casual elegance of his posture, that reminded Meir of Marcello Mastroiani, except that he was shorter and thinner with a forelock of curly gray hair—and while the tall girl, who had a pale, pretty face, stood listening and waiting with bored impatience, playing with her beads, they agreed on the price and the other details, and the man said, "Hang on a sec while I finish my sandwich and then we'll go. You can wait in the car in the meantime," and Meir got into the car, suddenly feeling so ill and exhausted that he had to stop himself by force from lying down on the seat while the moving man finished his sandwich and his drink and went on talking for a few minutes to the tall girl, who kept twisting her beads, before he got into the car. He did everything with the confident indifference of a Jean Gabin, and while he was busy straightening the cushion on the driver's seat, he turned to the girl with the words, "I'll be back in an hour. Come then and we'll talk," and the tall girl said, "I'll try," with a discontented look, and the moving man took an old newspaper from between the two front seats and began wiping his hands and said, "Come. You won't be sorry. I'll be back in an hour," and the tall girl repeated, "I'll try," and began walking away, and the moving man stuck his head out of the window and called, "I'll be back in an hour. You come. I'll be waiting for you," and watched her walking away in the mirror while he wiped his hands on the newspaper, and then he turned to Meir and said, "She sucks," in a matter-of-fact tone of voice tinged with the same air of weary indifference and threw the crumpled newspaper out the window and added, "We're both men, aren't we?" and Meir said, "Yes," and the man started the car and said, "I fucked her when she was still half a child. I was the first one to get into her, and I'm still in there," and he put the car in gear and said, "But now I leave her a bit of money every time. So she won't go short," and while he was busy nosing the car out of the parking space, which he did with calm deliberation, he said, "She doesn't work at it on a permanent basis. Only now and then, you understand, when she's got the time and she needs something special—some dress for the new season or a pair of boots, something like that. Usually she works at the post office," and Meir said, "The post office?!" It sounded so funny and surprising to him, especially because of the nonchalant, matter-of-fact way in which it was said, that in the middle of his heavy, sick feeling he sensed a broad, happy smile spreading through him, and the moving man, without turning his head, said, "She works there mainly for the social benefits and the pension," in the same tone of voice that Meir found so amusing, and put on the brakes to allow another car to pass, and added, "All women today are whores," and then he changed gears and said, "I know that's not right. Not exactly. My wife, for example. But who knows, maybe she's one, too," and Meir said, "Yes," and the smile died away inside him and was swallowed up in the old pain yawning around and beneath him like a gray abyss.

At the intersection of King George and Dizengoff streets they stopped and waited for the green light, and the moving man lit a cigarette, and with the same serious, businesslike air, he said, "You saw me talking to her? I'm trying to fix her up with a friend of mine. He saw her and asked me to fix him up with her, so I'm trying to get her to meet us tomorrow night and bring a friend, but before that I want to make a date with her for today," and he pressed down on the gas pedal and said, "Tomorrow's tomorrow and today's today," and Meir said, "Yes, you're right," feeling wretchedly inferior and removed from life, especially now, with the weight of the illness crushing his body and his will, and as a prelude to asking the moving man to fix him up with her, too, he said, "She's got a terrific figure," and the man revved the engine and said, "That's true, although I've already had better, single and married too. Married women are in a class of their own," and Meir said, "Yes," and sank into gloom, and it occurred to him that perhaps this furniture mover was the other man, and although he knew for certain that it was quite impossible, this thought remained hanging over his head like a cloud, and the moving man, who hardly took his eyes off the road, said, "I've got one dame, for instance, from Holland. A Jewess, new in the country, she does a bit of nursing at a hospital, lives in north Tel Aviv, not far from the Peer cinema. What a body! All new, get me? You can tell at once that she's hardly been used. I'm the only one who has her," and he carefully passed a car as it turned into a side street and immediately added, "I like the feeling of exclusivity," in a tone of obvious self-esteem, and without turning his head, he asked Meir, "How about you?" and Meir, preoccupied with his own poisonous thoughts, said, "Yes. So do I." He said this with reserve and guided the mover to the furniture shop, and after concluding his business in the shop, he helped him, with shaky legs and the cold shivers, to load the sideboard onto the roof of the car and afterward to take it up the stairs and install it in the flat, and while Aviva, who opened the door for them, was busy admiring it and wiping the dust off it, Meir paid the mover and parted from him warmly, and then he went straight to the bedroom and got into bed and pulled the blanket over his head without even taking off his clothes. He was overcome by pains shooting through all his limbs and violent shivering fits, which did not pass even after Aviva covered him with another blanket and put a hot water bottle under his feet and brought him tea and two aspirins, for which he barely thanked her, he felt so cold and reserved toward her, and all he wanted was to fall asleep, but sleep eluded him and he lay there shivering, huddled under the two blankets, hostile to Aviva and longing for sleep, until at last it came and he fell into an uneasy sleep. In the morning, after bringing him a glass of lemon tea, Aviva suggested that he remain in bed while she phoned to ask the doctor to pay a house call, but he refused and said that he was feeling better and there was no reason for doctors, it was only a cold and it would go away by itself, but Aviva insisted, and in the end he gave in and said that he would go to the Sick Fund clinic himself and see Dr. Reiner.

Dr. Reiner, who had replaced their family doctor and whom Meir had never seen before, was a woman of about fifty with a full, feminine body and a heavy, open face. She examined him and found that, in addition to the mild infection in his throat and ear, he was suffering from high blood pressure, and Meir, who was very upset by the news, said that it was impossible and that he felt fine and that up to now there had never been anything wrong, and Dr. Reiner looked at him sympathetically—she had lively green eyes—and said that high blood pressure was a disease, which if not diagnosed in time could go on for years without the patient being aware of it until it suddenly manifested itself in an acute form, causing severe and irreparable damage to his health, and Meir said, "I understand," but in his heart of hearts he thought it was all a mistake and a misunderstanding, which would probably be cleared up in a day or two, and Dr. Reiner asked him his age and occupation, and Meir told her that he was forty-two and that he worked as a structural engineer, although the whole thing seemed absurd and irrelevant to him, and Dr. Reiner wrote down the details and said, "This is a disease that should not be neglected. From now on you'll have to take care of yourself." Meir said, "Yes," immediately and somewhat irrelevantly adding, "But I was completely healthy," and Dr. Reiner looked at him with her lively green eyes with their youthful expression and said that every sick person had been healthy until they became sick, and Meir said, "Yes, that's true," but it still seemed to him that it was all a mistake, and he said, "It's not possible," and smiled, and Dr. Reiner told him to go home and come back after he had recovered from the flu for another examination, since there was a faint possibility that the rise in his blood pressure was only a temporary phenomenon. And a week later, when he had recovered from the flu, Meir went to see her again, and she gave him a thorough examination and concluded once more that he was suffering from high blood pressure, and Meir, who had spent the intervening days turning the bad news over in his mind, unwilling for some reason to share it with Aviva, and had ostensibly begun to come to terms with it, asked her why it had happened to him, smiling slightly as he did so and not really expecting a reply, since he was interested only in the fact that it had indeed happened to him, which seemed to him very unjust and even outrageous, and Dr. Reiner said that there could be a number of reasons, such as heredity, bad eating habits, inactivity, mental stress, and perhaps other reasons not yet known to medical science, and in the end she added, "In the last analysis, we don't know very much," and Meir said, "I understand," and for a moment it seemed to him that he had accepted his fate and resigned himself to it without bitterness, and he looked at her big, mature, womanly face and asked her what he should do, and Dr. Reiner said, "Don't worry. You'll have plenty to do," and wrote down a list of tests he would have to undergo and prescribed several drugs and explained how to take them, and she also instructed him to cut down on salt and coffee and recommended that he try to change his eating habits, with the aim of cutting down on sugar and fats, especially animal fats, and to eat a lot of fruit and vegetables and try not to gain weight but to lose it, and she told him to come back in two weeks' time, after the results of his tests were in, so that she could see the effects of the treatment and decide how to continue. And Meir, his mood veering between glum resignation and an inexplicable insouciance, said jokingly that he had certainly not been expecting such a surprise and promised to follow all her instructions to the letter, and after thanking her and shaking hands and turning to leave, he paused and asked her with a smile if it was curable, and Dr. Reiner said that opinions were divided on this score: there were some doctors, for example, although they were still in the minority, who claimed that the disease could be cured by a suitable vegetarian diet, but the majority considered it a chronic disease that could not be cured—at any rate, and this was the important thing, it was clear that it could be checked and prevented from causing severe and irreparable damage, and it was this that they must aim for, and she gave him a level look and added, "There's no point in talking about perfect health, you know. It only leads to despair." And Meir thanked her again, and when he was already standing in the door he said, "I came in healthy and I'm going out sick," and Dr. Reiner smiled and asked him again to have the tests done without delay and come back in two weeks' time, and Meir said, "I intend to take care of it right away," and left.

Aviva accepted Meir's high blood pressure as a fact that, however regrettable, had to be faced without giving way to useless feelings of resentment and indignation and treated in accordance with Dr. Reiner's instructions, which was the way in which she related to all life's difficulties and troubles because her realism, the product of courage and honesty, was so deep-rooted that she never allowed herself to be seduced by illusory expectations, and was accordingly spared the bitterness of seeing every trouble and mishap as a mistake that could have been avoided or a malicious attempt on the part of life to do her in, which was so characteristic of Meir. She tried to reassure him and encourage him, first of all by trying to persuade him not to see his illness as a deliberate injustice perpetrated on him by fate or a catastrophe that might have been avoided but was now irreparable, and urged him to take all the tests and use his medicines and stop buying junk food in the streets, while she, for her part, would adapt her cooking according to Dr. Reiner's recommendations, and Meir was grateful to his wife for her talent for putting things on a practical basis, and despite the dark dregs of his hostility, he could not help but give way to the sense of profound closeness and appreciation he felt toward her. As for Pozner, whom Meir told the next day—embarrassed and uneasy not only because of Liora's presence on the balcony where they were sitting and drinking beer—he listened to him calmly and then, taking a sip of beer, said, "You seem resentful toward your body," and Meir, who definitely did feel that his body had done him an injustice, said "Yes," and Pozner said, "Everyone is doomed to get high blood pressure or some other disease. I can't understand what you're complaining about," and Meir said, "I don't know. About everything," because in the depths of his heart he really felt that life, or some supreme cosmic order in charge of human affairs, had treated him unjustly, picking on him, of all people, after he had been such a healthy, athletic boy, and Pozner, who had just come back from the beach and looked fresh and tanned, laughed and, lightly stroking the arm of the girl who up to two or three years ago had been his pupil, said, "Allow me to philosophize a little to the evening breeze," and Meir said, "Go ahead, I'm listening."

There was a barely perceptible wintry chill in the deepening and darkening blue air and big soft clouds piled up in the early evening sky—how Meir loved this twilight hour—and Pozner asked Liora, whose presence continued to embarrass him, for the matches and lit a cigarette and said that there was no such thing as perfect health because no such thing as perfection existed, and that health was actually an ideal state for which everyone strived while at the same time steadily and inevitably receding from it, since from the moment a person was born he moved further and further away from it the older he grew. And Meir, who listened willingly to Pozner's words, which were only indirectly related to his illness but nevertheless gave him a certain relief, said that this did not console him, and Pozner said, "I'm sorry. I have no consolation to offer apart from the facts of life," and immediately added, "That, at any rate, is my way of consoling myself," and burst into his hoarse, uninhibited laughter, adding as he laughed, "I can make up any theory I like and it will all be true," and he pinched Liora roughly on the arm, and Meir, indignant at this show of affection and at the mere fact of their being together, joined in his familiar laughter and said, trying to sound amused, "Still, it's a fact that there are some people who don't suffer from any diseases at all," and Liora, who was only a little older than Pozner's eldest daughter and worked at the International Telephone Exchange to pay her university fees, said, "Yes. That's true." Her naiveté angered Meir, and he nodded to her shortly and said, "Yes," and Pozner, with the vestiges of the laughter still on his face and in his voice, said with surprising seriousness, "Don't envy anyone. You haven't reached that stage yet," and immediately added, "You talk as if someone was discriminating against you," and Meir, pleased and encouraged by the unexpected, almost scolding directness of his tone, said, "Yes, you're right," and smiled and added jokingly, "But you have to admit that there are people less ill than me," and Liora said that in her opinion, too, he was exaggerating and she couldn't really understand what he wanted, and Meir, very annoyed by her interference, shrugged his shoulders and said rather incoherently, "I want to be the way I was in high school." And surprised and shaken by the words that came out of his mouth, he added, "I want to be healthy, like I was before, that's all," and smiled, and then he grew serious and said sadly, "If only I had exercised and gone swimming and kept to some sort of diet, it wouldn't have happened," and Pozner shook the ash from his cigarette into his empty beer can and said, "Rubbish! What happened is what had to happen," and Meir said, "Maybe you're right," feeling pleasure and admiration for Pozner's words and style, together with the lingering sense of unresentful inferiority at his friend's wisdom and breadth of knowledge, which had remained with him ever since they were at school together. For years Pozner had been preparing himself to write a book that would cause a worldwide sensation and would not fall short of Tolstoy or Pascal—nothing less would satisfy him—until he realized that he wasn't capable of it and abandoned the whole idea and devoted himself to teaching instead. A light breeze rustled the leaves of the tall tree whose dark crest reached the balcony, and the chill in the air increased, and something unclear, the movement of a head, perhaps, or something barely glimpsed in a secret, remembered thought, suddenly darkened Meir's mood, and Liora said, "Perhaps you should go and see a naturopath; they sometimes succeed where conventional doctors fail," and Pozner said, "That's not a bad idea," and gave her another affectionate pinch, and Meir imagined them in bed together making love—sooner or later this disagreeable moment always arrived—and said, "Maybe I will, who knows," and in an amused but joyless tone he added, "I have no desire to spend the rest of my life eating grass," and got up to go, but before he could leave, Pozner said, "Wait, I'll go down with you. I have to buy some cigarettes," and he turned to Liora and said, "I'll be back in a minute," and Liora said, "Okay, I'll be here," and accompanied them to the little hall, where she paused and turned to Meir and said, "You really should go to a naturopath. Why not give it a try?" and Meir said, "Okay, maybe I will. See you," and Pozner pinched her arm affectionately again and said, "I'll be back in a minute, don't run away," and they both walked out the door. When they were on their way down the steps, Meir paused and said, "You may be right, about what happened being what had to happen, but I still don't understand why it had to happen to me," and Pozner said, "You spend too much time thinking about it. The disease isn't the disease itself, but the thoughts about it," and they stepped outside into the dark street, and Meir, who loved Pozner although not in the same comfortable way that he loved Gavrosh, said, "Maybe you're right," and in a voice to which he tried to impart an amused, lighthearted tone, he repeated, "I'd like to be the way I was in high school again." There was something very pleasant and even moving in walking peacefully down the street with Pozner, and in the very fact of their friendship, which had lasted so long that it seemed to have gathered a momentum of its own, and Pozner said, "For that you'll have to be born again," and he tore a leaf off a hedge and suddenly said in a worried, serious tone, "I'm damned if I know what to do with her. I wish she would disappear of her own accord and put an end to the whole affair." Although Pozner's wife had broken off relations with him he knew that she would forgive him the moment he wanted to go back to her, but at the same time he felt a certain degree of responsibility for Liora, who was only a little older than his own eldest daughter, and he said, "I'll wait for her to finish her degree, and that's it," and Meir said,

"You're just stringing her along." They had discussed this matter dozens of times over the past few months and there was no longer anything new to say about it and Pozner, who was obviously troubled despite his lighthearted tone, said, "You can't keep love in a safe. I loved her, you know I did, but I don't love her anymore and there's nothing I can do about it," and then he stood still and exclaimed, "What an evening—just look," and looked around him as if he wanted to capture the evening in all its loveliness—it really was a lovely evening, precisely because of the unseasonable wintry nip in the soft air—and as he spoke he gestured with his hand, and when they began to walk again, he said in a slightly smiling, almost intimate tone that embarrassed Meir, who imagined he could hear something mocking or contentious in it, "You remember how you once wanted to write poetry?" and Meir said, "Yes, I remember," trying to swallow the words and make them disappear as quickly as possible, together with the embarrassing memory lurking somewhere inside him like the memory of a shameful act in some remote era of the past, and he turned on Pozner abruptly and said, "Tell her and be done with it." They were now crossing the road and approaching the café where Pozner intended to buy cigarettes, and he said, "I'd like her to understand for herself and disappear. That's all," and in a voice full of laughter he added, "People are so inconsiderate, they never do what's expected of them. It's terrible," and chuckled, and Meir said, "Yes, it's a scandal," and they both laughed lightly and Pozner said, "I'll tell her in two weeks' time. As soon as she finishes her exams," and he went into the café and asked for two packs of Time and took his change, and when he came out they lingered a moment longer and Pozner said, "Stop thinking about your blood pressure and why it happened to you," and Meir said, "Okay, I'll try," and Pozner said, "We think that if we say to ourselves 'chance' instead of 'necessity' or the opposite everything will be all right," and Meir said, "Yes," and Pozner said, "Don't believe it," and they gave each other a little wave and parted.

The streets were unusually empty for this hour of the evening, or so it seemed to Meir, and as he walked slowly under the old

tamarisks on Ben Gurion Boulevard, he said to himself that even
though it hadn't rained yet, winter had already begun, and as he
turned into Dizengoff Street and walked along it, he tried to remember if there was a basketball game or some other special program on
TV that night, which might account for the surprising emptiness of
the streets, and as he continued walking north, looking almost unconsciously at the pavement and the trees and the shops and houses and
taking them in, down to the most minute and elusive detail, with an
unfocused stare, while at the same time noting all the changes that
had taken place in them and remembering them before these
changes, like three photographs superimposed, one on top of the
other, his thoughts returned to his illness, which he knew was there
inside him although he could not feel it at all, and his spirits fell
because he somehow saw this illness, which was nothing worse than
high blood pressure after all, not only as an impairment to his health
but as a blight unjustly striking him down and mainly, which was the
most painful thing of all, as a shameful personal failure and an injury
to his manhood, and the bottom line of all this was that he was no
longer young and never would be again, and the only road ahead of
him, along which he was already being pushed, was the road leading
to old age, which had already tarred him with its brush, and death.
And his thoughts turned once more to his body, which felt like a
rather thick covering of flesh over the surface of which his thoughts
groped and beneath which, in the dark space that was the inside of
his body, they moved, and he was conscious of how slack and feeble
his arms and shoulder muscles had become, and how puffy and flabby
the flesh on his chest had grown, and his belly, too, with its funny little
paunch suspended like a small, swollen sack above his legs, which had
also dwindled and lost the sturdiness and agility that had seemed to
be theirs for all eternity, since this sturdiness and agility were the very
nature of those legs, just as they were the nature of all his other organs
and limbs, and of his body as a whole, with that delightful suppleness
that was its birthright and that had made it so pleasant and comfortable to inhabit. With an aching heart he remembered the strenuous
youth movement hikes and the cheerful army marches, not to men-

tion the basketball and football games for which his keenness had known no bounds, and he said to himself that all that suppleness and robust vitality were lost forever, and that this blighted, infected flesh would grow more and more withered and flabby and shapeless, and he could already feel it happening the moment the thought came into his head! He felt it like the dry movement of sand sifting through his flesh, and then shifting about in the dark space inside his body like grayish vapors, groping for the inner organs—heart, liver, lungs, stomach, intestines—hanging there as if on invisible hooks, and with frozen sorrow he stared at one of the houses next to the police station as he walked past it, and he saw the hut with the gray tiled roof and the sandy field full of little stones and bits of broken china and dry leaves and pieces of coal and the dilapidated fence that had once been there and that he would never see in their material form again, and at the same time he felt that inside his feet, as if inside the hollow shell of a chocolate doll, there was another pair of feet—his childhood feet, treading the pavement—the feeling was so vivid that he looked down at his feet and smiled, and after a moment, still subject to the same curious sensation of having two pairs of feet, he looked up again at the houses and the trees, which filled him with sorrow and pity. He had already passed the place where the hut and the field had once stood, and he said to himself that his life was running out and finishing, in fact it was already finished, and he had hardly done anything with it—he had a wife and two sons, one in high school and the other in the army, and he had an apartment and a steady job as an engineer with quite a good salary, and once, many years before, he had taken a trip abroad, and that was it, more or less—and he said to himself again that if only he had studied architecture instead of engineering, as Gavrosh had encouraged him to do, or at least if he had left the firm and set up his own, as he had intended doing and would have done, too, but for the economic slowdown and the Six-Day War, which had ruined everything, his life would have been much more successful and exciting, and with a feeling of growing despondency, his thoughts strayed to Raya and that wasted week in Haifa. From the moment he left Pozner's and began walking, he knew that sooner or later his thoughts would drag him in this direction, and the unwanted memory, which was always lying somewhere in the recesses of his mind like a dark stone, now came floating up to the surface and filled him with the familiar sense of dismal failure and impotence, which persisted in spite of all the old, increasingly untenable arguments he had advanced to justify himself over the years—the "spirit of the times," and the well-nigh sacred principles of working-class morality that had been so deeply instilled in him in his youth that they had become part of his being, or even the argument about the comradely obligations he owed her husband, Bentz, which was part of the same moral scheme of things—his obligation to his own wife for some reason seemed far less weighty, enamored as he was then of Maya-kovsky and that spirit of reckless bohemianism that rejected bourgeois respectability and all its institutions and beliefs with contempt, thanks to and in the name of the revolution, which apart from anything else, and perhaps above all, meant the liberation of feeling and instinct. With the perspective of time, the missed opportunity in all its bitterness seemed not less but even more cruel and painful to him, and he repeated to himself that if only he had made love to her then as he had wanted to—for they were alone with no one to disturb them, and she had been so eager and willing to submit to him and respond to all his desires—and not in that blind, unnecessary panic, he would have felt completely different now about life, but the opportunity was irretrievably lost, and not only because of all the years that had passed since then.

On the corner of Nordau Boulevard, where a cool breeze was blowing along the open street from the sea, he paused for a moment and wondered whether to turn off toward the sea and come back via Yarkon Street, but after a short hesitation he continued along Dizengoff, which at this point was completely dark and deserted, exhorting himself to pull himself together immediately and cast off useless regrets about the past and anxieties about the present and all his hesitations and doubts and begin to live vigorously and enjoy himself as much as possible, since a day that passed without pleasure, or even an hour, was time wasted. And he conducted a rapid survey of the world in his head, feeling a momentary wave of dizziness and panic as he did so, and concluded that it was so packed with pleasures he had not yet tasted that it was a pity to waste even a single minute, and he made up his mind to begin enjoying himself on the spot, and in a surge of exhilaration and optimism he decided to begin with the Oriental pastries that he had seen displayed in countless shops and kiosks all over town but had never sampled before, and thus to begin his new life, full of vigor and enjoyment, and as he hurried toward the Pèer cinema, he made up his mind that if he did not find what he wanted there, he would take a bus to Dizengoff Center or even to Jaffa.

Opposite the cinema, in a little kiosk, he found the pastries laid out on trays, each kind on a separate tray, and after hesitating for some time he chose two, each of a different variety, and made up his mind that he would come back every day and buy two different kinds of pastry until he had sampled them all, since he was not prepared to forgo even a single one. The kiosk owner wrapped the pastries in paper and held them out to him, dripping with oil, and Meir paid him and asked him what their names were, he himself called them all *baklava*, as if knowing the exact name was a vital part of obtaining the anticipated pleasure, but after a few steps the names had already grown confused in his head, and by the time he reached Ben Yehuda Street they had disintegrated into a jumble of meaningless syllables. The pastries themselves were so sweet that they nauseated him and he wanted to throw them away, but he told himself that he had to taste everything and devoured them down to the last crumb, and then he spat on his sticky fingers and wiped them with some leaves he tore from a hedge and walked along Ben Yehuda Street with his mouth full of an unpleasant, cloying sweetness but with the elated feeling that he had now embarked on his new life, until he couldn't stand it any longer and stopped at a café in Allenby Street and bought a bottle of grapefruit juice and gulped it down, swishing it around in his mouth to get rid of the nauseating sweetness. Then he continued on his way, uncertain whether to go straight home, for something painful drew him now more than ever before to Aviva's side, or, because of the very same pain, to call Drora and try to invite himself over to go to bed with her, but this time using the direct, even crude approach that seemed to him both more promising and also more appropriate to the new way of life he had now embraced.

And when he walked past the café where he used to sit regularly with Gavrosh in the evenings, and which they used to call "Pa's café" because of the appearance of the café owner and his wife—God knows how they ended up running a café in Tel Aviv—who looked like a couple of old-fashioned farmers from a *moshav*, he paused for a moment and inspected the place, which had changed hands in the meantime and was closed for renovations, and thought of the many hours he had spent here drinking beer, which was Gavrosh's favorite drink, listening to him, at almost every one of these meetings, which sometimes took place every day, endlessly and obsessively analyzing his tortuous relations with a married woman called Nurit, who was the mother of two children and who, according to Gavrosh, looked like the French actress Macha Méril, whose picture he always carried around with him in his wallet, where for some reason he shrank from keeping the picture of his real love, who had consequently remained engraved on Meir's memory in the form of Macha Méril. Meir had caught a glimpse of Nurit only once, and that purely by chance, because Gavrosh went out of his way to prevent them from meeting, as part of the anxious and shifty secrecy with which he surrounded this relationship, which gave him little pleasure and caused him much heartbreak and agony, not only the agonies of jealousy and hopelessness and doubt, but moral agonies, too, since the affair was in total contradiction to his clumsy and old-fashioned sense of the fitness of things, but he did not have the strength to break it off, and his conflicts and unhappiness touched Meir to the heart, because he loved Gavrosh and felt very close to him despite the difference in their ages. And he went on walking and left the dark café behind him, thinking to himself that it was important for Gavrosh to know that the café had changed hands and was being renovated, but also that perhaps it was a good thing he had been spared this grief. And when he crossed Frishman Street, where a cool wind was blowing from the sea, bearing the steady murmur of the waves with it, he thought about the bird that Gavrosh had pursued during those two rainy winter days in the region of Caesarrea, where he had gone to observe the habits of a certain species of waterfowl and suddenly come across this bird, if it really was the bird he thought it was—Gavrosh himself was not certain because he knew that the bird in question could not possibly be in Israel at that season, and the distance and misty gray air had blurred his vision—and he pursued the bird through the cold, wet plantations and between the fish ponds and through the muddy fields whipped by piercing winds, trudging desperately through the mud in his boots, which grew as broad as a goose's feet and as heavy as lead, along the foothills of the Carmel as far as Atlit, where it disappeared from view in the stormy rain and the dark, as if it had been swallowed up in the murky air, and all his searching, which lasted for another whole day, was in vain. Meir did not remember the name of the bird Gavrosh had hoped this bird was, or even its appearance, which Gavrosh described to him very vividly, with a boyish enthusiasm that seemed a little strained by now, and not very well suited to his ravaged face, with its lines of age and weariness and the little bags of sagging skin under the eyes, on another rainy day in the kitchen of Gavrosh's parents' flat, because in spite of all the youth movement nature hikes and the years on the kibbutz, and despite all Gavrosh's persistent efforts to convert him, his attitude toward nature had remained abstract and lacking in any kind of intimacy, so that all he remembered of Gavrosh's description was the stubborn, back-breaking pursuit in the rain and mud under a somber sky, and the fact that the bird was very rare—to himself he called it a Colibri because this was the most exotic bird's name that he could think of—and the fact that it had a prominent red mark somewhere, but he could not be certain whether this red mark was on its breast, as he thought he remembered, or on its head, or perhaps its tail, and this irked him greatly because from the moment that Gavrosh died, every little forgotten detail connected with his friend became important to him. If only he had suspected that Gavrosh would die less than two years later, he would have listened to him attentively and questioned him about even the smallest and most insignificant details concerning his actions and views and engraved them firmly in his memory, but Gavrosh died unexpectedly from a cerebral hemorrhage that no one could possibly have predicted, and when Meir stood with Aviva on the edge of the silent group of mourners gathered around the open grave—Pozner had not joined them, on the grounds that he refused to take part in religious rituals—scanning the crowd in vain for Macha Méril and trying to identify her by his memory of the picture, he raised his eyes and saw the rows and rows of white tombstones between the heads of the people, and beyond them the expanse of still-empty golden sand stretching to the cemetery wall and beyond it into the distance, at the end of which he could clearly sense the presence of the sea. It was all so utterly different from the shady graveyard on the hillside in Nazareth, with its old stone wall against which they had sat in the shade of the softly murmuring pines, eating their fruit and sandwiches in the profound stillness steeped in the smell of earth and resin and fallen pine needles. In front of them in the distance they could see part of the Valley of Jezreel and the blue mountains beyond it, and Gavrosh, who was almost ten years older than Meir and worked as a geologist, crumbled a little clod of earth between his fingers and said, indicating the view before them with a slight movement of his head, "Look at the valley—have you ever seen anything so beautiful?" and bit into his sandwich, and Meir said, "It's marvelous," and the view of the mountains and the valley really was marvelous, with all the flavor of Eretz Israel compressed into the sight and the smell of the air and the trees and something emanating from the earth underneath its carpet of pine needles. The stillness and the pure, clear air were wonderfully pleasant and soporific, and Meir looked at the dense blue air and wished that he could fly away and dissolve into the infinite blue spaces, and Gavrosh gathered a few pine needles in his hand and crushed them between his fingers, and then he said that people who lived in nature, and he had met a few of them during the two years he had spent working as a fisherman in a village in Holland, knew from childhood that death was a part of life, as integral a part of it as the taste of salt was part of seawater; they saw it around them every

day in the animals and plants, and grew to understand that it was not
an accident or a mishap or something in contradiction to life, and that
their lives were only minute particles of something begun long before
they came into the world, something that would go on long after they
died and became part of the earth they now walked on—which was
exactly as it should be—and that this was why they did not complain
so much, for all the sorrow and pain, at their own deaths or the deaths
of those close to them, or at any rate the thought of their lives coming
to an end did not make them bitter and desperate, and Meir said,
"Yes," and bit into a tomato, which squirted juice onto his shirt, and
asked what people like himself, who were not close to nature, should
do, although the truth was that all this did not really concern him at
all because, even though he knew in theory that everyone, including
himself of course, was doomed to grow old and die, in practice he felt
that he was immortal and that he would go on living forever. He asked
only to please Gavrosh and thank him for showing up at the kibbutz,
where life had become difficult and full of conflict, owing to the fact
that he and Aviva were about to leave, in the dusty Nature Protection
Society jeep, and persuading him, almost against his will, to come
along on this trip with him, and Gavrosh said, "You can come close
to it. All it takes is the will and a little effort. Nature is open to
everyone." Meir said, "Yes," without really meaning it, and threw a
little clod of earth aimlessly in front of him, and then the midday
silence fell again, deeper and quieter than before, and a gentle drowsiness settled on them, and Gavrosh opened his shirt and sprawled out
with *Rameau's Nephew* unopened in his hand and said that when he
looked into this transparent air and penetrated far, far beyond its
physical limits, he sensed not only how small and transient man was,
and how lonely in the vast, insensible spaces of the cosmos out of
which he had somehow emerged, but also to what extent he was the
product of a blind and insignificant combination of circumstances,
and Meir, who felt drunk with drowsiness in the clear, still air, asked
languidly, "What does that mean?" and Gavrosh replied, "It doesn't
mean anything. It's frightening," and glanced at a bird flying past,
and Meir said, "Yes," and stretched out on his back on the ground.

He felt no interest whatever in the subject, and Gavrosh's words sunk indifferently into the pleasant, drowsy lassitude filling his body, and he repeated, "Yes. It's very frightening," and for a moment he thought of asking Gavrosh if they should really leave the kibbutz, and if he should go and study architecture, but he didn't ask him, partly because he knew what Gavrosh's answer would be, but mainly because he didn't have the strength to rend the silence surrounding him, and he abandoned himself to it and to the quiet desire spreading through him to go on lying there forever on the earth, covered with fallen pine needles, or to take off and fly away, and he felt as if there was no difference between lying on the ground and soaring into the infinite blue sky. Gavrosh, too, sank into silence, but after a while, quite suddenly, he said that perhaps he should break off his relations with that married woman with two children, and Meir said, "Maybe you're right," and Gavrosh turned over onto his side and said, "Do you really think so?" and Meir, who was half asleep and felt as if everything was happening at a distance from him, said, "Maybe not," and went on looking up at the crest of the tree swaying slightly above him, and Gavrosh said, "No, there's no point in carrying on like this," his furrowed face full of sorrow, and then he said that the trouble was that he loved her very much, and Meir said, "I know," and Gavrosh threw a pinecone at something, and after a long interval he said that her husband had been offered a job in France and they intended to take the offer, and afterward he said that he hadn't seen her for three weeks, and his ravaged face filled with anxiety, and he added immediately, "What if she falls in love with her husband again in the meantime?" and Meir, making a weak effort, said, "She won't fall in love with him, you've got nothing to worry about," drawn to sleep as powerfully as if its gravity was equal in force to that of the earth he was lying on, and Gavrosh ran his fingers through his hair and said, "I haven't got the strength for it anymore," and turned onto his back again, with his face to the treetops high above them and his hand playing idly with *Rameau's Nephew* lying at his side.

After crossing Mendele Street, Meir went into a little café to phone Drora, but as he was about to dial the number, with his finger

already in the dial, he was overcome by a feeling of impatience and
distaste for all these stratagems and ploys, so exhausting and devious
and contemptible, and he was seized by powerful longings for Aviva
and an urgent need to feel an intimacy and security that required no
tricks and ploys, and with a feeling of relief he stopped dialing Drora's
number and phoned home, and when he heard Aviva's voice he was
filled with happiness and told her that he was calling from a café and
asked her what she was doing, and she said, "Nothing special. A bit
of ironing," and asked him, with a note of surprise in her voice, if
anything was the matter, and Meir said that nothing was the matter
and asked her if she felt like coming down and taking a little walk with
him, the streets were almost empty and the weather was fine, and if
they felt like it they could go and have a drink somewhere, and she
asked "Now?" and the note of surprise in her voice pierced his heart
and heightened his eagerness and he said, "Why not, come on," and
waited for her to agree, but she still hesitated and said that she wasn't
properly dressed, and he said, "It doesn't matter. Come just as you
are," and about fifteen minutes later they met in front of the Chen
Cinema and walked down Dizengoff Street, and then along King
George Street and Ben Zion Boulevard to the Habima Plaza.

They strolled along at a slow, leisurely pace, and he realized how
much he loved these old streets where he felt so at home, and walking
with Aviva filled him with happiness and serenity, everything was
suddenly as peaceful and harmonious as he could wish, and he felt the
tender evening air lapping them in its loveliness and thought of
turning into Ehad Ha-am Street or Rothschild Boulevard, drawn by
the desolation of these beloved old streets, but Aviva wanted to walk
in the direction of the livelier streets, and they walked around the
museum and then crossed the road and walked along Chen Boulevard,
talking about his office, and especially the Youth Center he was
working on, and about the plant where Aviva worked as an expert on
optical instruments, and about their money problems and their sons,
the younger son at home and the elder son, Roy, doing his national
service, who was thinking of signing up for a stint in the regular army
in spite of Meir's objections, and about the government and the

economic and political situation, all in the same spirit of peaceful conciliation that was in the air and that enveloped them, too, and when they reached the end of the boulevard, they crossed the street and sat down on the wall of the fountain in the middle of the big, open square and looked contentedly at the quiet, distant traffic, until Aviva said, "It's getting cold," and cuddled up to him, and he hugged her lightly and said, "Why don't we have something to eat? There's a place with blintzes near here," and Aviva, with his arms still around her, said, "I don't feel like eating. But I'd like something hot to drink," and Meir got up and pointed to a café across the road and said, "Come on, that place is supposed to be great," and they crossed the empty square and went into the café.

Aviva ordered hot chocolate and walnut cake and Meir, who decided, with her approval, to suspend the not very strict diet he had been on for the past couple of weeks, ordered cappuccino and chocolate cake, and as they sat eating and drinking and chatting and praising the cakes and the place, which was tasteful and elegant and full of the fragrance of coffee and freshly baked cakes—the cappuccino and chocolate cake were delicious—Meir glanced at a couple sitting a few tables away, and after a moment he looked at them again, as if in spite of himself. The man was not particularly good-looking, but he had an air of carefree confidence, in his sporty, striped shirt, and all of a sudden, without knowing why, Meir felt something darkening inside him, as if an imperceptible shadow, which up to now had been somehow hiding in the air, had gathered around him and seeped into his body. There was nothing to arouse his suspicions about the man with the self-confident air, but the shadow went on seeping into his flesh, filling the hollowness inside him with darkness and gloom and covering his face, which grew dull and closed up, and he withdrew into himself, poisoned by bitter memories and hostility, until Aviva noticed and asked if anything was wrong, and he said, "No, nothing," and made some remark in praise of the cappuccino, and Aviva repeated, "What's wrong?" and Meir said, "I told you, nothing," and Aviva said, "Okay," and went on drinking her chocolate as if nothing in fact was wrong, even though both of them could already feel the gloom hanging heavily in the air, and Meir said, "I'm a little tired," and went on artificially prolonging the conversation with his thoughts on something else entirely. When they had finished eating and drinking, he paid the waitress and they left the café in a strained silence broken by one or two forced remarks, which only emphasized the estrangement yawning between them, and they crossed the municipal square, where a few dogs were running about in the dark while their owners stood chatting on the sidelines, and Aviva, who could no longer bear the ugly atmosphere of anger and hostility, asked him again to tell her what was wrong, and Meir, his arm resting on her shoulder without any feeling at all, said, "Nothing. I'm tired, that's all," and Aviva said, "If you don't want to tell me, don't, I won't force you." Meir said, "That's fine by me," and entrenched himself in his silence and thus, without a word or a glance, keeping his eyes straight ahead and his arm coldly on her shoulder, he walked stiffly at the side of this decent and loyal and far-from-adventurous woman, whose single aberration had been filling his days and nights with confused and bitter thoughts for many months now without his being able to come to terms with her behavior or understand how she could have gone to bed with a strange man half an hour or forty-five minutes at the most after seeing him for the first time in her life. She was so domesticated that it would never have occurred to him in his wildest fantasies that she was capable of hurting him with an adventure of this kind, but after the first shock had worn off, together with the consternation and devastating pain and humiliation, a feeling of excited wonder and awe began to erupt from the boiling lava of his injury and hostility, and even a painful, but at the same time, agreeable admiration—he was more attracted to her now than ever before—of the boldness and independence she had shown by giving in to the lust of the moment and allowing herself to experience this chance adventure, which he longed to emulate, although he felt his own ineptitude so keenly that it was hard for him to admit it, and which enflamed his imagination and his jealousy of her, and especially of the hated stranger. He cursed him and wished that he would die, but at the same time he felt for him too, as for his wife, a poisonous and painful, but at the same time, undeniable admiration, and in the vortex of these violent emotions he felt that he himself had to repeat, if possible in the very same way, the act his wife had committed with that man, for only then would the wrong be righted and the injury his wife had done him be canceled out, and when he masturbated he went over the act in detail and made love to his wife in the form of the other man, and thus, together with the searing pain, he found some sort of consolation.

When they entered Masaryk Square and crossed the dark little park, he could no longer restrain himself and said, "How did it happen? You know what I mean," and Aviva said, "I knew it. It's beginning again," in a tone of impatience and despair, and Meir said, "I want to know how it happened," all his inhibitions collapsing at once in the seething tide of his pain and hostility, and Aviva said, "Can't you leave it alone," and Meir said, "No. I want to know who the man you made love to in the car was," with something helpless and imploring in his hostile, insistent voice, and Aviva said, "I never told you that I made love to someone in a car," and Meir said, "So was it in his house then?"—by now he was begging, and Aviva said, "Why must you keep on dragging it up over and over again? It's enough already, leave it alone," and Meir said, "No. I want to know," and repeated his question, and Aviva said, "I told you everything I wanted to tell you and that's it. I don't want to talk about it anymore. It bores me to death," and Meir said, "But you went to bed with someone." The saliva stuck in his throat like a ball and there was a faint, anxious note of hope in his voice and Aviva said, "Yes," and Meir, who was hoping against hope that she might deny it, felt the ground slipping away and the abyss of pain and defeat gaping despairingly at his feet again, as if he had just heard it for the first time, and he asked, "Who was it? Someone I know?" and Aviva, who had given up hope of putting an end to this futile, exhausting exchange, said, "No," and Meir asked, "Someone from work?" a question he had already asked twenty times, and Aviva said, "No," and Meir said, "Was he tall and handsome?" and Aviva did not reply, and Meir repeated, "Was he handsome?" as if he was pleading for his life, and

Aviva stopped and turned to face him and said, "Why do you have to keep on dragging it up? Leave it alone, it's enough," and Meir said, "Tell me, what do you care? Was he handsome?" and Aviva said, "I've already told you what I had to tell you. And I'm not saying one more word. It only makes things worse," and Meir said, "Why did you do it?" He said this in a tone of heartbroken reproach, hoping for an admission of guilt, or at least an expression of sorrow and regret, but Aviva said, "Because I wanted to," in a hard, impatient voice and started walking again, and Meir walked behind her, flooded by a renewed wave of insult and anger, and they walked for a while without saying a word until Meir said, "Do you ever think about it?" and Aviva said, "I never think about the past, you know that," and Meir, with a glimmer of relief flickering faintly inside him—he knew that she was telling the truth—hesitated for a moment, uncertain whether to keep on, but he couldn't stop, and in the end he said plaintively, "I know you think about it all the time," and Aviva said, "Don't make me laugh. I'd forgotten all about it by the next day," and Meir felt relief spreading through him and gradually dispelling the insult and hostility, only the matter of the "next day" still embittered his soul. If only she had forgotten it immediately, the very next minute, or at the very most, the next morning, he would have been happy, but nevertheless he was ready to be appeased and to embrace her in a spirit of reconciliation and gratitude, only something stopped him, and he went on walking next to her gloomily without saying a word until Aviva suddenly softened and pressed up against him and said, "Please let's forget it and put it behind us," and Meir said, "All right," and put his arm limply around her shoulder, and Aviva said, in a playful, conciliatory tone, "I don't understand what you want," and Meir, with a faint hint of a smile in his voice, said, "I want what happened not to have happened, that's what I want," and Aviva smiled and said, "But you do everything you can to make it happen all over again," and nestled up to him, and Meir, who now felt quite consoled, said, "I know," and immediately, as if deliberately leaping into a dark, rocky chasm, asked, "Did you enjoy it?" and felt as if he was going to suffocate with the intensity of the suspense, and Aviva said, "It's not important," her voice gentle, and Meir said, "It's important to me. Tell me, what do you care? Did you enjoy it?" and felt the sweat breaking out on his forehead with the panic and suspense, and Aviva said, "No, I didn't," and Meir felt an immense flow of happiness and thankfulness washing away the vestiges of the insult and hostility, it was what he had longed to hear, and he hugged her to him in a passion of joyful reconciliation, flooded with gratitude and pride in his wife, and Aviva said, "You're just making yourself and both of us miserable. Leave it alone. Why must you keep coming back to it?" and Meir said, "I don't know," everything inside him glowing with relief and pleasurable feelings of purification and love—if only she had never gone to bed with that man in the first place, his happiness would have been complete—and Aviva said, "I told you it was nothing, that I'd forgotten all about it ages ago," and Meir said, "Enough, enough, I've finished with it," and pressed her to him. And in fact he did feel as clean and purified as if some malignant infection had left his body, and they turned into Bograshov Street, where a wind was blowing into the open street from the sea, and went home, where they found Amnon, their younger son, sitting in the big room watching television, and Meir joined him for a few minutes while Aviva made the bed, and then he went into the bedroom and got into bed with her and embraced her, and afterward, full of tranquil happiness, he took *The Bermuda Triangle* and read it for a while until he fell asleep.

A few days later he went to the Sick Fund clinic for an ECG whose results were good, and then he went to see Dr. Reiner, who examined him and found that his blood pressure had stabilized at a satisfactory level, and when she gave him the prescription she reminded him again of the importance of taking his medication regularly, and in the end she asked him casually if he played any sports —there was something a little less affable in her manner this time, as if her thoughts were elsewhere, or perhaps he was only imagining it—and with a feeling of disappointment he said, "I walk a lot, if that can be called a sport," and Dr. Reiner said that that was very good, but that he should take up something else as well, a little more active, like swimming or basketball, and Meir, whose anxiety about his health was now somewhat allayed, so that it seemed like a cloud somewhere on the horizon, which though real and menacing enough was still so far away that he could ignore it, said, "I'll try," and shook her warmly by the hand and thanked her and left. It was a soft autumn day with a few light clouds scattered here and there in the sky and something immeasurably delightful in the transparent blue air, and as he left the clinic and strolled at a leisurely pace down the fresh, bright street, he suddenly sensed a very delicate, almost imperceptible scent lightly brushing his nostrils, or perhaps it was only the memory of the smell that he called the scent of youth, that scent of the world that only the young are capable of sensing in all its subtle nuances, and like a dog picking up a scent, he stood twitching his nostrils and trying with all his might to pick up and revive the scent of youth, which had suddenly broken out and crossed the barrier of the years, and sense once more that sweetness and intoxication, with its finely tuned responsiveness to every fleeting nuance and shifting current in the air, and its suppleness, and the thrill of young love, and above all the incomparable feeling that everything was open and everything was possible, and at that moment he felt a sudden desire to cast off all his obligations and give himself an unexpected holiday for no reason at all, and as he abandoned himself to the feeling of freedom and pride and the giddy sensation of the world with all its pleasures opening up before him, he decided to go to the Paris Cinema and take in a morning show and afterward, perhaps after a short stroll through the streets, to go and have lunch at a restaurant, and in the meantime, since there was still an hour to go before the show began, he walked along Ben Yehuda Street and went into a bookshop to ask about Ken Stevens's new book, *Industrial Building and Construction*.

The shop was deserted except for the two saleswomen sitting behind the counter and chatting, and Meir was able to stand and browse at his leisure through the book, which he found on the architectural shelves, and after making up his mind to buy it, he put it aside and went on scanning the shelves with the same leisurely air, removing a book from time to time and browsing through it and then putting it back, feeling that he had made a complete break with the daily routine imposed on him from outside for the sake of something higher, private, and more spiritual. And after browsing through a few history books, especially about Israel, and archaeology and philosophy books and also a few cookbooks and poetry books, wishing that he could read them all and with no aim in view but the pure delight in his freedom, he caught sight of *The Joy of Sex* and took it down with an absentminded air, and his face stiff with the effort to maintain an expression of indifference and cover up the signs of embarrassment that he felt as keenly as if he were doing something perverted and wrong, he turned over the pages, at first in panicky haste and then more calmly, and studied the explanations, all in big, clear letters, and the seemingly innocent but actually very stimulating drawings illustrating the various positions of lovemaking and copulation—*Cuissade, Croupade, Flanquette*—words he had never heard in his life, which gave rise in him to a feeling of inferiority and deprivation. "With a woman who has good vaginal muscle control it can be fantastic for the man, but for her it is unique, giving her total freedom to control movement, depth and her partner . . ." the words ran before his eyes, filling him with excitement, and he sensed the arousal and embarrassment covering his face like a layer of hot jelly. On no account did he want anyone to see him like this, now it was brutally plain to him just how great his ignorance of sexual matters was and how much he had missed: *"Pompoir,* the most sought-after feminine response of all. She must close and constrict the Yoni until it holds the Lingam as with a finger . . ." He had never heard of the "Yoni" and the "Lingam," and his regret for what he had missed broadened and deepened, "opening and shutting at her pleasure," "A woman who has the divine gift of lechery . . . will almost always make a superlative partner," "The knack lies in playing on your partner like an instrument, alternately pushing them forward and frustrating them . . ." For a moment, as he studied the book, it occurred to him to buy it and take it home so that he and Aviva could use it to help them improve their sex life, which, after he had perused the book, seemed to him dull and impoverished, and he put it down and took up *Behind the Male Myth* by Antonio Pietropino, whose name sounded to him for a moment like a deliberate distortion, perhaps for the sake of a joke or a publicity stunt, and Jacqueline Simonard, and paged through it almost unconsciously, pausing from time to time to read a few sentences, and then studied the statistical tables, which interested him more than anything else, the results of a survey taken of four thousand men, and as he read he tested himself in relation to the questions that had been put to these anonymous interviewees— "What gives you the greatest pleasure in foreplay? What can your partner do to increase your pleasure? Be more active during sexual relations—34.4%; engage more in oral sex—24%; touch my genitals. . . . How do you feel about having sex with a woman older than yourself? How frequently do you have sex?"—and here there was a detailed comparison with the findings of the Kinsey Report and the Hunt Report, of which he had never heard, and also a special column noting the ideal number of times (a week) for different age groups, which interested Meir especially because he had recently been a prey to fears that he might become impotent because of the medication he was taking for his blood pressure, and already it seemed to him that he could discern symptoms of weakening desire and diminished potency, and he would have gone on studying the tables in spite of his embarrassment, but when one of the salesgirls got up and came over to the bookshelves he closed the book and put it back on the shelf, and with a face as calm and casual as he could make it, he went to the counter and paid for the book by Ken Stevens and went out into the cool fresh air and walked to the Paris and saw the movie, and when it was over he came out into the light, agreeable rain, which was falling slowly, moistening the air and wetting the pavement, and he decided to forgo the restaurant, which seemed to him to be going a bit too far, and went to have lunch at his mother's.

His mother hurried to the door with her usual quick shuffle, opening it with her elbow because she was holding a steaming little pot in her hand with a kitchen towel, and when she saw him she gave him a welcoming smile and said, "I'm glad you came, come in, come in," and hurried back to the kitchen, where she was standing and cooking in the clean, empty flat still full of the fresh coolness of the morning, which gave rise in her, as always, to a mood of tranquil melancholy and pangs of secret longing intensified by the light rain, and she abandoned herself to her constant and in a certain sense even enjoyable regrets for all the things she had done wrong in her life or the chances she had missed, and the wishes and yearnings, most of them incurably romantic, that still stirred in her soul, even though she no longer believed in their fulfillment, and she prayed that no one would come and deprive her of this fragile peace and quiet—one ring at the doorbell was enough to bring it all down in ruins at her feet —and as she sliced the eggplants and turned the rissoles over in the pan and salted and stirred, she listened effortlessly to the strains of the *Rio Flamenco,* the record she had bought on that tender day at Algeciras, shortly before embarking on the ferry to cross the little blue bay and return, after a three-day trip, to Gibraltar, the toylike town that now seemed to her like an incredible dream, where she had ended up purely by chance living in Number 9 King's Yard Lane, on the third floor, and where she had miraculously been granted something of those wishes and desires after she had already despaired of everything and been drained of her strength and the remnants of her vitality by the unendurable disappointment of her life in Eretz Israel, the beloved land to which she had come with her mother as a girl, almost a child, at the beginning of the thirties, drawn by the spell of songs and stories, and a vague, romantic Zionism, and the passionate yearning of youth for redemption and the building of a new world.

And to the delightful strains of the music merging with the soft autumn air drifting in through the kitchen window and the hissing of the fat in the pan, she walked slowly down the stairs, the wicker shopping basket on her arm, and in the always unfamiliar dimness and coolness of the stairwell, paused for a moment at the mailbox to see if there was a letter from Meir or Rifka, and full of happy, solemn suspense, like a little girl going to her first day of school, emerged into King's Yard Lane. Every day the same suppressed excitement returned, every day she wondered at it anew, every day she felt the same fear lest it disappear like a dream, and before she set out she glanced up at the little street behind her, this was a part of the ritual of leaving the house, and glimpsed the narrow little street and the grayish-white Rock looming steeply over the town—and then she turned around and with a glad, ringing step and a feeling of freedom that filled her with wonder, she walked along the narrow street with its low colonial houses, full of little shops, most of which were owned by Indians and Jews, and a subdued, commercial bustle, which invariably reminded her of Nahalat Benyamin Street in Tel Aviv. For a moment she paused outside Ben Zaken's shop, nodded to Ginger, peered into the window of the Indian clothes shop, said a polite "Good morning" to Mr. Watson of the rather provincial department store, full of happiness at all these little actions, and at the same time, with the solemn, festive feeling that never left her, she gazed, more lingeringly now, at the tranquil alleys winding up the slopes of the Rock projecting into the straits, on the other side of which, a little blurred, Algericas lay encircled by brown hills. After the photographer's, opposite the Spanish restaurant, where they had dined on the unforgettable evening of her birthday—she hadn't wanted it because she didn't like ceremonies, especially those of which she herself was the center, but her husband had already reserved a table and invited the chief engineer and his wife, and she did not consider herself free to refuse and spoil his pleasure—she turned and walked in the direction of the wharf and the docks, and although the area was unfamiliar, she felt supremely confident and ready for adventure, and even exhilarated at the idea of having unexpectedly lost her way. She came to a little open square and paused for a moment to look at the wharf, with the warehouses and shipyards, and listen to the sounds of work—the banging of hammers and the whine of drilling and buzz of sawing—coming from them, and then she strolled slowly through the unfamiliar alleys to Africa Point, passing an old cinema and crossing a miniature square whose little garden moved her almost to tears, and sensing on her face and her bare arms and in every fiber of her being the pleasure and freedom saturating the sights and colors and the blue air with its pungent smell of the sea, the smell of seaweed and rust, and she wished that she could fly away and dissolve into the blue spaces, somewhere in whose depths perfect happiness awaited her. And thus, sweetly straying, she reached the place where the two oceans, the Mediterranean and the Atlantic, met and from where on a clear day you could see the bluish coast of Africa, but when she came to the place itself, her memory failed her and everything grew blurred and she stopped strewing salt on the slices of eggplant and strained her memory to make it yield the place with the blue sky spreading softly over the bay and the straits, but as if to spite her, the sight so vital to her happiness eluded her and remained buried somewhere in the dark depths of her memory, until for a moment—although there could be no doubt of its existence, for she had seen it with her own eyes—the suspicion entered her mind that it had all been nothing but a mirage. But then, still shrouded in a delicate web of melancholy, she reminded herself that soon, in a few months' time, she would be there together with her husband, who had already been to the travel agent to inquire about fares and flights and returned with a pile of brightly colored brochures, making the trip seem imminent and real, and when she was there she would see everything again in precise and vivid detail and engrave the sights in her memory, where they would remain forever, vivid and distinct, together with the sounds of the Spanish melodies, which like the old Polish tunes of her childhood, all kinds of mazurkas and folk songs, and the songs of her youth, full of vibrant hope and Zionist longings, stirred the deepest chords of her soul, a romantic soul brimming with tender yearnings for the past, when everything was still good and full of promise, a past that had vanished, but which in some hidden and mysterious way seemed to infiltrate through invisible pores in the air and come back to life, metamorphosed, in all kinds of undefined places—little towns in Europe, real or imaginary villages on riverbanks or seashores, and sometimes even a little house with an overgrown garden in Rashi Street or Hameilitz Street in Tel Aviv—and for the life of vagabond freedom in which that past should somehow have been reincarnated, and of which she had been robbed by her home and family and relations and friends and also by the country itself, Eretz Israel, which had worn her out and disappointed her, and which together with her family and friends and relations had turned into the wall against which all her wishes and fantasies had been dashed. She had found herself suddenly an exile in her own land, so much so that she wanted to fly to the ends of the earth, but to her despair, she was tied to it not only by her memories and the dreams of her childhood and visions of her youth but also by the bonds of heartbreak and bitter resentment that the dreams had not come true and the visions had not been realized, and in the course of the years all this turned into the burden of her life and its substance, and she was filled with a creeping despair and a profound nihilism and the wish to be rid of this life, which had treated her with such shocking injustice and left her disillusioned and without hope. But her deep love for her mother, who had died, and her sense of responsibility toward all the people connected with her —her husband, Meir, Rifka, Bill, her brother in Canada, and all the other friends and relations—stopped her, and even filled her with energy; she was convinced that if ever she failed in the performance of any of her duties, or if she died, none of these people would be able to go on existing, and everything, all the frameworks of life and family relationships, would collapse, and this spurred her on, almost against her will, and gave rise to a spurious vitality, which had recently been reinforced by the projected trip to Gibraltar bursting like a bright sunbeam into her life, for she longed for the place where the sweetness of the past, with all its as-yet-undisappointed hopes, had somehow merged with her wishes for the future, of which she had not yet despaired, and she believed that if she went there a miracle would take place and her life would be purged of the weariness and despair that had infected it and she would be renewed.

At the same time, however, even while she and her husband were busy planning their trip and making the initial arrangements for it, she secretly doubted that she would ever reach Gibraltar, the place of her heart's desire, where nobody would be able to disturb her peace with an unexpected ring at the doorbell, and Meir came in and stood in the kitchen doorway and asked her how she was, and she said, "Just fine, as always," and he took off his jacket and put it on a chair in the little room, stealing a glance at his grandmother in the regal portrait on the wall, and after rubbing his hair dry in the bathroom, he went into the kitchen and sat in his usual place, and his mother repeated, "I'm glad you came. Lunch will be ready soon," and asked him how he was and Meir said, "Everything's okay," and told her about his visit to Dr. Reiner, and his mother, who listened to him while she busied herself about her cooking, said, "You must look after yourself. It's not a joke." She said this with real concern but in a completely routine way, and at the same time she stirred the soup and laid a place for him on the table, and when she placed the plate of soup before him after wiping the table, she said, "A letter came from Rifka," and immediately added, "I was beginning to worry, we hadn't heard for nearly two months," and Meir, immediately aware of the discreet nudging in her voice despite her matter-of-fact tone, said, "I really should write to them." There was an apologetic note in his voice, and he felt uncomfortable and so full of resistance to his mother that for a moment he was sorry that he had come, and he tasted the soup and said, "What does she write?" and his mother said, "Nothing special. They're working hard, but they're quite content. The children are as usual. Semedar is going to school, and Uri has begun to play the clarinet," and she took the last rissoles out of the frying pan and put the pan into the sink and asked him if he wanted another helping of soup, and Meir said, "No, no. It was delicious," and the feeling of impatience and irritation that had accompanied him from the moment he entered the house overwhelmed him because the business of writing to his sister, which hung over him like a shadow, made him angry, and the whole thing repeated itself with every letter he had had to write to her for the past five years, since she had gone with her family to settle in Boston, where her husband had completed his studies and then gone to work for a computer company, not only because writing letters had always been an onerous chore for him but because his relations with his sister, which were generally good, and even warm, had lost all real content and become hollow and forced, and whenever he sat down to write to her, after endless delays, he realized anew how little he had to say to her. His mother, who was perfectly well aware of his feelings because she shared them, although she would never have admitted this even to herself, since it contradicted what family feelings were supposed to be, removed Meir's empty plate and said, "You really should write to her. After all, how many sisters have you got?" and set a plate with two rissoles and some rice and gravy before him, with a bowl of her eggplant dish on the side, and said, "It's got hardly any salt in it. I'm very careful so you don't need to worry," and Meir said, "I'll write, I'll write." He was angry with her and just as angry with himself, and his mother—no power on earth could have prevented her from going on, although she sensed the resistance in his voice—said, "I wouldn't like them to leave the country for good," and Meir, who felt an unclear impulse to push her away and even to hurt her, said, "They'll live wherever it suits them to live," and his mother said, "Of course. But I'd like them to live here," and stretched out her hand for the radish lying in a saucer at the other end of the table, knowing with the intuition that never failed her that he fancied some, and asked him if he would like a few slices on the side, and Meir nodded his head and said that he would slice it himself, and stretched out his hand to take it, but his mother said, "It's nothing," and rapidly sliced the radish and gave it him on a little saucer with a sprinkling of salt and said, "I'd like them to live here, in this country, that's what I'd like." She knew that the chances of this happening were growing increasingly slim, especially now that Alex had an excellent position with a big computer firm, and if anyone had asked her why, she would have been hard put to find an answer, since she herself no longer really believed in the need for keeping the family together or the importance of living in Israel. Her attitude to the family had become reserved and full of conflicts and her attitude to the country so full of resentment and disappointment that she would have liked to run away to the ends of the earth herself, but at the same time she felt a gnawing need for them to come back and live in Israel, since their emigration would constitute not only a proof of grave failure but also a dark blot on the family, and as if to herself, she added, "If everyone leaves it will be very bad," and put a little dish of stewed apples in front of Meir, who said, "Let them live where they like. As long as they're happy," the battle around the letter was wearing him out, and his mother said, "Yes of course," realizing that he was right and trying to agree with him, and then she said, "Who would ever have imagined that that Begin would rule here? Ben Gurion and Berl Katznelson would turn over in their graves."

There was a sound of footsteps on the stairs, and she added, "That's not what we came here for. Not so that the Revisionists would ruin everything," and she wanted to add something else, but the ring at the doorbell cut her short and she said, "It's Bill," and hurried with the pot of rice in her hand to the hall to open the door, where Meir heard her saying, "Good morning, Mr. Bill," in English and with true joy in her voice, and he took another spoonful from the bowl of apple compote, which she had left on the table, and a moment later Bill appeared in the kitchen doorway with his round flushed face wreathed in a boyish smile as usual. Meir greeted him warmly and said, "How are you, Mr. Bill?"—like his mother, he felt a profound and happy affection for him, and Bill grinned and said in his heavy American accent, "I'm fine. And you?" and Meir said, "Thank you," and Bill said, "Very nice, my dear," and sat down at the table opposite Meir, standing the huge box of chocolates he had been carrying under his arm against the wall, and said in a curious mixture of English and rusty Yiddish, "A country of *gonifs*! I can't wait to get back to Miami," and Meir's mother smiled and said, "There's no lack of thieves in America, either," and as she wiped the table in front of him with a damp cloth, she added, "You've come at just the right time. You'll have your lunch in a minute," and Bill said, "Who told you that I wanted to eat? I was in the area to buy something for Weiss's daughter and I just dropped in to say hello. I'm leaving directly," and Meir said, "Sit for five minutes. Your business won't run away," and his mother said, "I've got meat soup with a little rice and very good rissoles and stewed eggplant. You can go as soon as you've eaten, nobody will stop you," and Bill said, with his boyish grin, "If you're so eager," and took off his jacket and went to hang it on the chair in the hall—from the side his head, with its sparse gray hair, looked like a rugby ball and made Meir smile in amusement every time he saw it—and he came back and said, "I don't know what I've been doing here for three years among these Jews," and Meir's mother said, "And

what would you have done for three years in America?" and poured
some of the soup she had warmed up in the meantime into a bowl
and added a little rice, and Bill said, "Nothing. But I wouldn't have
been here. That's something isn't it?" and he laughed his hoarse,
throaty laugh, which always amused Meir, and his mother joined in
with a light laugh and placed the soup carefully in front of him and,
with a frank, affectionate smile on her pale face, said, "Eat, eat. Who
knows how many more opportunities you'll have to taste soup like
this? Miami isn't Israel," and Bill said, "Thank God," and burst into
his loud, hoarse laughter again and added, "I'll remember this soup
every day in Miami and I'll remember Israel too, and thank God that
I'm not there anymore," and he began to eat, after salting the soup
liberally in spite of vociferous protests from Meir's mother, who had
recently become convinced that salt was the cause of all illness and
who now hurried into the bathroom to turn off the tap in the basin
where she had been soaking two shirts before washing them later by
hand, and when she returned she said, "You won't go." She could not
believe in the reality of his departure, in spite of all his talk and even
in spite of the preparations he had already begun to make for the trip,
not only because she loved him as a friend and felt more comfortable
in his company than with anyone else, there was something so refreshing in his manners and the freedom of his thought and the way in
which he never imposed himself on others and never allowed others
to impose themselves on him, but because she felt a profound affinity
with him as a kindred, but luckier, soul who had realized her own
deepest wishes and fantasies in his vagabond bachelor life, wandering
over the face of America from town to town and trade to trade,
entering into instant, casual relationships and breaking them one
morning without undue thought or distress and moving on to some
other town, sometimes at the other end of the country, to find a new
place to live, a new occupation, and a new set of casual relationships,
and thus, simply by virtue of his free and easy, undemanding and
uncommitted style of life, refuting all those apparently essential habits
and needs, loyalties and conventions and dogmas that had so embittered her own life—and all with such utter, unconsidered naturalness,

without a trace of exhibitionism or striving for effect, that it filled her with excited admiration and affectionate envy—and she wished with all her heart that she could be like him and follow the inclinations of her heart, even to a far lesser extent.

When he turned up in Tel Aviv one day with the intention of settling in the country it had caused a lot of surprise, because most of his acquaintances and the friends of his youth, and there weren't so many of them left, had forgotten his very existence, and at any rate none of them could credit him with feeling any Jewish, let alone Zionist, sentiments, and they could scarcely believe he felt the sentiments of friendship that he said had overtaken him in his old age, since he had hardly kept in touch even with his two brothers and three sisters in America, where he lived without contact with any Jewish community or any kind of Jewish life at all, so that in the course of fifty years of living in America, among Americans and all kinds of Irishmen and Mexicans, he had turned into a *goy* himself and almost completely forgotten Jewish ways and customs and also Yiddish, and together with them that faint and imperceptible, but nevertheless distinct, aura of Jewishness that tells you, like a scent in the air, that someone is a Jew, had faded and dissolved, and this goyishness surrounded him in Israel too, and when he decided to leave the country and return to America, Meir's mother was shocked and saddened far beyond any sense of personal betrayal and flooded by a wave of anguished longing because she knew that on his return to America he would disappear from her life forever and she would never see him again. This was a certainty that she could not and would not accept and thus, up to the very hour of his departure, she denied the possibility of its taking place, and at the same time, echoing his own joking tone, she tried to persuade him to change his mind and abandon the plans, which in the depths of her heart she not only understood but sympathized with, for she herself was an exile in her own country and wanted to run away from it to the ends of the earth. She removed the empty soup bowl from the table and said, "What have you got waiting for you there? Here there's a Jewish sun, Jewish rain. And Jews. And what have you got there? Nothing." A faint, barely perceptible strain

of lyricism crept into her humorous tone, and then she added matter-
of-factly, "Over here you can live like a lord with a few hundred
dollars. And there? You'll be lonely and miserable as an ant, nobody
will look at you." And Bill, who seemed momentarily embarrassed by
her serious tone, said, "I'd rather be lonely as an ant in America than
not lonely here in Israel among all these Jews," and he laughed again
until his face blazed red as a fire, and Meir's mother, who felt defeated
and above all hurt and offended, laughed lightly and said, "As you
please, Bill, we don't force anyone to stay here against his will. And
if you promise to behave yourself we may even agree to take you back
again," and although the shadow that had darkened her face lifted a
little, Meir could feel the sorrow and conflict tearing her soul apart
behind the lighthearted tone and laughter as if they were his own, and
Bill laughed and said, "Okay, I'll write it down behind my ear," and
Meir's mother put a dish of apple compote in front of him and said,
"I suggest you leave your clothes here. In any case you'll be back after
a month," and Bill smiled and said, "I don't intend taking anything
with me from here," and drew the apple compote toward him and
added, "I'll be damned if I understand how anyone can live here,"
and Meir's mother looked at him affectionately and said, "Look at us.
We live here," and Bill said, "You're really crazy," and took a spoonful of compote and said, "Mm, very good," and Meir's mother, who
had begun to clear the dishes off the table in order to get it ready for
her husband's lunch, said, "Doesn't it bother you to live in the
Golah?" and Bill said, "This is the greatest *Golah* of all, and Meir
said, "So you don't want the Jews to come here?" and Bill said, "Only
the ones I hate," and burst into loud laughter. Meir laughed with him
and his mother, who was trying to maintain an air of reserve, could
not stop herself from smiling and said in a conciliatory tone, as if she
wanted to soften his heart, "You're not going anywhere, Bill. You're
just talking," and Bill, also in a gentle, serious tone, said, "Yes, I am
going. I want to live in the *Golah*. I'm used to it already. I'm like a
man who's used to his old suit. I haven't got the time to start getting
used to a new one," and the next minute they heard heavy footsteps
on the stairs and Meir's father came into the kitchen wrapped in his

shabby old coat, with a cloth cap on his head and his old lunch box under his arm, his face gray with weariness, and Bill turned his egg-shaped head toward him with his face wreathed in a smile and said, "Hello, Mr. Lifshitz," and Meir's father looked at him blankly, with a forced smile on his strained, tired face, which immediately resumed its dark, gloomy expression, and in a hollow, uninterested tone said, "What's new?" and without waiting for a reply turned his back on them and went into the little room and took off his coat and scarf and put them on the table with his cap and lunch box and came back into the kitchen and remarked, "It's raining," and sat down in his usual place, and Meir's mother set a bowl of soup before him the moment he sat down, and he turned to Meir, who stood up to go, and said, "Aren't you working today?" and Meir said, "No. I had some things to take care of," and his father said, "Are you going already?" and Meir said, "Yes, I have to. Aviva's waiting for me," and thanked his mother for lunch and praised her cooking, and put on his coat and said good-bye and went out into the slow, gentle rain.

It went on raining lightly, with short intermissions, for two days, with sudden gusts of wind and cold, but on the third day everything suddenly cleared up and the weather was so fine that it seemed like the middle of spring, with only the shortening of the days and the sharp nip in the air toward evening to show that winter had arrived, and straight after work Meir went to the bank, where to his disappointment he found a young man wearing a skullcap sitting behind the counter instead of Aliza, and as soon as his turn came he asked the new teller if she had been transferred to another department, but the teller said, "No, I believe she's not well," and Meir said, "I'm sorry to hear it," and a week later he went into the bank again and found her sitting in her usual place. The minute Meir set eyes on her he felt his lust flaring up, together with the memory of the other man, which lay dormant inside him like a dull, nagging pain that never let up, and he stood waiting for his turn, nervous and tense, and in the meantime, with an expression of indifference, he furtively inspected her crude young face, with its fleshy, provocative lips and its bored, vapid expression—it was precisely the vapidity and insolence, and especially the vulgarity, that attracted him and made him think of some cheap movie-starlet or chorus girl or pin-up girl, uninhibited by any considerations of morality or education or cultural refinements, or, of course, feeling, and utterly available for the wildest and crudest sensual pleasures, as described in *The Joy of Sex*, and he felt how much he desired this vapid young woman, who seemed to him the very incarnation of the provocative boldness of youth. His face was burning, and it seemed to him that it was actually giving off a silvery steam, and although this made him feel embarrassed and uncomfortable, he could no longer control his thoughts, and he said to himself that he would give a great deal to have her as his playmate, and then he thought—the man in front of him was insisting on clarifying some point or other, to Aliza's undisguised annoyance—of how he would ask her to go to the movies with him, and later, after having something to drink in a café, he would take her to a hotel, he was sure she would not refuse, perhaps one of the hotels in Yarkon Street between Bograshov and Allenby, but closer to Bagrashov, since the proximity to Allenby would make him feel uncomfortable, and there he would spend the night with her and lie with her in the *Flanquette* position, or perhaps the *Cuissade*, the names had become confused in his head, but he remembered the ink drawing of the position as it appeared in *The Joy of Sex* very clearly—her back turned slightly away from him and his one leg between hers—and in the meantime the man in front of him finished his business and turned to go, but even before he walked away, Aliza made a disgusted face and said, "That character eats me up with his eyes," and Meir held out his bankbook to her and said, "Some people are like that," and Aliza said, "Those married types are the worst—they've only got one thing on their minds," and Meir, wishing desperately that he could somehow convey his agreement with this general sentiment to her, nodded slightly and said, "Yes," and asked for five hundred pounds, and then, as she was writing the transaction down in his bankbook, he smiled and said, "I'm married, too, you know," and after making sure that there was nobody next to him, he asked her jokingly if she would go to the movies with him, and Aliza laughed and pushed the money and the

bankbook over to him on the counter and said, "It's all up to date."
There was an amused and slightly mocking expression on her face, and
Meir, who imagined that he could hear a note of contempt in her
voice and now wanted to obliterate every trace of his words as quickly
as possible, thanked her, feeling as if he had fallen into a puddle and
covered himself with muck, and took the money and the bankbook,
and said, "So long, Aliza," with exaggerated heartiness and so loudly
that he sounded to himself as if he were shouting, cursing himself for
having come into the bank at all, he could have put it off for at least
one more day, and she said, "So long," and turned to the next
customer, and Meir wanted badly to make some witty remark to
correct the bad impression he had made up to now, but he couldn't
think of anything, and cursing her silently, he walked out into the
street, where it was already dark.

At first he felt a momentary sense of relief that it was all behind
him, but after walking a few steps the feeling of embarrassment at
having made a fool of himself for nothing came back, and as he walked
on, with no aim but getting away from the bank, he went over what
he had said and what she had said and how she had looked at him
and how he had looked at her, and it all seemed so feeble and inane
and especially irrevocable that he felt disgraced forever, but when he
turned into Gordon Street, with the feelings of shame and disappointment still burning inside him, he said to himself with a hint of
complacency that she had not, in fact, turned him down, but on the
contrary, she had smiled, apparently in consent, and he went over the
whole scene again in his head, every facial expression and tone of
voice, in order to decipher the intentions hidden behind every single
detail, and concluded that if he went back and made the same pro-
posal more firmly it was almost certain that she would agree, and he
decided that next time he went to the bank that was just what he
would do.

A few days later in the office, close to midday, when Drora came
up to his desk for the red ink and at the same time took a sip of his
coffee, something she was in the habit of doing with a few of the other
men in the office, too, Meir asked her to go to the movies with him

that evening and she immediately agreed. Overwhelmed by the ease
and speed of his success, he flipped eagerly through the newspaper to
see what was showing and suggested that they go to see the Kurosawa
movie playing at the Zafon, but soon afterward, when the first flush
of victory had died down, he was flooded with anxiety and doubts, and
shortly before closing time he went up to her and suggested that they
go to see *The Detective with Four Faces* at the Dekel instead, but no
sooner had he seated himself behind his desk again than he regretted
this too, and he was sorry that he had not suggested going to the Ofir
or the Orly instead, and he was so eaten up by regrets that he grew
despondent about the entire project and even thought of making
some excuse and calling the whole thing off, but that evening, after
buying two tickets in the last row, he stood waiting for her at the
corner of the movie theater building in the entrance to a toy shop,
which was already closed, trying to efface himself as far as possible and
staring expressionlessly at the bus stop on the other side of the road.
Hardly anything was left of the first panicky flush of victory, let alone
the exciting pictures painted by his imagination—everything had
somehow been crushed and corroded by his inner conflicts and anxieties, and at the same time, as the minutes passed and she did not
appear, he began to worry that she might not show up at all. She was
a little late and Meir, who saw her the moment she got off the bus,
lingered for a moment in his hiding place and then walked toward her
with a slight wave of his hand, an embarrassed smile plastered over
his face like a mask of dry mud, and said, "I'm so glad you came,"
and shook her hand, and Drora asked if he had been waiting long, she
was wearing a black turtleneck sweater and black trousers and she
looked very attractive, and Meir said, "No, only about five minutes,"
and asked her if she wanted something to drink. His voice sounded
hollow and full of embarrassment to him, and his movements and the
sensation of his body as a whole disappointed him and made him feel
that everything was spoiled because he didn't have the right carefree,
nonchalant approach, like the other man, for instance, and when she
said that she had already had something to drink before leaving home,
Meir, wanting with all his heart to put off going into the movie theater

for a few more minutes, and trying desperately but without success to overcome the stiffness and clumsiness he sensed in his voice and movements, said, "Then let's get some chocolate to keep us going," and Drora said, "Whatever you like," with no sign of tension in her voice or her fresh, open face, as if there was nothing out of the ordinary in their being together like this, and he went into the little café he had noted when he was buying the tickets and bought a bar of chocolate and a packet of mints, and they went into the movie theater and sat down.

To Meir's relief, the hall was already dark, and when the commercials were over and they started showing the movie, he took his arm off the back of the chair and squeezed her shoulders very slightly, as if by accident, feeling a stiff bubble of embarrassment surround him like a yellowish halo of buzzing gnats, and when he encountered no hint of resistance, he tightened his embrace, his tension growing even more acute, and after a moment during which he sat without moving or breathing, he drew her closer to him, again as if absentmindedly but at the same time with obvious intent, and as he went on pretending to watch the movie, he felt the first, confused inklings of victory stirring inside him, and with them a partial relaxation of the tension that had not abated since he had asked her to go to the movies with him, and he had a fleeting, rather blurred and impressionistic vision of himself going up to her flat with her after the movie and lying with her in the provocative position depicted in *The Joy of Sex,* and with a light caress he moved the finger of the hand embracing her shoulder over her chin and along her jawbone and throat, and she laughed lightly, and he quickly joined in, at the same time tightening his embrace and drawing her closer to him—the freer he felt, the more tender and refined his attraction toward her became—and she moved slightly and as if by accident laid her hand on his knee and rested her leg against his, and the utter naturalness with which she did this sent a wave of warmth and anticipation surging through him so wonderful that for a moment he was lost to everything but the physical contact between them, and then in the midst of his joyful arousal it flashed through his mind that perhaps Aviva too had behaved like this with the other man, and the very thought hurt him, and he pressed Drora tightly to him and kissed her on the head in order to cleanse himself of all painful thoughts, and she rested her head on his chest and said, "That feels lovely," and he said to himself that it had been a great idea to ask her out and kissed her on the corners of her lips and afterward, with demonstrative sincerity, as if he were acting in a movie, he gazed at her face in the darkness, and she felt his eyes on her and looked up at him for a moment with a smile and then dropped her head onto his chest again. Meir, who was now uncomfortably aware of how much all this resembled something in a Hollywood movie, relaxed his embrace slightly and sat up straight and crossed his legs, the film bored him to tears, and he thought of the problems with the Youth Center and tried to find ways of dealing with them, but everything unraveled and dissolved and eluded him like wisps of smoke, and he thought about Gavrosh, with his face as wrinkled and withered as an apple dried in the sun, and how much he missed that weather-beaten face now—if only he could pull him out of the chasm into which he had been swept! His suspense and arousal evaporated, his embraces grew mechanical, and suddenly he felt fed up with the tedium of sitting there uncomfortably next to Drora, and in his anger and disappointment he thought how unfit he was for this role, from one minute to the next the whole business was turning into a burden and a nuisance and also into something ridiculous, and all he wanted was for the idiotic movie to be over, and only the picture from *The Joy of Sex,* which had been engraved so deeply on his memory, the woman lying with her back half turned to the man and the leg next to him slightly raised so that his upper leg was lying between her two legs and on her belly while he embraced her from the side, remained with him like a signpost of desire floating to the surface of a dark and murky sea of anxiety.

The movie had ceased to interest him to such an extent that he wasn't even looking at it anymore, and he thought again of extricating himself from the whole situation after taking her for coffee some-where and going home as soon as he had seen her to her door, and Drora laid her hand on his knee again, and again he felt moved, and for a split second he saw the entrance to his apartment and the big room with its furniture and pictures and potted plants and the particular shade of the walls with the light on them, and Aviva, who was most probably sitting on the sofa reading or watching television, and he wished he could be there with her now, he felt no guilt or self-reproach and also no resentment or hostility, but only the desire to be in her company, which was so agreeable and necessary to him, and Drora said something in a whisper and put her hand on his hand, which was lying motionless on her thigh, and with complete naturalness played a little with his fingers, and he thought about her for a moment with warm affection and felt a despairing disappointment in himself for being so unfit for adventure and romance, and smiled at her in the dark and felt the smile freeze on his face.

Outside the rain-charged air felt pure and fresh and Meir, who was happy and relieved to be outside in the fresh air, put his arm around Drora's waist, exactly as he had imagined doing, and said, "I love this weather," and Drora said, "Me too," and Meir kept his eyes open for a cab as they walked down the street and asked her if she wanted something to eat or drink, and she said, "I'd like something to drink, to wash the taste of the movie out of my mouth," and Meir, very put out by the fact that he had not been the first to say something critical about the movie, suggested going to a bakery, he knew an excellent one on Milan Square, where he would buy a cake and they could take it up to her place and have coffee there, and Drora said that she would have been glad to, but she was afraid it might be awkward because her brother and his wife, who were the owners of the flat where she lived, had come into town the day before for a short vacation from Eilat, where her brother worked in something connected with the quarries, and they would most probably be there now, and Meir, who immediately felt disappointed and cheated, said, "What a pity," and went on smiling in order not to lose face, and keeping his arm around her waist as if nothing had happened, he wanted to keep things on a cordial footing with all his heart, he said, "You see how bad it is not to have a place of your own," and laughed lightly, feeling vaguely relieved in spite of his disappointment. Drora said that he was right but that he, too, did not have a place of his own, and Meir smiled and said, "Yes, indeed," thinking longingly of his home and wishing that he were already there, and he stepped over a big puddle and said, "We could have had a ball," and then he smiled a broad, frank smile, admitting defeat, and said, "Pity," and pressed her to him and gave her a playful kiss on top of her head, hoping that Aviva would be awake when he got home so that he could enjoy her company for a while, and Drora said, "I'm sorry. That's life," and suggested going to have something to drink in a café, and they crossed the street and walked down Yehuda HaMaccabi Street for a bit— Meir did not like the area or feel at home there—and went into a café, where he ordered coffee and cake for both of them, and afterward he saw her to her front door and parted from her with a friendly kiss, doing his best to express his affection for her, and especially to deny his disappointment, and with a feeling of relief he walked home along the streets, which were already quite deserted, and when he was one street away, the rain started pelting down in a furious flood, and he quickened his step and began to run through the puddles that had already formed under the heavy downpour.

Aviva was sitting on the corner of the sofa, mending a dress and watching a news program on television, and when Meir came in she asked him if it was raining and he said, "It's pouring. I got caught in it on the corner," and he took off his coat and hung it on the back of a chair, where it dripped onto the floor, and walked into the room and asked, "How's the program?" and Aviva said, "Not bad. Quite interesting," and Meir said, "I'm glad you're still awake," and Aviva said that in fact she had thought of going to bed, but then she decided to stay up and get a few things done that she had been putting off from one day to the next. She showed no sign of suspicion, and when Meir said, "There's no one like you," he really meant it, he was so happy to find her awake that nothing, no suspicion or unhappy memory, could mar the happiness and gratitude he felt toward her simply for being there, and he went into the kitchen and emerged with a glass of cold milk and two cookies and said, "I took in a movie at Ben Yehuda, I decided to go on the spur of the moment," and he sat down in the armchair, the faint embarrassment that he could hear in his voice slightly marring the blissful feeling of security that wrapped him round like a warm shawl, and Aviva asked him to turn the volume of the TV down a bit and asked him what the movie was like and he said, "Boring. American rubbish with that Raquel Welch. I should have left in the middle." There was a flash of lightning and a heavy roll of thunder, and the rain pelted down harder than before, and Aviva raised her head from her sewing for a moment and looked at the dark window and then she said, "What's troubling you so much?" and Meir said, "Nothing in particular," and after a slight hesitation he added, "This business with my blood pressure, and especially the medication," and Aviva said, "They've got new drugs today. Don't worry, everything will be all right," and he said, "Damn them and their drugs," and for a moment, full of anger and dejection, he had a powerful urge to tell her that he had spent the evening with Drora and shatter her security and peace of mind. Suddenly he was plunged in gloom and full of rebelliousness and resentment against himself and her and the evening he had wasted so idiotically, and against Drora too, for leading him up the garden path, and he stood up and took the empty glass back to the kitchen; outside the rain was still pouring down in dense, heavy sheets, and when he returned to the room he sprawled out in the armchair and looked mindlessly at the TV screen and felt his anger and disappointment being absorbed, although not without a trace, in a sense of pleasant domesticity and repose, and after the late-night news he made the bed and with a delightfully pleasant feeling of conciliation cuddled into the quilt and took up *The Bermuda Triangle* and waited for Aviva to finish her sewing and come to bed. And when she came into the bedroom a few minutes later, after finishing her work and putting everything away, they chatted a while and then she curled up into her quilt and put her head on the pillow, after patting it into place as usual, and said that she had a hard day ahead of her and Meir said, "Go to sleep. I'll take care of lunch tomorrow, you don't have to worry about it," and when he turned around a few minutes later to read her something from the book, she was already fast asleep, and he looked at her for a moment, flooded by a warm feeling of intimacy and compassion, which melted his bitterness, it seemed to him forever, so that for a moment he wondered if this was indeed the woman who had delivered him such a fatal blow, and he put his hand carefully on her shoulder under the quilt in order to express his feelings and also his gratitude, hoping she could feel it, although she lay without moving, and after a moment or two he turned over and went on reading *The Bermuda Triangle* and listening to the rain falling incessantly outside.

A few days later, in the evening, Meir went to visit Pozner, and while Liora was busy studying in the next room, the two of them sat in the kitchen and chatted, and Pozner said that he was apparently going to continue living with Liora—he simply didn't have the strength to look for a new apartment and move all his things, and he didn't have the least desire to live alone either, and he stood up to make coffee, and Meir said that he understood, and asked for tea, and added, "This business with my health is really getting me down." And Pozner said, "You talk as if somebody promised you something and broke his promise," and Meir said, "Yes, that's how I feel," and Pozner put the tea in front of him with a plate of cookies, and then he took his coffee and sat down opposite Meir and said that we always tended to see things as if there were some hostile and unjust intent behind them, whereas from the point of view of justice and perhaps of nature, too, there was nothing but chance and arbitrariness, which was in fact the only law that existed. He spoke in a confident and even scolding tone, and his words pleased and encouraged Meir, especially the note of reprimand in them, which he saw as an expression of patronizing sympathy and closeness, which was exactly what he had hoped for, and in a humorous tone he remarked that he was afraid of becoming impotent as a result of the medication he was taking, and Pozner said that there wasn't a man in the world who didn't suffer from impotence in one form or another during the course of his life, which was a well-known fact and one that he could substantiate from his own personal experience. He said this so directly and naturally, without a trace of irony or amusement, that Meir was overcome with gratitude, and all he wanted was for Pozner to say it again, and in the meantime he said, "I hope you're right, but the fear is real nevertheless," and Pozner said, "Have you ever heard of a life without fear?" —every sentence that passed his lips made Meir happier than the one before, and he said, "No," meekly, trying to squeeze the last drop of comfort from the conversation, and took a sip of tea and added in a tone of disguised resentment, "I look healthy, I feel healthy, and I'm sick. That's what eats me up," and Pozner took a cookie and said, "Would you prefer to look and feel sick? I don't understand what you want," and Meir said, "Why couldn't I have gone on being healthy?" and Pozner said, "You talk as if someone promised you perfect and eternal health," in a tone of impatient rebuke, and Meir smiled and said, "Yes, that's how I feel," and still smiling, he added childishly, "If only I knew why it had to be me," and Pozner leaned forward to take the cigarettes that were lying on the stove, and at the same time he said that one of the most wonderful and memorable things in Nadezhda Mandelstam's book was how Mandelstam kept telling her that no one had promised her that she would be happy—he knew that suffering, if you could put it like that, was the true substance of life, and happiness was only a blessed, accidental flickering, and Meir, who enjoyed this kind of talk, said, "I'm not talking about happiness, only about health," and Pozner said, "It's the same thing. There are no guarantees in life," and stretched out his hand to take the matches lying next to the stove and lit a cigarette and said that in the end life was what a person made of it, in other words an expression of the will or the personal viewpoint of each separate individual, which was exactly the way it should be, and he shook the ash off his cigarette into his empty coffee cup and added that life had no moral content or purpose as such, all we could say about it with any degree of certainty was that it was organic material moving in space and changing over time, and even if it did have a content or purpose in itself, we would not be able to know what they were, since man was incapable of transcending his own being and really knowing what was outside him, so that the only knowledge was his own knowledge and the only truth his own truth—he was the measure of all things, and this enabled him and in fact obliged him to be free and do whatever he wanted to with his life.

Here Pozner fell silent while Meir, who had been hanging on to his every word, waited, moved and excited, and after a moment his friend added in a grave, confessional tone that this, in any case, was how he saw life: he did not know or understand what it was, and although once he had wanted very much to know what it was and tried to direct it toward the goals and achievements that seemed to him the highest and most exalted, like saving the world and writing books of eternal value, he now knew that it was a waste of effort and that there was no point in trying to direct life, it was better to give it a free rein and let it take its own direction—it would reach the stable sure enough without any help from us. His gravity was not diminished by the slight ironic smile that crossed his face from time to time, as if he was expressing in these words, without evasions or beating around the bush, something that touched the very roots of his being, and this encouraged Meir, not only because it somehow put Pozner in the same position as himself and expressed a priceless kinship, but because, without Meir himself knowing how or why, it stirred something in the tangled undergrowth of his own soul, and quivering inwardly with emotion, he said with a faint, wry smile that he could on no account understand how a healthy body could suddenly become sick, and Pozner blew the cigarette ash off the table and said, "And how a living body becomes dead—that you can understand?" and Meir said, "It really is a dirty trick," and then, overcome by an urge, which could no longer be denied, to confess his pain and insult, he looked at Pozner and said, "What would you do if your wife went to bed with somebody else?" Suddenly the words that had clamored so loudly in his mouth only a moment before sounded embarrassingly weak and insipid—he had wanted to say "fucked" or "screwed," but something inside him refused, and he broke off a bit of a cookie and added that it would never have occurred to him that Aviva was capable of it, especially not with a stranger, a man she had never set eyes on before, and that if only he knew at least where and how it had happened it might be easier, and he asked Pozner what he should do, although the question already seemed superfluous, the whole thing sounded so simple and trivial, even to him, and Pozner said, "Nothing," as simple as that, and Meir was beside himself with happiness, for this was exactly what he had longed to hear. And Pozner added that if it had happened to him he might never have left home in the first place, and a very delicate, tremulous note of sorrow crept into his voice, or so it seemed to Meir, and at that moment the door of the room opened and Liora appeared in the kitchen doorway and said, "That's it. I'm done for the day. I'm worn out," and Pozner said, "Come and sit with us," and Meir, who suddenly felt glad to see her, joined in Pozner's welcoming smiles and even pulled the stool out from under the table, and Liora smiled her thanks and said, "I'm famished," and Pozner said, "There's tomato soup in the fridge, it only has to be warmed up," and Liora said, "Good idea. With black bread it's fantastic," and Meir, with a sudden surge of gaiety, said, "I'm crazy about soup," and Liora took the pot of soup out of the fridge and said, "It'll be ready in five minutes," and began to clear the cups and sugar bowl off the table, and Pozner grabbed her by the arm and said, "Isn't she something?" and Meir smiled in embarrassment and said, "She certainly is," suddenly feeling surprisingly glad of her presence and sympathetic toward her, and Pozner let go of her arm and without any preliminaries, as if he were replying to a question, said that our minds were constructed in such a way that they did not allow us to dwell on the terrible dangers of existence or on death, the knowledge of which stirred inside us continuously, like the movement of shadows under the crust of the earth.

Liora, who had cleared the table in the meantime and laid down a wooden board with a black loaf on it, said, "Are you talking about death and diseases again? What's so interesting about them?" There was a note of resentment in her voice, and Meir was embarrassed, since it seemed to him that her resentment was directed mainly against himself, but this embarrassment did not spoil his good mood, and Pozner caught hold of her arm and said that they were like children whistling in the dark to chase the evil spirits away, and he laughed, and Liora freed her arm and said, "I simply don't understand you," and stirred the soup, whose warm smell spread through the little kitchen, and then she turned to Meir and said, "The only thing that's wrong with you is a bit of high blood pressure," and Meir said, "Yes, you're right," feeling a need to apologize, even though she was wrong, and realizing that the whole subject was so remote from her and so alien to her that there was no point in going into explanations, and a moment later she set the pot on the table and dished out the soup, and Meir drew the bowl toward him and stirred the steaming soup and said, "Just what the doctor ordered," speaking very emphatically in order to express not only his sympathy for her but also the fact that he was in good spirits, despite her remark, and he lifted the spoon to his mouth and blew on it and tasted the soup and said, "It's divine." And afterward, while they were eating, he said in a humorous vein that he would never have imagined that the body that had been the source of all his pleasures and joys could become his enemy and a source of annoyance and anxiety, and Liora said, "You talk as if you were somebody else," with a puzzled air, and Meir said that that was how he felt and added in a reflective tone that he felt as if he had been separated from his body, which had betrayed him and made his sick, and that because of the illness inhabiting his body he himself felt like a stranger in his own body, which felt like something alien and separate from him, like a kind of shell in which he was imprisoned, and which, if only he could, he would actually like to shed and be free of, and Pozner said that according to a number of religions that was just what happened to you when you died—the spirit cast off the body and was liberated from its coils—and Liora said that it wasn't very nice to listen to someone talking like that about his body and suggested that Meir go to see a certain naturopath, and Meir shrugged and said that he didn't believe in it, but Liora went on trying to persuade him and described the miracle this doctor had performed for a friend of hers, after all the other doctors had given up hope. She spoke with passionate conviction, and Pozner, who confirmed Liora's story, said, "Give it a try. What can you lose?" and Meir shrugged his shoulders, feeling pressured and threatened, and said, "Maybe

you're right." It was obvious that he was saying so purely and simply
so that they would leave him alone, but Liora would not let it be and
said, "What will it cost you to try? Perhaps he'll be able to cure you,"
and Pozner—who usually dismissed all unorthodox practices such as
meditation and astrology and all theories advocating abstention and
asceticism out of hand and almost on principle, together with all
Indian beliefs, whether authentic or invented by various gurus and
maharishis, who were all frauds and charlatans and racketeers in his
eyes, and who included all forms of vegetarianism in this category too
—to Meir's surprise, now took sides with Liora and enthusiastically
praised natural diets and natural medicine as well, which he claimed
had definite advantages over conventional medicine in the curing of
disease, especially cardiac and vascular diseases, and he said again,
"Give it a try. I'm sure it will help you," and Meir, succumbing at
last to their confident advocacy, said that he was willing to try and
asked Liora for the naturopath's number so that he could call him the
next day, feeling his willingness growing into unreserved optimism
inside him, and Liora said that she didn't have the number herself,
but that she would get it from her friend and went over to the
telephone to call her immediately, and Meir said, "I'll phone him first
thing in the morning," and as he wrote the details down in his
notebook, he said, "I'll do whatever he tells me to."

Outside the streets were cold and deserted and the sky was dark
and cloudless, and when he reached the corner of Bograshov and King
George streets, he paused for a moment and wondered if he should
turn and walk down to the sea, the sound of whose dull roar reached
him where he stood, but for some reason the thought of the sea made
him feel vaguely uneasy, and he went on walking along King George
Street until he reached the old sycamore trees, then he turned up
Bograshov. There was a bitter cold in the air, which seemed to be
emanating from the street and the dark houses, and he buttoned his
coat and raised his collar, and as he walked down the empty street,
unthinkingly taking in the sight of the old houses, with their dark
yards and faded fences and here and there a bush or a tree rising up
like a column of darkness, he was seized by powerful longings for his

grandmother, with her heavy, wrinkled face the color of the pages in an old book, shining with intelligence and humanity, and he said to himself, in so many words although without moving his lips, that it was impossible that she did not exist somewhere—and he did not mean in her grave, which he had never visited—it was impossible that she had evaporated and turned into nothing, because in that case it would mean that she had never existed at all, and he remembered her perfectly, her appearance and her touch and her smell, the smell of her face and clothes and sheets, and even the characteristic shuffle of her slippers; she was more real to him than anything in the present, and at that very moment, even as the words formed in his mind, he saw her somewhere in the distance as a featureless figure strolling along a rift full of darkness yawning like a velvety valley between the stars, as calmly as if she were walking down Peretz Smolenskin Street, and as he scanned the sky in pursuit of her and tried to keep the figure in the familiar gray Sabbath dress and the felt slippers before his eyes, on no account could he see her dressed in any other way, he said to himself again that she could have gone on living, although she had been about eighty-five when she died, as far as he was concerned her death would always have been premature and unjust, and he knew that if only she had gone on living, everything would have been different, since in her time everything had been good and full of flavor. And as he walked down the deserted streets, abandoning himself to the sweetness of oblivion and wrapped in the melancholy of the heartfelt longings that filled the infinite spaces between him and his grandmother, he was suddenly overwhelmed by a flood of sorrow for his own death, which up to now had been hiding, as it were, inside his sorrow for his grandmother like a shadow within a shadow, and the sorrow soon turned into a frantic panic and a gnawing, numbing fear. And as he approached Ben Zion Boulevard, he saw himself surrounded on all sides and trapped by this death, which he saw as a kind of blackness filling up all of space and immensely strong, pursuing him stubbornly and single-mindedly in order to swallow him up, and in his panic he escaped from the earth into the star-strewn darkness of the sky, and for a moment he felt relief, but only for a moment, because right away, in the midst of his relief, he knew and felt that death would overtake him wherever he was, even if he hid in a narrow crack at the end of a dark cavern in the tiniest and most remote star in the entire, infinite universe. And as a renewed wave of panic surged through him, he realized that he was bound to death with a stout, tight rope, like the rope that lifts pails of sand and concrete into the air on the scaffoldings of building sites, one end of which was tied securely round his waist, while the other was in the hands of death, who was only teasing him by letting out the rope a little to give him the illusion that he was free to fly, but who could pull him back again whenever he wanted to, in another day or even another second, and as soon as this thought crossed his mind, he felt death tugging the rope and pulling him back.

The next morning, before he left for work, Meir phoned the naturopath and asked him for an appointment, if possible for the very next day, and the naturopath, with a slight sneer, or so it seemed to Meir, said that the earliest appointment he could offer him was in a month's time, and it was only after repeated pleas and arguments about the urgency of the situation that he relented and unwillingly agreed to see him in ten days' time, at six-thirty in the morning, and Meir was obliged to be satisfied with that, although he now felt that the matter was intolerably pressing and urgent and regretted not having called the naturopath immediately after Liora had first recommended him.

Ten days later, at six in the morning, Meir left home on his way to the naturopath, and as he walked along the cold streets, which were still almost deserted, he felt full of suspense and anticipation and ready to submit to any difficulty and sacrifice that was required of him for the sake of the new life, a life of health and freshness and longevity, that awaited him.

The naturopath, who had only recently opened his clinic, invited him into the consulting room, a large, old-fashioned room with high, bare walls painted halfway up in dingy oil paint, which, apart from an old desk and a bed covered in white oilcloth, contained nothing but two plain chairs and an old brown cupboard, upon which stood

a number of jars of the kind once used to pickle cucumbers, full of
a dark green liquid, and a diagram and two color photographs that
looked like maps of the hemispheres hanging on the walls, together
with two framed certificates attesting to the educational qualifications
of their owner and the fact that he was a naturopath. There was only
one window in the room, and this high, curtainless window added to
the general impression of utilitarian bareness and asceticism.

Meir sat down opposite the doctor, an elderly man with a wiry
body, a sharp weather-beaten face, and a mane of thick, silvery hair
with a peculiar greenish tinge, like the color of olive-tree leaves, who
sat down at the desk and tidied the few papers lying on it with brisk,
vigorous movements, remarking as he did so, as if to himself, that the
sea this morning had been wonderful, if a little stormy, and then
turned to Meir and asked him what had brought him there, and Meir
replied that he suffered from high blood pressure, and lately also from
a certain feeling of lethargy, and in addition, he remarked with an
embarrassed smile, he would like to get rid of the little paunch that
had developed over the past few years. The naturopath listened to him
gravely, nodding from time to time, and in the end he said, "Of
course. It had to happen," and asked him his age and occupation and
how long it was since his high blood pressure had been diagnosed, and
after glancing at the results of the various tests that Meir had brought
to show him, he took a magnifying glass and a little torch out of his
desk drawer, moved his chair up to Meir until their knees were
touching, and asked him to open his left eye. Meir did as he asked,
and the doctor raised the magnifying glass to his eye and looked
intently into the pupil, illuminating it with his flashlight, and then he
did the same with Meir's right eye, and then he repeated the whole
performance with the left eye and then the right eye again, and in
the end he put the magnifying glass and the flashlight down and
informed Meir, who was anxiously waiting his verdict, that his heart
was fine, he was prepared to guarantee it, and the same went for his
liver and gallbladder and lungs, but that he had observed impairments
in the blood vessels and also in the right kidney that required immediate treatment before the damage became irreparable.

Plunged into gloom and anxiety and already seeing his kidney eaten away in his imagination, Meir asked, as if he had not heard properly the first time, if it was the right kidney that was affected, and the naturopath, who seemed offended by the question, as if it called his diagnosis into doubt, rose from his chair and, with a patronizing expression, invited Meir to step up to what looked like the two maps of the hemispheres of the world but which, according to him, were actually maps of the inner organs as they were seen from the pupil of the eyes, and with condescending patience he explained the order of the organs to Meir—the gallbladder, the lungs, the liver, the heart, the blood vessels, the various glands—and how he could discern every impairment in the functioning of any of these organs as he looked through the pupil of the eye, and Meir said, "That's amazing," with a growing feeling of disbelief, and the doctor said, "I can see everything through the pupil of the eye, even cancer." He said this with the complacent superiority of a successful man, and when they returned to the desk, he replaced the magnifying glass in its leather case and said that in general it was possible to say that blood vessels became clogged due to the layer of fat covering them from inside, which made them narrower and forced the blood to flow harder and faster, and this in turn led to a more serious blockage of the blood vessels and was the source of a great many fatal health problems, but there was no need to panic since this process could be arrested, and some of the damage that had already been done could even be reversed by the right diet and, in the specific case of blood pressure and kidney problems, also with the aid of two natural remedies extracted from a certain kind of plant, which had to be brewed and imbibed like tea, with astonishing results, and as he spoke—everything he said sounded so clear and self-evident—he took hold of Meir's hand to take his pulse, and then he took a notebook out of his desk drawer and remarked that all organic diseases, and all physical impairments, which in fact were also diseases, like the loss of hair and teeth and the weakening of vision and hearing, were the results of years of neglect and an exploitative attitude toward the body: people seemed to think that their bodies were their slaves, with appalling consequences that were sure to manifest themselves sooner or later, but this was apparently the way of the world and there was nothing to be done about it, people never learned from the experience of others but only from their own suffering, and thus it happened that they came to veganism only after their bodies were already full of rubbish and filth and completely poisoned—and he wrote something down in his notebook, as if he had only just remembered it, and said, "People treat their bodies as if they were trash cans," and wrote down something else, and said that he himself could serve as a living example of all this, since he had come to veganism only after the age of forty, when his body and health were already in a very bad state, whereas if he had begun to keep a strict vegetarian diet before, at the age of twenty or even thirty, he would have accomplished far greater things, but he did not say what these things were, although it was clear that he meant achievements in the field of health, and Meir, to whom the doctor's words sounded logical and convincing, and of course encouraging— especially his example about himself—although at the same time his skepticism and even his ridicule did not leave him for a moment, suddenly felt how his body was rotting away, full of rubbish and filth like the streets next to the Carmel market, and he nodded his head slightly in agreement, and the naturopath said, "People are blind. They get up in the morning with their mouths full of a bad taste and their stomachs full of gas, and they can't understand the reason," and he added immediately, "You have to listen to nature. Nature is the best doctor," and Meir nodded again and said that he wanted to begin the cure right away and asked the doctor what he had to do, and the doctor said, "First of all, you have to rid your body of the dirt," and Meir said, "Of course, I understand," and waited not only submissively but even eagerly for the naturopath to impose a drastic diet on him.

The naturopath reflected for a moment—the greenish color of his hair was the thing about him that made Meir most uneasy—and playing with his pen, he said that the best possible treatment was a total fast for two weeks, to begin with, followed by two weeks of natural juices, which would immediately rid the body of all its accumulated poisons, but he would have to refrain from recommending it in this case since Meir was not a strict vegetarian or vegan, and his body was unaccustomed to such stringent measures, and although Meir, who was excited by the prospect of purging himself and gaining perfect health in one short effort and could already see himself in his imagination turning his back on his former corrupt way of life and entering a new and completely different era, asked the doctor to allow him to try this drastic treatment, he refused to be moved, listing all the difficulties and complications involved, and promised that in a few months' time, after Meir had completed the initial, more moderate treatment, and his body was stronger and more accustomed to a natural diet, he would recommend the fast. Sorry that he had not turned to veganism years ago, Meir overcame his disappointment and submitted unwillingly to the postponement of the fast, which now seemed to him like the indispensable key to health, since it, and only it, promised a total reversal of his situation, nothing less than which would satisfy him. The naturopath, counseling patience, drew up a writing pad and prescribed eight natural remedies, explaining their properties as he wrote down their names in Latin, together with a list of the recommended nutrients, with occasional comments on the recommended way of cooking them, and Meir, whose spirits suddenly plummeted at the sight of the list, which included hardly anything that he knew and liked, tried to soften the blow by suggesting all kinds of vegetarian foods that he hastily called to mind, such as nuts and dried fruits and milk, but the doctor rejected all his suggestions irritably and even scornfully—with regard to milk, he remarked rather contemptuously that it was good only for babies, and even honey, which popped unexpectedly into Meir's head at the very last minute, when he was already holding the grim list in his hand, and about which he eagerly inquired, was dismissed out of hand with the words, "If you want to kill yourself, go ahead and eat honey,"—and afterward, perhaps in order to soften the depressing effect of his words, he said, "Perhaps in a few months' time. First you have to get strong," and Meir, who was bitterly disappointed, said "Okay," and suppressing his disappointment, he folded the list and put it in his coat pocket, together with the prescription for the herbal remedies with their Latin names to be brewed and imbibed twice a day, and after paying the doctor and thanking him, he rose and, joylessly but full of hope and resolution, left the house.

On his way home, in the clean, fresh streets, which had just begun to wake up, this exalting feeling of hopeful resolve went on throbbing inside him, obliterating the embarrassment and the last, faint traces of doubt, until he felt as if he were being borne aloft as he walked, healthy and cleansed and full of renewed suppleness and youth, but when he passed the bakery in the square, with its display window full of bread and rolls fresh from the oven, filling the clear morning air with their aroma, he thought of buying himself a fresh poppyseed roll baked to a turn, with a brown, bursting crust, as a final farewell to his life up to now, and postponing the veganism till Sunday, in order to finish off the forbidden foods that Aviva had already prepared and that were waiting in the fridge, since it was a pity to throw them out, and in order, above all, for the last time in his life, to enjoy his mother's gefilte fish with fresh challah bread and her *klops* and fried meat, not to mention her wonderful butter cookies, and perhaps he would ask her to prepare *cholent* and stuffed *kishka* for him, too, this Saturday—all this seemed to him quite logical and irreproachable, and he said to himself, albeit with a divided heart, that nothing would happen if he postponed his diet for three or four days, and if his polluted body became a little more polluted, for in the last analysis, how much did three or four days of pollution count in comparison with more than forty years, and it was only by the purest chance that he had gone to see the naturopath today, when he might just as well have gone to see him in three or four days' time, or even in a week. But when he turned into Pinsker Street he recovered his former resolution and decided that he would not postpone the strict vegetarian diet and he would follow the doctor's instructions to the letter, and he said as much to Aviva when he told her about his visit to the naturopath and gave her the list of permitted foods.

Aviva, who was on the point of leaving for work, listened attentively and, after glancing at the list, said that she would help him to maintain the diet to the best of her ability, but she advised him to forget about it since he would never be able to stand it and even if he did succeed, it would only be at the cost of perpetual tension and resentment, and she added that in general she didn't think it was a good idea for anyone to go around all the time full of tension and resentful thoughts about food and what he was missing every hour of the day, or full of guilt and self-reproach at every crumb of food he put into his mouth—it was unnatural and she couldn't believe that the cost was worth the benefit—and afterward, as she got ready to leave the house, hurrying now, she remarked that as a rule she was against going to extremes, and especially against resolutions that were impossible to keep, since they led only to anger and despair, and she didn't believe at all, as he knew, in miracle cures and all kinds of shortcuts, which gave rise to high expectations and at the same time to tension and bitterness, and she was surprised at him—surely he knew himself well enough to know that all this wasn't for him?—but Meir insisted that he intended to keep strictly to the diet, which he was confident he would be able to do without tension or bitterness, and Aviva put on her coat and said, "I hope you're right," and before leaving, she added that people who set their sights too high often ended up giving in completely, which was exactly what she was afraid of. And Meir, whose respect for her shrewdness and presence of mind made him all the more irritated at her skepticism, said, "You'll see," and parted from her in a spirit of annoyance and slight hostility and went to the fridge and took out a carton of yogurt, one cucumber, and a few leaves of lettuce, which was his breakfast according to the new diet, with a cup of unsweetened tea to follow, and he began to eat very slowly and with great concentration, trying to enjoy the feeling of his improving health as he did so, and as he stood before the big window chewing the cucumber cut into rounds and the dreary lettuce leaves, leaving the yogurt to the end, he tried to sense the renewed vitality surging through his body, and even imagined that he could indeed discern its traces, when suddenly, in the middle of these endeavors, he felt a grim amusement and laughed at himself and turned to the rich blue winter sky, with its sun as yellow as an egg yolk from days gone by, and the whole world with its mountains and seas and infinite spaces and all the pleasures that he had not yet tasted and would not taste anymore, and with a joyless heart he suddenly said out loud, "Good-bye, wonderful gefilte fish. Good-bye, cheese omelettes. Stuffed *kishka* and *cholent,* good-bye falafel and *techina.* Good-bye honey cake and poppyseed cake. Good-bye all the pleasures of life," and he bit sadly into the tasteless lettuce leaf and reminded himself in a loud, reproving voice: "But being healthy is a pleasure, too. And walking down the street with a light step or climbing stairs without becoming short of breath. There are other pleasures in life besides eating!" By the time he had finished eating the lettuce, however, and stood drinking his unsweetened tea and looking out at the winter morning bathed in yellow sunshine, the effect of these encouraging words had already worn off, and a mood of grim depression settled on him as he saw his life becoming empty of content and stretching out before him like a sad, gray desert without a tree, a bush, a flower, or a bud, and full of restless longings for food, his heart wrung with self-pity, he asked himself what was the point of such a life— a life without boiled or fried meat, without *klops* and rissoles and fried eggs and cheese, without ice cream or whipped cream, and above all without bread, ordinary slices of bread and butter, not to speak of a well-baked roll with halva, the very thought of which plunged him into a gloom so black that he almost wept. But when he took up his briefcase and got ready to leave for the office, he recovered and said to himself that his despondency was temporary: in a few weeks' time, when his body had been purified, refreshed, and healed, and he had become accustomed to the new diet, his joy of life would return even more intensely than before, and thanks to the new vegetarian regime he would restore his health and lengthen his life and free it of many anxieties, and in the summer, after getting rid of his paunch and acquiring a tan, he would look as young and lithe as he had after his army service, and once again he was filled with hopeful resolution.

The day passed with agonizing slowness, time seemed to have emptied out and frozen with every minute longer and more desolate than its predecessor, and nagging thoughts of food never left him for an instant, but he controlled himself, and only in the evening, after the news, he said to Aviva that he would love something good to eat and Aviva said, "Then eat," and Meir said, "No, I can't," dying for her to prove the opposite, and Aviva said, "A glass of milk and a spoon of honey won't do you any harm, believe me," and he said, "I've already had my rations for today," and waited for her to go on pleading with him, afraid that she might persuade him to cross the borderline he had been battling all day long to preserve, while at the same time longing for her to do so, but Aviva only shrugged her shoulders and repeated what she had said to him in the morning—that she was against anyone going around all day long tense and full of frustrated thoughts about food and what he was missing, suffering from feelings of guilt and self-reproach, which in her opinion was worse than the illness itself. Meir listened to her with an expressionless face and a sense of bitter betrayal and then said coldly, "Okay, I understood you the first time," and feeling all his latent hostility toward her flaring up again, together with furious resentment against the naturopath with the silver-green hair, he stared stonily at the television screen for a while and then, with a muttered "good night," went into the bedroom and got undressed and lay down with the newspaper.

At the end of the week, three days after his visit to the naturopath, exhausting and oppressive days during which he struggled grimly against the temptation to break his diet, Meir went up to his parents to ask them how they were and to weigh himself and get the gym teacher Gerda Altshuler's address, as he explained to himself, although he knew, in spite of all his desperate efforts to deceive himself, that this was not his true intention and that he should keep away because he would not have the strength to withstand temptation and every step he took was bringing him closer to his doom. He approached the house and climbed the stairs in a mood of sulky submission to his fate, but nevertheless he still believed that he would behave with restraint and abstinence, and indeed, when his mother opened the door, he told her that he had come for only a few minutes, to see how they were and to weigh himself, and he crossed the little hall and passed the clean, empty kitchen without blinking an eye and went into the big room, where his father was sitting and watching television, and sat down on the edge of the sofa, glancing with perfect indifference at the butter cookies lying on the plate, and after exchanging a few words with his parents, he stood up and went into the bathroom to weigh himself and saw to his astonishment and disappointment that he had lost only one kilo—judging by his suffering, he was sure that he had lost at least a kilo a day—and he examined the scales and adjusted them and weighed himself again, but always with the same result, until he went back into the room feeling defeated and depressed and sat down on the edge of the sofa, doing his best to ignore the cups of tea and the wonderful butter cookies, and told his parents the news in a plaintive and resentful tone, wondering as he did so if he should stretch out his hand and take one of the cookies off the plate. His mother, immediately on the alert, said that losing one kilo was just fine, there was no need to lose any more—in her heart of hearts she was pleased that he had not lost any more, since although she knew that losing weight was good for him, something inside her rose up in protest at the idea—and she added, "Why be in such a hurry? Is anyone chasing you?" and his father nodded in confirmation without taking his eyes off the screen, and after a heavy pause, full of conflict and inner struggle, she took the bull by the horns and very cautiously, in a guilty, apologetic tone and as fearfully as if she were treading on the edge of a precipice, said that she knew she shouldn't offer him anything to eat, but nevertheless she would like him to taste a bit of meat with a dish of peppers on the side. When Meir, who had already resigned himself to his doom, did not immediately refuse, she pressed her advantage and remarked that it was very lean meat, without a scrap of fat, and Meir, still putting up a pretense of struggle, smiled weakly and said, not very firmly, that it was against doctor's orders and would ruin his diet, and his mother said that once couldn't ruin anything and suggested that he come with her to the kitchen and see for himself how lean the meat was before making up his mind.

Meir got up and went with her to the kitchen, remarking that he hadn't actually decided to be a strict vegetarian for the rest of his

life, but he still wanted to go on giving the experiment a chance to
see if it would really have a beneficial effect on his health, and his
mother took the dish of meat out of the fridge and held it out to him
and told him to see for himself, or perhaps he would prefer a piece
of fish, the fish was very lean too, and Meir repeated, "You're ruining
my diet," and without expressing his consent by so much as a hint,
sat down at his usual place and asked her about Bill, totally ignoring
what was about to happen, and his mother said that he was still talking
about going back to America and apparently making practical arrangements as well, but that she still hoped he would stay in Israel,
and she put a plate with a hefty piece of meat on it in front of him
and next to it a slice of *klops,* and Meir drew the plate toward him
and, without looking at it, began to eat and asked her what gave her
grounds for this hope and went on eating with a noncommittal air,
as if it were someone else eating, and his mother said, "I simply don't
want him to go away," and put a dish full of boiled carrots in front
of him and added two or three spoonfuls of rice, and Meir said, "I
understand," and smiled, but all his thoughts were concentrated on
the desperate effort to distance himself from his eating, which filled
him with gloom and fury against his mother, who had tempted him
to eat, and against himself and against the naturopath, with his pale
green hair, and against his very enjoyment of the dishes, which only
a few days before he had renounced in such exaltation of spirit, and
against the whole world, including Aviva, and in a last, desperate
attempt to save the situation, he tried to convince himself that the
meat and the *klops* and the peppers and the carrots and even the rice
were really very unfattening, except perhaps the bread, and that one
little accidental deviation was incapable of causing serious, irreparable
damage. He told himself that he would rectify whatever slight damage
was caused by imposing even further restrictions on himself for the
next three days, by abstaining from apples or cracked wheat, for
instance, but the feeling of defeat went on embittering and poisoning
his soul and he pushed away the remnants of a slice of bread and said
to himself that he had never sworn to be a vegan, or any kind of
vegetarian either, and he had no obligation to keep to the diet he had

submitted to of his own free will—he was free to keep to it or deviate from it or even to give it up completely—and for a moment he felt a sense of relief and drew the half-eaten piece of bread toward him and said to his mother, who had seated herself in her usual place next to him, after putting on the kettle to boil, that he intended to begin exercising—he said this in a tone of reserve, which barely disguised the anger and resistance he felt toward her for making him eat, and his mother said that it was a very good idea, and if only she could, she too would begin to exercise. Even before he opened his mouth, he had known that she would rush to agree with whatever he wanted, and this instantly aroused all his irritation against her, for her oppressive devotion and her humble kindheartedness, sweeping him against his will into a murky whirlpool of hostility, and making a strenuous effort to soften the chilliness of his tone, he asked her about Gerda Altshuler, the gym teacher from Berlin, with whom he had exercised for a time as a boy and who had shown a particular affection for him and who was so different from his mother, with her big but supple body and her heavy, swarthy face, radiating confidence and a natural, unforced freedom toward the world, and his mother looked at him in surprise and said that she had been dead for a number of years already, at least five, and when the kettle whistled, she got up to make the tea and asked him if he wanted any, and then placed a plate of the delicious butter cookies on the table together with two cups of tea, and Meir said that he didn't want any tea and that he wouldn't have any cookies, and finished his meal with a glass of water from the tap. This resolute refusal lifted his spirits a little and raised his hopes for a moment, but before he parted from his parents, after sitting and watching the news with them, he stole into the kitchen and quickly snatched a handful of crumbly butter cookies from the blue plastic jar—he could feel their crumbliness and even their taste on the tips of his fingers—and hardly pausing to chew, he gobbled them down as if the rapidity with which he ate them somehow canceled out the act of eating itself, and afterward, as if nothing had happened, he said, "Good-bye," and with a heavy heart, full of resentment and anger, left the apartment.

Slowly and drearily, day followed day as the battle dragged grimly on, in a world that had turned into one endless mine field, leaving him without a moment to spare from his efforts at abstinence and from the interminable calculations—calculations concerning the food he ate and the frequency with which he ate it and calculations concerning the point and efficacy of his actions—which turned his life into one futile, bitter sum. Whenever he went into the street, whenever he visited his parents or friends, and of course whenever he was at home, he was engaged in fighting the exhausting battles of a lost war, in which, as he very soon realized, even his most decisive victories were only temporary stations on the inevitable road to his defeat. He felt his blood filling with poison as a result of his conflicts and failures, which multiplied intolerably, for when he did not fail in deed he failed in thought, until his whole life turned into one dense defeat, and overcome with anger and despair, he repeated to himself in his endless inner debates that the whole business of veganism, however logical it might sound, was utter nonsense and in contradiction to human nature as it had taken shape during thousands or perhaps even millions of years. And even if the whole of humanity, including the greatest doctors and scientists and scholars, were wrong, and only a handful of vegans were right—which was quite impossible and didn't make sense—he preferred to count himself among the masses of mankind, together with the greatest doctors and scientists and scholars, and to be mistaken along with them, and take the risks that they took in living an unhealthy life; and he said to himself that even Gavrosh, for all his closeness to nature, had not become a strict vegetarian, and also that the very wish to live without pollution was an inhuman wish, since the corruption of the flesh was an integral part of human life, and you might even say that a life free of all impurities was in a certain sense no different from death, not to mention the fact that a life devoid of pleasure was not worth living, however healthy it might be, and he went on to remind himself that you only lived once, which changed everything, an argument he repeated to himself dozens and perhaps hundreds of times, for even though it made him uneasy in its vulgarity and banality—it was the argument of shopkeep-

ers and taxi drivers and all kinds of people of whom he disapproved
—it was nevertheless, and to exactly the same degree, decisive and
undeniable. And on his way home from work one day—he had grown
into the habit of wandering aimlessly about the streets in search of
a refuge from the baited trap which his home had become—he
suddenly understood that his desire to restore the youthfulness to his
body was as fatuous as it was hopeless, and the same thing applied,
essentially, to his health, and in any case it meant losing his life in
the vain endeavor to retain what could not be retained and postpone
what could not be postponed, and even if he could attain his goal, it
would be only on a partial and temporary basis. In the last analysis,
what were five or ten or even twenty additional years of life in comparison to the unimaginable vastness of the eons of time, which would
go on after he no longer existed?—especially since even then, in spite
of all his efforts and renunciations, he would never know if his life had
indeed been lengthened, even by a single hour, or if this was exactly
the span of years and days and hours that had been allotted to him,
and which he would have lived even without the abstention and
sufferings he had imposed upon himself in the battle for this life,
which could be lived only once and no more, and in any case when
he was lying in the ground it would make no difference at all, and no
one would give a damn if he had been a vegetarian or not, or if he
had kept his diet or broken it.

The clear and simple logic of these arguments would convince
him and fill him with peace and happiness, but not for long, since
right away, sometimes at the very same moment, he would be overwhelmed once more by a flood of anger and despair sweeping everything before it, and he would say to himself bitterly that all this
veganism wasn't worth a damn and the only thing that would do him
any good would be the ability to live with complete, impudent freedom, according to his instincts, which was the right way to live and
the only way of life he really aspired to, like Aviva, who had gone and
fucked a man in a car, or God knows where, a man she had met only
half an hour or forty minutes before, in his car or some cheap hotel
or perhaps in his house—if only he knew where and how it had

happened! Again and again in the misery of these somber and joyless
days, in the painful and provocative pictures created out of the darkness of his ignorance, he tried to imagine the man's face and figure
and the most minute details of how he embraced her and kissed her,
how she took off her clothes, and how he stroked her stomach and
thighs, and how in the end he went to bed with her. All his fury and
hostility were directed against Aviva, whereas the man himself gave
rise in him mainly to feelings of envy and defeat, for he too could have
behaved in the same way, and with even greater freedom, with Raya
in that long, narrow room, when she was so ready and willing to give
herself to him and submit to all his desires—with a touch of his hand
he could have intimated to her, when she came back and stood next
to the bed after throwing her clothes onto a chair, to turn her back
to him, and then to put one leg on the chair and bend slightly forward
and lean on the table, and very slowly and lingeringly, while stroking
her belly and thighs, he could have looked and seen what he was dying
to see, but he lay with his eyes closed, too frightened to do what he
wanted so urgently to do, because something, some miserable cowardice or simply the lack of a vital life force, prevented him from doing
it, just as it prevented him from breaking this rotten diet. And in an
evil mood of black disappointment, he contemplated his life, all he
needed was one quick look because it was all there inside him in all
its details, with his youth and young manhood—full of joyful hikes
and adventures and lofty, romantic idealism, slightly tinged with
anarchism, the product of youth and the spirit of the times, everything was so ardent and full of faith and freedom then, and it was all
somehow personified in the figures of Lenin and Mayakovsky and
"The Cossacks of Kuban" and he too had even tried his hand at
writing a few poems in the same admired style—and with his conventional, bourgeois present, which would also be the mirror of his future,
unless he looked sharp and shook himself free of it with all his might.
On no account could he understand why he didn't finally rid himself
of the bloody veganist diet, which was already so full of holes that after
three weeks almost nothing was left of it, despite all his bitter efforts
and sufferings, but for the yogurt and cucumber and dreary lettuce

leaves in the morning and the two glasses of tap water after lunch—
all the rest lay in ruins at his feet, poisoning his life with guilt. But
he continued to advocate veganism, nevertheless, and to see himself
as a vegan, albeit a temporary and sinning one, and this turned his
life into a maelstrom of anger and bitterness, in the midst of which
he was continually assailed by feelings of angry hostility toward Aviva,
the guilty woman who had betrayed him and fucked a stranger, and
toward himself, for not putting a stop to the bloody diet and beginning to lead a life of unfettered freedom according to his instincts,
and for the feeble way he had behaved with Raya in that long, narrow
room, the crowning failure and fiasco of all the other miserable failures
of his life, and especially against the naturopath with the greenish-
gray hair, for whom he felt only scorn and contempt and whom he
denounced as a thief and an ignorant charlatan. And one day, in a
moment of insight, he said to Pozner, to whom he was presenting,
perhaps for the hundredth time, all his complaints about the diet,
cursing the naturopath as he did so, that the truth was that it was only
because of his scorn and hatred for this fraudulent doctor that he was
going on with this bloody diet, and he would go on with it until the
doctor burst—he smiled as he said this, and Pozner smiled back and
asked him if the doctor knew about it, and Meir said, "No, but I don't
care," in an obstinate tone of voice, with the vestiges of the smile still
hovering on his lips.

A few days later, one rainy evening, as he emerged from the
cinema where he had fled to find a refuge from his sufferings—an
exercise of the kind to which he was becoming increasingly addicted
—and stopped outside the entrance to button up his coat and
straighten his cap before stepping out into the cold, steady rain, he
saw Dr. Reiner standing not far from him and waiting for the rain
to stop. For a moment he thought of slipping away and pretending
not to see her, but it seemed to him that she had recognized him, and
so he overcame his embarrassment and turned to her and said, "Hello,
Dr. Reiner," and she smiled and said, "So we meet again. You were
sitting a few rows in front of me," and tightened the scarf around her
neck and asked him how he was feeling, and Meir said, "Okay," and

stole a glance at the rain, wishing it would let up so that he could say good-bye and leave, and Dr. Reiner, who was evidently fed up with waiting, opened her umbrella and said, "This rain's not going to stop. Come along, I'll give you a lift, my car's parked not far from here," and Meir thanked her and said there was no need, he had a bus almost to his front door, and she said, "It's on my way. Come on, the car's just around the corner," and set off, and Meir said, "Okay," although he would have preferred to go by foot, and began walking behind her, his head slightly bowed in the cold rain, which the wind was blowing into his face, and as soon as they turned the corner, Dr. Reiner pointed to the Volkswagen Beetle parked a few yards away, saying, "Here she is," and strode rapidly down the street, which was exposed to the wind and flooded with water, holding the umbrella in one hand and keeping her coat collar closed with the other, and quickly opened the door and sat down and opened the other door and said, "Get in," and Meir took off his cap and tried to shake the raindrops off his coat and got in and sat down. Dr. Reiner unbuttoned her coat and said, "What a rain," and then added unexpectedly, "It's not a good idea to neglect treatment for high blood pressure. It doesn't get better by itself, you know," and Meir hesitated for a moment and then said, feeling very uncomfortable, "To tell the truth, I went to see a naturopath. I decided to give it a try," and Dr. Reiner said, "It's the latest fashion. Have you taken up jogging, too?" and Meir, who could hear the smile in her voice, said, "No, not yet," and with a smile of complicity in her mockery, he repeated, "I wanted to give it a try," and Dr. Reiner put the car in gear and said, "I hope you're enjoying it," and started off. The faint, amused smile did not leave her face, and Meir said, "It's depressing me to death," in the same lighthearted tone, and Dr. Reiner gave him an amused glance and asked, "Are you a masochist then?" and Meir, with a mildly challenging note in his voice, replied, "They say it helps," and Dr. Reiner said, "Certainly. But only in certain cases. In others, it can do fatal damage," and she stopped at a traffic light and then added, "There are lots of things that help that we don't do. In the last analysis, people do what they want to do with their lives," and Meir said, "Yes, but veganism keeps the body clean," and waited expectantly to hear what she would say, and she gave him a smiling glance and said, "Who says the body has to be clean?" and passed another car and added, "We know so little about the body that there's no point in going to extremes," and Meir —her words were music to his ears—asked, "So you recommend that I stop it?"—he wanted to hear her say so in so many words—and Dr. Reiner said, "I'd be sorry to deprive you of the feeling that you're doing something important for the sake of your health," and smiled, and Meir said, "I understand," and asked her to stop in front of the house with the high hedge, and when he opened the door of the car, after thanking her, he said, "I'll see you tomorrow, Dr. Reiner," and Dr. Reiner said, "Tomorrow I'm in Jerusalem," and Meir said, "The day after tomorrow then," and thanked her again and got out of the car.

Filled with a tremendous sense of relief, as if some unbearably heavy weight had been lifted from his chest, and so jubilant that he wanted to cheer, he waved to her as she drove off, and then, feeling that he had been saved and his life was about to begin again, he bounded joyfully up the stairs. And two days later he went to the clinic and Dr. Reiner gave him a thorough examination, and as she wrote out his prescription, she remarked that she was very much in favor of losing excess weight and eating a balanced diet, she had no doubt that these two things were good for your health, especially for people suffering from a certain category of diseases, such as cardiac and vascular disorders, but there was a big difference between that and veganism. Meir said, "Yes. I have the feeling that my veganist experiment is over," and took the prescription and thanked her and left.

That evening, when he went up to his parents' to celebrate his freedom, he felt buoyant and happy, as indeed he had been feeling every minute of the day since he had stepped out of Dr. Reiner's car and stopped being a vegan, and only the sight of his mother's pale face as she opened the door, with its expression of lifelessness and resignation, which even her weak, forced smile could not disguise, worried him and gave rise to an anxiety he did his best to suppress and ignore, since he was determined not to allow anything to mar his happiness and good spirits. She invited him into the kitchen so that she could give him something to eat—at long last he could eat without feelings of anger and guilt—and he told her to sit down and said that he would serve himself, intending in this way to demonstrate his feelings of concern and closeness to her, but she refused, of course, and laid the table and set the dishes of food before him, and even cut his bread for him as usual, and he sat down and ate, and his mother sat down beside him and said despondently that after fifty years of living in the country she still felt like a foreigner and a displaced person, especially since the Revisionists with that Begin had come to power, and she really wished that she could leave and go somewhere else, never mind where. And in a very somber tone she added, "This isn't my country anymore," and stood up to put the kettle on to boil, with something ugly and sickly that Meir had been doing his best to avoid seeing, spreading over her pale face, and when she resumed her seat, she said, "Bill's going back to America in two weeks' time," and it was obvious that this was the immediate cause of her dejection, and Meir, still stubbornly trying to ignore her gloom and her ugly, sickly pallor, said, "He's not going back so quickly, it's all talk," and his mother said, "No. This time it's serious. He's already found a buyer for his flat and is making arrangements for the journey," and Meir, who was enjoying his food and wanted to go on enjoying it without worrying about her depression, said, "Let him make them. He's not going yet," and his mother said, "I'll miss him very much, I've grown so accustomed to his being here." She said this in utter simplicity and at the same time in a tone of such desolation that it seemed as if her life were coming to an end, and she took an orange from the bowl and began to peel it apathetically with a knife, and as she peeled the orange and ate one segment after the other, she said that she wasn't cut out for this life since too many things, among them trifling and unimportant ones that had happened many years ago, went on troubling and depressing her as if they had happened only yesterday, and it was still possible to do something about them, and the truth was that the more the years passed, and they passed with terrible swiftness, the less she understood the nature and point and purpose of life—especially since

her mother's death, when a vast emptiness had suddenly gaped all
around her and she felt as if she were drifting aimlessly without
anything to hold on to, and her soul trembled within her—or maybe
it was because of the winter and the particular quality of the cold this
year, which reminded her of the cold when she was a girl. She put
a segment of fruit into her mouth and afterward, as if she were laying
down a heavy burden, she said that actually she would like to die, and
Meir, who had been vaguely following her movements as she peeled
and ate the orange, suddenly and with the vivid immediacy of a vision,
saw in his mother's movements, as if they were disembodied shades
concealed like a soul in a body, the movements of his grandmother
in all their concrete uniqueness—the way she had of peeling and
eating an orange and of cutting and salting and of pouring and stirring
tea and turning the pages of a book, and her actual person, too,
surrounding these movements, and in that same split second, flooded
with tender longings for his grandmother, he realized that when
someone dies, he takes with him not only his own particular image
and voice but also the special, unique movements in which he was
embodied, and which for one fleeting moment had seemed to come
back to life, although they were really gone forever.

Two weeks later, on a clear, cold winter's evening, Meir's mother
gave a farewell dinner for Bill, who had already packed his few remaining possessions in two small suitcases, after giving all the rest of his
belongings away to his friends and neighbors, and all the people she
had invited sat around the table laden with his favorite foods, which
she had been busy cooking since early that morning. Close to mid-
night, when the guests, a few landsleit and friends of his youth, felt
that the evening, after proceeding in a spirit of cheerful nostalgia, was
now drawing to its inevitable end—an end they did their best to
ignore, as if they were going to meet again in a few weeks' time—
Meir's father turned to Bill and, with a jovial smile that did nothing
to disguise his seriousness, said that now that he had drunk the special
brandy with the taste of their old hometown that he had prepared for
him, and eaten the gefilte fish and the *cholent* with the stuffed *kishka*
and tasted the raisin *kugel* and the cheesecake that his wife had

cooked especially for him, he proposed that he give up the whole idea of leaving, for why should he drag himself all the way to Miami when in any case he would be back again in two weeks' time, and maybe even less. Bill laughed all over his ruddy, childish face and shook his rugby-ball-shaped head in embarrassed amusement, and Meir's mother, who had been busy all night long serving and slicing and clearing away and washing up and seeing that nobody lacked for anything, and had only just sat down to drink a cup of tea, joined in and said, "Stay, Bill. Stay and imagine that you've been there and back. No one will think the worse of you for it," and Bill, whose perpetual smile had disappeared from his childish face, leaving it looking naked and as if it didn't belong to him, said, "No, it's too late," and Meir's mother said with a smile, but at the same time with a refusal to let go so profound that it seemed as if her whole life depended on it, "It's too late to go," and Yitzhak Kantz said, "We're not getting any younger, Bill. Why start running around the world by yourself at this stage of your life?" and something heavy and oppressive, which up to now had been held at bay, settled on the company, with only Bill still attempting to deny the oppression of the parting and separation that was almost upon them, and he laughed loudly and said, "I'm not going to run around the world. I'm going home to America." A slight tension spread through the room and hung disguised but palpable in the air, and Meir's father said, "America is the *Golah*," and the rebuke and even anger in his words, although he tried to suppress them, were very evident to the rest of the company, who shared his feelings. Suddenly the thing that up to now they had managed to deny and ignore, and that divided them despite themselves, was upon them, and Bill said, "And what have you got here? The biggest *Golah* of all!" and laughed hoarsely, but he, too, sensed the shadow that had fallen between them at the parting of the ways, and Meir's mother, who was cut to the quick by his words, even though she identified with them so strongly, said, "This is our country," and Bill, without taking in what she said, or without wanting to, perhaps, said, "I want to live in the *Golah*, I like it," and with a loud, confused laugh, he waved his empty glass in the air and cried,

"Long live the *Golah*!" But all this did nothing to hide his panic as he suddenly realized that the departure, which up to a few hours before had been no more than an intention, was rapidly becoming a reality whether he liked it or not, and he rose from his chair as a sign that it was time to leave—most of the other guests too were already getting up, and one or two were even putting on their coats—and went up to Meir's mother, who felt her heart contracting with the intensity of her sorrow and loss, and placed his hand affectionately on her shoulder, and after asking to be remembered to Meir and Aviva and putting on his coat, he shook hands with the departing guests and kissed Meir's father and his mother, who waited until everyone was gone and then washed the dishes and put everything away, singing, "And perhaps it never happened at all" softly to herself, as she was in the habit of doing when she felt her soul sinking within her, and a few weeks later, at the end of winter, she died.

PART TWO

Meir's mother died suddenly and without any warning, apart from a bout of flu that forced her, after stubbornly ignoring it for as long as she could, to take to her bed for the first time in years, but after two days in bed, before she had properly recovered and despite the pleas of his father, who took care of her devotedly, she got up as soon as he left the house and resumed her household duties, and the next day she was taken to the hospital, a fact that Meir discovered only that evening when he dropped in to visit his parents on his way to Pozner's. His father opened the door with a deflated air and a worried, helpless look on his ravaged face, and said, "It's good you came," and still standing in the hall—the flat was disagreeably silent and dark, except for a light coming from the kitchen—he told him that they had taken his mother to the hospital that morning, and Meir, surprised, asked him what had happened, and his father said that she had taken a turn for the worse and the doctor who examined her had ordered her immediate hospitalization.

His voice was frail and hollow and full of impotence and complaint, and Meir said that everything would be all right and there was no reason to get into a panic, and he went into the kitchen behind his father, who invited him to sit down and have a bite to eat, but Meir said he wasn't hungry and remained standing, leaning against the marble-topped table—finding himself alone like this with his father in the empty flat made him feel extremely uncomfortable—and asked him what exactly had happened, and his father took a bite of bread and cheese and told him again, this time in greater detail. There was something horribly lonely and helpless in the way he looked and spoke and sat and in every movement he made, and Meir, with a barely perceptible note of impatience in his voice, said that doctors nowadays were in a big hurry to send people to the hospital whether it was necessary or not, which was a well-known fact, and there was nothing to worry about, and indeed he himself felt not worried but harassed, and he was sorry that he had come to visit his parents instead of going straight to Pozner, and he moved away from the table and went into the bathroom to weigh himself, and when he saw that he had not gained any weight, and perhaps even lost a bit, he experienced a feeling of satisfaction and went back into the kitchen to say good-bye to his father, and after a moment's hesitation, he went to the cupboard and nonchalantly took a handful of butter cookies from the blue plastic jar, as if he wasn't really aware of what he was doing—on the way upstairs he had definitely decided not to do it—and then he sat down, as he had felt obliged to do from the moment of taking the cookies, on the stool opposite his father, who drank his tea with long, noisy gulps and recapitulated the course of events from the moment his mother had fallen ill to the moment he left her in the hospital. All his strength and suppressed violence were exhausted, and he looked so frightened that Meir was embarrassed and assured him again that there was nothing to worry about and that everything would be all right, and then he said good-bye and went away with the nagging feeling that he should have stayed with him a little longer, at least until the beginning of the evening news. The next day, as soon as he came home from work, Meir phoned his father to find out how his mother was feeling, the obligation to do so had been nagging at him since morning, and his father, who had just come home from his second visit to the hospital that day, said that there was no change in her condition but that she was apathetic and depressed, and that he had spoken to her and tried to take her mind off things, mainly about their coming trip to Gibraltar, and that this had cheered her up a bit, and in the end he said that she had repeated her request for nobody to visit her, and Meir acceded to this request with a feeling of relief, unlike Aviva, who bought a bunch of flowers and paid her a short visit that evening, and the next day too, in the afternoon, while Meir, whose equanimity had begun to fray a little at the edges, phoned a friend from his kibbutz days who held a high administrative position in the hospital and asked him to drop into the Internal Ward and put in a good word for his mother, and the next day, in the middle of work, he went to the hospital to speak to the doctor himself and find out exactly how things stood, and especially to take advantage of his friend's intervention in order to get them to take a special interest in his mother's case.

It was a sunny winter's day and Meir, who had only taken an hour or so off work, strode purposefully down the hospital corridors looking for his mother's ward until he came to a glass door with the name of the ward printed on it, where he stopped for a moment and wondered whether to turn around and go away again—after all, his mother had explicitly said that she didn't want anyone to come and visit her—but then, after studying the sign again, he slowly and gingerly opened the door and saw his mother lying on a white bed right in front of him, in the opposite corner of the wide, brightly lit lobby of the ward, one of her legs exposed with the knee comfortably bent and her face raised motionless to the ceiling. He stopped just inside the door, and as he looked at her, a doubt crossed his mind as to whether it really was his mother, because the pillow on which her head was resting, and especially the tubes to which she was connected, partly hid her face, but instead of approaching the bed to see for himself, he took a few more steps toward the nurses' desk, where he stood leaning on the counter, and looked at her again. But he was still unable to decide whether it was really her or only someone who resembled her in the posture of the leg and the shape of the hand lying limply at her side, and the black hair peeking out from the edge of the pillow on the pale and insufficiently clear bit of face, and especially in something elusive radiating from her body, and after a moment he turned to the nurse sitting behind the counter and introduced himself and inquired about his mother, slipping in an embarrassed reference to his friend and the fact that he was taking an interest in the case as he did so, and the nurse, who was busy with various lists, glanced in the direction of his mother's bed and said politely and matter-of-factly that her condition was not good and that she would apparently have to be moved to Intensive Care, and turning her head in his mother's direction, she suggested that he go up to her, but Meir said that he didn't want to disrupt the hospital routine by making a nuisance of himself outside of visiting hours, he would come back to see her later in the day during visiting hours, and the nurse said, "You're not making a nuisance of yourself, but it's up to you," and Meir waited a minute and said that he had come only to find out how she was, and once again, in the same embarrassed and roundabout way, mentioned his friend and the fact that he had made inquiries about his mother, and the nurse said, "Yes, he spoke to someone here. I think it was Dr. Appelboim," and after answering the phone, she repeated that his mother's condition was not good and that the next twenty-four hours would be critical, and then she looked down at the papers in front of her again. Meir retreated slightly and sent a farewell glance in his mother's direction, but instead of leaving he went on standing near the counter with one hand resting on it because he felt that he had not yet done his duty, and he looked at the nurse and then across the lobby at his mother, who from time to time shifted her raised leg slightly and also her head—she seemed very peaceful and serene—and he wondered if he should go up to her and disrupt her tranquillity, and especially if he should speak to the nurse again and ask her to keep a particular eye on his mother, since that was what he had come for, after all, and also to mention his friend again, this time firmly and clearly, since the way he had mentioned his name

before made him feel painfully disappointed in himself, but then he
demurred and said to himself that the nurse was busy and that interference of this kind was liable to provoke resistance, and rightly so,
and that in any case they would look after her properly, at least as well
as they looked after anyone else, and that there was no need for any
prompting from him, and after glancing at his mother again, he
turned away, but as he approached the glass door an orderly pushing
a large covered instrument came through it, and he waited because
something told him that this orderly was on his way to his mother,
and in fact, he pushed the instrument to her bedside where he
removed the cover, plugged it into the wall, tested it briefly, and then
attached it to her body and switched it on, doing everything without
haste and in a casual, routine way, and then he lit a cigarette and stood
there joking and chatting with one of the nurses while keeping one
eye on the machine. Meir, who was so eager to be out in the fresh
air and mild winter sunshine that he could already see himself in the
street outside the hospital walls, hesitated for a moment and then took
up his position leaning against the counter again, where he stood
looking at his mother and at the orderly, who seemed to him to be
doing his work inattentively and negligently, with a growing sense of
impending disaster.

Full of this sense of dread, which gave rise in him to a feeling
of panic and the need to do everything he could to avert the danger,
while at the same time increasing his desire to escape—if the orderly
with the instrument hadn't suddenly shown up he would have been
well away by now—he thought again of approaching the nurse behind
the counter, and the orderly and all the other nurses, and asking them
to take especially good care of his mother, and he rehearsed what he
should say to them, trying out different tones in his head—first a firm
tone and then a pleading, almost imploring one—but he stayed where
he was, with one hand resting on the counter, and said to himself that
the fact that they were relaxed and smiling didn't mean that they
weren't doing whatever was necessary, there was no doubt that they
were doing just that—after all, it was their plain and simple duty to
do so, and in any case his request would do no good, and it might even

do harm because it was liable to arouse their anger against him, and consequently against his mother. In the end, with the same bored, practiced, well-drilled movements, the orderly detached his mother from the machine and exchanged a few words with the nurse—Meir caught only the movements of their lips and heads and the enigmatic expressions on their faces, as if everything were happening behind a glass wall—and the nurse covered his mother with a thin white blanket and called another nurse to help her push the bed, and he wanted to go up to his mother and say something to her, or just to touch her shoulder, but he went on standing without moving and looked at them and at the bed until they disappeared behind the doors at the end of the corridor, and then, after a slight hesitation, he turned to the nurse behind the counter and asked her to tell his mother that he had come to ask how she was, and the nurse said, "All right," and made a note of it, and he said, "Thank you," and after hesitating again and taking a step away and then stopping, he asked her to write down his telephone number, with the request that if the need arose they should get in touch with him first and not his father, and the nurse said, "All right" again and wrote the phone number down, and he thanked her again and left the hospital with a feeling of relief and also of oppression.

Little gray clouds were scattered over the blue midday sky, and Meir walked slowly in the mild winter sunshine toward the municipal square, enjoying the touch of the cool fresh air and the feeling of freedom stirring in his body and filling him with joy, but as he walked he felt the dread and fear which lay somewhere inside him like a lump of granite rising up and spreading through all the hollows of his body like leaden smoke, and his face grew grave and hard, as if it had been covered by an extra layer of scaly skin, and he withdrew into his shell, remote and separate from everything around him, and with a not unpleasant feeling of isolation and seclusion, existing and not existing within his shell, he contemplated the trees and houses and cars and the crowds of people strolling along the streets, which were bathed in the golden sunlight. When he reached the square he paused, unable to make up his mind whether to continue along Gordon Street and drop in to see his father, who might be taking his afternoon nap by now, in order to tell him that his mother had been transferred to Intensive Care, and he decided to put it off until he came home from work, but as he was waiting at the bus stop he changed his mind and went to see his father.

The moment he pressed the bell, he heard the frantic shuffle of his father's feet, as if he were sitting and waiting tensely for him to ring the bell, and he was filled with rage, as usual, and then the door opened and his father was standing before him in an unbuttoned shirt and loose trousers, his face dark with worry and confusion. They went into the little room, and Meir told him that he had just come from the hospital, where his mother had been transferred to the Intensive Care department, that things didn't look good, and that he was going to phone his friend at the hospital as soon as he got home from work and ask him to speak to one of the doctors in charge of his mother's ward and request that she be given special treatment, and his father said, "Yes, yes, do it," all the strength and vitality seemed to have evaporated from his frightened body, leaving only a shadow of his tyrannical violence hanging in the air, like the stifling fumes of a smoldering fire, in the form of sullen resentment and a mute demand for pity. He said, "Do it," in a voice of despair and clung to Meir with his eyes, giving him a look full of desolation and desperate appeal, as if he really had it in his power to perform a miracle and save her, and added, "I begged her to stay in bed a few days longer. Where was she running to?" and Meir said, "Everything will be all right. There's nothing to worry about," and said good-bye to his father and went back to work.

Late that evening, when Meir and Aviva came home from visiting friends, their son Amnon told them that someone had phoned from the hospital an hour before and asked them to come at once because his mother was sinking fast, and they went out again immediately and stopped a cab, and shortly afterward they were already walking down the deserted hospital corridors to the Intensive Care department, where they found his father in the passage, in front of the white door of the ward, huddled and helpless in the glare of the

neon lights, almost lost between his brother and his brother's wife,
Aunt Chava, and Zimmer's widow and another distant female relative, whose faces, stiff with panic and shock, thawed a little when they
saw Meir and Aviva, who approached and greeted them with nods and
a few murmured words. Meir sat down next to his father, who looked
at him imploringly, and for a moment an abject expression of gratitude appeared in his dull, defeated eyes, as if the very fact of his late
arrival held out some promise of salvation, but it disappeared again
immediately, leaving no trace on his stunned and despairing face, and
Meir put his arm limply around his shoulders and turned to Zimmer's
widow, who was sitting on the chair next to him, her fleshy face
swollen with unshed tears, and asked her how she was, and then he
said something to his uncle, who was sitting on his father's other side,
and something to the distant female relative, and after that he fell
silent and sat there without a word, looking at the wall opposite him
and at the closed double door of the ward, with its two round windows
like empty portholes, and occasionally into the depths of the corridor,
which looked like a deserted tunnel, while Aviva conversed in whispers with his aunt and from time to time with his uncle, who suddenly
stood up and began pacing to and fro with his hands behind his back,
and then sat down again. All their attention was concentrated on the
door, somewhere behind which, in one of the white rooms none of
them had seen, surrounded by all kinds of instruments and machines,
his mother lay dying without anyone being able to save her. None of
them doubted it or hoped for a miracle, and all they could do was wait
in resignation or terror for the final announcement, which they were
now quietly doing, while Meir, withdrawn into his silence, tried in
vain to take in what was happening—his mother's death—and clarify
it to himself, but despite his efforts, it eluded him like a slippery puff
of smoke or shrank from the touch of his thoughts and disintegrated
into pointless details, leaving him with a heavy feeling of disappointment and shame; and he felt himself growing remote and opaque like
a mollusk in its shell, while the void yawning around him filled with
indifference, which spread like grayish vapors through his chest and
expressionless face and his arm, lying like an empty pipe on his father's

shoulder. Even through the thick cloth of the Sabbath suit he was for some reason wearing Meir could feel the frantic panic and numb helplessness filling all the pores of his father's body and corners of his soul until they themselves became his body and soul, and he tightened his arm slightly around his shoulder as a sign of sympathy and drew his body a little closer to himself—a defeated body stunned with despair, which from time to time gave vent to an unintelligible mutter or sigh immediately swallowed up by the neon-lit emptiness of the corridor.

Finally the doors parted with a light, almost soundless push, and a young doctor with a black mustache appeared. They all froze and stared at him in silence, and the doctor paused in front of the door and looked at them uneasily, as if he was searching for some unfamiliar face, and then took one or two steps toward them, and Meir's father rose to his feet, together with the others, and stood with his shoulders slumped, looking at him with dead, imploring eyes. The doctor, who looked to Meir like an Argentinian, raised his shoulders in a slight, apologetic shrug, and his glance slid uneasily over the little group standing side by side without taking their eyes off him, and in a silence so intense they could hear the noise of the pipes inside the walls, he said in a voice no louder than the silence itself, "It's over. She's dead," and then he raised his shoulders again in the same slight shrug and looked away. Meir stood without moving, stonily supporting his father, who uttered a deep groan and clutched his head, and Zimmer's widow began sobbing softly, her eyes red and her whole face streaming, while his uncle and aunt and Aviva just went on standing there numbly, like the distant female relative, who kept muttering something to herself, and the doctor, addressing himself mainly to Meir and Aviva, said that if they wanted to they could go inside in a moment or two to see her for the last time, and then he said a few words about the cause of death, and something else, too, as if he were trying to detach himself from them as gently as he could. And in the subdued, barely perceptible confusion, like the ghostly movement of the shadows of leaves on a wall, which came with the relaxation of the terrible tension of waiting, Aviva turned to Meir and asked him quietly if he wanted to go in to see his mother, and Meir said, "No, I don't want to," in a hard voice and recoiled slightly from his father, who suddenly sagged and crumpled like an empty bag of skin and dropped into his chair with harsh, dry sobs, repeating over and over, "No, it can't be true. She killed herself and she killed us. I begged her to stay in bed a few more days," and his uncle, who was now supporting him, tried to quiet him, but without much conviction, and the distant female relative joined in dimly, but his aunt put her hand on his shoulder and said, "Let him, let him. He must cry," while Zimmer's widow wept without restraint and kept repeating tearfully, "She was a wonderful woman, there was no one like her," over and over to herself and to his uncle and aunt and Aviva and Meir himself, who nodded unwillingly and then walked away from them all as if to be alone with his grief. He did not want to hear anything or say anything, and he stood there in his isolation, watching out of the corner of his eye as Aviva and his aunt disappeared after the doctor behind the white door, oppressed by a feeling of disappointment that he could not overcome, for everything seemed so thin, even forced, and very far from the terrible grandeur, sublime and yet utterly private and personal, reaching down to the depths of his soul and rolling like dark thunder in its recesses, which should have been present in everything at the moment of his mother's death. A few minutes later, when Aviva and his aunt came back, his uncle stood up and put his hand gently on his father's shoulder and said, "Let's go," and his father raised his head slightly and looked at him in bewilderment, as if nothing would induce him to accept the fact that just like that, at this very moment, an ordinary and undistinguished moment, everything had irrevocably ended, and his uncle said again, "Come on, let's go," and placed his hand under his elbow and gave him a gentle nudge, but Meir's father went on sitting in his chair, not obstinately but dumbly, looking with dull, imploring eyes at his brother and sister-in-law and at Aviva and Meir, who quickly looked away, and his uncle said in a coaxing tone, full of self-justification, "There's nothing more for us to do here," and Zimmer's widow, her face swollen with crying, looked around her and said, "Only a few days ago she came to borrow a little oil," and Aviva put her hand gently on Meir's father's back and said, "We have to go now," and took his arm, and with his uncle holding the other arm they started walking slowly, followed by the others, down the deserted hospital corridors toward the exit. And as they walked, Meir was seized by the sensation that the air was beginning to gape around him and that the ground under his feet was opening up and moving away on either side of him and he was walking on air in an empty, gaping void, together with the nagging feeling that they had forgotten something that they should on no account have forgotten, but that it was now impossible to go back and get it.

Next to the exit Meir's father suddenly stopped and asked if they shouldn't get some sort of certificate before they left, and Zimmer's widow said that they would probably need something for the funeral, and Meir's father said, "There won't be any funeral. She's donated her body to science." He said this defiantly, and Meir's aunt said, "What?!" and his father repeated, "There won't be any funeral, that's what she wanted," and this time, too, he said it in the same tough, argumentative tone, as if he was trying to give offense, and he asked again about the certificate, and Meir, who vaguely remembered his mother saying something years ago about this wish of hers—she didn't want anybody fussing over her, she was revolted by the beadles and cantors and the rest of the religious paraphernalia, and by religious rites in general when they were imposed upon or adopted by people who were not themselves believers—now felt, after hearing it in so many words from his father, relief and even happiness at having been let off the business of the funeral and burial rites, and his heart filled with a warm pride in his mother, who by this final act had made herself free, something she had aspired to all her life without daring to do it, and proved that she really was a woman who went her own way without paying any attention to the conventions and expectations of society, an exceptional, even a bohemian woman. He asked them to wait and went to inquire at the administration desk, where he was told that both the matter of the death certificate and the donation of the body to science could only be arranged the next day, during office hours, and he rejoined the huddled little group waiting at the exit, with the uneasy feeling that they had forgotten something still nagging at him, and told his father, and they went out into the chilly night air, where all at once he was overwhelmed by a feeling that did not replace the previous one but merely pushed it a little to one side, that something crucial had happened in his life and nothing would ever be the same again. He quickly called a cab, and when it came and they got in and drove off, he sat withdrawn into himself in the back seat, staring stonily through the window at the dark houses and streets, and he saw his mother lying on the hospital bed in the pink hospital pajamas, covered with a white sheet, alone in the room with the lights out, behind the wall of the deserted corridor, and his heart contracted; and then he remembered his grandmother, whom he suddenly saw in all her concrete reality, more real than his mother, in her black kidskin shoes with the bump at the joint of her big toe, and her woolen Sabbath dress, her heavy face the color of old newspaper, and her velvety cheeks full of a grieving sorrow too heavy to endure for the death of her daughter, but she did not cry, because she was somehow, thanks to her age or perhaps her wisdom, beyond all that. When they approached the house, after dropping Zimmer's widow and the distant female relative on the way, Meir's uncle said to his father that he would sleep there with him, and Meir's father said, "I'll sleep alone," and his aunt said, "No, he'll sleep with you," but his father was adamant, and his uncle said, "All right, we'll talk about it when we get there," and Meir, his hand resting on Aviva's knee, felt as if all this was somehow directed at him and they all expected something of him, but he didn't say a word and went on staring stonily out the window at the dark, desolate streets, and when he and Aviva came home, only a few hours after going out, he knew that everything had changed forever.

The next morning, after bathing and breakfasting and phoning the office to tell them, without going into details, that he wouldn't be in that day for family reasons, he went to his parents' house to see his father and get the papers he needed in order to make the necessary arrangements. And as he walked up the streets he knew so well, still stepped in the somnambulistic sensation of weightlessness and dislocation, the solemn, dreamlike feeling that had been with him from the moment he woke up in the morning, he gazed at the pavements and the streets, the houses and the hedges and the little square with the spreading trees and the kindergarten and the shoemaker's, all of them wrapped in a delicate web of dreamy solemnity, and was filled with calm wonder at the fact that they were still there, since he felt that they belonged to his mother and were identified with her to such an extent that their existence depended on her walking past them and seeing them, and the same was true of many other parts of the town, of its streets and skies, and this increased the sensation of weightlessness and dislocation, which had something rather pleasant about it and which grew more intense as he entered the lobby of his parents' building and walked up the stairs.

His aunt opened the door and said that his uncle had gone to work and that she would stay until evening to tidy up and cook and take care of everything, and Meir, who was very pleased, thanked her laconically and went into the little room where his father sat in an armchair in the dim light with photographs of his mother scattered over the couch next to him, and after asking him evasively how he was—his father did not answer, but only waved his hand in helpless rage—and making a few more meaningless remarks, he himself did not know why he made them, and all he felt was impatience, he spoke to him about the arrangements that had to be made, trying to maintain the matter-of-fact tone he had rehearsed on the way, and made a list of the things that had to be done—get the death certificate, arrange to have the body donated to science, get the death notices printed, phone his sister in Boston, let Roy know through the Town Major's office, and afterward he stayed on for a while, walking from room to room as if he was tidying up and then sitting down for a moment and trying halfheartedly to talk to his father, whose defeated face was stunned and whose eyes were lifeless, and who slapped his thigh or the arm of the couch from time to time and said that it couldn't be true and that she had killed herself and killed them and that it was an unheard-of calamity. A stubborn refusal to look at his father, and especially to look at the photographs of his mother lying next to him on the couch, overpowered him to such an extent that he was unable to even glance in their direction, and in the end, after putting it off as long as possible, he asked his father for his mother's identity card and the document about donating her body to science, took a few cookies from the blue plastic jar, and left.

The hospital was now flooded with light and bustling with people and activity, not a trace of the desolate mystery and infinite loneliness of the night remained, and as he walked down the corridors, following the instructions of the clerk at the reception desk, to the ward where his mother had died, and approached the place with the chairs and the cylindrical ashtray where they had sat waiting, he was overwhelmed by the feeling of tension that had accompanied him since setting foot on the hospital grounds. Although he very much wanted to do so, he did not stop to look around him, but carefully opened the white door with the two empty portholes, upon which his attention had been concentrated for a number of hours the night before, and with a pounding heart, without looking to the left or right, he crossed the short passage and went up to the little desk behind which the department secretary was sitting, and when she turned to him after concluding her telephone conversation and asked him what he wanted, he told her that his mother had passed away the night before —he wanted to say "died" but, for some reason, shrank from the word —and that a few years before she had willed her body to science, he had the document to confirm it with him, and he had come to make the necessary arrangements, and feeling the same pride that he had felt the night before, he took the document out of his pocket and set it down before her. The secretary glanced at the document, for a moment he was afraid that there might be a signature missing or some other flaw in the document and the whole business of the donation of the body to science might fall through, and then she asked him for the name of the doctor who had treated his mother the night before, and Meir said that he didn't know his name but that he was a young man with a black mustache and a foreign accent, probably from South America, and the secretary nodded her head and dialed a number and spoke to someone on the phone, and afterward she asked Meir to sit down and wait a few minutes until the doctor was free. He sat down on an empty chair and waited with his hands folded in his lap, looking at the walls and the doors into the rooms, and as he did so he was carried away and abandoned himself to the feeling, which had been stirring inside him from the moment he entered the ward, that in one of these rooms, perhaps even the room on the other side of the wall against which the back of his chair was leaning, his mother was still lying and waiting for them to take care of her request and turn her over to science—the feeling was so vivid that it seemed to him he could actually sense her shadowy figure through the wall, which made him uncomfortable, because no distance had intervened between them as yet, apart from the distance of a few hours and the knowledge of an event that had penetrated only the surface of his mind and disrupted the routine of his life a little.

The doctor with the black mustache came in and they shook hands. Yes, he remembered him from the night before, and Meir told him why he had come, feeling the same flash of pride again, and the doctor nodded his head, he was very helpful and polite, and after looking at the document, he said that the hospital would take care of everything and see to it that her request was carried out, and Meir hesitated for a moment and asked him what exactly his mother had died of and if there had been no possibility of saving her, and the doctor said that she had died of a heart attack and it had been impossible to save her. The doctor's words calmed the doubts that had been nagging at him all morning and that he wanted with all his heart to deny, and after wondering whether to ask him if he could see his mother before they transferred her, Meir shook the doctor's hand warmly and thanked him and turned around and walked with a light step out of the ward and down the corridors, which were now as familiar to him as if he had trodden them countless times, and left the hospital with a good feeling that everything had been taken care of. And as he walked down the sunlit streets—it was a lovely spring day—experiencing once more the somnambulistic sensation of agreeable weightlessness and dislocation, and thinking proudly about his mother, who had willed her body to science, a mild feeling of uneasiness crept into his heart, as if something had not reached its conclusion and remained hanging in the air like an interrupted cry, and although he tried to deny this feeling and dismiss it, it would not go away and accompanied him until he went into the bank, which at that hour was almost deserted, and saw Aliza. She was sitting on the edge of a desk, leaning slightly sideways, holding a cup of tea and a doughnut in her hands and chatting vivaciously to the girl sitting behind the desk, and when he approached and said, "Hello, Aliza," she interrupted the lively conversation in which she was absorbed to smile at him and say, "I'll be with you in a minute," and Meir said, "That's all right, I'm not in a hurry," and stole a quick glance at her legs, which because of the way she was sitting, were exposed to above the knee. He didn't take his eyes off them even when she rose unwillingly to her feet and sauntered over to her place behind the counter, still holding the cup of tea and the doughnut in her hands, and as she did so he realized that she had ugly legs, which gave him a feeling of satisfaction, but as soon as she sat down behind the counter he felt attracted to her again, and he went on feeling attracted to her even after reminding himself that she had ugly legs, and remembered reading somewhere that mourning and train journeys awakened sexual desire, and said to himself that at this very moment, without a thought for anything, he would gladly have taken her to a hotel or any other place and gone to bed with her.

At about midday, after handing in the death notice, to which the clerk at first objected, insisting for some reason that he write "passed away" or "departed this world" instead of "left us," and notifying Roy through the Town Major's office, Meir went home and put through a call to Boston to his sister, who for several minutes could not take in what he was saying, and then, after realizing that there would be no funeral, said that she would be there within the next few days and asked him to give her regards to their father in the meantime, and afterward he intended to go and have lunch with his father—the thought that it was his duty to do so had been oppressing him for several hours—but Aviva, who had come home early from work and was busy warming up the meal she had prepared for their lunch, said that she would go instead and that he should eat at home and lie down to rest. He himself had not realized how tired he was, but the signs of exhaustion, and especially the tension of which he was not even aware, were very evident behind the calm and routine behavior, and after eating his meal alone—Amnon had gone with Aviva—he lay down on the bed with the newspaper, and within a few minutes he fell asleep, and only toward evening, after taking a shower and drinking a cup of coffee, all of which he did very slowly and drowsily, did he set out for his father's; but when he reached the corner, two houses away from his parents' house, he turned around and started walking toward the sea. A pleasant twilight shade covered the streets, which were full of people, and he sauntered slowly with his hands behind his back, effortlessly taking in the sights—everything was still suffused with the beauty of the spring day—his feeling of calm well-being gave way to the feeling that just behind him, right behind his back, like a scene from a war movie so vivid that he had only to turn his head to see it, lay piles of rubble, with here and there the charred wall of a house, a lopsided pillar, a fence, or a devastated tree standing in the ruins, and that there was only one fresh, green area left, ending somewhere not very far ahead of him in the pure blue sky above the sea, which lay hidden behind the belt of limestone hills, creating the illusion that beyond the hills lay a blue void, and then he felt as if he were standing on a strip of richly patterned carpet, long and narrow like the carpeting of a corridor, which someone was rolling up behind him until it touched his ankles, and as he walked down Ben Gurion Boulevard in the gathering shade of the tamarisks, still absorbed in these thoughts and scenes—everything around him was as usual, but at the same time everything seemed to be drained of its content, and beyond the outer skin of ordinariness an unclear emptiness yawned —he sensed with a pang of anxiety that his mother's death had exposed him to the terrible dangers of existence, and mainly to death, from which, simply by her presence, she had protected him, and he said to himself that now that she was dead it was his turn to die.

His parents' flat, both the rooms and the hall and the kitchen, was crowded with the friends and relatives who had come to condole with his father, who was sitting dazed and haggard in the big room, shuffling through the pile of photographs of his mother on the low table in front of him and explaining what was in them in a voice hoarse with tears and helplessness—here she was in the Young Socialists' League, and here she was with her hoe in front of their hut, and here she was in her white blouse with Ita, and here she was in Gibraltar, at Africa Point, and here she was in America next to the Niagara Falls, look how happy she was—interrupting himself from time to time to raise passionate, imploring eyes to the people sitting around him, and full of amazement and indignation, as if continuously buffeted by new waves of pain that he made no attempt to control, allowing his pain and despair to break out and flood him shamelessly and without restraint, to recapitulate the events of the last days of her life. He did this with a grim, soul-shaking determination to get at the true cause of her death, which in his restless groping in the dark he kept attributing to something different, because she was a strong, healthy woman without any complaints at all—he stressed this repeatedly—and her sudden death was, in his opinion, not only illogical but above all, shockingly unjust, as he kept furiously and brokenheartedly repeating, especially in view of the fact that in a few weeks' time she would have gone with him to Gibraltar and made her greatest wish come true, a fact that drove him wild and drew forth a savage jumble of sighs and groans and broken cries of protest every time he repeated it. There was something dark and violent about all this, and there was a bitter and harshly aggrieved tone in his voice as he kept repeating that if only she had died after the trip to Gibraltar her death would have seemed a lot less tragic to him, and he would have gritted his teeth and borne it in silence, since when all was said and done everyone had to die sometime—but things hadn't turned out that way, and it was all because of the flu, in the end he latched onto the flu violently and obstinately and said over and over again that it was the flu that had killed her, and that if only he had been at home he would never have allowed her to get out of bed and nothing would have happened, but he was at work and he didn't know that she would get out of bed, and he wiped his pale, clouded face, which had grown uglier, with a handkerchief, a bit of white spittle had gathered at the corners of his mouth, and aimlessly shuffled through the photographs and said, "She died like a bird, in absolute silence, without uttering a sound. If she had stayed in bed, nothing would have happened. I begged her to stay in bed. In two weeks' time we would have bought the suitcases for the journey. She killed herself and she killed us," and he repeated this again and again, hitting his thigh and the arm of his chair in helpless rage.

The guests sitting in the room listened to him sympathetically, and some of them tried to soothe and console him, which only fanned the flames of his rage, while Aviva and the aunt served tea and cake, with Zimmer's widow occasionally giving them a hand, and Meir entered the room and responded to the handshakes and muttered condolences of the visitors and then went up to his father and asked him if he wanted anything and sat down on the end of the couch, and after sitting silent and withdrawn for a while, he got up to help Aviva and the aunt with the tea and the empty cake plates because he couldn't stand the sight of his father, with his face that had grown so ugly, or the sound of his tearful complaints. There was something shameful and even contemptible, in his opinion, in all this, it was not in this undignified way that he would have liked his father to bear his grief, and he felt impatient and disgusted and wished that he could go away in order not to have to witness the demeaning spectacle, or at least slip out of the room and be by himself on the dark balcony overlooking the yard, but he went on carrying the glasses of tea and slices of lemon and teaspoons to and fro until he was detained by Yitzhak Kantz—he had never been sure if he was a member of the family or just a compatriot from the old country—who accosted him on his way to the kitchen, with a face full of complaint and concern, together with his wife, whose face expressed the same feelings, and said that he would like a word with him, and they stood in the corner of the little room, which was relatively deserted at the time, and Yitzhak Kantz said that it was inconceivable that his mother would not be given a decent burial, and his wife, who was even more excited than he, said, "Where will she be? Where?" and Yitzhak Kantz said,

"It's a scandal. What will become of her body? She was an unusual woman, that's true, but this is going too far. A person has to be buried somewhere," and his wife said, "There has to be a grave, a person has to have a grave! Don't you understand?" She was beside herself, and Meir, who had listened to all this with tolerant scorn, shrugged his shoulders and said that it was his mother's wish, and Yitzhak Kantz's wife said, "Then it was a stupid wish," and Yitzhak Kantz said, "She's dead now, but there are the living to be considered," doing his utmost to sound reasonable and persuasive, and Meir, who was actually beginning to feel sympathetic toward them and their arguments but didn't want to say so, said, "She didn't want a religious service, she hated all that stuff," and Yitzhak Kantz said, "What's that got to do with it? I'll talk to your father. She has to have a funeral," and Meir nodded, although he knew that nothing would come of it, and said, "Go ahead, talk to him. But it won't help. He'll do exactly what she wanted," and feeling vaguely uneasy, he put his hand on Yitzhak Kantz's shoulder as a sign that the conversation was over and said, "Leave it alone. After all, it's what she wanted," and turned his face as if he heard someone calling him and slipped tactfully away to the kitchen where Aviva, noticing his restlessness and tension, suggested that he leave everything and go out for a little walk and come back later to take her home, and when Meir asked her if she really thought it would be all right, she said that it would be perfectly all right and suggested that he drop in to see Pozner, and Meir said gratefully, "Okay, then. I'll go in a little while," and after making a few more trips between the big room and the kitchen, he slipped out of the house without saying a word to anyone.

He found Pozner alone in the flat reading Asimov's *Foundation*, which he had taken up in the middle of correcting some math tests, and as soon as he saw the welcoming smile on his face, he decided to postpone telling him about his mother's death for a while and said, "I hope I'm not disturbing you," and Pozner said, "I want to be disturbed, I've been waiting for someone to come and disturb me for hours," and put the book down on the table and asked Meir if he wanted a cup of coffee, and Meir said, "Yes, with pleasure," and they

went into the kitchen. Meir sat in his usual place and Pozner put the
kettle on to boil and washed two cups, cursing the endless math and
physics tests, and saying that he liked teaching but that all these tests
took all the pleasure out of it, and Meir thought of taking advantage
of the pause in the conversation when Pozner took the kettle off the
gas and began pouring the boiling water into the cups to tell him
about his mother's death, but he felt embarrassed at not having told
him the moment he arrived and decided to wait until he finished
making the coffee and sat down, and Pozner said that to be honest,
under the social and educational conditions in which the school operated today, tests were an unavoidable necessity because most pupils,
like most people—including himself—operated on the principle of
immediate gratification and without exams they wouldn't learn anything or attain the accomplishments society had decided to demand
of them as a condition for accepting them as members, and he put
the coffee on the table with the sugar bowl and a bottle of milk and
said that the problem might possibly be solved if teachers could
transform learning into a personal adventure and a game, which is
exactly what he himself had tried to do when he first began to teach,
mainly for the sake of his own enjoyment, but for the most part
without success, and he took a plate of cake down from the top of the
fridge and put it next to Meir and said, "Cut yourself a piece," and
sat down and said, "Perhaps it just isn't possible. It seems that life has
to consist of some boring parts, and there's nothing you can do about
it. As far as that's concerned, I'm beginning to come around, unwillingly, to Russell's way of thinking," and Meir, who knew that he had
to tell Pozner about his mother's death but sensed that the opportunity to do so was slipping further away from him with every minute
that passed, said, "Yes," and added, "In other words, it's a lost cause,"
and waited for Pozner to see for himself from his face, where his grief
must surely be stamped like a dark shadow, and Pozner said, "Yes,"
and poured a little milk into his coffee and stirred it, and said that
nevertheless it was worth trying to destroy the system as a whole, with
all its principles and goals and frameworks, and adopt the methods of
A. S. Neill, for example, which had once been used on the kibbutzim,

or to return to the ways of the Middle Ages, as proposed by Ivan Illich, who had become his most recent enthusiasm, but that was no longer a question of the school as such, but of the structure of society as a whole, and even then he was inclined to think that in the end everything would revert to the way it had been before, and he lit a cigarette and said, "I like characters like Ivan Illich," and started telling Meir about *Medical Nemesis,* which he had finished reading a few days before and which had made a big impression on him, and he said that it was a fantastic book, especially the part about pain and the alleviation of pain, and stood up to close the window, through which a cold wind was blowing, and Meir said, "The cake's delicious," and thought of taking advantage of this propitious moment, but then it, too, seemed unsuitable to him, and altogether he felt that it was already too late to say anything that would not sound silly or embarrassing— he should have told him the minute he came in the door. Pozner said, "Liora certainly knows how to buy a cake," and he smiled and sat down again and said that he had never thought of pain as having a history, but this became quite clear the moment you removed it from its physical dimension and transformed it into a spiritual and human experience, and this discovery alone would have been enough to make reading the book a riveting experience, and if only he could he would write a book about the history of pain, which would actually amount to the history of culture, and he shook the ash off his cigarette into his empty coffee cup and said that from the spiritual point of view, if we took our cue from Ivan Illich, there was no difference in principle between the experience of pain, which was one kind of suffering, and the experience of death, each could be perceived as something with a personal-spiritual meaning or a profound religious meaning, or as something technical, as it was seen by modern medicine, which consequently robbed it of the profound personal and spiritual meaning it could have had and prevented people from accepting pain or death as a vital and significant part of their existence and endurance in the world. He broke off a piece of cake and said that actually this wasn't the fault of medicine but of modern civilization as a whole, since medicine naturally acted in its spirit and according to its beliefs, one of which—perhaps the most harmful and dangerous—was the belief that medicine had it in its power to do anything, not only to put an end to disease and pain but also to prolong life endlessly, since death itself was perceived as a disease, or a kind of accidental misfunction, and all this in the faith that there was nothing that couldn't be solved because everything was a technical matter, which was what the metaphysics of our day amounted to. Meir nodded and said, "Yes," feeling that his time was running out, and beginning to prepare himself to take his leave, and then he added, "I'm afraid of pain, I must admit," and smiled, and Pozner smiled too and said, "So am I, but I envy people who can bear pain and relate to it spiritually, if I can put it that way," and in the same breath, as the vestiges of the smile disappeared from his lips, he said that he knew that he would never write a book, and after a moment he said, "Or maybe I will?" and then he said that he didn't care anymore, he no longer had any ambitions of that nature and it was possible to live without writing books, too, in any case there were too many of them already, and then he said, "The truth lies somewhere between the two," and dropped his cigarette butt into his cup and suggested moving into the other room because the cold in the kitchen was beginning to get to him, and Meir, who wanted to say what he had to say and leave—his uneasiness at his absence from his parents' house was growing increasingly oppressive with every moment that passed—accompanied him into the room and sat down in an armchair while Pozner sat on the bed, leaning against a pile of cushions, and began talking about politics. Meir said something, too, although not much. He knew that he had to get up and go and observed himself procrastinating with impatient disappointment—he already knew that he wasn't going to tell Pozner about his mother's death, unless maybe he did it at the very last minute, just before he left, and he went on waiting, with diminishing hope, for Pozner to notice the shadowy mark of grief stamped on his face and ask him what had happened, but all Pozner said was "That Begin and his phony self-righteousness, all it amounts to is the Messianism of shopkeepers, he turns everything into a circus —religion, Judaism, the Holocaust, Eretz Israel. It's a disgrace." He said this in a lighthearted tone and Meir said, "Yes, it's a scandal," and a moment later he said, "I have to go," and stood up, and Pozner said, "Where are you running to? Stay a little longer. Liora will be back soon and make us something good to eat," and Meir said, "I can't. I should have been home long ago. I've got a lot of work to do," and he turned toward the hall, and Pozner said, "You're forcing me to go back to those bloody tests," and stood up to see Meir to the door and stopped and said, "Just a moment. Before you go, come and see what Liora brought me," and he smiled bitterly and opened the door into the other room and switched on the light, and there in the corner, in a wooden box full of sawdust, lay a puppy, which Pozner regarded sourly and said, "That's all I needed—a dog in the house," and he bent over slightly as if to see him better, and when he straightened up again, he said, "I hate having a dog in the house. It drives me crazy. But what can I do? I won't leave the house just because of some stinking dog," and Meir, who was feeling angry and upset, said, "It's a nice little dog," and Pozner said, "I wish he'd go to hell," and kicked the box and then paused a moment and added, "I hope he dies, and the sooner the better," and laughed, and they went out of the room and lingered for a moment in the hall in front of the door before saying good-bye.

It was a cold, dark evening, and to Meir it seemed particularly cold and dark, or perhaps it was only the emptiness of the streets that made him think so, and as he crossed Dizengoff Street, before turning back to his parents' house, he decided to go on walking for a while and overcome the uneasiness he felt at prolonging his absence and shirking his filial duties—he had no doubt that his father had already asked for him more than once, and this thought fanned his anger, and he tried to clarify in his mind why he hadn't told Pozner that his mother had died, his failure to do so gave him no peace, and he continued along Gordon Street as far as Ben Yehuda, where he turned left, but before reaching Ben Gurion Boulevard he changed his mind and decided to go back, and he took a shortcut through the dark synagogue yard into Byron Street, and from there to Jean Jaurès. A dense darkness crammed the spaces under the luxuriant foliage of the ficus trees and covered the trees themselves, so that they seemed to disappear into their own darkness, and Meir was once again, more intensely now, gripped by a feeling of uneasiness at the thought of his mother not having a funeral. The fact, which only this morning had seemed so right and logical to him, and filled him with such admiration and pride in his mother, had now been transformed against all logic into a source of uneasiness and nagging sorrow, and this perplexed and embittered him because it was in total contradiction not only to his convenience and expectations but also to his convictions and beliefs, and once again he saw his mother lying in a dark hall, like the empty kitchen of a kibbutz, with tables and stainless steel sinks, everything polished and gleaming with cleanliness, on a high table covered with a thin sheet; there was a steely chill in the hard, transparent air, and he felt the metallic chill that she felt in his own flesh and shuddered, and he heard the low, continuous roar of the sea not far off and suppressed the scream inside his head and said to himself firmly that it was a mistake and that she should have been given a proper funeral.

When he arrived at his parents' house all the lights were still on, but the visitors had all left except Aviva, who was standing in the kitchen washing the dishes and putting them away, and his uncle, who opened the door, and his aunt, yellow with misery and fatigue, sitting in the big room with his father, who was still sitting in the place he had occupied since the beginning of the evening, drained and stunned and so insensible of everything around him that he scarcely responded when Meir greeted everyone brightly and sat down between his father and his uncle, stealing an uneasy glance at his father as he did so and praying silently that he wouldn't begin talking about his mother or his tragedy, or groan either—he could already feel the anger and resentment bubbling up inside him, and he quickly said something in an excessively loud voice about the cold and the dark outside and about the streets being more empty than usual. Although he wasn't really talking to anyone, he was ostensibly addressing his uncle, who remarked that people had apparently not yet recovered from the winter, while his aunt said, "It may still rain, it's not over yet," and

Meir said, "I can remember rain at Pesach, and even at Shavuoth,"
and he told them about a quite heavy rain that had fallen one year
on the kibbutz during the harvesting season and how they had all gone
out in the evening to take the hay to the barn so that it would not
get spoiled, the thought of saying good-bye to his father was preying
on his mind because he would have to kiss him or press his hand or
at least touch him, and he tried to find some encouragement in the
thought that Aviva was there and would somehow come to his rescue,
and his uncle told them about how a heavy shower had once fallen
on the first of May, during the May Day parade, and as he spoke he
kept looking at Meir's father, who sat staring stonily at some invisible
point in front of him and said nothing. Meir, too, looked at his father
and felt his resentment flaring up at his silence—if only he would say
something or at least nod his head, and his aunt nodded and said,
"Yes, I remember it as clearly as if it was today," and Meir said,
"There's no point in having all the lights on," and got up and went
out of the room and walked through the flat switching off all the
unnecessary lights, and then returned to the big room and asked his
father if he wanted anything to drink. There was half a glass of tea
standing before him, which looked as if it had been standing there
since the beginning of the evening, and his father said, "No, I've had
enough to drink," and Meir said, "Something cold, perhaps?" knowing even before he asked that his father would refuse because he was
angry with him for staying away, and his father said, "I don't need
anything," and Meir said, "Good," and his eyes crept like a spider
over the pictures on the yellowing walls and the evergreen philoden-
dron and stopped at the bookcase, time stood still in the room, and
he went up to the bookcase as if his eye had fallen on a book he was
looking for, and as he put out his hand, wondering which book to take,
Aviva came in from the kitchen and said, "That's it, everything's
clean and tidy," and she went up to his father and put her hand
affectionately on his shoulder and said, "We're going," and his father
said, "Go, go. Good night," and touched her with his hand, and Meir
retreated from the bookcase in the direction of his father and the
doorway and said, "Good night, Dad"—no power on earth could have

forced him to kiss him or even touch him, as he felt that it was his duty to do, he didn't know where all this was coming from, but he detested him and wished that he would die—and then, with well-concealed haste, he said good-bye to his uncle and aunt, and as he crossed the threshold of the room he felt the beginning of relief in the midst of the anger and weariness, as if he were approaching a patch of cool shade on an oppressively hot day, and Aviva, who had lingered a moment with his aunt to make arrangements for the next day, caught up with him in the passage, where he was waiting for her. On their way home he told her about his visit to Pozner and how he hadn't said anything about his mother's death, giggling in embarrassment as he did so, and Aviva said, "Then you must phone him when we get home and tell him. It would seem strange if he found out from the papers," speaking in a calm, encouraging tone of voice, and Meir shrugged his shoulders, and when they got home he phoned Pozner, and after hemming and hawing he told him that his mother had died the night before, his tone was apologetic and diffident and he giggled in embarrassment again, and Pozner said, "You're crazy. Why didn't you tell me when you were here?" and Meir said, "I don't know, some devil got into me," he couldn't stop giggling and Pozner said, "You're crazy. Your mother's just died and I sit and lecture you like an idiot about Ivan Illich and pain," and Meir said, "Never mind. It doesn't matter. In any case, there isn't going to be a funeral. She donated her body to science," he felt more embarrassed and idiotic with every word he uttered, and Pozner said, "You should say things like that right out, not wait for the other person to guess. It isn't right," and Meir said, "Next time," and laughed pointlessly, he couldn't understand what had gotten into him, and Pozner asked him if he needed help with anything, and Meir said, "No, no. Everything's taken care of," and asked him to tell Liora, and Pozner said, "Okay, I'll see you tomorrow."

The next day Meir went back to work, feeling a need to carry on as usual, and as soon as he entered the office, as he had decided in advance, he told the chief engineer and his secretary, and the engineer who worked in the same room with him, that he had been absent from work the day before because his mother had died, suppressing the embarrassment that overcame him again as he spoke and trying to sound as if he were talking about some ordinary daily event, and afterward, when the initial shock had died down and a number of his colleagues came into his office to express their condolences, he told them briefly when and how it had happened, and settled down to work. He felt quite free to act as if nothing had happened, and in fact he did not sense any sorrow or grief but only that peculiar, very tenuous sensation, almost abstract but at the same time constant and real, of weightlessness and dislocation in a world where, apart from his mother's death, everything was normal—a sensation that grew more and more intense until it encompassed him like a gigantic, invisible hat made out of thin, transparent skin, inside which he moved alone, indifferent and set apart from the rest of the world. Toward evening, after coming home from work and taking a shower and changing his clothes, Meir went to see his father, who was sitting in the armchair in the little room—the pile of photographs of his mother at his side—staring into space with a defeated expression on his face. The light of the setting sun coming through the slats of the blind painted yellow-orange stripes on the dark walls and on his father, and Meir, who had hoped to find other people there, his uncle and aunt at least, paused at the door and said, "Hello, Dad"—he had come on his own, although he would have much preferred someone to accompany him, but Aviva had not yet come home from work while Roy had arrived filthy and exhausted from the army only moments before Meir had set out—and his father looked at him helplessly and nodded his head, which irritated him immediately, and he paused for a moment and said, "Should I put on the light?" and his father said, "Not yet. There's plenty of time," scarcely moving his lips as he spoke, and Meir sat down at some distance from his father's chair, facing his profile, and after looking around him aimlessly and paging through the newspaper, he asked, "Do you want anything?" careful to avoid asking him how he was—for what could he reply?— and not even glancing at the photographs of his mother on the table, and after a few minutes, when he received no reply, he repeated, "Do you want anything, Dad?"—the way his father was sitting slumped in his chair, miserable and defeated, was driving him out of his mind —and his father said, "No, nothing," and Meir said, "Maybe a cup of tea," noting with a pang his failure to introduce even into these few words a single drop of warmth or intimacy, not to mention love or at least pity, even though this man sitting opposite him without moving in the dim room was so very pitiful, and his father said, "I've just had some," and Meir said, "I'll put the kettle on anyway. You can make up your mind when it boils," and he stood up and went into the kitchen, feeling that he could not bear to go on sitting opposite his father for another minute. Slowly, dragging out the time, he filled the kettle and put it on the gas, and then he put fresh tea leaves in the pot and filled the sugar bowl to the brim, waiting impatiently for the sound of footsteps on the stairs and for someone, anyone at all, to come into the flat, and he ate a few cookies, which he took out of the blue plastic jar, and then he went back to the room and sat down again, and as he gazed past his father's profile in the strips of light, which had very quickly grown blurred and gray, waiting eagerly for the sound of footsteps on the stairs—Roy should be arriving any minute now—or at least the whistle of the kettle, he searched frantically for something to say before his father could begin talking about his mother and his plight, which he sensed he was about to do, and said that Roy had arrived from the army, where he was stuck in the Sinai on army maneuvers, and that he would be coming as soon as he had taken a shower and changed his clothes—nothing better occurred to him for the moment—and then he said something about Aviva's problems at work, his voice sounding strained and dry as dust in the gray, darkening room, and at the sound of the whistle he got up and went to turn off the gas, and when he came back to the room and sat down, he asked his father again if he wanted a cup of tea, and his father shook his head, and after a moment he said, "What a disaster, what a disaster," and beat his hand helplessly against his thigh, and then he said, "What will I do here without her?" and Meir knew that there was no stopping or distracting him now, and at the same time he felt a warm current of feeling and the wish to say something consoling to him, and his father said, "The flu killed her," and passed his hand despairingly over his lips and said, "If she hadn't gotten out of bed, nothing would have happened," the strips of light had been almost entirely absorbed in the darkening walls and curtains, and then he said, "If I'd known that she would get out of bed I would never have gone to work," and raised his beaten eyes slightly and added, "But how could I have known?"—he was talking not to Meir but to nobody, into the void that had suddenly gaped around him and swept his life into its great darkness, and in which, in that great darkness, lonely as an ant and forsaken for all eternity, he twitched and jerked, blind and helpless as an amputated body.

Meir felt that he had to say something, never mind what, but he was overpowered by an obstinate, denying silence, and his father said, "She died like a bird. Without a complaint," and Meir turned his head carefully and looked outside, and his father said, "If she had only lived to go to Gibraltar—I would have borne it in silence," and then he said, "In two months' time we were supposed to fly. She could have been the happiest woman in the world, she wanted to go there so much," and he beat his thigh again, and Meir turned his face and let his eyes slide lightly over his father's face and then fixed them on the dark wall opposite him—the way his father kept despairingly hitting his thigh was driving him out of his mind—and his father said, "We've suffered a mortal blow," and sunk into a silence so prolonged that it made Meir uneasy, and unable to endure the dismal silence, he exerted himself to say something about his work, cursing his father in his heart and loathing every word that came out of his mouth and at the same time listening eagerly to the sound of footsteps on the stairs, which he had no doubt were on their way to the apartment— they weren't Roy's, but he didn't care—and his father suddenly roused himself and said, "She killed herself, and she killed us," and nodded his head heavily. Meir rose and went out to the hall to receive the newcomers, and he shook hands with Israel Shuster and his wife, Ita, and with the neighbor who had arrived with them, and after exchanging a few mumbled words, accompanied them to the little room, where they shook hands with his father, and Israel said in a weak voice that they had seen the news in the paper only that day, and they sat down on the couch and Ita said, "What a tragedy, it's terrible, I can't believe it," and she asked how it had happened, and Meir's father let out a groan so deep it seemed to come from the bowels of the earth, and in the voice of a stranger, unimaginably despairing and broken, he said, "I'm a finished man, Israel. They've chopped off my head"—they had been close friends since they arrived in the country in the days of the Young Socialist League and Working Youth, and for many years they had worked together too—and Meir asked them if they would like some tea, and without waiting for an answer he hurried to the kitchen, where his father's voice reached him dimly as he went over the whole thing again from the beginning in a voice hoarse with suppressed rage and pain, which increased in volume and choked on tears, making Meir withdraw into himself in fury and disgust, and after making the tea and lingering a while in the kitchen—if only he could have escaped to the ends of the earth!— he took it in to them with some slices of cake, having decided not to offer them the butter cookies because they were too precious to waste.

Israel and Ita, helpless and embarrassed, tried tactfully to console his father, while the neighbor sat stiffly with a glum expression on her face, and Israel even went up to him and laid a friendly hand on his arm and said in a coaxing tone that it was a terrible tragedy, no doubt about it, but that he must be philosophical about it, as the French said, and his father said, "What's it got to do with philosophy? She's dead, and that's all there is to it," with a savage note of barely suppressed rage in his voice, but Israel persisted, he loved him and wanted very much to help him, and in a soothing, coaxing voice— it was obvious that he was very distressed—he said that everybody had to die sooner or later, that was life, but Meir's father cut him short, he didn't want to hear, and in an uncontrolled voice, his face contorted with fury, he said, "I don't know about everybody. I don't care about everybody. All I know is that she's dead and I'm alive," and in a furious shout he added, "I'm not interested in everybody! She shouldn't have died!" and Israel said, "You're right, you're right. But we have to go on, we have to go on." He said this in a solemn, fateful tone, while Ita looked on with eyes full of bewilderment and fear, and his father, frantic with pain and rage—there was something wild and hostile in his flushed face—went on shouting that there had never been a tragedy like this one, not ever, it was the worst tragedy that had ever happened in the world, and that if only she had lived to go to Gibraltar, as she had dreamed of doing, he would have held his peace and never said a word, but the way things were it was the most terrible injustice that the world had ever known, and Meir, fixing his eyes on the balcony of the house opposite, listened, together with the other people in the room, shocked and embarrassed and expressionless, to this desperate cry of despair torn from the depths of a soul maddened by its irreversible and arbitrary loss and the horror of its own perdition, which dashed Israel's words to pieces, sweeping them away like flotsam and jetsam in the vortex of a raging flood, and beat helplessly against the darkening walls: a cry for everything—for his wife, who had suddenly and for no reason, cruelly and maliciously, after nearly fifty years of marriage, during which they had grown into one creature, been torn away from him so that he was left alone— a blind and amputated body jerking convulsively in the dark—for the future, which had all at once been swept away, with its plans and secret hopes that all kinds of things that had been missed would somehow still come to pass, and sunk into the valley of the shadow of death and turned into a land of desolation and eternal solitude; and for the past too, whose best and happiest moments, like those immortalized in the photographs on the table, for instance, had also sunk into the darkness of this end and turned into bitter, heartbreaking signposts on the road to his terrible and unjust ruin, and in the end he collapsed, with desperate sobs racking his whole body, and Meir suddenly stood up, as if there was something urgent he had to do, and shut himself in the lavatory, where the sound of his father's sobbing still reached his ears.

He took an old newspaper from the basket and leafed through it aimlessly, taking in a sentence here and there, pausing for a moment on a headline or a picture, until his eye was caught by the following paragraph: "If you are proud of being normal, you are probably a rather gray person living in the usual frustration of unfulfilled dreams," claims Varda Raziel-Weizeltier at the beginning of her new book *Tzipor Hanefesh (The Bird of the Soul)*, which deals with popular psychology. And she goes on to explain: "To be 'normal' means to be an invisible man from the point of view of society, the 'average man.' " On the assumption that "we all suffer from psychological symptoms to one or another extent," and with the unequivocal assertion that it is "absolutely impossible to be ambitious, normal, and happy!" the writer prefers to call those situations in which the reader will identify himself as reacting, thinking, and tormented by the general name of "a positive as opposed to a negative life-style, rather than 'normal' and 'abnormal,' " and he put the newspaper on his knees and stared at the door—his father's voice was growing more subdued—and glancing from time to time at quotations from the book, he tried to make up his mind if he was normal or abnormal, and to this end he tested himself to see if he was "gray" or "not gray" and if he lived in "the usual frustration of unfulfilled dreams" or not, and if he was "visible" or "invisible" from the point of view of society, a question he found it very difficult to answer, and also if he was "responsive" or "unresponsive"—this question, too, like most of the others, he found it difficult to answer unequivocally, which disgruntled him a little: on no account could he understand from what the article said whether he was supposed to aspire to the "positive life-style," which was apparently supposed to replace the definition of "normal," or rather the "negative life-style," and he didn't mind if he would have to face the fact that he was unhappy too—on the contrary, this was one of the only points that encouraged him to think that perhaps, in the final analysis, he was, after all, not normal. His father's voice had died down in the meantime, and when he returned to the room, where the daylight had finally faded, he found him sitting in the gathering darkness, still and dazed, with Israel and Ita, as drained as he was, sitting opposite him—the neighbor had already gone—and waiting in the oppressive silence for the moment when they, too, could get up and leave, and he put on the light and asked them if they wanted anything, and Israel said, "No, no, thank you.

We've already had something to eat and drink"—their teacups were still half full—and he added, "We'll have to be off soon," and a few minutes later when Roy came in, they both stood up and said good-bye to his father and left.

On Friday, when Meir left the office at the end of the day's work and turned up Ahad Ha-am Street, where the sense of the approaching Sabbath filled the air, so that it was already possible to feel the impending emptiness of the streets at the heart of the midday bustle, he felt a pang of longing for his mother, whose death, despite the suddenness and denial, was beginning to establish itself as a fact, albeit one that left a delicate train of strangeness behind it, and as he walked with calm detachment down the street, unthinkingly taking in the sights around him—it was a part of the town that never failed to stir his heart—he said to himself that this would be the first Saturday without her, and at almost the same second he felt, in his very body, how the knot holding and uniting the ends of all the threads had come undone and the long, narrow carpet, like the carpet in a corridor—for some reason this was how he imagined it—beginning somewhere in a distance so remote and shrouded in a darkness so thick that the eye could not penetrate it, and reaching all the way to where he was standing, was becoming unraveled, for the time being only at the edges, but forever and irreversibly, because it would be impossible to weave the threads together again and reconnect him to his father and his wife and his sons and his sister—who had called from Boston to say that because of something to do with the children she would be coming a few days later, since in any case there was no funeral and no reason to arrive on any set date—and to her husband, for whom Meir had never felt anything but polite reserve, and also to her children, one of whom, the little girl, he had never seen except in the photographs his sister sent about once a year to their parents; and to his various uncles and aunts, some of whom were already dead or had gone far away or changed so much in their appearance that they had become strange shadows of their former selves, giving rise in him to uneasiness and revulsion; and to his parents' acquaintances and compatriots and friends, ancient comrades from the Young Socialist League and the Labour Party, unforgettable faces from old photographs and long-ago visits to the house, which seemed to have taken place only yesterday, brothers and closer than brothers, or comrades for a time—how those bonds and intimacies had comforted him and warmed his heart before they had gradually, and in the natural course of time, dissolved; and to Bill Gorman, with his flushed face and his rugby-ball-shaped head, who had disappeared somewhere in America without writing a word or leaving an address, and who didn't know about his mother's death and would probably never know, either, until he himself died in his vagabond solitude, if he hadn't already died in some tenement or Jewish old-age home, and while he was still absorbed in these thoughts he was again assailed by the feeling that something that had sheltered and protected him had been removed and that all at once, for the first time in his life, he was completely exposed to the terrible dangers of the world, and that now, with the death of his mother, it was his turn to die, since she, by the very fact of her existence, had separated him from death. And then, with the same movement of thought and feeling, he said to himself that not more than four days, or the equivalent amount of hours or minutes—it wouldn't be difficult to calculate the sum—had passed since her death, and nevertheless they were already separated by all the distance in the world, and that even if he gathered all his strength and ran until he was breathless, he would still be like a man running after his own shadow cast on the ground before him, and he would never catch up with her until he himself was swallowed up by the same darkness into which she had been plunged, and he decided to turn into Allenby Street in order to escape the melancholy pressure of these thoughts, and turned into Balfour Street and walked along it in the shade of the spreading ficus trees. A flock of children burst gleefully out of school while others still ran about shouting and laughing on the playground, and he paused to look at them until they dispersed a little and cleared the pavement, and when he started walking again it occurred to him to go into one of his favorite restaurants and have some *cholent* and stuffed *kishka* in order to lift his spirits a little, and a suppressed smile, full of mischief, spread through

him, and he quickened his steps, which grew lighter and more buoyant, as he imagined the little display window with the dish of dum-
plings and the dish of boiled meat and the plate with the stuffed
kishka reposing on it like a coiled snake, and he said, almost audibly,
to himself: "I'll eat it in her memory," and the smile broadened and
spread under the skin of his face, and afterward he said, "After all,
she'll never make me *cholent* and stuffed *kishka* again," and the smile
grew even broader and burst out of his mouth and he was filled with
hearty, soundless laughter.

Meir went up the old gray stairs and entered the restaurant, and
after peeping into the big, rather dim dining room—it was all exactly
as he remembered it, nothing had changed—he went back into the
entrance hall and sat down facing the street, which was visible
through the high door, the view of Allenby Street was necessary to
complete his sense of well-being, and although he knew precisely what
he intended ordering, he studied the menu intently until the waitress
came, when he ordered *cholent* and stuffed *kishka* and horseradish
and a bottle of beer. The woman wrote his order down on a piece of
paper and went away, and he fixed his eyes on the street and gazed
serenely at the ceaseless traffic and movement, glancing from time to
time at the menu—he loved everything about it, even the shape of
the print and the written letters, until the waitress returned and put
his order in front of him, together with a plastic basket holding slices
of fresh *challah* bread, and he thanked her with demonstrative
warmth and examined the plate, a beam of happiness spreading
through him and radiating from his smiling face, and picked up his
knife and fork and repeated to himself that he was eating the dish in
memory of his mother. Very carefully, not yet as part of the eating
itself, which he wanted to postpone as long as possible, but in prepara-
tion for it, he cut a piece of brown potato, and then put it in his
mouth, pausing a moment to repeat to himself, once more without
any sorrow, that now that she had died he would never again have the
chance to sample these dishes with the special flavor she imparted to
them, and a pleasant wave of sadness engulfed him at this banal
thought, and he smiled and pinched off a bit of bread and kneaded

it lightly between his fingers and looked at the street, and afterward he began to eat, thinking to himself that when somebody died, he took with him from the world not only his image and voice and movements but also the special and unique flavors that were somehow inherent in his tongue and palate, and afterward, as he was eating— the *cholent* and stuffed *kishka* were delicious—and looking from time to time at the street and mulling over this thought, which gave him a melancholy kind of pleasure, he saw his mother again in the same dark hall, which resembled the clean, empty kitchen of a kibbutz, with its tables and gleaming stainless-steel sinks. It was a fresh, transparent darkness, and he saw her in the form of a pale, featureless shadow, although he knew without any doubt that it was she, but then he immediately said to himself that she couldn't possibly have been there for the past two or even three days, since the place was fixed in his mind as a temporary lodging only, and he tried to locate her somewhere else in his imagination, but she kept shifting about and wandering restlessly from place to place—all the places he imagined were too vague and abstract to hold her—until he brought her back to the clearly defined hall, where he had no doubt that she had really been immediately after her death, and she stayed there for a moment and then revealed herself to him in the still, silent depths of the Sargasso Sea, which looked to him like the Dead Sea, but so much bigger and deeper that it seemed to be set in an infinite space, and was covered not with a haze of brownish-bluish-grayish mist but with enormous fields of seaweed, filling him with a mysterious fear, and then, in almost the same split second of thought, she turned into a thin, dark blot, something like an inkblot, which cracked and disintegrated into tiny particles and was transformed into a silver-gray cloud the color of cigarette ash—it was she, of that he had no doubt—which spread and rose into the clear air under the amazing blue of the Tel Aviv sky, from the east, over the municipal square, and then from the south, and then, unexpectedly, the north, from the direction of the Yarkon River, with a swaying, gliding movement full of sudden swerves, like a vast flock of starlings in autumn above the fields of the kibbutz, very gradually, perhaps because of the wind, expanding and losing its tenuous unity until in the end it thinned and dispersed and disappeared, some of its particles borne away on the wind to continue drifting somewhere in the ever-darkening vastness of space, whose spherical emptiness was studded with stars and blazing pools of gas, and some of them falling to the ground and merging with the clods of earth or the leaves of plants or the water, where they drifted down into the blue-green depths, gently borne on almost imperceptible currents, until they touched the bed of the sea, which was as soft as a cradle of water and sand and caressing fronds of vegetation, and surrounded by dense darkness and fearsome rocks inhabited by deep-sea fishes and sea animals, threatening in their appearance and primordial silence, and here, after measureless eons of time, after percolating through the delicate mesh of capillaries, capillaries of air and earth and vegetation, which he saw as the tangled threadlike rootlets of a stalk of wheat, but immeasurably bigger, of course, they would reunite and resume their former shape, and for a moment he experienced a sensation of satisfaction and joy at the thought that time would triumph in the end, but then he said to himself plaintively —the happy smile had already vanished from his face—that if only his mother had not donated her body to science and they had given her a funeral, she would have stopped her wanderings and there would be one, defined place where she would be known to be and would always be and where he could have gone to honor her memory or, at least, where he could have concentrated his mind when he thought about her, and he stole a glance at the big girl with the untidy yellow hair and the bored, tired face who entered the restaurant and very hesitantly, with lowered eyes, sat down at the table in front of his with her back to him.

There was something neglected and despairing about her, as if she had been abandoned and thrown into the street, and she immediately aroused his curiosity, together with a feeling of affection, mingled with pity, and the wish to protect her and shelter her, as well as the memory of the old pain, although dimmer and more remote than ever before, as if the wound had imperceptibly healed, and he tried to attract her attention with little coughs and taps of his knife and fork on his plate, and to catch her eye, but she ignored him and sat closed and withdrawn into herself, as if she were afraid of everything in her surroundings and wanted to detach and efface herself, and he went on looking at her stubbornly, as if he were determined to force himself on her attention, but to no avail, and only when the waitress approached her did she turn her head slightly and raise her eyes, and he caught a glimpse of her face, and for a split second he also caught her embarrassed, evasive eyes, and as he looked at her with a friendly, expectant air, it occurred to him to take her to the office—it was Friday and they had all gone home and he had a key—and when the waitress went to bring her order, he shifted his chair a little, as if to straighten it, and invited her to join him at his table, but she refused politely, and Meir, who felt disappointed and a little offended too, said, "Okay," and went on eating as if nothing had happened, but from time to time, in spite of himself, he stole an encouraging glance at her back, longing with all his heart to tell her who he was—his family and background and origins, his profession and opinions—and persuade her of the honesty and purity of his intentions, in which he thoroughly believed—and he kept on glancing at her until he had finished eating and paid the bill, and he took up his briefcase, and when he was already standing at the door he paused and turned his head, as if to make sure that he hadn't forgotten anything, and stole one more look at her before leaving.

The traffic had died down somewhat, and although there were still cars and people in the streets, everything was gradually thinning out and winding down, so that it was already possible to sense the desolation and emptiness, which up to now had been hidden, as it were, beneath the busy traffic, rising to the surface and taking over the street in the impending Sabbath gloom that was already hovering in the air, and Meir, walking slowly with a trancelike sensation of endless suspension in time, crossed Brenner Street and Sheinkin Street, glancing as he passed at the market, which was as empty and deserted as the streets, and at the continuation of Allenby Street and the end of Nahalat Benyamin Street, which were also emptying out and gradually surrendering to the coming desolation, and he turned into King George, a street that his mother must have walked down hundreds and perhaps thousands of times and that somehow, and not only because she had crossed it so many times, he identified with her and her life more than any other, regarding it and a few of the other streets around it as nothing but extensions of his own self, and at the sight of the street, which suddenly lay before him, steeped in the sadness of the late Friday afternoon, all the way down to the ancient sycamore trees and beyond them, he was flooded by a melancholy sense of communion with this vulgar street, which was so close to his heart in all its shabbiness and provincial ugliness, as if it, precisely it, with its dusty, tasteless shops, most of which were already shut, and its peeling old houses with their borrowed, slightly ridiculous beauty, which had crumbled and fallen into ruin together with them, and its people, the teeming throngs of petty tradesmen and shopkeepers, almost all of whom had gone home by now and abandoned it to emptiness and desolation till Sunday—as if this street somehow contained the very essence of the soul and spirit of the city, and he said to himself that his mother would never walk down this street again or see these crumbling houses with their seedy shops, and nobody would feel her absence or know that she was gone. And in the sudden dread that overwhelmed him he felt a tremendous desire to erect a pillar of stainless steel that would soar into the heart of the sky and mark for generations to come the fact of his mother's existence and the place that she had occupied in the endless stream of the generations, the thought that his mother's memory would cease to be, as if she had never existed, filled him with panic, and he raised himself to the top of the sky and looked down from there at the darkness lying in the past of the little spot of light below, within whose bright circle many familiar faces were illuminated, and at the throngs of people pressing closely up behind them, many of whom he recognized as friends and relations and acquaintances, whose faces were already becoming a little blurred, and at the ranks of those standing shoulder to shoulder behind them, who were rapidly growing indistinct and losing their identity as webs of darkness enfolded them and they merged into one another, turning into one block of darkness eternally submerged in the shadow of the valley of death, where no light would ever penetrate, and then he looked toward the even greater darkness on the future side of the little spot of light, where fitful flickers of light revealed faces that were featureless but nevertheless not anonymous, as though their familiar features, which were still inherent in the formlessness of embryonic matter, could somehow be surmised before, at a distance of half a pace away, they darkened and turned into a multitude of black spots, vast beyond number, merging and floating in one dark torrent between the immeasurably broad banks of the river, which stretched into the distance until it was incorporated in the original darkness pouring dense and heavy out of the obscure depths of the past and rolling into infinity, whose endlessness he felt like the sensation of wetness in water, and he crossed Borochov Street and walked in the shade of the sycamore trees and passed the Heruth Party headquarters in "Fort Ze'ev," a place that always made him feel uneasy, and thought of crossing the street and walking through Mish'ol Ya'akov, he liked this quiet alley with its smell of pines and cypresses, and taking a look at the one-storied house where many years before, in the pink room overlooking a backyard overrun with weeds, his grandmother had lived. As he stepped off the pavement into the street, a car stopped behind him with a screech of brakes, which made him jump aside in alarm, and the driver stuck his head out of the window and said, "This is a street, mister, not a beach," and Meir said in confusion, "I'm sorry, I was thinking about something else," and the driver said, "If I wasn't such a careful driver, you would have been a goner by now and I would have spent a few years in jail," and he smiled, and Meir recognized him as the furniture mover from Turkey and smiled in embarrassment and repeated, "I'm sorry. I wasn't thinking," and the moving man said, "Never mind, never mind," and asked him if he wanted a ride, and Meir said that he was on his way home and he would walk the rest of the way, and the moving man put his car in gear and waved and drove off with Meir waving after him.

Surprisingly soon, his father's friends and acquaintances, apart from a handful of individuals, stopped coming to offer him their condolences, making do with an occasional phone call instead, and when Meir went up to see him, usually in the early evening, he would generally find him sitting alone in the light armchair in the stifling little room—he never opened the door leading to the balcony, and for the most part he refused to pull up the blinds, too, on the grounds that he was cold, although the weather was growing warm, and even hot—listening apathetically in the gloom to the radio or staring indifferently into space with the newspaper on his knees, or sometimes in the kitchen sitting and eating his solitary meal or washing the dishes after it, and he would sit down opposite him, stiff and reserved, and after making a few routine opening remarks about his work and Aviva and the children and so on, trying his best to maintain a matter-of-fact and, if possible, even lighthearted tone and to steer the conversation into the channels of a normal family exchange about ordinary family matters, he would go on to discuss the political and economic situation, speaking too loudly and with forced vivacity and endeavouring to avoid anything in any way connected with his mother's death, for fear that his father would begin to talk about her and his terrible loss. His father would hardly react, apart from an occasional nod or blurted word, or suddenly, quite unexpectedly and out of context, he would start speaking in his hollow voice about his mother and how she could have been saved if she had only stayed in bed for another day or two, which was precisely what he had begged her to do, and in a voice full of grievance and pain, sometimes with dry, strangled sobs—his tears were beginning to dry up by now—he would point out again how happy she could have been now, for it was in these very days that they should have been setting out on their trip abroad, and sometimes he would hold forth, speaking with yearning and pain, about her life and deeds, her exceptional personality and beautiful soul, and Meir would withdraw into his shell, and while he listened to his father with a stiff, denying face, without saying a word or even nodding now and then to show that he was paying attention, he would abandon himself to the feelings of loathing and disgust to which his father gave rise in him and allow himself to be swept away on a tide of hostility and rage.

The only feelings evoked in Meir by his father's despairing helplessness and frank, desperate need—he demanded pity and succor as if he were a baby suddenly robbed of his favorite toy—were ones of impatience and anger, and at the same time he was filled with indignant irritation at the expression on his father's ravaged face, which he had shamelessly abandoned to misery and old age, and at his shrunken, wasted body, and the slackness of his posture and gait, not to mention his frail, brittle voice, so full of tearful complaint and impotence that it maddened his son beyond endurance. He wanted to be as miserable as possible and he wanted the whole world to see how miserable and beaten he was, but Meir wanted him to behave differently and keep up appearances too, and day by day he waited, angry and hostile, for his father to collect himself and behave with restraint, or at any rate not to impose the burden of his despair and terrible, unyielding solitude on the rest of the world, for then he would be able to feel some respect for him, and even affection. But how could he? All his days and nights, for almost fifty years, had been spent at the side of this woman until they had become one creature, and suddenly she had died and he had been truncated and turned into a mutilated piece of a human body—but all these things, which Meir repeated to himself more than once during the increasingly oppressive summer, as he went to visit his father full of anger and tension, and as he left him after these depressing visits embittered and exhausted, and of course also as he sat there opposite him, did not soften his heart, or melt the shell of stubborn resistance, which he tried to break through every now and then, in fitful and fleeting bursts of remorse and contrition, and with the help of the crumbs of sympathy or affection, real or imaginary, which he endeavored to squeeze out of himself, to say something consoling—a sentence or two, no more, or even, in a moment of grace, to put his arm around his father's shoulders. But something resistant, as if a shriveled devil had taken possession of him and hardened his heart, prevented him obdurately from saying anything that held the slightest hint of intimacy, and above all he refused to exchange a single word with him about his mother—he shrunk from this in fear and panic as if there was something prohibited or pregnant with danger about it, just as he shrank from any physical contact with him, with his body, his clothes, or any of his personal possessions—and he tried to engage him in conversation about other things in order to cheer him up a little and express an attitude of sympathy and concern by these means, but his father was not interested in anything except the death of his wife, and in the course of the summer he sank into an apathy from which he only fitfully and unexpectedly bothered to rouse himself, and all the efforts of Meir's uncle and aunt, Zimmer's widow, and Aviva to extricate him from his condition were in vain.

And thus, after making a few opening remarks about his work and health, Aviva and the children, and talking at the top of his voice about some political or sporting event or public scandal, or some other subject that he would rack his brains to find, Meir would surrender to his father's blank, hateful silence and take up the newspaper, and the two of them would sit facing each other in the empty, desolate apartment, all of whose rooms, but for the little one where they usually sat, were dark and still, or else they would move into the big room and sit joylessly watching television, which instead of giving them the anticipated respite from their silence and estrangement, only made the feelings of loneliness and alienation worse than before, and in order to extricate himself, if only for a few minutes, from the horror of sitting there with his father, Meir would go into the kitchen to make them both a cup of tea, taking advantage of the opportunity to help himself to one or two of his mother's wonderful butter cookies, which in spite of all his efforts to curb his appetite were becoming fewer and fewer, so that after a couple of weeks he could already begin to see the bottom of the blue plastic jar, and every time he took one now he would say to himself that very soon the cookies would be finished and there would never be any more of them until the end of time, because when she died his mother had taken their unique and inimitable taste, which was inherent in her fingers and her tongue, with her, and once, when there were only a few cookies left in the jar, he decided that he would never eat the last cookie, but put it away and keep it so that something of her, unique only to her, would go on existing, but one day, when he was in the kitchen waiting for the kettle to boil while his father sat apathetically watching "The Muppet Show" in the big room, he couldn't control himself any longer and he ate the last cookie, and then he collected the crumbs, which were even more delicious, with a teaspoon and ate them all, letting them dissolve slowly between his tongue and palate while he concentrated on trying to extract the last drop of flavor and crumbliness from them and to absorb them into his palate so that they would stay with him forever, and when he finished eating he closed the jar and put it back in its place.

In the middle of the summer Meir's father gave in to his uncle and aunt's pleas and went away with them to spend a week in the country, and in obedience to his request Meir went over to the apartment after a day or two to see that nobody had broken in and that everything was in order, and as he approached the building, with the dusty hibiscus hedge in full summer bloom and the evergreen ficus trees at the entrance, and glanced up at the closed blinds as he walked along the quiet street, which was already full of shade at the end of a hot summer's day, he was seized by suppressed excitement, for a veil seemed to have been unexpectedly drawn aside, and he saw his mother sitting upstairs in the silent, empty flat, where a very pale ray of light had penetrated a slit in the blinds and lay on the wall, filling the big room with the reddish-gray glow of the setting sun, and she was clean and her hair was combed, as if she had just emerged from the shower and changed into fresh clothes for the evening, and she was holding *To the Lighthouse* in her hands, and there was a cup of coffee and a thick slice of cake on the low table next to her, and she seemed boundlessly serene and content, for there was no one to disturb her and rob her of her enjoyment and her freedom, and he went upstairs, and although he knew that there was no one in the flat, he was full of joyful expectation, and he passed his hand over the locked door and tried the handle, and even peered through the peephole, and then, after pausing a moment to listen, he turned on his heel and went slowly down the stairs and into the shady street and started walking in the direction of Gordon Street. The houses, with their entrances and balconies, the trees and bushes in the yards, even the color of a wall, a curtain, a blind, or the shifting shades of the light in the street—all of it, down to the subtlest and most elusive detail, was so familiar to him that it seemed not to exist in actuality at all but to emanate from his own soul, for there, and only there, did it exist in the fullness of its true reality, and in the pangs of longing for his mother, which encompassed him in this street at this hour, he understood, not by deductive logic or emotional intuition or any mystic faith, which was foreign to his spirit, but with a knowledge that was almost tangible and self-evident, the product of a yearning and a need that could not be subdued because nothing could deflect them or take their place, the strength of the conviction of those who believed that a person close to them who died did not vanish from the world as if he had never been in it, since it was impossible that someone who had existed exactly as they did, eaten and drunk and read newspapers and walked in the streets, and who was so dear to them that the very point and purpose of their lives were inextricably bound up with his, and the reality of his existence was identical with the reality of their own, had ceased to be—he had simply gone to another place, somewhere in the vastness of the universe, and there, in the fresh, dim mists of a land both boundless and clearly defined, with mountains and valleys and fields and lawns, under a mild, fixed sun, he went on existing forever like a gray shape of air in his own form and image, living the same life as he had lived before but at peace and without bodily needs, in the same way that the past goes on existing in the present, in any case that was the way he saw his mother at this moment—and this, too, was the source of their wish to die, for only in their deaths would they be united again with the one they so craved and needed that it was as impossible for them to be separated from him as it would be for them to be separated from themselves.

And he turned into Gordon Street, which at this twilight hour was crowded and steamy as a carnival, with the tension and lust palpable and vibrating in the hot air between the men and women filling the streets in their light, revealing summer clothes, and he looked covetously at the girls and women passing him in the street,

although he kept his face blank, and then he took in the girl standing
next to him at the pedestrian crossing, for some reason she looked to
him like a tourist, and thought to himself that she was attractive and
he would like to go to bed with her right now, at this very hot and
sticky moment, in his parents' flat or anywhere else, and when the
light changed he let her cross before him and inspected her hips and
legs until she disappeared among the crowd, and he continued along
Gordon Street, thinking to himself that he would give anything for
his mother to come back to life, even if it were for only a day, and
the moment he had this thought a tremor of happiness passed
through him, as if it had already come true, and he glanced at the
Haute Coiffure hairdresser's with its fake Spanish decor and said to
himself that he would give five years of his life for it to happen, and
then, with the joy of the meeting still fluttering in his chest, he asked
himself if he would give ten years of his life and he answered, "Yes,"
and a suppressed doubt trembled inside him for a moment, and then
he asked himself if he would give fifteen years—he knew that he
should not ask himself this question, but nevertheless he asked it as
if something outside himself was forcing him to do so—and he paused
for a moment to think, for some reason he felt obliged to tell himself
the truth, and he said, "No," and immediately, in a panic, he said,
"Yes," and again, "Yes," and tried to wipe out the memory of the
"No," but to no avail, the "No" went on reverberating inside him,
as annoyingly persistent as a slogan on a wall still showing through the
fresh coat of whitewash painted over it, and a feeling of gloom and
panic overcame him because he had suddenly and unexpectedly been
forced to realize that his love for his mother was not as unconditional
and unreserved as he had believed it to be, and the joyful emotion
which had encompassed him only a few moments before faded and
disappeared, leaving behind it disappointment and shame.

A little later, when he was sitting with Pozner on his untidy
balcony and having a beer, Meir told him in detail about what had
happened, laughing as he did so, but the laughter did nothing to cover
up his embarrassment, and in the end, with a confused smile still on
his face, he said, "Which means that I don't really love my mother,"

and Pozner said, "Did you really think that you loved your mother more than yourself?" and Meir said, "Yes," and they both smiled, and Pozner shook the ash off his cigarette over the balcony railing and said that this was nonsense, and that ninety-five out of a hundred people would have given the same reply and that what was generally true of humanity could not be inhuman. He said this lightly, but his intention was serious, and afterward he changed his tune slightly and said that a man could ask himself such questions only if he was prepared to face the harshness of the answers, which in a certain sense were inevitable because they confronted us with the truth that there were no bonds that were unconditional and unreserved, and even in the bond between a mother and child a moment was likely to come when a split second of doubt was revealed, and that this, in a certain sense, was perhaps the very essence of humanity, since in the last analysis man was imprisoned in himself and attached to himself in the crudest and most elementary sense of the words, and so he remained in spite of all his connections and relationships with others. And with a light, casual gesture, which was somehow absorbed into his words, he threw the cigarette into the yard and said, "At the same time, of course, people sacrifice their lives for others and for all kinds of things almost every day," and smiled very faintly and ironically, and Meir said, "Yes, I understand," but he did not feel reassured.

Toward the end of summer Meir decided, with Aviva's whole-hearted encouragement, to go abroad for a few weeks in order to rest and recover from the tension and gloom that were depleting his strength, and in order to enrich himself with cultural experiences—museums, theaters, concerts, famous buildings, and so on. It was nearly ten years since his last trip abroad, which had also been the first, and of course, which was actually the thing that stimulated his imagination above all, in order to experience wild and uninhibited sexual pleasures, since in Europe he would once more, if only for a short time, be independent and free from all constraints. A few days before his departure, Meir went to the clinic to have a checkup and get a prescription for his medication from Dr. Reiner, and as he was about to thank her and stand up to leave, she told him that she was thinking of making some alterations in her apartment, but before she started breaking down the walls she would like to get some professional advice, and she asked him if he could recommend someone to her, and Meir said that he would be glad to advise her himself, and the next day, after work, at the appointed time, he arrived at her apartment, and after telling him what she wanted done, Dr. Reiner invited him to have a cup of coffee, and they sat in the living room, with its book-lined wall, and spoke about the renovation of the apartment and about her sons. Meir was able to answer most of the questions she raised on the spot, but there were a few problems that needed to be discussed more thoroughly, and he promised to phone her within a day or two to tell her what he had come up with, and then they spoke about foreign travel, and Dr. Reiner told him about her younger son, who had finished his army service a few months before—she had another son and a married daughter, too—and taken off with two friends to tour the rivers and lakes of North America, and on his way back he planned to go to Europe and spend some time with his father, who had been living in England, where he had been working as an electrical engineer in a hearing-aid laboratory, for the past few years, and from there he would return to Israel, and Meir said, "I envy him," and Dr. Reiner said "Why should you? You're going yourself," and smiled, and Meir said, "Yes, but it's not the same thing, you know," and he added, "I'd like to travel and travel without stopping," and Dr. Reiner said, "Do it, then," and Meir said, "Something always happens to prevent me. Either work or money or health or something else. You know how it is," and she looked at him with her bright, lively eyes and said, "I love traveling. Once I used to travel a lot, but not so much over the past few years," and then she asked him about his itinerary and he told her in general outlines, but without going into details, since her son's trip made him feel uncomfortable about his own, and shortly after that he left.

On the eve of his journey, after parting from Pozner, who asked him to bring him D. L. Crook's *Volcanoes and Volcanic Activity* from London—he wrote down the particulars for him and said he was sure he would be able to find it at Foyle's—Meir finally went to say good-bye to his father, after postponing the visit for days and putting it off from one hour to the next because he knew that he would have to kiss him or at least shake his hand. They sat in the little room, and while Aviva was making tea in the kitchen he told his father in a loud, jovial voice what he had taken with him and how he had packed it all and then he told him, perhaps for the tenth time, where he planned to go, all in the same loud, strained, vivacious tone, and afterward they watched the news on television and spoke about politics while Meir waited for the right moment to say good-bye in the briefest, most casual way possible, and then, while Aviva was exchanging a few remarks with his father, he took the opportunity to go to the toilet, and when he came back he remained standing at the door, there was no point in putting it off any longer, and said that they had to go now because he was leaving early in the morning, and his father stood up and approached him to say good-bye and told him to take care of himself and Meir, paralyzed by panic, said, "Yes, I'll try to. Don't worry," and put out his hand and shook his father's limply, certain that he was waiting expectantly for him to kiss him, and then, as they were standing in the hall next to the front door and saying their last good-byes, with his father warning him again and again against all kinds of dangers and asking him to take good care of himself, he lifted his hand and patted his father lightly and casually on the shoulder, a deliberate but at the same time seemingly accidental pat, and immediately removed his hand and said, "Good-bye, Dad," and turned around and walked quickly out of the door, where he waited for Aviva to say good-bye to his father and join him, and the next morning he flew to Amsterdam.

PART THREE

A fine rain was falling slowly as the plane landed on the wet asphalt of the runway early in the afternoon of a dull summer's day. Meir took his blue suitcase from the conveyer belt, the heavy, green shoulder bag had been with him on the flight, and walked over to the tourist information booth. He went up to the girl behind the counter and told her that he had the address and phone number of a place in Amsterdam where you could get a bed and breakfast—Pozner had recommended it to him after staying there several years before—and asked her how to go about booking a room there. The girl offered to phone for him, and Meir gave her the note with the address and phone number on it. She glanced at the note and said that the phone number was wrong, since it had only five digits, whereas all the phone numbers in Amsterdam had six. Meir expressed his surprise and told her that he had received the number from a friend who had lodged there himself, but the girl, who was very pleasant and helpful, glanced at the note again and repeated firmly that no such phone number existed, and remarked that if only he had the Christian name of the man in addition to his family name—Van Essen—she would have been able to look him up in the telephone directory. Meir took the note back, upset and downcast but still trying to keep calm and maintain the cheerful frame of mind of a carefree tourist, and asked her if she could recommend any other lodgings that were not too expensive, and the girl said that all the places on her list were relatively expensive, but that the tourist office in town, close to the terminal and railway station, had the addresses of cheaper places. Meir hesitated for a minute or two and then decided to go to town.

The journey to town was pleasant enough. The bus, which was clean and comfortable, drove between brown-green fields and water canals softly shrouded in a grayish, rain-saturated mist, and dappled by broad patches of shade cast by the clouds moving across the sky. Here and there were little cargo boats, a crane, a tractor ploughing a field, and Meir, sitting close to the window, felt his composure, albeit a little ruffled, returning, and with it an expectant happiness, and from time to time he cast a glance at his blue suitcase, which was lying with the rest of the luggage, and at a man in an elegant blue suit sitting a few seats in front of him, on the other side of the aisle, who was smoking one cigarette after the other and kept on turning around to look at the back of the bus, and who looked to him like an Arab. Meir fixed his eyes on the calm, flat landscape and said to himself firmly that everything was going to be all right, there was no doubt about it, and that he was in Holland and would soon be in Amsterdam, a city he had always wanted to visit, where he would be able to relax and have a good time, and in the meantime he should concentrate on the scenery and enjoy the sights and the journey.

The Amsterdam Tourist Office, a not-very-large room in a one-story building that looked like a hut, was crammed with people, most of them young and from Africa and Asia, with a few unkempt young Americans, Swedes, Germans, and Italians among them. They were all clustered in three noisy, jostling lines in front of a counter behind which sat three young girls trying politely and with the utmost patience to meet the requirements of the people in front of them, who were behaving rudely and even with an undercurrent of violence. Meir stationed himself glumly in the middle line, which seemed to him the shortest, his face stony with despair. The moment he walked into the room he knew that he had made a terrible, fatal mistake in not booking a room at the tourist office in the airport, and that his whole stay in Amsterdam, and perhaps in London, too, was doomed to failure. He looked at the people pushing and crowding him from every direction, there was not one remotely familiar face among them, and he said to himself bitterly that if he had booked a room at the airport, as he could easily have done, he would already be in his room, and in a little while he would have gone out for a stroll in the city, after a shower and rest, instead of standing here sweating and suffocating in a crowd of shoving strangers. He wiped his sweating face and looked expressionlessly at the girls behind the counter and the people standing in the line in front of him, whose ranks seemed to be swelling instead of diminishing, and in his despair it occurred to him to go back to the airport and find a room through the tourist office there, in order to correct his mistake and start his visit to Amsterdam off on the right foot.

On his right, in the line only one step away from him, two Arabs were standing and conversing loudly, and he tried to keep his profile toward them and efface himself as much as possible, while furtively turning the airline label attached to the handle of his suitcase with his name and address on it back to front, and again he thought of going back to the airport to book a room, but he went on standing in the stationary line, wrapped in an impenetrable feeling of foreignness, and clinging tightly to his suitcase and the green bag hanging heavily from his shoulder. In the end, after waiting for what seemed like hours, with his back and legs hurting and his whole body bathed in sweat from the stifling heat, he decided to get out of there and try to find the address that Pozner had given him. At least it was in some sense familiar to him, at any rate more than any other place in the city stretching anonymously around him, chilly and gray, because Pozner had stayed there for a number of days a few years earlier and praised the proprietor for his hospitality and sympathy toward Israel, and he extricated himself from the throng of people and went into the street.

Someone told him that Rokin Street was situated behind the Dam Square, and that it was not too far to walk, and he set off down the broad street crowded with people and traffic, the right side of which was lined with garish shops selling cheap, modish clothes and pornographic literature, bars and movie theaters with huge, flickering signs, and big cafés overflowing onto the pavements and crowded with men, most of them Arabs and Africans—at any rate they were the most conspicuous—who were sitting there drinking and necking indifferently in full view of the passersby with women who looked for the most part like prostitutes or spaced-out tramps. He walked on without pausing, almost without turning his head, his suitcase in one hand and his green bag on his shoulder, harried by the feeling that at any moment, because of some trifle, a chance look or gesture, he was liable to land himself in trouble, and all he wanted was to get as far away as possible from this wanton district with its smell of violence, where everything he saw filled him with hostility and disgust, and find himself a place where he could put his things down and take a shower.

On the other side of the Dam, which he barely glanced at in passing, in a broad street, depressing in its lack of charm and commercial grayness, which reminded him a little of Yehuda Halevi Street in the sector next to Allenby, at the end of a long row of houses in a very narrow alley that looked more like a passage between two houses than a street, he found the address he was looking for. Straining his eyes in the disagreeably dim light, which seemed to emanate from the walls of the houses and remain stuck there between them, he read the name on the heavy wooden door and then put down his case and wiped his face and rang the bell in tense anticipation. After a moment he heard a muffled voice coming from somewhere overhead and then slow, shuffling footsteps, and a few moments later the door opened and an emaciated old man with his hand in a bandage appeared. Meir nodded in greeting and said that he had received his address from a friend and that he would like to stay there for three days, and the old man nodded and said that he did in fact have a room to let, with bed and breakfast, but that it was occupied at the moment by a couple of tourists. He spoke in a quiet, apologetic tone and Meir, beside himself with disappointment, said, "I thought I would be able to stay here," the thought of going back to the tourist office filled him with a terrible despair, and the old man lingered on the doorstep, evidently wishing that he could help him, and repeated apologetically that he had no vacancies, and said that it was necessary to book in advance, especially at this time of year, and Meir said, "Yes, I see," but nevertheless he asked him if he couldn't squeeze him in somehow, at least for one night, and the old man said, "No, no, I'm sorry," and after apologizing again he suggested that Meir try the Hotel Rokin on the other side of the street.

The Hotel Rokin had the vulgar, seedy air common to cheap and even dubious hotels in commercial and entertainment districts or near railway stations, and everything about it aroused Meir's disgust: the mean facade that greeted his eyes as he crossed the deserted street full of a damp, misty twilight; the old sign; the few steps leading from the street to a kind of little porch; the long, narrow passage with little pictures—landscapes of Holland apparently, hanging on the walls leading from this porch to the cramped reception desk, behind which, in the light of a yellow lamp, stood a handsome young boy with a pleasant face and a certain air of casual elegance. Meir told him what he wanted and the clerk said that there was only one room available that night, a double room located outside the building, two streets away on the other side of the canal, in the annex, and he showed Meir a color photograph of the room and remarked that it was very clean. Meir leaned on the counter and examined the photo, which showed a double bed with a pretty counterpane and a chest of drawers and a vase of flowers and two chairs and a basin and a mirror, all very pleasant and cozy-looking, but he hesitated because there was something about the atmosphere of the hotel that made him uneasy, and because the room itself was located outside the actual hotel building, and especially because the price mentioned by the clerk was far higher than—almost double—what he had imagined it would be, even more than the sums mentioned by the girl in the tourist bureau at the airport, which were considered high, but he was worn-out and shivery from the waiting in line and the walking and the cold clinging to his flesh and invading his body, which was sticky with sweat and dirt, and the idea of going back to the tourist office, with the Arabs and Africans, or wandering blindly through the streets with his suitcase and bag searching, perhaps for hours, for somewhere else to stay in this strange city already sinking into the melancholy grayness of a cold, drizzly evening—he could feel it invading the hotel and creeping up the long, narrow passage—was too fearful and depressing to bear.

The young reception clerk did not press him but seemed indifferent to the whole affair, as if he were sure that within a short space of time someone else would turn up to take the room, and in the meantime he turned to an elderly couple who had appeared at the bottom of the steep wooden stairs and took the key for his room from the man, who asked him something in broken English. The clerk answered him and the man said, "Thank you," and turned to the woman, both of them were all dressed up as if they were going to the theater or a concert, and said, "I told you, come on," in Hebrew, but the woman stood her ground and said, "Ask him about the Jewish restaurant," and the man said, "What the hell does he know about Jewish restaurants? Come on," and she said, "He knows. The hotel belongs to a Jew, doesn't it? Ask him. What do you care?" and the man said impatiently, "What do you need a Jewish restaurant here for? Haven't you got enough in Tel Aviv? Come on, let's go," and the woman said again, "Ask him, I want to know." They spoke in lowered voices, and Meir, who was listening to their conversation with a blank face and averted eyes, felt his objections to the hotel dissolving, and after they had finished their business and left, he told the clerk that he would take the room, having made up his mind that the next day he would find himself a cheaper room in a pleasanter hotel, and the clerk said, "Okay," and with the help of a little printed sketch he explained how to get to the room, and then he explained that the annex was only for sleeping and that he would have to return to the main building for breakfast, and in the end, before giving him the key to the room, he demanded payment in advance for the night and Meir paid him and took the key and a brochure issued by the Municipal Tourist Office, which the clerk gave him, and went to the annex.

The room, which was at street level and opened right onto the pavement, did not look exactly as it did in the photograph, but it seemed clean and pleasant enough, and Meir locked the door behind him and looked around it for a moment, feeling the strangeness like a wall of congealed air, and then he put his suitcase down on the chest of drawers, and without taking off his shoes lay down on the big bed. Through the window, which overlooked the pavement, with the canal flowing a few steps away, he heard loud voices and a burst of laughter as a group of youths approached, and as they passed the low window, which was the only one in the room, it seemed to him for a moment that they were walking right through the room, and when the sound of their footsteps receded he got up and closed the window and drew the thick cream-colored curtains, and went back to the bed and lay on it for a while with his eyes closed, sensing the strangeness of the bed linen through his clothes—all the strangeness in the world was in their touch—and the strangeness reverberating in the little room, which was full of a dense, heavy silence encompassed by the fainter silence of the rest of the annex, where it seemed to him there was not a soul stirring apart from himself, and afterward he stood up, and taking his green bag, which he was afraid of leaving in the room, he went to the shower at the end of the passage.

After he had showered and changed his clothes, he returned to the room, which now seemed a little more familiar, and lay down on the big bed again and tried to fall asleep, but the noise coming in the window from the pavement and a muffled, steady roar in the distance, which seemed to him to be coming from the outskirts of town, together with a maddening, obstinate wakefulness, kept sleep at bay, and he tossed and turned, trying in vain to hold on to the weakening skeins of sleep, until in the end he opened his eyes and turned over, and as he lay on his back passing his eyes over the ceiling and the walls, empty but for the picture of a seascape with a ship and a sunset on the wall next to the bed directly above his raised knee, and over the curtain and the gleaming basin with the mirror above it, he wondered if he shouldn't get up and go for a walk in the town and find the red-light district, with the prostitutes sitting naked in the windows waiting for customers, and perhaps go in to one of them, an Indonesian or a Chinese, and he tried to work out how much it would cost and said to himself that but for the exorbitant price of the room, so much higher than he had expected, there would have been no difficulty about the prostitute, and consoled himself with the thought that he had taken the room only for one night and that the next morning he would find himself a different room, cheaper and nicer than this one, and once again he regretted not having reserved a room while at the tourist bureau at the airport, when it would have been so easy to do it, and he put his head down on his arm, the strangeness of the room with the dingy white of its walls, which had seemed to have softened somewhat, was after all insoluble, and decided that tomorrow and the next day he would cut down on his expenditures and save money for the prostitute—the difference between two extra nights in this hotel and two nights in the new place would more or less cover it, he imagined—and he looked at the basin, whose gleaming cleanliness warmed his heart a little and made him a little happier, since there was something homey about it, and concluding with a bitter smile that this room had robbed him of the prostitute, he took the map of the city and turned onto his side and spread it out in front of him: the city looked to him like a spider's web, and after reconstructing the way he had come from the tourist office next to the terminal to the hotel, he let his eyes wander to other streets and canals and tried to read their foreign, unpronounceable names and fix them in his mind, but the thoughts of the prostitutes in the windows persisted, like the dull, steady roar in the distance, and merged with the feeling of loneliness and strangeness—or perhaps it was only his weariness—and aroused his lust, and he thought about Raya, who suddenly popped up in front of him as if she had materialized out of thin air, and about how he had lain with her in a terrible panic, in haste, harried by a paralyzing sense of sin, on no account could he forget or forgive himself for that shameful panic—after all, they were alone, all alone, and he had had all the time in the world at his disposal. And he saw her in that long, narrow room with the wall, which were too high and painted a drab beige, and with the murky brown light filtering through the curtains on the barred windows—someone had walked past in the courtyard singing in Arabic or perhaps it was the radio—and with the revolting woolen bedspread, and afterward he saw her taking off her bra and her white panties, he shrank from seeing her in her nakedness, but nevertheless he stole a glance in her direction, unable to restrain himself—how he wished that he had her with him now so that he could do what he had wanted to do then and could have done and did not do, again and again he tormented himself with the memory of his shameful panic and haste, especially in view of her unexpected willingness to abandon herself to him and to carnal pleasures without any inhibitions, and he felt more and more stimulated, and with his eyes closed, the map of the city still spread out before him, he gave her a hint and she opened her legs and bent down slightly and leaned lightly on the table, and he looked at her vagina, his face burning with a dull fire, and afterward, with a gentle but firm movement, he put his hand there and stroked her, and slowly, tense and concentrated on the pleasure gathering and intensifying to bursting point, he rose to his feet and stood in front of the basin, and gazing dreamily as if through a sweet mist at his face in the mirror, he ejaculated, and afterward he cleaned himself and rinsed the basin, washing it very well and doing his best to make it as clean and gleaming as before, and tidied himself up and took his green bag and went out into the street, which was still shrouded in the same frozen gray dusk. For a moment he stood in the quiet street, staring apathetically at the canal and the heavy foliage of the trees lining it, and considering which way to turn in the city spread out around him like a great gray blot, with distances and directions he could not gauge, and then, overcoming his inhibitions, he turned south, in the direction of the terminal, and began walking along the canal toward Rokin Street and what he referred to in his thoughts as the "dirty district."

He stepped out briskly and seriously, as if he had some specific destination in mind, hardly turning his head to look at the buildings lining the canal or the passersby, who were few at first in this quiet section of the street, which was mostly occupied by silent houses and deserted office buildings, and afterward, almost from one moment to the next, turned into a crowd filling the main street and the little streets and alleys intersecting it. They thronged the little cafés and the dim bars with their strange names and the boutiques and shops selling posters and paper novelties and the sex shops with their display windows full of sexual appliances and garish magazines, and the many record shops with their deafening music blaring forth in all directions, and they clustered in little groups here and there, most of them sinister-looking Africans and Asians and Arabs, and of course young Americans and Europeans flaunting their decadence, while others leaned against the railings, staring vaguely around them in the deafening blare of the music, or wandered aimlessly about in couples or in groups. All of them looked so filthy and careless that they immediately aroused Meir's hostility, but he glanced at them only in passing, because he was concentrating on finding the prostitutes in the windows, and as he pushed his way through the crowds of youths, intent on this vain search and deafened by the music, which did not stop for a second, he kept exhorting himself to stop a while, slow down and relax and enjoy Amsterdam, and in the end he slowed down and stopped looking for the prostitutes, and even halted at the corner to inspect the view of the street and houses before him, making an effort to enjoy it and impress it on his memory.

After walking on for a while, straying disappointedly through the labyrinth of little streets and alleys without seeing one single prostitute in a window, until he began to wonder if this was the right district for them, he came unexpectedly on the street lining the canal again, which for some reason gave him a moment's satisfaction, and he turned and continued along it in a southerly direction beyond the tumult and crowds to a section of the street that was quiet and completely deserted, full of the seedy ugliness and neglect of an abandoned slum, until he reached a place where the street and the canal beside it ended abruptly at the bleak back wall of an old house with moss and weeds growing out of the cracks of its bare red bricks, and he saw himself suddenly trapped with no way out. The damp air was full of a heavy, menacing silence and a dense smell of stagnant water and mold and slime, but instead of stopping and turning back he quickened his pace, as if he were being pursued, and with sullen determination, the green bag dragging heavily on his shoulder, crossed a little wooden bridge that suddenly loomed up in front of him and entered a very narrow alley. From the first few steps he took into this alley, lined with a row of gloomy houses on either side, he knew that he had made a bad mistake and that he should have turned back into the street lining the canal and returned with it to his room, now he felt more trapped than ever before but he hurried on, quickening his steps in the muck of the squalid alley, and as he did so two blacks emerged from a doorway not far ahead of him, and after lingering for a moment in the door, as if they were parting from someone or wondering which way to go, they turned and started walking toward him. In the panic of the moment, he thought of turning on his heel and retracing his steps, but he went on advancing at the same brisk, resolute pace until he passed them, and after a moment or two he suddenly emerged from the alley into the broad, noisy street that led from the tourist office to Rokin Street, and his spirits lifted in relief, he was so happy to see the sordid street, and without a pause, his face and neck and whole body bathed in sweat, he turned and started walking north, full of shame at the foolish panic that had taken hold of him and disappointment at not having seen a single prostitute in a window, and then he stopped to wipe his face and the back of his neck with his handkerchief and told himself firmly to slow down and take in the sights of Amsterdam. After the Dam—this time, too, he did not pause to inspect it and gave it only a weary glance in passing, but he promised himself that the next day he would come and look at it properly—he saw a couple in their forties advancing toward him in what seemed to be a great hurry, even at a distance he could see that they were Israelis, and as they hurried past him the man stopped and asked him in Hebrew, twisting his face into a would-be ironic leer,

"Where's the street of the red lights here?" and Meir instantly shrugged his shoulders as if he couldn't understand him and went on walking, his face stiff and expressionless, and crossed to the other side of the street, passing opposite the Rokin Hotel, which was already shrouded in darkness and gave him a feeling of reassurance and even well-being, and afterward, at the intersection of Rokin Street with a number of others, he crossed the street again and stood on the bank of a rather wide canal, on the other side of which was a whitewashed boat house with steps leading down to a little jetty with a cruising launch next to it, with everything—the steps and the boat house and the jetty with the launch and the surrounding bit of canal—brightly illuminated in the fast-gathering darkness. Meir leaned against the iron railings, slipped the green bag off his shoulder, put the bag on the ground, and looked wearily at the boat house and the man in the captain's uniform who was standing at the top of the steps and nodding affably at the tourists stepping cautiously down into the launch, and at the still, dark green water, which was illuminated by the lights of the launch anchored next to the jetty and in which the headlights of passing cars were fitfully reflected. It was already almost completely dark, and Meir, who was tired to death, repeated to himself that he was in Amsterdam, but no response of happiness or excitement stirred in him and broke through his weariness and gloom, and he repeated it again, emphatically, and looked around him at the wide, deserted street and the blank facades of the buildings, which had already sunk into cloudy darkness, and once again he was filled with regret at not having booked a room through the airport, which for some reason was connected in his mind with his failure in the matter of the prostitutes, and he tried to cheer himself up with the promise that the next day, even before breakfast, he would go to the tourist office and get that other, cheaper and nicer room, and on the very same impulse of thought it flashed through his head that the whole trip to Amsterdam was a pointless mistake, a thought which he indignantly rejected, and he raised his coat collar as a cold wind began to blow down the street and said to himself that in any case he didn't have to stay here for three days, as he had originally intended, and that he might well take an earlier flight to London, where he had friends waiting for him.

A fine drizzle began to fall, caught from time to time in the headlights of passing cars, and Meir hoisted the green bag onto his shoulder and made for the dark alley beyond the canal and the white boat house in order to return to his room, and as he walked in the light, drifting drizzle down the dark alley, which as he had guessed, led to the street lining the canal where the annex was situated, he said to himself that Amsterdam was a wonderful city, as everyone knew, one of the most beautiful and agreeable cities in Europe, and that he had a whole list of places to visit—a number of museums and interesting buildings and parks, the Portuguese Synagogue and the Royal Palace and Rembrandt's house, the prostitutes in the windows, and more—and that it would be a shame to leave before he had completed it, who knew if he would ever be here again, and he stopped in front of the hotel, which was sunk in heavy silence and darkness except for a dim light filtering through the glass in the thick front door, and took out his keys and opened the door—all the other residents had evidently gone out to enjoy themselves—and went into his room.

For a moment he stood in the room and looked at the furniture and the dingy white walls, discovering another little landscape on the wall to his right, next to the wardrobe, and then he slipped the green bag off his shoulder and removed his coat and sweater and shirt, which were all soaked in sweat, and washed himself in the basin, and after that he hid his wallet under the pillow and undressed and got into bed. The thick silence, which seemed to be more and more tightly compressed between the walls and seemed to surround the whole house and the bit of road in front of it and the trees and the canal, was broken from time to time by loud voices or bursts of laughter and sometimes by fitful bursts of loud, merry music, which seemed to be borne on the wind from very far away, but like air cleaved by a plane passing through it the silence immediately closed up again, as thick and heavy as before. Meir switched on the night lamp above his head and leafed through the Cook's Tour Guide he had obtained from the receptionist, with the picture on the cover of an elderly Dutch couple in national costume smiling, and glanced at the pictures—one of them, of rounds of yellow cheese arranged on wooden stretchers in a square in Alkmaar, attracted him particularly, and the names of recommended restaurants and shops, he did not have the strength or patience to do anything more than skim through the pamphlet, and then he studied the street map again and planned his route to the Stedelijk the next day. He ran his eyes aimlessly over the map, trying again, without much success, to take in the names of the streets and canals, and began thinking about Aviva, who seeped imperceptibly into his thoughts like drops of water soaking into dry ground and gradually spread until she dominated them, and he thought about her with feelings of closeness and need in the knowledge, which came to him with a sudden clarity, that she was the only bit of solid ground in his life, which was rapidly being eroded and swept away, and for a moment he saw her as a bit of brown and gray earth with a few chalk stones and clumps of grass on it somewhere beyond the abyss of infinite darkness stretching between the wall of this hotel and Tel Aviv and separating them from each other, and at the same time he listened attentively in the hope of hearing the approaching footsteps of a pretty tourist or chambermaid coming to knock on his door and invite herself to spend the night with him.

When Meir woke up early in the morning, everything was enveloped in a profound, almost rural silence, and he got up and washed and dressed himself without dawdling and took his green bag and went quietly into the street on his way to the tourist office, since he had decided to relieve himself of his worries about the room before breakfast in order to prevent them from poisoning his whole day, but he loitered in front of the hotel for a moment to breathe in the crisp morning air and the smell of the trees before setting off. The silence was so deep and soft that he wished he could float through the gray-blue light lying like a mist on the canal and the trees so that the tapping of his footsteps would not disturb it, and he felt the special pleasure that he had anticipated feeling in Amsterdam, until he arrived at the tourist office and discovered to his astonishment that it was locked and deserted. From a notice on the door he learned that the office opened at nine, and he remained standing outside the locked door, incredulous and completely at a loss—for some reason he had been sure that they were open twenty-four hours a day, and afterward, without a trace of his former happiness and feeling that someone was deliberately wrecking his plans and hopes, he began walking back to the hotel. He branched off the main street, the one leading from the terminal to Rokin Street, and walked along the side alleys parallel to it, where only a few people were to be seen sweeping the street or hurrying to work, bitterly calculating that if he had to go back to the tourist office at nine o'clock to get the new address and make the arrangements about the new room, and then go back from there to Hotel Rokin to get his things and go to the new place and get settled in there, his whole program for the day would be ruined, and with it his whole program for his stay in Amsterdam—he had intended spending the morning visiting the Stedelijk and the Van Gogh Museum and walking back along the Amstel to visit Rembrandt's house and the Portuguese Synagogue—and when he reached the place where, according to his calculations, he was supposed to turn left in order to return to Rokin Street and the hotel, he kept on walking, it was still too early for breakfast, and walked to the end of the street, which was a very narrow commercial street, almost an alley, still wrapped in the profound early morning stillness, and there he turned left and emerged, as he had anticipated, at the Rokin Street intersection, not far from the section of the canal with the white boat house, and he stood there leaning on the iron railings on the street corner. There was a kind of archway with a bell tower just behind him, and as he stood looking at the sleeping streets and enjoying the view and especially his own enjoyment of it, of which he was very conscious, he thought that if only he had booked a room while he was at the airport he would be really happy now, the idea of the hassle ahead of him kept buzzing through his thoughts like an angry wasp, and then he crossed the intersection, where trams drove past at regular intervals with a pleasant, monotonous clatter, and he entered a narrow, dirty street and walked along it for a while, it was full of morning shadows and completely deserted, and then stopped in front of the window of a sex shop and slowly inspected the articles on display—artificial sexual organs and sexual appliances and provocative bras and panties and journals and posters—until he heard a faint noise and saw a worker coming toward him from the other end of the alley on a bicycle, and he walked away with an empty face, as if he had never stopped there at all, and passed movie theaters and all kinds of shops, which were all shut and deserted, without stopping, and at the end of the street he turned left and found himself opposite a small park, and then he turned left again, circling the same block of buildings, and a few minutes later he came out on Rokin Street again and walked along the iron railing of the canal leading to the white boat house in the direction of the hotel, which still looked seedy and sordid to him as he approached it, but less so than the day before. And when he climbed the few steps to the little porch overlooking the street and walked down the long, dark passage with the little landscapes on the walls, a faint feeling of belonging, or at least of not being a stranger, stirred in him reassuringly, and the elderly couple from Israel popped into his mind again, together with the fact that the owner of the hotel was a Jew, and he decided to save himself any additional fuss and bother—in the last analysis, how did he know that the new place would be any better than this one?—and stay where he was.

There was now a female receptionist behind the desk, and Meir introduced himself as a hotel resident and said that he had decided to stay there for another two days. The receptionist, a pleasant-looking woman in her forties, nodded and asked him to wait a moment and after looking through her papers said that he would not be able to remain in his present room because it was booked, and Meir, to whom this came as a surprising and also insulting blow, said that he liked the room very much, and he wanted to say a lot more, he didn't know exactly what, but he was so taken aback that words escaped him, and the receptionist, with a very pleasant, polite expression on her attractive face, nodded understandingly and said that she was sorry and remarked that they were very full at this time of year, and Meir said, "I understand," and with a bitter feeling of relinquishment—at this moment the little room was as dear to him as if it were the one and only

place he had left in the world—asked her to give him another room in
the hotel, although he was not yet resigned to the loss of his former
room and believed that somehow he would go on staying in it, and the
receptionist said that at the moment she didn't have any rooms at all
but that it was very possible that something might become available
soon, and she suggested that he come and see her again after breakfast,
and Meir, who now felt a wave of panic and despair surging through
him, asked her if there was no room for one single person in the entire
hotel, asking this question in an aggrieved and imploring tone, as if he
had been betrayed and banished, and the receptionist repeated that
something might become available and that he should come to her
again after breakfast, and Meir said, "Okay. Thank you," but he went
on standing by the desk and after a slight hesitation urged her again,
very awkwardly, to do her best to find him a room, remarking as he did
so that he was from Israel, and the receptionist promised him that she
would do her best, and Meir thanked her with exaggerated heartiness,
he wanted very much to ingratiate himself with her, and with a heavy
heart climbed the steep, narrow wooden stairs to the dining room,
which was on the second floor.

There were already a few people in the little dining room, among
them the elderly couple from Israel whom he had seen the day before
when he first arrived at the hotel, and he stood at the door searching
for a place where he would be as isolated as possible, the tables in the
corners and next to the tall windows overlooking Rokin Street were
already taken, and then he sat down and put the green bag on the
floor at his feet and while he was waiting for breakfast to be served
surveyed the other guests with a blank, expressionless face. Most of
them seemed pleasant and respectable enough, and some of them
were even talking, in politely lowered voices, in Hebrew, but he did
not let on by so much as a slight inclination of his head or a hasty
glance that he understood what they were saying and sat there apart
and withdrawn into himself, sunk in his worries and the bitter sense
of injustice stemming not only from the fact that he already saw
himself as a rightful resident of the hotel but also from the vague and
illogical but nevertheless persistent feeling that this was Holland after

all, and he was an Israeli, and the owner of the hotel was a Jew, and
at the same time he said to himself that all this was his punishment
for not taking a room through the tourist bureau at the airport. In the
meantime the waitress arrived, a fresh young girl with long honey-
colored hair and a tight black sweater, who looked like a glamour girl
straight out of a comic book, and Meir decided to shake off his worries
and bad thoughts, at least until after he had eaten, and he gave her
a frank stare and even tried to catch her eye, and at the same time,
while she was going in and out with trays of food, he buttered a thick
slice of bread and spread a fragrant slice of cheese on it and bit into
it and smiled to himself in enjoyment, trying with all his might to
abandon himself to the pleasure of eating, but a few minutes later he
found himself struggling once more with the worry and nagging
thoughts, which toward the end of the meal, as the time for his
sentence to be passed approached, had grown into a torrent of anxiety
raging beneath the strained surface of his serenity and enjoyment of
his food. As he ate, he looked covertly around him at the people sitting
and eating and the people coming through the door, in a sluggish
trickle as if they were still wrapped in warm webs of sleep, and
gradually filling the room. Among the stream of people, most of whom
were in couples, some even with children, was a burly, rather elegantly
dressed man of about forty with a black mustache and black hair and
pale, olive-colored skin, who stood out for some reason as different and
separate from the rest, and Meir, who noticed him the moment he
came in, said to himself immediately that he was an Arab. He stopped
at the door and surveyed the dining room with a slow, heavy look, an
undisguised expression of proud, bitter hostility and fierceness on his
tough, somber face, and then sat down at an unoccupied table not far
from the door and waited to be served, and Meir covertly brought his
leg closer to his bag and stole a glance at him and repeated to himself
that he was an Arab, and for some reason this thought made him feel
uncomfortable, and he said to himself that he was probably a gangster
from South America, but after another look he could not rid himself
of the definite impression that he was an Arab, which may have
stemmed from the expression on his face or something else, undefina-

ble but nevertheless real, about him, and he felt a new uneasiness mingling with his other worries and anxieties, but at the sight of the unconcern of the rest of the breakfasters he decided to put it out of his mind, saying to himself that perhaps he wasn't even an Arab after all, and afterward he said to himself, "And if he is an Arab—so what?" and went on eating with an expression of indifference on his face.

After the meal he went to the receptionist, who was talking on the phone, and when she was finished she said that she had a room for him, and Meir thanked her very much, feeling the heavy tension melting inside him and his heart lifting with relief and gratitude, and she went on to say that the room was in the main building, on the top floor, right under the roof, but that it, too, was a double room and available for only one night, and Meir was taken aback, a shadow darkened his happiness, and he asked her, as if he had not heard what she had said, if she didn't have any other room here or in the annex, and she said no, everything was booked up, and remarked that another room might become available the next day—it was up to him to decide if he wanted to take a chance. She was very friendly and made no attempt to influence him and Meir, who now wanted to get the whole business over as quickly as possible, said, "Okay, I'll take it," and asked her what he should do with his things, and the receptionist told him to go and fetch them right away and bring them to the desk because they had to prepare the room he had slept in for its new occupants, and at noon he could come and take them up to his new room, and Meir thanked her again and hurried to the annex and took the blue suitcase and parted from the room in which he had spent the night with a feeling of sorrow, and still believing that somehow, God only knew how, he would come back to it, he returned to the hotel, where he deposited his case with the receptionist and went out into Rokin Street and began walking with a light, brisk step toward the Stedelijk.

He proceeded north on Rokin Street, the green bag on his shoulder, until he reached the intersection with the archway and the bell tower, which he had passed before breakfast, and without pausing, following the route he had mapped out the night before, he continued along the broad, commercial street with its tall buildings, many of them modern, containing shops and restaurants, bank branches and commercial firms, and the trams passing at regular intervals down its center. The air still had a crisp, early-morning freshness, but the traffic was already brisk and lively, and as he walked with his green bag on his shoulder, glancing at the buildings and shop windows and the trams and cars and the faces of the passersby hurrying about their business, and along the canals flowing past on either side, he suddenly noticed that his gait had grown tense and rushed, he could feel the tension in his face and loins, and he told himself to slow down, to stop every now and then, and to look around him in a leisurely way in order to absorb the sights of the city and enjoy its beauty, and he slowed down and from time to time forced himself to stop and stand still and look intently at a shop window or the facade of a building, or a stone-edged canal with its bridges and green trees, and repeated to himself admiringly, "What a wonderful town, what a beautiful sight," but his intent gaze, which took in the most minute details, seemed to slide helplessly over some glassy surface coating all the sights that lay before him, unable to penetrate to the things themselves and sense their reality, which appeared to exist above and beyond these details, or to extract one single drop of pleasure or excitement from them. Everything seemed to get lost on the way from them to him, but he repeated to himself, "What a wonderful city, what a beautiful sight," and continued on his way to the museum.

After wandering for a long time through the spacious halls of the Stedelijk, where every once in a while one of the exhibits brought a smile to his lips or gave rise to a faint feeling of pleasure, and sometimes even a hint of emotion, he went down to the cafeteria, where he decided to rest a while and refresh himself before going on—he was determined to take in all the galleries without skipping a single one—and he sat there with his cup of fragrant coffee and cheesecake, exhausted by all the walking and concentrated looking, his body sinking leadenly into itself, and as he drank the coffee he looked dully at the men and women going in and out or sitting around the white tables, all of them looking fresh and happy and relaxed, and all of them well-dressed, not necessarily elegantly but in a way that expressed some elusive quality he would never be able to comprehend and define, let alone emulate, and the feeling of strangeness and utter isolation that had surrounded him all the time and trailed behind him like a very delicate, almost imperceptible train of murky air, thickened —precisely now, during these moments of relaxation in this pleasant, cultured place—and he felt as if not only he himself but they too saw him as alien and apart from them, and irremediably so. And he looked at the statues in the garden on the other side of the vast glass wall of the cafeteria, and especially at the monotonous, repetitive movement of an iron statue standing on the smooth lawn made of pegs and ceaselessly turning wheels, whose arm, a kind of slightly curving pipe, acted as a kind of moving fountain, and he tried to discover, by strained and patient observation, if there were any changes, even the very slightest, in the movement of the statue, or whether it was absolutely and endlessly repetitive. His gaze was trapped by this monotony and riveted to it, and sunk in contemplation he thought that this movement, endlessly repeating itself, would go on even after he was dead, and as he sipped his coffee with his eyes fixed on the statue he saw himself dead, while the statue continued its repetitive movement against the background of these green lawns and spreading trees and wisps of cloud moving slowly, with melancholy patience, over the gray sky, and someone else, not he himself but someone resembling him totally in appearance and thoughts and feelings, sitting here in his place, in the same clothes and the same posture, one leg crossed over the other, one hand holding the emptying cup of coffee and the other resting limply on the table beneath which, close to his feet, stood the green bag, and contemplating, just like him, the constant, repetitive movement of the statue and trying, just like him, to see if there were any changes in it, and he felt as if he had a double who would be born one of these days, he could actually feel him in all his body, as if it were the double and not he himself who was filling it even now like the stuffing in a pillow, and that it was this double who was following the movements of the statue, and a gentle, mischievous smile spread through him at these thoughts, which had something consoling about them. For a moment he thought of taking his bag and going upstairs again and completing the tour of the halls he had not yet visited, and he tried to work out the direction he was facing, whether it was west, as he instinctively guessed from the movement of the clouds, which seemed to be coming from that direction, or perhaps it was east—there was nothing to be learned from the look of the sky or the light, which was full and unfocused, or perhaps the clouds came up in the north here and moved southward, in which case he was facing north, but the more he turned it over in his mind the more he kept coming back, like the stubborn needle of a compass, to his original conviction that he was facing west, because it was from that direction that the clouds continued to rise until they gradually covered the sky and it began to rain, not very hard, a rain which in some obscure way was close and familiar to him, and he said to himself, "A Tel Aviv rain," and looked at the rain, whose drops spattered on the glass and trickled down the wall beyond which the fountain of the statue continued to move and scatter its water aimlessly in the misty air. The low, merry laugh of a young woman sitting not far from him with a man in a sporty white suit, perhaps her husband, attracted Meir's attention, and he glanced at them and at his watch and said to himself that if he wanted to visit the rest of the museum he had better do it now, because it was getting late, but he went on sitting where he was, so unwilling to get up that the very thought of it depressed him, and after a few minutes he stood up and bought another cup of coffee and sat down at his table again. All he wanted was to go on sitting in this clean, quiet place, in which for all its strangeness he felt comfortable, and he would have gone on sitting there till evening but for the fact that last night he had planned to walk along the Amstel and visit Rembrandt's house and the Portuguese Synagogue—he had already decided to put off the Van Gogh Museum to the next day, after the Rijksmuseum—and but for the thought, which gave him no peace, that he had to be back at the hotel at lunchtime to transfer his suitcase to his new room. He did not want to put this off a moment longer than necessary, not only because he feared for the fate of his suitcase, lying unguarded in the hotel lobby, but mainly because it was quite impossible for him to tour the city without knowing that there was a specific place that was his—not knowing this gave him a feeling of rootlessness and uneasiness that undermined what little will and ability to enjoy the sights he still had left, and a few moments after his second cup of coffee, which he finished drinking impatiently, and in spite of the continuing rain, he took his bag and left the museum.

A few minutes after twelve, in obedience to the receptionist's instructions, Meir entered the hotel, worn out with walking and wet with sweat and rain, after having wandered aimlessly along all kinds of streets and alleys and canals in the obstinate drizzle, which soaked him to the marrow of his bones, because he didn't have the patience to take shelter and wait until it stopped, or go into a café or take a tram somewhere or other, and he stopped only once at a bookshop, where he paged distractedly through one book after another, so impatient that he could hardly read the titles and the names of the authors, and it occurred to him to buy a couple of postcards and write a few sentences to Aviva and the children on one of them and to Pozner on the other, and he did so—it was a good idea and gave him an excuse to stay in the shop a few minutes longer, and then he put them away in his bag and went out into the rain again. Standing in front of the reception desk in the hotel were a couple of Middle Eastern youths with a young girl or woman, it was hard to tell, sitting between them shrinking with fear and hopelessness, small and scrawny as a famished alley cat, in a dirty white dress, looking at them with frightened, submissive eyes, and weeping fitfully in a weak, wailing voice, the tears leaking out of her like weak spurts of water from a ball with holes in it, despite the strenuous efforts she made to suppress them for fear that she would be punished by the two men, in whom, especially the taller of the two, they seemed to give rise to some irritation. The two youths, long-haired and filthy in their cheap, fashionable rags, which looked as if they had not taken them off for days, were speaking in French to the receptionist, who asked Meir to wait until she had finished with them and with the girl, to whom they addressed occasional words of encouragement and reassurance, perhaps promises too, alternating with scoldings and threats, ap-

parently trying to persuade her to do something, the taller one even
gave her arm a vicious, stealthy squeeze, eliciting a stifled scream and a
burst of tears, and afterward, when they had come to some kind of
agreement with the receptionist and with the girl, they spoke to each
other in Hebrew so that no one would understand them. Meir stood
and listened, hearing and not hearing, with an expressionless face, as if
he didn't understand a word, and the receptionist waited patiently, and
the tall youth, who looked as if he was under some intolerable strain,
told the other one that he could have her for two weeks and another
three thousand gulden, and when the latter did not react but stood
leaning against the counter calmly chewing his fingernails, the tall one
said in a nervous, wheedling voice that he was prepared to add another
thousand, and grabbed him urgently by the arm and said, "Be a pal.
She'll bring you at least ten in two weeks. Add it all up, you'll have
fourteen. That's more than I owe you," and the second stood his
ground and demanded five thousand immediately and another two
when he gave the girl back. He was perfectly calm and collected and
the tall one, realizing that there was no point in pleading with him said,
"You're killing me," and gave in, and the second, satisfied, stopped
chewing his nails and stole a glance at the girl and asked the tall one to
persuade her to wait until they came back for her, and the tall one said,
"Don't worry, she'll wait," and the second said, "And if she doesn't?"
and asked the tall one to frighten her, and the latter put a vicious
expression on his face and spoke to her harshly in French, holding her
arm so tightly that her face twisted in pain and she let out a groan, and
then he spoke to her nicely and stroked her hair and said something to
the receptionist and paid her, and the two men parted from the girl like
a concerned father and mother and walked out of the hotel, and the
receptionist wrote something down while a very slight expression, no
more than a faint shadow, of disgust crossed her face for a moment, and
then she took a key and came out from behind the counter and told
Meir to follow her and headed for the stairs.

Meir took his suitcase and followed the receptionist up one flight
of steps after the other on the steep, narrow staircase, as dark as the
stairway of a tower, admiring her shapely, athletic legs, until they

reached the top floor, where she opened the door of his room and gave
him the key and Meir, hoping very much that the bitter man in the
elegant suit was not staying in one of the adjacent rooms, thanked her
and entered the room and locked the door behind him. The room,
which contained a double bed and a table and two chairs and a
cupboard and washbasin, was much smaller than the previous one,
and the sloping ceiling created the impression that it was also much
lower, but on the other hand it had a certain feeling of intimacy, and
especially of utter isolation. Through the one small window in the
sloping ceiling there was nothing to be seen but rooftops and a square
of gray, rainy sky, and for some reason this made him feel peaceful
and secure. He put his suitcase and shoulder bag in the cupboard and
took off his wet shoes, and after washing his face, dropped onto the
bed and lay on his back looking mindlessly at the gray sky, and then
he closed his eyes and tried to fall asleep, but something kept him alert
and wide awake, and in the end he got up and went to shower in the
shabby little bathroom at the end of the passage, which he crossed
with a hasty step on the way there and back, anxious to prevent the
bitter man in the elegant suit from discovering which room he was
staying in, and then he lay down on the bed again with his eyes closed,
and after a while he opened them and saw swollen rain clouds sailing
very slowly across the square of the window, and then he closed them
again and tried to sleep. The silence all around was absolute, with only
the steady roar, like the subdued roaring of a heavy sea, coming from
a distance, and after a long and exhausting battle with his sleepless-
ness, he opened his eyes again and looked miserably at the bit of wall
in front of him without a thought in his head. The weariness of his
limbs combined with his restlessness to turn his wish for sleep into
an irritable, impatient yearning, and the silence, which deepened and
arched until it was like an inverted abyss threatening to suck him in,
merged with the feeling of strangeness rising like invisible vapors from
the obscure ends of the gray, rainy city and advancing down the dark
passage and cramped lobby and up the ugly staircase, and seeping into
the room until he felt unwilling and unable to remain there, and he
thought of getting up and going to have a *rijsttafel* at the Chinese

Corner, as he had planned on doing the night before, and after one more attempt to fall asleep he got up and dressed, tired and nervous, and with a feeling of relief he left the room and locked the door behind him.

It was raining heavily, with a thick layer of clouds darkening the sky and shutting out the daylight, and after Meir had deposited his key with the receptionist he stood at the end of the passage, where the dense gloom blotted out the little landscapes, staring hunched and indifferent at the dark sky and the rain coming down in sheets and veiling Rokin Street, where there was no sign of life but for the trams passing with monotonous regularity and stopping for a moment at the deserted station and continuing on their way. And as he stood there a rather fat girl with a big head and a Doris Day haircut emerged from the depths of the passage and joined him in the doorway, and after staring for a moment at the deserted street and the rain, she said, "It's raining," and Meir said, "Yes, it's raining," and the girl, who was dressed in the most tasteless, provincial way and looked like a melting cream cake in her tight-fitting clothes, said, "How long is it going to go on?" and Meir, whose face and clothes were getting damp in the water-saturated air, shrugged and said, "Who knows?" and the girl gave him a friendly smile and asked him where he was from and Meir told her and she said, "Oh, yes, Israel, I know," and then she said, in the same friendly way, that she was from the U.S.A., from Michigan—her pink whipped-cream face was that of a provincial housewife, and she was not at all like the beautiful American girl he had imagined accompanying him on his wild, free round of pleasures—and that she had come to Holland with her parents to visit a village not far from The Hague, she mentioned the name but Meir failed to catch it, where her family had lived before leaving to settle in America, and where some of them were still living to this day, while others had scattered in various directions, and Meir said, "That's very interesting," feeling both interested and full of vague longings, and asked her when all this had happened, and she said, "About a hundred and fifty years ago," and he repeated, "That's really very interesting," and wondered why this rather plain and completely unsexy girl attracted him so much, precisely for these reasons, although not to go to bed with her but only to sit next to her and look lingeringly at the slit of her vagina as she lay on her back with her legs apart, and he undressed her in his mind while she glanced at the street, in the direction of the terminal, and said, "This rain isn't going to stop until evening," and added that she was waiting for her parents, who were due to arrive at any minute with their luggage, and then asked him what the hotel was like, and Meir said that it was fine, and added immediately, "It's very clean." The thought that she and her parents would be staying at the hotel gave him a good feeling, and the girl said, "It makes that impression," and at that moment a cab drew up and stopped in front of the hotel and she said, "Here they are! They've arrived," and she called and waved and turned to Meir and said, "Nice to have met you," and descended the steps with a kind of waddle and hurried over to a man with a big head and gray hair who emerged from the cab and embraced him quickly in the rain, which had somewhat abated, and then she embraced her mother, who got out of the other side of the cab, and Meir raised his coat collar and ducked his head and stepped out into the rain-swept street.

The Chinese Corner was almost empty at this early hour, which made Meir feel so uncomfortable that except for the fact that he had decided to have an Indonesian *rijsttafel* at the Chinese Corner, and that one of the waiters had already seen him and given him a slight nod, he may well have turned around and left, and he stood in the doorway of the large hall wondering in which row and at which table in all the many rows of tables to sit, until the waiter who had noticed him came up to him and with perfect politeness and without uttering a word pointed to one of the tables, and he sat down and put his green bag on the empty chair next to him, and while he was waiting for the waiter to come and take his order he inspected the large hall, full of a dim green light like the smell of incense or herbs and a strange, uncomfortable, feline stillness, with the other hall splitting off from it, and the heavy furniture, it too shrouded in the same greenish shade, and the lean, lithe Indonesian, or perhaps Chinese waiters, whose smooth, greenish, expressionless faces created an impression of polite distance and hidden slyness, two of whom, or perhaps three, were busy serving, with soundless steps and neat, deft movements, a jolly party of Indonesians, or perhaps Chinese, consisting of adults and children and old people, all of them festively attired, sitting around a number of adjoining tables, who had apparently gathered to celebrate some family event, and as they ate and conversed in lively but subdued voices to the accompaniment of a delicate tapping of chopsticks, occasional exclamations or bursts of laughter rose abruptly from their table, dying away with the same suddenness that they had arisen —but in all these sounds, including the soft footfalls of the waiters and the short sentences they uttered, there was something snatched and somehow introverted, and they did nothing to disturb the strange silence that gave rise in Meir, together with the exotic and impenetrable feeling of foreignness, to a disagreeable sense of mystery and the hatching of sinister plots. One of the waiters, perhaps the one who had directed him to his table, came up and placed a menu before him, and he studied it purely for pleasure, since he knew exactly what he was going to order, and after a while a different waiter came to take his order, and then there was another interval—everything proceeded at a calm, leisurely pace, which he did his best to enjoy—until the first waiter returned and placed a hot plate next to him, and in the end, after what seemed to Meir a very long interval, he came back again and without uttering a word, with the same marvelously neat, quick, unobtrusive movements, set out thirteen little bowls holding a variety of dishes and a larger plate of rice before him. Meir thanked him with a nod, to which the waiter responded with a slight movement of his head before vanishing as instantly as if he had melted into thin air, and then inspected everything in front of him with a feeling of satisfaction and bewilderment. The eagerly awaited *rijsttafel* was now before him, but he did not know the right order in which to eat the tempting dishes, a fact that seemed to him important if he wanted his enjoyment to be complete, and in the end, after hesitating a while, he began to eat without any order at all, at first very slowly, making an effort to taste the special flavor of every dish and savor it to the full, and then voraciously, and although he kept urging himself to control himself and eat slowly, for he wanted to get the maximum enjoyment possible out of this meal and he had all the time in the world to do it in, he found himself again and again gobbling greedily and bolting his food, at the mercy of a wild, uncontrollable impatience, and as he struggled unsuccessfully against this panicky haste and expressionlessly scanned the hall and the waiters and the other diners, whose ranks had gradually swelled, sitting and eating without doing anything to alleviate the strangeness or disrupt the silence, he sensed with increasing despondency how his enjoyment was disintegrating and diminishing until there was nothing left but the exhausting effort to finish the food remaining in the dishes and get out of the restaurant as quickly as possible.

The Dam was once more thronged with young boys and girls sitting in little groups and smoking and staring into space or making love indifferently in the cold, pale sunlight that had broken through the clouds, and the streets and alleys roundabout were crowded, too, everything seemed to be waking up, and Meir stood in front of the restaurant for a few moments looking around him and hesitating—according to his plan he was supposed to go to Rembrandt's house and the Portuguese Synagogue now—and in the end he decided to go for a short stroll through the "dirty district" in order to digest his meal and see the filth and the decadence and especially the prostitutes in the windows, for it was unthinkable that he should be in Amsterdam without witnessing this spectacle, and stepping out briskly, without stopping or turning his head, his green bag on his shoulder, he set off and walked from one street to the other. The narrow streets were muddy after the rain and a cold, enervating wind was blowing, but they were packed with people nevertheless, and the same deafening music was tearing the air to shreds again, and as he walked he felt the profound weariness from which he imagined he had recovered overcoming him again, and despite the cold wind he began to sweat, and he looked around for a quiet spot where he could sit and rest a while. For a moment he thought of going back to his room to shower and rest, but the thought of the hotel repelled him and he decided not to go back till evening to sleep, and he went on walking through

the little streets, which were becoming emptier and quieter, and
crossed a small, rusty bridge and walked along a pleasant, narrow
street and turned into the next street and passed a neighborhood
square, the whole district made the impression of a working class
neighborhood, and after that he passed a few buildings that looked
as if they were up for demolition, and walked along an open lot, at
the end of which, near the bank of a broad canal, were large piles of
rusting junk, and paused for a moment to look at the desolate landscape; even though it was not far from the city center, the desolation
gave him the feeling that he was standing somewhere on its outskirts,
and as the sky darkened again and the cold wind blew harder, he
began walking down the broad street with the empty lots on either
side of it until it merged into another street, which he judged by its
breadth and traffic to be a main road. He had the feeling that if he
continued along this road he would reach the part of the city that had
seemed to him from his study of the map the day before to be
particularly quiet and attractive, and which he had intended visiting
anyway, and in the meantime it began to rain, but he did not stop
to take shelter and continued walking in the rain, which soon turned
into a heavy downpour, crossing a big new bridge over a very broad
canal and quickening his steps until he was almost running, with the
rain beating on his head and pouring down his face and soaking into
his clothes and shoes, toward the high white buildings looming ahead
of him in the distance, blurred by the curtain of rain, and when he
reached them he took shelter under a jutting roof next to a commercial company or agency for something or other, and after shaking off
some of the water, he was wet through, and wiping his face and head
with his handkerchief, he stood and stared at the rain shrouding the
broad, deserted street and the high white buildings as thickly as a fog.

The air was very damp and cold and it penetrated his wet shoes
and clothes and made him feel miserably uncomfortable, and as he
stood there staring at the rain, which seemed so heavy and steady that
he imagined it would continue falling for days on end, he thought that
in Israel the sky must be blue and clean and full of light, and he saw this
sky in front of him stretching as far as the eye could see like a gigantic

sheet of cloth, from the direction of Israel toward the place where he
was standing, over the Sharon and Tel Aviv and the seashore and the
gentle loam and limestone hills, and as it came closer, gradually growing grayer and gloomier until it was as dark as the sky above him, and he
sat down on the step and took the map of the city out of his bag in order
to get his bearings and locate his exact position, hoping by these means
to overcome the cold and the boredom that were beginning to wear
him down, and he spread it out in front of him and looked at it, and
afterward he walked under the roof to the edge of the building to find
out the name of the street, and he saw that it was Sarphati, and he
looked at the map again to find the street and as he did so it occurred to
him that this Sarphati was a Jew, it seemed to him that he had heard his
name in his history or literature lessons at school, and a warm, happy
feeling of closeness and belonging spread through him and cracked the
wall of impenetrable strangeness and foreignness, for all at once, as if by
the wave of a magic wand, this cold, deserted, rain-swept street was
transformed into something close to him, which in some abstract sense
belonged to him, just as he himself belonged to it, and this feeling did
not disappear or diminish even after he had failed, despite all his efforts
in the boredom of waiting for the rain to stop, to remember a single
detail concerning this Sarphati, who, considering the length and
breadth of the street named after him, must have been an important
person—at first he was sure that he was a poet, a descendant of the
exiles from Spain, and then he thought that he was an important statesman, and after a moment it seemed to him that he was a philosopher,
like Spinoza, or perhaps he had invented something in the field of
optics, and two office girls ran out of the building to a cab waiting for
them opposite the entrance, and he watched them until they got into
the cab and it drove away and disappeared around the corner, and
wondered what to do with the time ahead of him—it was nearly three
o'clock and there were another five hours to go until nightfall. And
while he stood staring apathetically at the deserted street and the rain
—now he was sure that Sarphati had been an important politician,
something like Disraeli—he thought of the postcards he had written to
Aviva and Pozner and decided that as soon as it stopped raining he

would go to the post office and mail them, and from there perhaps he would go to Rembrandt's house or at least the Portuguese Synagogue, and he opened the map again and planned his route, and after a while the rain abated and turned into a light drizzle, and he glanced at the map again and put it back into his bag and raised his coat collar—he didn't have the patience to wait until it stopped completely—and stepped out of the shelter of the roof and began walking toward the city center.

Meir walked from one street to the next, huddled into his wet coat, trying to sense the right direction by intuition, for some reason he refused to take a tram, and in the end, after straying at length in uninteresting streets, he suddenly arrived at the Rokin Street intersection with the archway and the bell tower, where he stopped for a moment to look at his map, and then walked a little farther, and instead of crossing the street and continuing to the post office, he turned right and went to the sex shop in front of which he had stopped that morning, and walked past it with an innocent air, slowing down to look through the open door and note that the shop was almost empty, and then continued to the end of the street, where he stopped and retraced his steps and entered the shop, which apart from the salesman, a young boy who was sitting at the back of the shop with his feet on the table in front of him reading and listening to music through a pair of earphones, contained only two well-dressed middle-aged men, who looked as if they might be clerks or lawyers or businessmen, standing well apart from each other and isolated in their separate corners, absorbed in the perusal of the pornographic magazines that were displayed on the stands and shelves together with various appliances—contraceptives and instruments for accelerating sexual activity and intensifying pleasure and desire, artificial sexual organs for the purposes, apparently, of stimulation and masturbation, and also specially designed panties and bras. Meir advanced slowly along the stands and shelves, furtively inspecting the various sexual appliances, which aroused his resistance and disgust, particularly the artificial sexual organs, at the sight of which he sneered dismissively to himself, and then he stood still, put the shoulder bag on the floor, and began paging poker-faced through the pornographic magazines, whose explicit color photographs of beautiful naked women in lewd postures and of copulation in pairs and trios and groups in the most fantastic positions aroused him to such an extent that he felt his face burning and he was sure that it must be covered with a bright blush that everyone could see. And in the midst of his embarrassment and excitement—not for a moment did he forget the presence of the other two men and the salesman in the shop—he wondered whether to go into one of the black-curtained booths at the back of the shop and see a pornographic movie for a small payment, but in the end he decided to put this off to the next day since there was something about the idea of shutting himself up in one of those black-curtained booths in the middle of the day and in public that made him feel uneasy, and he went on looking at the pornographic magazines until he gradually became aware that his first flush of excitement had dulled and it had all imperceptibly turned into a rather boring contemplation of more and more naked bodies of women in postures that repeated themselves and more couples copulating in ways he had already seen over and over again, but nevertheless he went on paging through the magazines for a while before looking around him and then retreating slowly into the street, where a very thin rain, as fine as dust, hit him feebly in the face, and he crossed the Rokin Street intersection on his way to the post office.

The intersecting streets were now crowded with people and cars, and this lively traffic too joined the first, still very faint, signs that the day was beginning to decline into evening, and Meir stopped next to the archway with the bell tower and glanced at his map and then walked a little farther down the street and turned into a rather narrow pedestrian mall running parallel to Rokin Street, which was jammed with shops and boutiques, and as he walked through the crowds of people thronging the mall at this time of day it seemed to him that he could see the bitter man in the elegant suit standing in a little crowd in front of one of the shop windows. His face was turned toward the window, but Meir could recognize him from his profile and something undefinable but at the same time absolutely unmistakable emanating from him, and he stopped as if he had just remembered something, and after hesitating for a moment turned around discreetly and walked away. He strode past a number of streets with a purposeful, preoccupied air, as if he had really remembered something he had to do, and then he stopped on the bank of a canal, his legs aching with tiredness, and stared glumly at the dark, still water and the trees and houses on the other side, the more he went back over the scene in his mind the more uncertain he now was that the man in front of the shop window was really the bitter man in the elegant suit from the hotel—he had only seen his profile, and that he had barely glimpsed before it was hidden by the passersby—and he was overcome by a feeling of shame and despair, and as he glanced at the map and continued on his way to the post office, he felt a wish to return to the mall from which he had so shamefully fled a short while before and to find the man he had seen there and ascertain if he really was the bitter man in the elegant suit or somebody else, and if it really was he, to go up and stand right next to him, shoulder to shoulder, and maybe even exchange a few words with him on some pretext or other—he felt that this would be an act of great and, in a certain sense, even crucial significance, but his legs were so stiff and numb with weariness that they could hardly carry him, and the thought of going back all that way in order to find someone who had almost certainly moved on a long time ago and vanished without a trace, sunk like a stone into a thick pile of dust.

In the post office—a big building, grand in the old style—Meir bought stamps and dropped his postcards into the mailbox, and then he went to the kiosk in front of the building and bought two sandwiches with yellow cheese, and a bit of fruit, a bar of chocolate, and a danish pastry to keep for the evening and the night, which he already knew he would be spending in his room in the hotel, and he packed it all into his green bag, and then he stood on the edge of the pavement and looked at the streets in front of the post office and wondered which way to go and what to do with the time that was left before it got dark. He felt too drained and exhausted to contemplate

even a short visit to the museum or the Portuguese Synagogue or
anywhere else, and he spread out his map and looked at it, feeling very
reluctant to go back and incarcerate himself in the hotel yet, or to
return to the center whose steady roar he thought he could hear rising
up and hanging condensed in the cold air like a frozen cloud of smoke,
and which gave rise in him, now more than in the evening and night,
to the feeling that it was the very essence and embodiment of the
violence seething under the calm, pleasant facade of the city; and
after a rather lengthy study of the map, he turned and walked toward
the streets to the east of the post office, where he had not yet been
and which seemed to him from the map to be particularly quiet and
pleasant, and with a heavy, weary tread—the numbing pain in his legs
had spread to his waist and back—he wandered aimlessly through
these streets, gazing dully at the houses and trees and waiting for the
evening, the signs of whose approach he could feel becoming more
and more apparent as he caught every additional mote of darkness
dissolving in the air, every additional crumb of stillness or hint that
the traffic was slowing down—but still it did not come. He stopped
on one of the little bridges and removed his heavy shoulder bag and
leaned on the railings and stood and looked with immeasurable weariness at the black houses with the high windows and the tall green trees
reflected in the water of the canal, which was as stagnant as the water
of a swamp, and he felt in his despair that his trip was irredeemably
spoiled, and all because of that business of the room—ah, if only he
could begin again from the beginning! And he tried to cheer himself
up by whispering, "Amsterdam is a wonderful city. Look and see.
Look at this beauty all around you and delight in it," and he waited
for some revelation to illuminate his eyes and stir his soul and flood
him with the rare emotion and delight, which he so longed for and
which he should have felt but did not feel, and asked himself if it was
in this narrow canal with its dark green, motionless water that the
beauty of the city lay hidden, or perhaps in the rows of trees with their
soft green foliage on either side of it, or perhaps in the house opposite
him with its gable and tall, white-curtained windows, and as he gazed

languidly at the house he asked himself what the people living in it, or even the people living in the flat on which his eyes were fixed, were doing now—were they eating an early supper or a late dinner, speaking of this and that as they did so, or watching television, or quarreling, or was the husband dozing in his armchair with the newspaper as was his habit at this time of day, did they have children and how many, and where did they go to school, and what did the father and mother do, if she worked outside the house at all, and whether they were satisfied with the neighborhood, and in general whether it was considered a good or a bad neighborhood, respectable or disreputable, or perhaps neither but a little unconventional or bohemian, like Nevei Shalom or the area around Rothschild and Ehad Ha-am and Melchett streets in Tel Aviv, and he turned his head and looked around him as if hoping to find the answer in the appearance of the houses and trees and the few shops, and then he looked far down the canal, in the direction of the harbor, where it opened out in a wonderful perspective with more trees and houses and the edges of the sky sloping down to meet them in the background, and he skirted the whole city in his mind as he imagined it from poring over the map, and tried to guess the directions of its growth and the character and flavor of its neighborhoods—where the upper classes lived, the rich and the members of the administrative and technological and intellectual elites, and where the ordinary people lived, where the students and the artists and the workers hung out and where the most pleasant streets were situated, or the most prestigious or unusual ones, or the most unpleasant and run-down ones, where respectable people were afraid to venture alone, even in broad daylight, and he felt the impenetrable, uncompromising foreignness drifting toward him from every direction and closing in on him like a wall beginning right next to him, in the cold air touching his body and reaching all the way to the blurred boundaries of the city. He saw the city limits as a winding borderline beyond which green-brown fields and canals of dark water stretched as far as the eye could see, all the way to the edges of the sky covering the whole country like a dark tent—oh, how he wished he could be in Tel Aviv at this very minute, if only for a single hour,

and he imagined a narrow strip of steel crossing the vast gray expanse
of the air and connecting him for a moment to Aviva, and a gentle,
consoling joy nestled tenderly inside him, and afterward he remembered his dead mother, her memory brought no pain or sorrow with
it but feelings of closeness and happy longings, and he tried to think
about her, but the thoughts disintegrated and became confused with
all kinds of other thoughts, and with the feelings of missing and
longing, and to a certain extent even with the miserable strangeness
and loneliness, and they all combined and merged and were swallowed
up in the apathy of an immeasurable weariness. The numbing pain
in his legs spread to his waist and back until he felt that they were
as stiff and brittle as if they were made of clay, but he went on
standing and looking at the trees and houses and canal, which darkened and dimmed before his eyes as they sank gradually into the
blessed evening dusk. He felt an agreeable sensation of weakness and
profound indifference seeping into him and he abandoned himself to
this feeling in the wish that it would not be disturbed, when suddenly
a small car stopped a few feet away from him and the driver stuck his
head out of the window and called out in Hebrew, "Hey, what are
you doing standing there by yourself?" and grinned, and Meir, very
taken aback by the unexpected familiarity of this address, turned his
head and looked at the unknown man sitting alone in the car, examining his face in the attempt to ascertain if he was perhaps a childhood
friend from his youth movement days or someone from the army or
the kibbutz or the Technion, and he even took a step forward and
bent down a little to see him better, and the man, who was about his
own age, kept on looking at him patiently with a friendly grin on
his face and said, "You're an Israeli, aren't you?" and Meir nodded
his head very slightly and stiffly, as if he was admitting something
against his will, and the man, somewhat embarrassed by Meir's chilly
response, laughed lightly, as if he had won a victory anyway, and said,
"It's obvious," and waved and drove away.

In the emptying street in front of the hotel Meir came across the
elderly Jew strolling back and forth in the evening breeze, and without
a moment's hesitation, as if it was the most natural thing in the world,

the man turned to him and said, "Good evening" in Hebrew, and Meir, who was embarrassed because he had intended slipping into the hotel and ignoring him completely, replied, "Good evening," feeling as guilty as if he had been caught red-handed, and the Jew asked him how he was enjoying himself, not as if he really wanted to know but in order to start up a casual conversation, and Meir said, "Fine." His legs were caving in and all he wanted was to reach his room and wash himself and go to bed, and the Jew said that he and his wife, too, were having a wonderful time, and that during the two days they had been in Amsterdam—they had come by train from Düsseldorf—they had already managed to visit most of the important museums, two synagogues, and nearly all the other places of interest, and they had also gone for a cruise on the canals, and in fact they had actually covered the town, and if they hadn't booked the room for another night, they would have flown to London that very evening, and Meir said, "Yes, I understand," and leaned against the railing of the steps leading to the little porch, a feeling of relief and serenity spreading through him owing to the very presence of this Jew, the incongruity of whose respectable suit and hat and whose poor Hebrew, with its East European accent, did nothing to prevent him from feeling, completely unexpectedly, a warm sympathy and closeness toward him, and he wanted to linger on in his company and felt a sense of regret and even distress at the fact that this man and his wife were leaving the next day, and the Jew said, "Never mind. No use crying over spilled milk. We'll fly tomorrow," and Meir said, "It doesn't make any difference. What does it matter? Instead of sleeping there tonight you'll sleep here, that's all," and he asked him what their room was like, looking for a way of coming closer to him and expressing his sympathy, and the Jew said that he had no complaints and asked Meir what his room was like, and Meir said, "Not bad at all," wishing there were some way he could persuade him to stay on with his wife for one more day, and he asked him what they were doing this evening, and the Jew said, "Nothing. I wanted to go to a movie, but my wife's afraid. And I am too, a bit. The whole town's full of Arabs and all kinds of black gangsters. Who knows what can happen to a person," and he lit a cigarette—it was getting darker, and a bitter cold filled the air—and

Meir said, "Yes, it's not such a nice town, specially around here." He felt a tremendous weariness dragging his body to the ground but was prevented from going up to his room by something that kept him riveted to this Jew and would not let him bid him good night, and the Jew nodded and said that it was like that all over the world, and he blew out a cloud of smoke and asked Meir if he had come from London, and Meir said that he was flying there in two days' time, and the Jew said that his wife was afraid they wouldn't find a room there because they had heard that this year London was filled up, and it was obvious that he was worried, too. And then he told Meir how they had arrived in Amsterdam by train from Vienna, but not directly because before then they had gone through half of Germany—Munich, Stuttgart, Frankfurt, Bonn, Cologne, Hanover, Hamburg, Düsseldorf—and all by train, and to prove how much they had saved by traveling in this way, he made a comparison between train fares and air fares, and then he subtracted the costs of sleeping in hotels and eating, and went on to compare the prices of all kinds of things that they had purchased on the way and things that they had not yet purchased but intended purchasing, especially in London, because it was well known that prices were lower there than anywhere else in Europe, especially the prices of clothing and electrical appliances, and Meir stood leaning against the railing of the stairs and listening, straining himself to the utmost but not catching everything that was said because of his terrible tiredness and the cold and the aching pains in his legs and back, and from time to time even putting in a question or a comment as a signal that he was listening and to encourage him to go on, he so wanted him and his wife to stay on for one more day, that was all he wanted, only one more day, and in the meantime the wife appeared, very friendly and full of worries, and Meir exchanged a few words with her, too, and afterward he parted from them both, and wishing that something would happen to keep them there for one more day, he went into the hotel and climbed the steep wooden stairs to his room.

The moment he locked the door of the remote little room, which seemed to float in the air of the Dutch night detached from everything, he was enveloped by a feeling of coziness and serenity at the sight of the

white walls and sloping ceiling, with its little window defining the familiar space containing the basin and brown wardrobe and double bed,
which still bore the impression of his body; it was his exclusive territory,
at least until the next day, when he would have to look for another
room, something that he refused to think about for the moment, and
he removed the green bag from his numb shoulder and slipped off his
shoes, feeling the sweet pleasure spread through his aching feet, and
washed himself sketchily at the basin, and then he took the provisions
he had bought at the kiosk for the night out of his bag and arranged
them on the chair next to the bed, with the map and the Cook's Tours
brochure on the bed itself, and lay down on his side and began to eat.
And as he ate slowly and with relish, his eyes wandered over the map of
the city, which was already clearly etched on his memory, with its
fanlike shape and the lines of its roads and canals and the green patches
of its parks, and once again he read the names of the streets and canals,
difficult, alien names which evoked no echo in him, purely as a means of
whiling away the time, since he had long ago despaired of reading them
properly and finding some kind of point in them, and afterward he took
the Cook's Tours brochure, with the smiling Dutch couple on the
cover—the steady roar from the south suddenly grew louder and more
distinct like a cloud of buzzing insects borne closer on a changing wind
—and for the umpteenth time he studied the various tours and excur-
sions: a tour of three and a half hours to the windmills and Edam, "This
tour is to"—here there were three words apparently in Dutch, which
he could not make out—"a community of forty little houses north of
Amsterdam on the banks of the river Zaan. At the end of the eigh-
teenth century there were seven hundred windmills here, only five of
which are left. The houses are built of green beams with sloping roofs
and white-washed windows," a picture of three haughty windmills and
a bit of sea graced the top of the page, and a few pages farther on, after
the tour to Antwerp and Brussels, which he immediately dismissed,
came the tour to the Zuider Zee, which but for its length, nine hours,
he may well have taken, first of all for the visit to the dam, "twenty
miles of a Dutch engineering feat, which was completed in 1932 and
constituted the first vital step in reclaiming 600,000 acres of agricul-

tural land." The tour to Hoorn, "a 17th-century merchants' port" whose name he seemed to remember from somewhere, attracted him too, although not as much as the tour to Alkmaar, with the picture of the ancient square and the wooden stretchers laden with cheeses as round as millstones, a pity it took seven and a half hours, and also not as much as the afternoon tour to The Hague and Delft, which lasted only four and a half hours, one hour longer than the tour on the opposite page to the bulb fields of Keukenhof, "where as far as the eye can see the fields are one magic carpet of crocuses and hyacinths and tulips, blazing in a joyous burst of color," and for a moment he saw before him, with the aid of the colored photograph in the brochure, infinite fields of flowers blazing like beacons under the grayish blue sky. The cheese sandwich was absolutely delicious, and he wondered if he should eat the second one right away or keep it for later; he thought that perhaps tomorrow he would go to Keukenhof—the whole tour only lasted three and a half hours—and see these glorious fields of flowers and be refreshed and delighted, for what could be more refreshing and inspiring than fields of blazing flowers stretching as far as the eye could see right up to the horizon, and as he looked at the picture with the brilliant flowers and the blue stream with the pretty little wooden bridge crossing it, he could already feel something of the delight awaiting him there, and he took the last bite of his sandwich, and as he munched it, glancing again at the description of the tour and the picture of the bright flowers and the stream with its little bridge, he sensed how much these fields of flowers stretching over the flat fields to infinity would bore him, and he took the bar of chocolate and broke off a piece, having decided to keep the other sandwich for later, and reflected that it would have been preferable if there were only one field there, one flower bed, or even better, a few flowers scattered here and there in a meadow where you could lie down in the grass with your head on the ground, even if it was alien ground—and he could immediately sense just how alien it was—and abandon yourself to the soft touch of the grass and the air as time passed idly by, but then he asked himself what would happen, if he really took the tour to Keukenhof, to the visits he had planned for the next day to the Rijksmuseum and Rembrandt's house and the Portuguese Synagogue—now he was sorry that he had not carried out his program for today in full—and what about the visit to The Hague and Edam and Delft and the seventeenth-century merchants' port of Hoorn, and the dam and Alkmaar and the ancient square in the photograph, which suddenly seemed to him the most attractive place of all and the one he should go to first, although he wanted to go to all of them without exception and stay in them long enough at least for a cup of coffee and a piece of cake and a leisurely stroll down the main street. He turned the page and broke off another piece of chocolate and studied the restaurant advertisements again, "Ristorante Roma" and "China" and "Neptune" and the coffee shop with the Dutch name and the sign of the rampant lion, and listened to the steady roar in the distance and the various noises coming from the street and rising from the hotel itself—the opening or closing of a door, footsteps, voices, something banging, water splashing—and followed, with growing suspense, the footsteps slowly ascending the stairs.

At first they were distant and muffled and he wondered if he was only imagining them, and then the thought crossed his mind that it was the fat American girl from Michigan coming up to his room to make love to him, and he even began to expect her, for now it seemed to him that she had definitely taken a fancy to him during that short conversation at the end of the passage, and already he saw her slipping away from her parents on some excuse or other and climbing very softly, on tiptoes, up the steep wooden stairs, and he waited in eager expectation to hear the knock on the door, and in the meantime he said to himself that if only Raya had been here with him now he would have been able to make up for everything he had missed then, but he would have been glad to have the receptionist with the nice, athletic legs too, or any other woman, if only she would lie next to him and let him do whatever he desired, and he tried to concentrate on the brochure and the tours to Alkmaar and the dam on the Zuider Zee as if he wasn't expecting anyone, and then, as he stared at the words on the page and went on listening, the steps grew heavy and distinct until there was no longer any doubt that someone was coming up the stairs and was already only one or two floors away, and it occurred to him that perhaps it was the bitter man in the elegant suit coming to confront him in his room, and in the panic of the moment he thought of getting up and switching off the light as if there was nobody there or quickly putting on his shoes and going downstairs, the room was a trap with no way out, but he went on lying there without moving, his eyes fixed unseeingly on the brochure, and listened to the footsteps until they were swallowed up in one of the rooms below him and the door was closed and locked behind them.

After he had calmed down a little, he got up and went and stood joylessly in front of the basin, compelled by the urgent need to relieve his anger and his shame and find some solace, and after he had relieved himself without joy and cleaned himself up, he pushed the empty chair under the door handle and got undressed and lay down under the blankets, noting with satisfaction that the sheets were clean and fresh, and their touch pampered him and gave him pleasure, and he took the second cheese sandwich and ate it, repeating to himself, as he had already done several times that day, that under the facade of almost rustic peace and pleasantness in this city there was a seething violence about to erupt, and the chief agents of this violence were the foreign riffraff from the Third World, Arabs and Blacks and Asians—he added the two Israelis with the scrawny girl from the afternoon to the list but excluded himself—who were a festering sore spreading through the body and spirit of Europe, which because of guilt and cowardice, and perhaps simply shortsightedness, allowed them to do whatever they liked with her, until in the end they would bring her down and ruin her, like the barbarian tribes had done to Rome. He broke off another piece of chocolate and switched off the light and closed his eyes, congratulating himself on his foresight in buying provisions for the night, and before he fell asleep he tried to think about Aviva and about his plans for the next day. Again and again, in a stubborn, exhaustingly repetitive circle, he outlined his route—the Rijksmuseum, Rembrandt's house, the Portuguese Synagogue, the prostitutes in the windows, the Amsterdam Historical Museum, a cruise along the canals—and he remembered that in the morning, in other words, not too many hours from now, he would have to vacate the room, and he was filled with resentment and anxiety and all at once everything, life itself, turned into something temporary and not worthwhile, and as he tried to put all this out of his mind by thinking other, positive thoughts, and fall asleep, he was flooded by a wave of regret for not having booked a room at the airport, regret so bitter and malignant that he wished he could go right back to Schiphol and begin the whole visit to Amsterdam from the beginning, and he turned his face to the wall and looked at it in the darkness, and wondered whether he shouldn't shorten his stay here and fly to London tomorrow, to his friends who were expecting him, and for a moment he was sorely tempted by the idea of putting an end to these wanderings from pillar to post and saving himself from the misery of further alienation and loneliness by this one redeeming act, but he immediately put the temptation behind him and decided to carry out his plans for his stay in Amsterdam to the full, without skipping a single thing. His shame and dejection at his fears and suspicions in the matter of the footsteps did not go away but only seeped down to a deeper level, where they collected like a pool of discontent, and he put the light on again and got up and ate a pear, and then he rinsed his mouth and brushed his teeth and went back to bed.

Meir woke early, after a deep, sound sleep, a fact that he pointed out to himself with some satisfaction as he went on lying in bed with his eyes closed, half awake and half asleep, steeped in the pleasant feeling of a Saturday morning on a fine autumn day in Tel Aviv. In the first moments after waking he imagined that he actually was in Tel Aviv, but little by little the sense of the strange, imprisoning room filtered through to him, together with the desire to hurry outside into the fresh air, and in the meantime he remembered that he had to vacate the room this morning, and the anxiety, which up to now had existed only as a slight tension in the delicate network of tissues beneath the surface of his face or chest, overwhelmed him completely, and he got up and shaved and dressed and packed his things. He was so sorry to leave this cozy, isolated room, with its sloping ceiling and its little window, through which a few nearby rooftops and a strip of sky were visible, that he could hardly bear to part with it, and after making a thorough inspection to see if he had forgotten anything, he went down with his luggage to the receptionist, who was sitting behind the desk in the cramped, deserted lobby and reading, and after wishing her a hearty good-morning and giving her a very bright smile he asked her about a room for the night, to which she replied that there was nothing available at the moment but that he should come back to her after breakfast, and he put his suitcase down next to the wall, in the same place where he had left it the day before, and went outside. Since it was still too early for breakfast, he decided to go for a stroll in Rokin Street and the little streets to the west of it, which he had passed through yesterday, on his way to Sarphati Street, and for which, for some reason, he felt a certain affection, hoping that now, in the tranquillity of the early morning, he would discover the beauty of the city and delight in it, but the nagging anxiety about the room would not allow him to look around at his leisure and enjoy the beauty and serenity of the streets and alleys, and in the end he cut short his stroll and hurried back to the hotel. It was still a little too early for breakfast and the dining room was deserted but for one lady, who resembled Indira Gandhi in her features and hairstyle, sitting and writing a letter, and a blond boy and girl looking silently together at a map, and Meir hesitated for a moment and then sat in the farthest corner next to one of the tall windows overlooking Rokin Street and looked out of the window at the street while he waited for the young waitress to appear. And in the meantime, very calmly and unhurriedly, other people came in—an Italian family with two children, a smiling young couple, perhaps Swedes or Germans, and two girls in tight, faded jeans, together with the elderly couple from Israel, who stood looking around for a place to sit and responded to Meir's friendly smile and nod of greeting as if they were old aquaintances, and his heart contracted at the thought that they were leaving and he would remain here alone, and a moment or two later, as if he had popped up out of thin air, the bitter man in the elegant suit appeared and sat down immediately not far from the door, in the same place as the day before. Meir had been waiting for him in suspense, hoping against hope that he would not appear, and he turned his face away and looked out of the window in pretended indifference, but he could not stop thinking about him or shake off the sense of his presence, which he felt like the steady pressure of a hand on his shoulder, and from time to time he turned his head involuntarily and gave him an ostensibly absentminded, neutral look and took in the tough, somber face with the expression of arrogant, bitter hostility and nastiness, and for a moment he hoped that he would not get a room in the hotel and would have to go somewhere else, but after breakfast, which he bolted down without enjoying it at all, the receptionist told him that he was in luck, since someone had canceled his booking at the last minute and a room had become available for him, a double room again, on the fourth floor, but that it was occupied at the moment and he should come back to her at noon, when he would be able to transfer his things to the new room. Meir thanked her, there was no point in starting to look for a new hotel for one night now, and asked her to give him the key to his old room for a few minutes because he thought he had forgotten something there, and when he came back to return the key, he saw the bitter man in the elegant suit in the cramped lobby standing at the corner of the desk and apparently waiting for the receptionist to finish talking on the phone, and Meir came down the steps and put the key on the desk in front of her and said, "Thanks," and without a pause or a glance in his direction walked past the bitter man in the elegant suit and down the narrow passage, which seemed longer than usual as he walked along it sensing the man's eyes on his back, and when he reached the little porch and descended the few steps to the street, he decided not to get the tram to the Rijksmuseum at the stop opposite the hotel, as he had intended doing, but to turn and walk in the opposite direction, make a detour around a few streets, and then get on the tram at one of the stops farther along the route. The apparently chance encounter seemed to him far from accidental and set his nerves on edge, and seething with animosity toward the bitter man, he carried out his plan to throw him off his scent and turned right into the first alley, and then right again, and continued along the quiet, narrow street parallel to Rokin as rain clouds began covering the sky and the air grew colder, and after a while he turned right again, coming out in the main street as he had

guessed, not far from the intersection with the archway and the bell
tower, where he stood and waited for the tram, already sensing signs
of tiredness in his legs perhaps left over from the day before, and when
the tram arrived he got in and bought a ticket and stamped it and
moved a little way into the tram, which was not very full, and then
he caught sight of the bitter man in the elegant suit sitting next to
the window a few seats in front of the place where he was standing,
looking out the window with his back to him, and for a moment he
thought of getting off at the next stop and walking the rest of the way
to the museum, or postponing the visit there to the afternoon, but
then he recovered, and with an expression of pretended indifference
he rode to the station he needed, where he got off in front of a broad
square planted with trees and walked to the museum, and when he
emerged again after nearly two hours he felt exhausted and dulled by
the solemn procession through the vast, dim halls of the palace, which
were full of splendor and noble works of art that demanded seriousness and reverence on the part of the viewer, and he felt strained by
the strenuous effort to take in everything in detail and be inspired,
while eagerly searching for a remotely familiar face in the crowds
of tired, serious people milling around him and moving slowly forward in a never-ending stream, so that he could pause for a moment
to pass the time of day and rest, and he stood outside the museum
in a daze, feeling the rain in the air and staring listlessly in front
of him.

He stood there for a few moments limp as a rag, with the cold
air soaking into his face and refreshing him a little, and then he set
out again and passed through the vaulted passageway under the palace
and proceeded at a very slow, leisurely pace, feeling rather agreeably
like a convalescent, down the street crossing the broad, pleasant park
opposite the museum, which was completely deserted and enveloped
in a uniform, silvery gray-white radiance shining through the bank of
clouds, and which looked infinitely broad and steeped in an archaic
calm, as if it were floating in some serene celestial domain, and he said
to himself, "What peace. What loveliness. Feel it, feel it," and he did
indeed feel it. But at the same time, as if under the surface of his skin,

or in some inner labyrinth, he felt tired and harassed at the thought of the long, cold, rainy day stretching out ahead of him, and he did not know how he would get through it in spite of Rembrandt's house and the Portuguese Synagogue and the Amsterdam Historical Museum and the cruise on the canals, and of course the prostitutes in the windows, whom he had not yet seen. He felt a terrible inner resistance to any more visits, never mind where, the very thought of it outraged him and made him want to scream with rage and impatience, and he bitterly regretted not having taken the tour to Keukenhof, or preferably to Alkmaar, with its charming ancient square, and concluded glumly that there was nothing for him to do but roam aimlessly back and forth and wait wearily for the day to pass. A light, cold rain began to fall and prick his face, but it did not stop him from enjoying the spacious, enveloping serenity of the park, and he wished that it would go on forever, and when it came to an end and he reached the broad, elegant street opposite it, he paused for a moment, feeling disappointed, and then turned left and began walking along the street. All of a sudden the rain started coming down hard, and after a few minutes of stubborn resistance he was forced to take shelter in the doorway of a shop selling photographic equipment, and while he stood there waiting for the rain to abate, he looked at the wet street and the houses and trees blurred in the misty rain and said to himself that this was the beauty of the town, and he tried to absorb the view in all its details—the houses and trees lining the street and the color of the mist in which they were shrouded and the park on the other side of the street and the houses in the distance—and engrave them on his memory without losing a single detail. He wanted to preserve the sight with all its details of color and smell and atmosphere in his memory forever, it seemed to him a matter of overriding importance to do so—as if not only the success of his stay in Amsterdam depended on it but the very fact of his having been there at all—and he decided to go straight to the travel agent as soon as it stopped raining and confirm his flight to London, which was the only practical thing he had to do during the day and the only one that aroused any interest in him, and as soon as the rain let up, he didn't have the patience to

wait for it to stop, he set out and started walking along the street
intending to turn left, and then a few streets later left again, until he
arrived at the tree planted square at the end of the main street, not
far from the *Rijks*, where he would take a tram to the center of town
and make the arrangements for his flight, and then go back to the
hotel to transfer his suitcase to his new room. But the streets grew
confused—he refused to look at the map because he wanted to put
his sense of direction to the test—and suddenly he found himself in
a market thronged with people, and he stood and looked around him
with a smile full of surprise, and even delight, and afterward he began
striding along the stalls of fruit and vegetables and eggs and cheeses
and shellfish and fish, the likes of which he had never seen before, and
sausages and meat, veal and pork and rabbit and game, and the stalls
selling clothing and haberdashery and household goods, pushing his
way through the crowds of people with a blank, closed face and
exhorting himself in vain to relax and enjoy the sights—nothing of
his momentary delight remained—and thus, with a tense, hurried
stride and the green bag pressing on his shoulder, he reached the end
of the market, where he turned around and strode back again until
he came out at the other end, emerging not where he had begun but
in a commercial street full of simple little shops, something like
Sheinkin Street or Nahalat Benyamin, and he walked along it with the
intention of reaching the tree-planted square, but after a while he felt
that he had lost his way, and he stopped and looked at the map and
even asked the owner of a little furniture shop standing in his doorway
for directions, and the man directed him gladly, and not long afterward he reached the square, worn-out with walking, and got onto a
tram and rode to the Rokin Street intersection, where he got off and
crossed two streets, the receptionist had marked the place for him on
his map the day before, and entered the travel agency. The place
exuded a warmth and elegance that made him wish he could curl up
in a corner and stay there without moving until his flight, and suddenly he felt not only exhausted and sloppy with his green bag on his
shoulder but also foreign and pathetic and embarrassingly out of
place, not at all the man of the world he had hoped to be, and within

the space of a few minutes, with the utmost nonchalance, one of the girls arranged for him to fly to London the next day.

He was so astounded by the ease and speed with which this had been accomplished, and so full of gratitude, that his spirits suddenly soared, and he thanked her and went out into the street—he hadn't been so happy since the plane dipped and he looked out the window and saw the fields and water canals and the tiny houses with their red and gray roofs coming closer all the time—and with a smiling face he walked to the hotel to transfer his luggage, but the room was not yet ready for him and the receptionist asked him to come back in an hour or an hour and a half, and he took it in good humor and left the hotel, and as he was going down the steps to the street he paused and wondered where to go, and in the end he went and stood at the tram stop and took the tram going back in the direction of the Rijks, and then, for no clear reason, perhaps because of the pretty view of a canal with a bridge and an imposing black house he glimpsed through the window in the distance, he got off again and doubled back and walked along the canal, which was not particularly distinguished from the other canals, and looked at the trees reflected in the heavy green water and the houses with their high windows, and said to himself that this was apparently the beauty of the city, and afterward he stood on a bridge and looked about him and tried to absorb the sights at his leisure and enjoy them, and while he stood there he asked himself where they were, the inspiration and delight, the tremors of excitement and pleasure of body and mind that should have filled him to the brim, to which he had looked forward so eagerly, and to which he had once been so susceptible that they came to him of their own accord—the sight of a house or a window, a piece of furniture or the cover of a book, the hint of a sound or smell in the air, had sometimes been sufficient to arouse him then—and he crossed the bridge and entered a tranquil little street and strolled along it aimlessly, and he remembered Gavrosh and the special bird, which had so thrilled him and which with his death had been transformed into a black silhouette somehow stamped into his being, and it was the same with his mother —for a fraction of a second he saw her with absolute clarity, with all

the sights she had absorbed during her life stamped into her like the
bird into Gavrosh, the sights of Poland and Tel Aviv and Gibraltar, and for a moment he tried to see them as she herself had seen
them, and he saw a tangle of twisting lines and patches of light and
dark, and he said to himself that the whole business of looking at views
was a total waste of time and also cruel and mean, if you couldn't take
them with you when you died.

He strolled at his ease, withdrawn but not tense, with only the
numbing tiredness weighing more and more heavily on him, and
stopped on a street corner and looked at a little café, intimately se-
cluded behind square windowpanes the color of thick honey in brown
wooden frames—there was something so intimate and so cultured and
European in the facade of the café that it attracted him, and after a
short hesitation he decided to go inside, not only because he wanted to
rest his body and legs, which were stiff and numb with weariness, but
mainly because he wanted to discover the source of the spirit and
beauty of the city. Very carefully, almost apologetically, he opened the
brown door, and after glancing around the café, which was full of a
pleasant brown dimness and soft silence, he stepped inside and sat
down close to the window, placing his green bag at his feet, and decided
that he would go on sitting there for a long time, perhaps until evening,
the place took his fancy so. He felt that something of the essence of the
spirit and beauty of Europe were indeed to be found here but that they
could only be discovered by idling, and that this idleness was in fact the
source and core of the essence he was seeking, which filled the quiet,
dim room like a special quality in the air and enveloped the people in it,
two elderly women conversing in low voices and an old man sitting in
the far corner reading a newspaper. And Meir relaxed in his chair and
waited patiently for the waitress, or perhaps she was the proprietress,
who approached him with leisurely steps and asked him courteously for
his order, and he ordered coffee and apple tart and looked outside at the
wet, deserted street, where a light rain had begun to fall, and the gray
strip of sky above the houses, until the waitress, who was a woman in
her forties with pale pink skin and neatly combed reddish hair, brought
his coffee and cake, and he thanked her with a polite nod, and sweet-

ened his coffee and poured in some milk from the little china jug, feeling or, so it seemed to him at least, the quiet, cultured atmosphere seeping into his body and soul, and trying to do everything very, very slowly in order to attain the desired idleness, and as he ate and drank he looked lingeringly at the square tables covered with checkered cloths and the walls with the little tasseled lamps projecting from them and the dark pictures, in which it was difficult to make anything out because of the dim light in the room, and at the two elderly ladies absorbed in their conversation and the old man with his newspaper and the waitress in her gleaming frilly white apron, and as he did so he felt an urgent desire to talk to someone, never mind whom, and he waited expectantly for one of those present, the old man or the waitress, perhaps, to turn to him and ask him who he was and where he came from, since he himself could not pluck up the courage to address them. He was as conscious of his foreignness as if it were a narrow sack in which he was confined, and he had no doubt that they were conscious of it too, and beneath the surface of his expressionless face his mouth filled with words quivering like little fish in shallow water and trying to break out, but he did not open his mouth and went on eating and drinking and looking at the waitress, who was busy doing something at the counter, cleaning or tidying, and he examined her body, which was not at all ugly but somehow neutral, lacking in any grace or vitality, and especially innocent of the least hint of sexuality or anything alluring, and the same went for her face, which seemed to have been molded neatly, but without any inspiration, from cheese, and he felt how this woman, as alien to him as it was possible to be, exuding the cleanliness and purity of a devoted, industrious housewife, whose heart had probably never been disturbed by any sinful thoughts, aroused him precisely because of this absolute strangeness and blank neutrality, and he imagined her naked, her white body more sexless than ever, and thought that he would give a great deal to have her lying naked in front of him in his hotel room, where he could sit beside her and look lingeringly, with infinite patience, for hours on end, at her genital slit with its black pubic hair, and as he was thinking these thoughts, the waitress bent down and disappeared behind the counter, and when she straightened up again, it seemed to him that she caught his eye, and he quickly averted his face and looked at the street. A light rain was falling monotonously and wetting the pavement and the street, and he let his glance linger there a while, and afterward, having finished drinking his coffee, he turned his face back and looked at the lamp with the tasseled shade on the wall opposite him, and the picture hanging next to it, a dark landscape with a few trees slanting in the wind and an obscure object, perhaps a hut or a haystack, and while he was looking at the picture, trying to discover the meaning of this mysterious object, and at the curtains and the flowerpots standing here and there on the window-sill or on a pedestal or the corner of a table, all in good European taste, he felt himself beginning to get bored with sitting there, and as his boredom thickened he began to worry about the way he was wasting his time—after all, he didn't have the chance to be in Amsterdam every day of the week, and there were still so many things he had planned to see and had not yet seen, and time was slipping away and vanishing without anything to show for it, and he felt an impatient desire to get up and hurry away, but he held himself back because he wanted to discover the taste of this European idleness and savor it and enjoy it to the full, and it seemed to him that he had not yet idled here long enough. Until he could bear it no longer and beckoned the waitress, who brought him the bill, and he paid her and took his green bag and went out into the cold, wet street and stood under the little roof over the café door, waiting for the rain, with its stubborn monotony, to stop descending from the gray sky, or, at least, to abate, but after a few minutes he got fed up with waiting and raised his coat collar and gripped the shoulder bag firmly to his body and set off, trying to keep as close to the walls of the houses as possible, and it was only when he reached Rokin Street, where a strong wind was blowing, beating the drops of water in the air into his face, that the rain abated, and he crossed the street and entered the hotel, where the passage and the lobby, and later the staircase, too, were dense with a thick, wintry gloom, and took his blue suitcase and followed the receptionist up to his new room on the fourth floor.

His clothes and shoes were drenched and his feet were cold, but he stayed in the room only long enough to look through the window at the bare, bleak cobbled yard with the somber back wall of the house next door looming over it—the room itself, which was long and narrow, was so ugly and off-putting that he preferred to look at it as little as possible—and then he went out again and locked the door behind him, consoling himself with the thought that tomorrow at this time he would already be on his way to London, and he handed his key to the receptionist and left the hotel and started walking to McDonald's, where he had decided the day before to have lunch today, but on his way there he made a slight detour and went to pay a farewell visit, as he put it to himself, to the sex shop, which to his surprise was full of people standing in front of the shelves and stands, silent and withdrawn, studying the pornographic magazines as gravely as if they were financial or scientific reports, or inspecting, and some-times actually fingering, the various sexual appliances, and he went in and joined them in looking at the pornographic magazines, his uneasi-ness somewhat alleviated by the fact that there were so many people there, and although he very quickly, after a short and embarrassing flush of excitement, began to feel bored and indifferent, he went on stubbornly paging through the magazines in the hope of stimulating and exciting himself, but after a few minutes more he resigned him-self to his disappointment and went to McDonald's, which despite the early hour, when he had counted on finding it quiet and empty, was packed with crowds of people, in total contradiction to his expec-tations and plans, and he left immediately and decided to walk around the surrounding streets in the hope that the crowds would thin out after a while. For a moment he thought of taking advantage of the delay to visit Rembrandt's house and the Portuguese Synagogue, which were about a fifteen-minute walk from where he was, but then he decided to put it off till after lunch, since he still had a lot of time to fill in until evening, but when he returned to Macdonald's after half an hour it was as crowded as before, and with a sullen feeling of disappointment and resentment, he took up his place in one of the lines, deciding that there was no point in going out for another walk, since it was unlikely that the situation would improve and he was beginning to feel hungry, too, and as he stood in the line he cheered himself up again with the thought that tomorrow at this time or two or three hours later his plane would already be landing in London. He bought a Big Mac and a container of French fries and looked around for a place to sit, but in all the restaurant there was not a single unoccupied table, and he went outside with his Big Mac and his container of French fries and stood for a moment on the pavement in front of McDonald's, the street and pavement were particularly filthy here, and wondered where to go to eat them.

He wanted to eat in a quiet, pleasant place where no one would disturb him, and he turned right and walked along the street, recollecting that he had seen a park at the end of the road the morning before, but when he reached the park, he didn't feel like going into it, it was so wet and desolate, and he walked past it without a pause and continued along the street perpendicular to it, and a few streets farther down he turned left, having decided to find himself a place in one of the little streets next to the canal near the annex where he had slept the first night, and when he reached the area he had in mind, he wandered about the quiet streets with the Big Mac and the container of French fries in his hand. The streets were indeed as quiet and pleasant as he remembered them, but in none of them did he find the place with the special rightness and felicity that he knew by instinct existed and that was actually nothing but a yearning or a mood, which he himself was incapable of defining but was able to recognize the moment he found it, and although he was very hungry by now he refused to give up and went on wandering from street to street, examining every wall and pavement and curb, until suddenly and quite unexpectedly he emerged at the sector of the canal with the white boat house at the end of Rokin Street, and he went up to the edge of the canal and stood there, leaning against the iron railing. Although it was not the place with the special, intimate feeling that he was seeking, a bitter resignation overcame him and he slipped the green bag off his shoulder and placed the Big Mac and the container of French fries on a block of concrete and began to eat. While he was eating, he looked listlessly at the green water of the canal and the passersby and the somber houses—a pale sun had broken through the veil of clouds and cast a chilly patch of light on the street—and thought longingly of Tel Aviv with its yellowy white houses, which looked as if they were made of old cardboard, and its bright blue sky with its sun as yellow as an egg yolk, like the sky in a child's painting, stretching like a gigantic sheet over the houses and the sand and the hills and the orange groves and eucalyptus glades and green fields, spreading and covering the red loam soil and hiding behind the little hills and stretching all the way to the blue mountains in the distance on the one side and the open sea on the other until it merged softly into the horizon, and he saw Aviva sitting in the armchair in the corner of the room with a cup of coffee and a book—he did not see her sharply and distinctly, but he knew that it was she because it was she whom he wanted to see, and then he saw Pozner, his face slipped away from him but he tried to hang on to it as long as he could, and he saw himself sitting with him on his untidy balcony the day after his return home and telling him that the whole business of tourism was to a very large extent a swindle, and Pozner saying that he imagined that there was something in what he said but that it was no different from a lot of other things, and perhaps one should relate to it like life itself, in other words—know that it was a swindle but at the same time behave as if it wasn't, which was the kind of thing that he had often heard from Pozner before, only this time he was offended because it seemed to him that the words were somehow directed against him and intended to expose his weakness, but he didn't really mind because the image of sitting on the balcony and the sounds of the Hebrew gave him as much pleasure and consolation as if he had withdrawn into his own cozy bed and covered himself with an old blanket, and he chewed the Big Mac and smiled to himself contentedly; afterward, still eating the last of the French fries, he wondered what to do with the time still left until it grew dark, and after some hesitation he decided that first of all he would return to the market he had liked so much in the morning, and which had given rise to a certain joy in him. In the last analysis it was in markets, perhaps more than anywhere else, that you could discover the essence of the spirit of a people, and he decided that this time he would saunter idly through the market, without rushing, so that he could absorb it and enjoy it, and after finishing his meal with a pear left over from the day before, he took the green bag and went to the tram stop at the Rokin Street intersection, and without asking anyone took the first tram going in the direction of the Rijksmuseum.

He bought the ticket and stamped it on the automatic stamping machine, deriving some satisfaction from the fact that this was already a matter of routine, but at one of the stops after the Rijks he suddenly changed his mind about the market and got off and crossed the road and stood at the tram stop opposite the one at which he had descended and got on the first tram that came, which it seemed to him would take him back to the vicinity of Rokin Street. His ticket was good for another whole hour, and he rode a few stations until he sensed that the tram was going in the wrong direction, and then he stood up and got off at the next stop and stood in the street looking around him as if he were looking for a specific address, doing this very seriously, as if he were trying to convince some invisible observer, and then, still searching for the nonexistent address, he crossed the road and boarded a tram coming from the opposite direction, still stubbornly refusing to ask anyone for directions, determined to gamble on his intuition and turning it all deliberately into a gloomy game in which he was determined to persist even if it meant traveling backward and forward for hours, and he got off and took another tram, coming from a different direction, and suddenly, quite unexpectedly, the tram turned into the Rokin Street intersection and continued along Rokin Street, and at the first stop he disembarked, pleased with the success of his gamble and the sight of the familiar surroundings, and at the same time completely at a loss because he had no idea what to do next. There was something embarrassing about standing on the pavement doing nothing among the people walking busily to and from and he crossed the road to the opposite pavement, without having any reason for doing so, apart from a vague feeling that there was something about the streets on the other side of the road that would suit his present mood, and he walked aimlessly from street to street, thinking about the time stretching ahead of him until evening and imagining it as a huge pile of empty, rusty cans he had to scale since it could not be circumnavigated or reduced by a single molecule, and in the helpless despair that overcame him at the idea of all the empty time he would have to endure, second by second, he tried to remember if he had no friend or acquaintance in this town, an acquaintance of his parents, perhaps, or a family relative, however distant and estranged, but in vain, and as he dragged his feet heavily and painfully along in an aimlessness that was itself a source of bitterness and humiliation, he was overwhelmed by a sense of such hopeless desolation and impenetrable alienation and unutterable weariness—the pain in his legs had once more spread to his hips and back—that he could actually hear himself whimpering with a plaintive, helpless sound inside his head, and he stopped at an ice cream van and bought himself an ice cream and went on walking, licking the ice cream and looking at the somber buildings, which seemed to be fortified against strangers, as if they were protecting some kind of intimacy, and he thought about the happy people living inside them—for there was no doubt that they were happy, wrapped as they were in the secure, intimate warmth of their families, like a blanket woven out of the calm, rooted routines of daily life, in their old-fashioned apartments, among furniture handed down from generation to generation—and he tried to imagine what one of them, looking by chance out of the window or passing him on his way home, would think of him, a sloppy-looking foreigner, dazed by fatigue and harrowed by cold and dejection, dragging himself about with a green traveling bag on his shoulder through the streets of this Dutchman's pleasant town, and trying with the despairing vestiges of his strength to uncover the secret of their beauty and find the connection that, however hidden, must somehow exist between himself and them. If only he could exchange a few words with this invisible Dutchman, even if only in his broken English! And why, in fact, shouldn't he beckon him from the window and invite him in or stop him in the street as he came toward him—when all was said and done, he wasn't as foreign to him as the Asians and Africans—and ask him where he came from and

what he did for a living—after all, he was an engineer and he had
studied history, the history of Holland or at least of Europe, included,
and read books like *Tilleulenspeigel* and admired the paintings of
Rembrandt and Brueghel and others, not to mention the great sympathy he felt for the Dutch and that they felt for Israel—and he looked
with disguised expectation at the man coming toward him, a plainly
dressed man with a long, friendly face, and then he glanced up at the
curtained windows and said to himself that it was impossible that in
all this city of hundreds of thousands of inhabitants he did not have
one single acquaintance.

His need to be in the company of someone with whom he was
even slightly acquainted became so pressing that he was afraid he
might suddenly scream, and he went into a large, tastefully decorated
bookshop—the streets he was walking through now were busier and
more central—but the books, which he had hoped would soothe and
distract him, gave rise only to impatience and irritation, and he paged
through them distractedly, and after a few minutes he left the shop
and crossed the road and walked along the same street for a while,
imagining that he was walking in the general direction of the terminal, which was the direction he wanted to take, and after that he
turned into a pleasant little street, where he stopped to buy two pieces
of airmail letters, and crossed a small square and continued walking
along the street leading out of it, and suddenly, after walking a
considerable distance, he stopped and stood still as if sunk in thought,
and then he turned around and began walking back. The heaviness
of his body and its aching weariness were too much for him to bear,
and the earliness of the hour filled him with despair. Here and there
he imagined he could discern the first, barely perceptible intimations
of evening, only to realize immediately, to his disappointment, that
it was only an illusion created by the gray, wintry weather, and after
walking past a few more streets with the same strained, exhausted
steps, he found himself in front of a café, which judging by its
appearance and the appearance of the few people, most of them in
their thirties or forties, sitting next to the windows around simple
wooden tables with a few barrels planted with flowers scattered among

them, seemed like an especially agreeable place, exactly the kind of place he had been looking for all this time. He went inside and walked down a few steps into a little hall with a large unlit iron stove in the center of it, full of a dim brown light, and sat down at one of the clumsy wooden tables next to the wall, slipped the heavy green bag off his shoulder, and looked around him at the people sitting, eating, drinking, and quietly conversing, most of them looked like students or lecturers, and at the walls covered with comical pictures and newspaper cuttings and all kinds of notes, as well as menus illustrated with caricatures, which he tried without success to decipher, and when the waitress came up to him, an elderly woman with gray hair combed neatly back from her large peasant's face, he ordered a beer and then unfolded the aerogram on top of the Cook's brochure, and as he drank his beer in small, leisurely sips, once again exhorting himself to do everything slowly in order to attain the desired sense of idleness, and also to rest and help the time to pass, he wrote a letter to Aviva and then one to Pozner. He wrote slowly, with a hankering heart, forming the words with his lips as he wrote, as if he were speaking to them, until he noticed two young men sitting at the table next to him looking curiously in his direction and he stopped. If only he could be in Tel Aviv now, at this summer twilight hour, even if only for a single hour, and see the throngs of men and women in their light summer clothes crowding the pavements and hear their voices and catch words and sentences, snatches of conversations, exclamations, and feel the touch of the steamy, sticky air, the heavy air of the height of summer unlike anything else in the world, gradually cooling down as evening fell and mingling with the lightest of breezes, so light as to seem almost imaginary, blowing up Frishman Street from the sea. And suddenly he had the feeling that this Tel Aviv and this summer were nothing but a memory of something that had vanished forever and that he himself was an exile for life, and a terrible panic flooded him, together with bitter, heartbroken longings, which did not go away even after he told himself that it was only his imagination, and afterward, when he had finished drinking his beer and writing his letters, he went on sitting there, trying to overcome the impatience that had taken hold of him again, and looking at the people sitting at the tables and the people coming in and going out, and the pictures and slogans on the walls, and the heavy wooden tables and the black iron stove with the thick chimney, and then again at the pictures on the wall, until in the end his impatience gained the upper hand and he looked at the map and outlined his route to the post office, paid for his beer, hoisted the green bag onto his shoulder and went outside.

The first shadows of evening, delicate as cobwebs, were faintly staining the light and air, and Meir, alert as a hound scenting its prey, knew that now the evening had really begun, and when he went into the post office and turned toward the appropriate counter in the big hall thronged with people, he thought that he could see the bitter man in the elegant suit standing there in line. This time too it was difficult to see him clearly because the people in line behind him obscured the view, but Meir was sure that it was he, even surer than before, a glimpse of his profile and his shoulders was enough, and he stopped and looked around him as if he was looking for the right counter, and then he rummaged in his green bag and coat pockets as if he had just realized that he had forgotten something he needed, and turned around and left the post office and began walking without knowing where he was going, full of shame and despair, because in his eagerness for the letters to reach Aviva and Pozner immediately, without delay, he imagined them falling into their hands the moment he dropped them into the mailbox, and now his urgent need to continue his conversation with them—for he felt that he had indeed spoken to them and heard them reply, or at least seen the attentive, responsive expressions on their faces—had been frustrated by this idiotic delay, interrupting their conversation and leaving his words hanging unanswered in the air. And as he prowled the streets in the vicinity of the post office with the intention of allowing a short time to pass before going back to post the letters, and trying in vain to continue the interrupted conversation in his head, it occurred to him to take advantage of this delay in order to visit Rembrandt's house and the Portuguese Synagogue, both of which would still be open long enough for him to get there in time if he hurried, and right away, with a sudden spurt of resolution and energy, he opened the map and plotted his route and set out briskly, feeling as invigorated and renewed as if all his weariness had vanished, and he visited both Rembrandt's house and the Portuguese Synagogue, and after he had completed his mission, filled with a marvelous sense of accomplishment and duty done, he returned to the post office and sent the letters, and then he turned away and walked through the streets, empty of all desire, and waited glumly for evening to fall and save him. Although his previous crushing fatigue had returned, he preferred walking to sitting, not only because he was too impatient to sit down, but also because he wanted to tire himself out and exhaust his strength to the utmost, and as he walked, he wished that he could talk to someone, never mind whom, about the trams or the weather, never mind what, as long as he could speak real words aloud and hear real words spoken aloud in reply—he had been silent for so long that for a moment he feared that he had lost the power of speech—and once more he was wrapped in a delicate web of longings for Tel Aviv, which he suddenly saw in all its details and all its loveliness, as if he bore the essence of the city, absolutely real and unique, within him, covered with a tender summer sky with a vague, elusive radiance at its edges and a half-moon peeping out between the branches of the tall lilac bush in the next-door yard, and although the streets were still bathed in full twilight, he decided to go back to the hotel and go up to his room and go to bed, because his aimless wandering was becoming more and more depressing and humiliating, and he could no longer find a single drop of desire, or of strength either, of course, to take one more step, and he opened his map and stood on the corner and looked at the name of the street and began walking back to the post office, in order to buy himself provisions for the night in the kiosk opposite it.

Again he bought two cheese sandwiches and two pears and a bar of chocolate, exactly what he had bought the day before, and for the sake of variety he added a candy bar made of nuts, and as he packed it all into his green bag, he felt an agreeable limpness and a ticklish feeling of satisfaction, because it was now quite obvious to him that his stay in Amsterdam was coming to an end, and he turned away and set off for Rokin Street and the hotel, but then he digressed and took a roundabout way, for he suddenly felt a wish to postpone the end, put it off a little longer, and he turned into a street that he sensed was parallel to Rokin Street and walked along it, as the daylight dimmed and the streets grew emptier and quieter, until he reached a little triangular park, a kind of broadening of the pavement and the street, with a few tall trees and benches in it. Very close by, just beyond the park and the pavement, was a hotel, not very large but very grand in an old-fashioned way, and he paused for a moment to look at it and then advanced into the park and sat down at the end of a bench whose other end was occupied by a boy of about sixteen or seventeen sitting and reading a book in the grayish-white twilight, and he took the green bag off his sweating, aching shoulder and looked at the facade of the hotel with its splendid, palatial balconies and its heavily draped windows and the massive front door made of wood with bronze decorations, and the tall, leafy trees deepening the twilight shade in the profound stillness and calm, and from time to time he glanced at the boy, very discreetly and with a hidden wish to express affection and the desire for closeness, and in a final flutter of vitality after he had already acknowledged defeat, he felt a faint tremor of desire to make one more effort to enjoy his stay here, mainly for the sake of knowing that he had indeed visited the city and enjoyed his visit, and at that moment a luxurious black limousine drew up outside the hotel and three men in elegant dark suits got out of it, he could see them quite clearly from where he was sitting, and by their appearance and gestures and gait he guessed that they were Arabs, and he said to himself that they must be sheiks from one of the Persian Gulf states, and when they went into the hotel and disappeared behind the heavy wooden door he said to himself that it was clearly a hotel for rich Arabs, and after what seemed to him a very long time during which he sat without moving, looking calmly in front of him, he overcame his hesitations and turned to the boy, they were alone in the darkening park, and asked him in English if he was from Amsterdam, keeping his voice as casual as possible, and the boy answered, "Yes. I came here with my parents when I was small," and he mentioned the name of the place they had come from, but Meir could not catch it, and he asked the boy what kind of a place it was, and the boy said that it was a large village not far from Amsterdam. From the start he was friendly and open and Meir felt very grateful to him, but he suppressed his feelings in order not to make the boy suspicious and asked him what he did in Amsterdam—he would have asked any question in the world, never mind how pointless, it was perfectly obvious that the boy was a student—in order to keep the conversation going, and the boy said that he was studying at a business college, and Meir told him that he spoke English well, and the boy smiled shyly and said that he liked languages and closed his book. Slowly but surely the dusk was thickening in the darkening foliage of the trees, although the street in front of the park was still bathed in the same gray twilight, and Meir told the boy that he was from Israel, and the boy said that he had heard of it, and Meir, in whom these words for some reason gave rise to a feeling of happiness and closeness and sharing, asked him how the people of Amsterdam could tolerate the thousands of wild, filthy tourists filling the center of their city, and the boy said that the people of Amsterdam were very tolerant, and besides they themselves did not usually come across them because they lived and worked in other parts of the town, and Meir said, "I'm a tourist, and I can't stand it. It's awful," and the boy smiled, his face already a little blurred in the dusk, and said, "A lot of people here earn their living from tourism," and Meir said, "Yes, I understand. But still, it's really awful," and he felt a fanatical, bitter animosity toward the vagabond rabble, as if there was something about them that threatened him personally, and the boy seemed to feel that it was up to him to apologize on someone's behalf, and he said that in two or three months' time when it grew cold most of them would leave the city, and he put his book into the briefcase next to him and stood up, and Meir stood up with him and hoisted the green bag onto his shoulder and said that he had to go to Rokin Street and the boy said that he was going in that direction himself, and they set off slowly side by side, so that from a distance they might have been mistaken for a pair of friends or a father and son, and when they reached the Rokin Street intersection by the archway with the bell tower, they parted with a friendly handshake, and the boy sprang over the iron railings and ran lightly across the road, where the traffic at this hour was heavy, and Meir stood watching him affectionately, as if he really were his son, and also gratefully, until he disappeared from view. He saw the bright lights of a movie theater in the street opposite him, a little way past the sex shop, and for a moment he thought of going into one of the black-curtained booths and watching a pornographic movie, which was one of the things he had promised himself he would do in Amsterdam, but he turned left instead and crossed a little street and then he crossed the intersection in the direction of the canal with the white boat house on the opposite bank, and even though the grayish twilight was still as bright as before, he decided to return to the hotel and go up to his room and by so doing to finally put an end to his visit to Amsterdam—if only it had been dark already he would have done so with a lighter heart—since he had already concluded it inside himself anyway and there was nothing else he wanted to see, except for the prostitutes in the windows, but he had already relinquished that desire, too, and he walked along the canal, hugging the iron fence, on his way back to the hotel, and as he walked he looked at the white boat house, in which the lights had already gone on, and at the tourists huddling on the little platform on top of the stairs and descending one by one with wary, hesitant steps to the boat, which was festooned with bright, gay lights.

He looked at them without any particular interest, as if from far away, and felt relief spreading through him and covering him luxuriously like warm, soft down at the thought that in another few minutes it would all be over, and afterward he passed a small Middle Eastern restaurant that was full of people, with a characteristic smell of grilled meat rising in the air, and he continued walking past the somber buildings, but the closer he came to the hotel the more he dragged his feet because the twilight, with its jellied gray-white light, went on shining stubbornly without getting any darker. Somewhere not far off life began to stir in anticipation of the night, as if it were somehow being born out of the restless tumult of the twilight, which would soon fade, and as he sensed these hidden stirrings he knew that the moment he entered the hotel he would set the final, irreversible seal on the failure of his visit to Amsterdam, and all because of his refusal to book a room through the airport as soon as he arrived, and especially because he lacked the talent for life possessed by Pozner, for example, or the Turkish moving man, who without any doubt, would have gone to take a shower now and changed his clothes and gone out to a restaurant, probably with some sexy girl he would have found for himself, perhaps the waitress with the provocative bosom or some liberated, adventurous Dutch or American girl, and later he would probably have gone to a movie and after the movie to the "dirty district" to enjoy himself there till late at night, going into nightclubs and getting friendly with some girl and making love to her, and at dawn he would have invited someone, a whore, perhaps, or even two, or the girl he met in the nightclub, to go back to his hotel room with him, and although Meir too now felt a desire to turn right into the narrow street and then left, and continue to the "dirty district," with only one block of buildings separating him from the hotel, he gave in and resigned himself and abandoned himself utterly to the exhaustion of his strength and will, but when he reached the hotel porch he went on walking, as if absentmindedly, until he reached the Dam, where the square and the buildings around it were still bathed in the same frozen radiance. If only it would get dark already, his surrender would not be so conspicuous and painful, but the pale, murky twilight went on shining frostily, and watching it vigilantly with owlish eyes, he turned right into one of the alleys, and after a while right again, and entered a narrow street where it seemed to him that the light was indeed growing somewhat weaker and darker, but in the end his attempts at observing and discerning confused him to such an extent that he could not make up his mind whether it was in fact the light that was fading and growing darker, or whether the darkness was caused by shadows owing to the narrowness of the street and the height of the gloomy buildings surrounding it, and he decided to stop thinking about the light because there was no point in wearing himself out with fruitless endeavors and also because he wanted to give himself a pleasant surprise when he suddenly realized, after walking a few more blocks, that darkness had fallen. And when after a while he turned right again, by now his legs and feet were nothing but malignant lumps of terrible, aching tiredness, and entered the Dam again, this time from a different direction, he saw that the light had indeed faded and dimmed, but not as much as he had anticipated, and he turned into Rokin Street and started walking toward the intersection, and when he reached the hotel, he stopped and leaned against the wall of a building, and stood without moving, stiff with stubbornness and lacking in any desire save the desire to see darkness fall, and looked at the hotel on the other side of the street, where a very faint, murky light on the point of dying was still clinging to the ugly facade with tireless obstinacy, until he felt that it would go on forever. And a sullen rebelliousness, hostile and obdurate, which was nothing but the last, helpless flutter of his broken will and sense of defeat and wretchedness, clenched inside him into the decision that he would stand without moving against this wall, with the heavy green bag on his shoulder, and go on standing there for a thousand years if need be, until the light faded and was swallowed up without a trace in the dark.

And then, very slowly and imperceptibly, he saw the light grow dim and softly shadowed, but it was still light, and then dull and darken as the spotlights of the boat house on his right grew brighter, and in the end darkness fell, and then he waited a few minutes more without moving, as if he wanted to make sure beyond a shadow of a doubt that the darkness was indeed complete, and confirm his victory, and then he moved away and crossed the street and went up the few steps to the hotel porch and entered the long, narrow passage with the dark landscapes, which the yellow light of the lamps illuminated together with the passage in all its depressing meanness, and he said to himself that his visit to Amsterdam was over. He said this firmly, word by word, and in the midst of the gloom and oppression he felt a profound relief, and he smiled warmly in response to a smile full of goodwill from the fat American girl, who was standing at the reception desk, apparently in the middle of arranging something, and asked her almost gaily how she was and how she was enjoying her stay, and she said that she was very well, and told him in schoolgirlish detail about the visit she and her parents had paid to Leyden and The Hague. They had hired a car and her mother drove most of the way, and he listened with little nods and looked at her pink whipped-cream face and her shapeless breasts and her body somehow squeezed into pants, how ridiculous and pitiful she looked in them, and thought about how he should invite her to come up to his room, whether to take her by surprise in the middle of her story or wait until she was finished, which seemed more logical to him, and whether to do it directly or by hints, which was the real problem, and the truth was that he was waiting for a hint from her, even the faintest and most indirect, but she went on telling him about the fabulous flower fields and the palaces, which America had nothing to equal, and then she told him about some ancient church with stained-glass windows, which she described as punctiliously as a conscientious schoolgirl taking a test, until he despairingly realized that she wasn't going to drop any hints because nothing was further from her mind, and that he wasn't going to make her any propositions either because he wasn't prepared to make a fool of himself and he didn't possess even a scrap of the impudent boldness he so admired, and which sometimes, here and there, he felt existed in him in spite of everything, gathering inside him and coming to a head and about to burst the bonds of false morality and consideration and the obstacles of cowardice and emerge into the light of day, juicy and wild, and in the end he took advantage of a moment's distraction and said good night and walked heavily up the steep wooden stairs, whose disagreeable dimness was only emphasized by the weak electric light, consoling himself with the thought that this would be the next to last time he would ever tread them again, and when he entered the ugly room on the fourth floor, in which he had spent only two or three minutes up to now, and shut the door behind him, he was flooded with an immeasurably profound relief, that sense of grace that comes to those who have given up entirely, until the surrender itself becomes the greatest and happiest victory of all.

The fat American girl had vanished from his thoughts even

before he reached the first floor, and as for the bitter man in the
elegant suit, he spared him not more than a passing, indifferent
thought as he crossed the lobby of the third floor, and the same went
for the feeling that all the residents of the hotel except him had gone
out to enjoy themselves, and after slipping the heavy green bag from
his shoulder and locking the door and leaning the chair against it,
which he did by now as a matter of routine, and washing at the basin,
and arranging the food he had bought for the night on the second
chair, next to the bed, and getting into bed with the map of the city
and the Cook's Tours brochure, and luxuriating in the touch of the
clean, stiffly ironed sheets, a great joy spread through all his body and
soul, too great to contain, tickling him and quivering inside him like
a peal of merry, irrepressible, childish laughter, and he dropped his
head onto his chest and drew up his legs and, full of happiness and
glee, rocked himself to and fro under the blanket and laughed in
delight. And after he had composed himself, but still flooded with
pleasure and delight, he ate his food and looked at the map of the city
spread out like a fan with its streets and parks and canals, all of them
engraved in his mind and familiar to him as if he had known them
for years, and he let his eyes skim over it for a while without any focus,
and then he followed the busy road leading from the terminal, it was
here that the town began as far as he was concerned, and continued
along Rokin Street, and turned at the intersection and slipped along
the Amstel, and paused a moment and retreated and located Sarphati
Street, and the street by which he had reached it, beginning at the
big dumping ground full of rusting junk, shortly after which he had
been caught in the rain, which had suddenly started coming down so
hard that it had forced him to quicken his steps, and then a little after
the big bridge, which he located with ease on the map, forced him
to run, until he took shelter under the jutting roof, close to the door
of the office, he remembered the desolation of the street vividly and
precisely and the wetness of the air and the cold and the smell of the
rain falling and making everything misty and blurred, and he racked
his brains in the attempt to remember and decide if Sarphati had
really been a statesman or something else, and skipped from there to

the Stedelijk and the Rijksmuseum, which he connected by means of
the park at the back of the Rijks steeped in its perfect, celestial peace,
at any rate that was the way he remembered it, and he skipped lightly
from there to the places that, according to the map, gave him an
impression of pleasantness and prosperity, and wondered why it had
never occurred to him to visit them, or for that matter the big park
that hit him in the eye every time he opened the map—the cheese
sandwich was delicious, even more so than the day before, and he
congratulated himself on buying two, and brought his eyes back to the
center, to the vicinity of the Rokin intersection, where he felt at
home, and looked slightly to the side and located the little street in
the area to the east of the post office, where standing tired and gloomy
on the neighborhood bridge and looking up the narrow canal in the
direction of the harbor he had seen the view open up in a marvelous
perspective of leafy trees and dark houses with the evening sky spread
out above them and sloping like the sides of a gigantic tent all the way
to the invisible borders of the town. He took the second sandwich and
bit into it with relish and quickly and easily located Rembrandt's
house and the Portuguese Synagogue, now he was glad that he had
visited them, and crossed Rokin Street again and located the Amsterdam Historical Museum, which was very close to the intersection and
the hotel, but he did not feel the least regret at not having visited it,
just as he felt no regret about the other places he had intended visiting
and not visited, the Van Gogh Museum and the zoo. Even his failure
to see the prostitutes in the windows in the "dirty district" gave rise
to no more than a moment's uneasiness, for by now, less than an hour
after shutting himself in his room and, to tell the truth, perhaps from
the moment he had entered it, he had left the town where he had
wandered so restlessly and aimlessly for three days behind him and
traveled thousands of kilometers away from it and its atmosphere and
sights—the streets and the leafy trees and the canals and bridges and
Rembrandt's house and the Portuguese Synagogue and the post office
and the pleasant streets to the west or east of Rokin Street and the
sex shop, with its shelves and stands full of pornographic magazines
and its black-curtained booths, and the trams sliding monotonously

past and the market—yes, far from the charming market, too, and from the fat American girl, who had remained standing by the desk and perhaps was still waiting there now for him to come back and invite her out, and from the waitress in the intimate café with the neatly combed reddish hair, God knows where she had suddenly popped up from, with her pale, sexless face whose features had vanished from his memory as completely as if she didn't have a face at all, and from the bitter man in the elegant suit, he too—all of them now seemed so remote and dim that for a moment he wondered if he had really seen them at all, he felt as if he was his own double looking, in decades or centuries to come, at the iron statue in the Stedelijk Museum, dispersing its waters with endlessly repetitive movements against the background of the rainy gray sky, and afterward he turned onto his other side and paged through the Cook's Tours brochure, and as he ate the chocolate—he had decided to keep the pears for later—he thought that on his next visit to Holland, if it ever took place, he would choose the tour to Alkmaar, "the wonderful background to the famous and picturesque cheese market," as it said in the brochure, and the ancient cobbled square and the wooden stretchers with the gigantic rounds of cheese like millstones in the picture did indeed look very appealing, and he would also choose the tour to The Hague and Delft, after all The Hague was the royal capital and he had heard that it was full of beautiful ancient palaces, and he turned the page and glanced at the bright, alluring colors of the flowers and the little brook flowing under the pretty wooden bridge and thought that perhaps he would also choose the tour to the bulb fields of Keukenhof, "where as far as the eye can see the fields are one magic carpet of crocuses and hyacinths and tulips, blazing in a joyous burst of color," and he listened attentively to the sound of footsteps coming up the stairs while his eyes rested motionless on the red and orange and yellow flowers and the blue water of the brook with the pretty wooden bridge, until the footsteps were swallowed up somewhere on the floor below and silence reigned again.

In the morning, after shaving and changing and packing and eating breakfast, which he enjoyed more than on the previous days, he left his suitcase with the receptionist and went out for a stroll in the surrounding streets, since he still had a few hours to spare and he had decided to take advantage of them for a farewell stroll through the streets that had left a particularly pleasant impression on him. It was a lovely Saturday morning and he felt fresher and more relaxed than he had felt since arriving in Amsterdam, and after two hours of a pleasant stroll, mostly in the streets to the east and west of Rokin Street, he returned to the hotel and settled his bill and picked up the suitcase and took one last look at the cramped lobby and the passage with the dark landscapes and the little porch, from which he surveyed Rokin Street as far as the intersection and the archway with the bell tower for a moment, and then walked to the tram stop and rode to the terminal, and early in the afternoon he flew to London, and a few hours later, on a cool but rainless evening, he arrived at the home of his friends, who had taken a room with bed and breakfast for him not far from Euston Road Station.

The next morning, it was a Sunday, Meir rose early and immediately got up and got dressed, feeling confined in the closed room and eager to get out and see the town, and after eating something and drinking a cup of tea he set out and walked along Euston Road, and then turned into Tottenham Court Road and Oxford Street, walking at a leisurely pace with his hands in his pockets and the map of London under his arm as he surveyed the heavy buildings and shop windows. The tranquillity of the almost deserted streets and the pleasant nip in the air gave him a sense of peace and even of suppressed joy, and even reading the names of the streets and shops, which presented no problems and which he began to do compulsively, was a source of extraordinary pleasure, but at the same time and in the midst of all this, like the mild after-effects of a passing illness, he went on sensing the restless malaise and distraction from which he imagined that he had recovered completely the moment he arrived in London and met his friends. He stood on the corner of Oxford Street for a moment and looked around him, and then he consulted his map and at the same leisurely pace walked to Hyde Park, and at about noon—he had arranged to have lunch with his friends at a

Chinese restaurant—he began walking back and stopped on the way at Regent Street Church, where he stood outside the door for a while listening to the sermon being preached by the priest to his well-dressed congregation on Jonah in the belly of the whale on closed-circuit television.

Lunch, which was surprisingly delicious and was eaten in an atmosphere of lighthearted gaiety, finished late, and when it was over Meir felt a great weariness and the same distraction again, with everything happening around him losing its clarity and vitality, as if it was taking place at a distance and behind a dull barrier of fog, but he said to himself that all this was a consequence of the tiredness and tension of his first day in London, and so he did not go back to his room to rest—he felt a profound unwillingness to be alone—but went home with his friends and spent the rest of the day and the evening with them. At half past eight in the morning, as he had planned the day before, he was already on his way to the National Theatre to buy tickets for the performance that night and for two additional performances. He went by foot, both for pleasure and as part of his sightseeing program in the town, and as he walked he felt fresh and full of energy and even elation, because there was something exhilarating in the wakening streets of this huge city and in the fine, cool weather and, of course, in the wonderful program of sightseeing that awaited him, but at the same time, as if to spite him, something of the dull tension and distraction remained like shadow accompanying him from the moment he got up in the morning and clinging to him stubbornly except for a few minutes at a time. On the corner of Oxford Street he stopped for a moment and consulted his map, and then he continued along Charing Cross Road, reading the names of all the streets on the way with enjoyment, to the Strand, where he turned onto Waterloo Bridge, and although he was in a hurry to get to the theater because he had a full schedule planned for the morning, he lingered on it for a while, gazing at the river and the heavy buildings on both banks, and then he hurried off again, but when he reached the National Theatre he discovered that there was already a line in front of the box office, which was still shut, and although the line was not a long one, only about twenty people altogether, he felt disappointed and sorry that he had not set out half an hour or even an hour earlier, and also worried that he might not get good tickets and that he might have to spend a long time standing in line and that his plans for the morning would be spoiled. For a moment he thought sulkily of going away and coming back the next morning at an earlier hour, but instead he got in line and tried to dispel his anxiety and disappointment by calmly contemplating the river and the white buildings on the opposite bank and by studying the map and working out the route for his morning's sightseeing. On the advice of his friends he planned, after buying the tickets, to walk along Victoria embankment to the Houses of Parliament and Westminster Abbey and return through Trafalgar Square and the National Gallery, and as he followed the route on the map, he put his hand in his pocket and discovered that in his rush to get out of the house in the morning he had forgotten his money in the pocket of his other trousers, and he was immediately plunged into terrible gloom and despair, mingled with bitter rage against himself and the world in general—all he wanted was to be transported at that very minute to his own house in Tel Aviv, and as he rummaged distractedly through his pockets in a turmoil of bitter emotions and panicky thoughts, he tried to decide what to do: for a moment he thought of trying to enlist the help of one of the people standing in line and the next he thought of explaining his predicament to the ticket seller and leaving something with him as a deposit, but the distinct feeling that he was a stranger to them and they were strangers to him, and even the fact that he was not as fluent in English as he was in Hebrew, made him dismiss these ideas, and in the end, his heart seething with despair and humiliation and a burning feeling of injustice, he left the line and, walking fast, almost running—he wanted to get back before the box office opened —he recrossed Waterloo Bridge and the Strand in order to change a traveler's check for a hundred dollars at a bank. Luckily, he had his traveler's checks with him, but when he got there he discovered to his dismay that the banks opened at ten, and after running from bank to bank, unable to resign himself to this stroke of malice, he was

obliged to overcome his furious despair and give up, and he stood
sweating and defeated outside the locked doors of Barclays Bank,
waiting for them to open together with some other people, who
seemed astonishingly calm and composed, without a trace of the
morning's energy and happiness left, trying to cheer himself up by
logical exhortations but all in vain: his despair and feeling of insult
deepened and with them the feeling that his whole visit to London,
never mind his plans for that day, was ruined.

And like an ill omen he experienced again, more distinctly, the
restless malaise, and after it the distraction and the feeling that something inside him was growing dull and he was becoming detached
from himself and his surroundings, and being enveloped in a balloon
of gray, porous air separating him from something in which he was
floating, like a dead embryo being detached from the placenta. After
buying the tickets, which he obtained without any difficulty, there was
only one person in front of him in line, he went back to Waterloo
Bridge on his way to Victoria and the Houses of Parliament, and in
the middle of the bridge he stopped and leaned against the railing and
looked intently at the river, whose gray water seemed almost motionless, and at the imperial buildings on both its banks, everything looked
so stable and enduring, and in this lingering contemplation he tried
to recapture the calm composure and the pleasure, if not the elation,
he had felt that morning when he left the house, but to no avail—
the dull, nagging worry and distraction did not leave him, nor the
malignant sense that everything was spoiled, and in addition to the
foregoing he was perspiring freely, apparently because of an unpleasant humidity in the cool air, which made him feel sticky and dirty,
and he wished that he could take a shower, and before tearing himself
away from the railing and beginning to walk, he took off his jacket
and folded it over his arm. At the end of the bridge, before turning
onto Victoria embankment, he decided finally to give up his program
for that morning's sightseeing—in any case, everything was spoiled
and ruined beyond redemption—and pay a visit to the British Museum instead, since the museum was on the way to his boardinghouse
and he had intended visiting it anyway, but when he reached South-

ampton he changed his mind and decided to go to Foyle's, which according to the map was not far off, and buy the book that Pozner had requested. The shop was packed with people, and Meir took a few steps between the stands on the first floor and then stopped and looked uncertainly around him, the press of people and books, and perhaps the stifling heat, too, which was worse here than outside, had made him feel faint the moment he entered the shop, and then he recovered and asked one of the salesmen where he could find books on geophysics, and he went up to the third floor, with the same feeling of strangeness and uncertainty, went straight to the shelves marked "Geophysics," and immediately, with frantic haste, as if someone were chasing him, began looking for the book. He skimmed quickly over the titles of the books at his eye level and took one out and held it in his hand, the sheer number of books gave rise in him to a feeling of panic and obscure anxiety, and with the book in his hand he skipped a few rows and bent down and began scanning the titles of the books on the bottom shelf, his face sweating and his spectacles misting over, and took out a book, not the one Pozner had asked for, and stood up to wipe his face and spectacles, and as he did so he felt the floor move and slip away from under his feet.

He leaned against the shelves and looked around him anxiously, waiting for the feeling to pass, but the movement, which seemed to him for a moment to be steadying, did not stop, and it was joined by a feeling that his limbs were becoming thick and heavy, and concentrating with growing anxiety on the movement of the floor and the lightness draining out of his limbs, he walked slowly, dragging his feet as best he could, to the desk of the person in charge of the department. Everything around him and inside him had suddenly receded into the distance and everything was happening with a maddening slowness and dullness, and he told the man at the desk that he wasn't feeling well and asked him if he could have a drink of water, he felt as if his face was rigidly encased in a shell of dry, taunt skin with two eyes staring frozenly out of it, and his voice, too, came out of his mouth with the same terrible slowness and sounded as hollow as if it were coming out of clay pipes in the depths of the earth. The salesman, a slender young man dressed with sporty elegance, who seemed embarrassed and put out, made a slight face, it was a handsome European face with delicately flushed cheeks, and said with a chilly politeness and reserve in which the disapproval was very evident, that there was no water here, but Meir, still holding on somehow to the two books, had already seated himself heavily on a chair two or three steps away, on the other side of the desk, because his feet, which had turned into two clods of gray earth, were incapable of bearing him, and he repeated in the same hollow voice that he felt ill and would like a drink of water, and the salesman, who had apparently resigned himself to the seriousness of the situation and the fact that he wouldn't be able to get out of it without doing something, turned away with obvious annoyance and hurried to the floor manager, who was sitting behind a large desk some distance away. Meir, who remained seated on the chair feeling his face growing stiffer and more numb and gray, contemplated them as if through a band of gray air surrounding him and separating him from everything around him, and felt a dull anxiety welling up inside him as he saw them whispering to each other and the young salesman pointing at him repeatedly, which he found very disagreeable, while the manager stared at him appraisingly, which he also found very disagreeable, but he nodded slightly in his direction, as if to confirm and reinforce what the young salesman was saying, although he couldn't hear a word of it, and also confirm the fact that it was him he was talking about, and after a few minutes the salesman appeared with a glass of water, and he thanked him with a nod, his lips were frozen and he couldn't move them, and took the glass with a heavy, lifeless hand and with a very slow movement lifted it to his mouth and drank. And afterward, with the same awful slowness, he put it down on the desk and went on sitting in the chair and waiting for the bad feeling to pass, while the young salesman and a few of the customers, and also the floor manager, stole curious glances at him and waited for him to get up and walk away, but he went on sitting there because the bad feeling did not pass, for a moment it seemed to him that it was passing but instead it grew worse, and as he sat there full of anxiety and completely absorbed in his body, out of which something was rapidly draining away, the books slipped out of his hand one after the other and he watched them slipping, one of them fell on the floor and the other remained hanging from his hand, and he wanted to stop them but he couldn't because he could no longer control his will or his fingers, which were numb and stiff, like his legs, which had grown bloated and gray, at any rate that was how he felt, and like his face, which had not only hardened, with the skin turning to stiff parchment, but which he could sense had also turned gray, and with it the envelope of air surrounding it. He looked at the young salesman, who looked back at him unwillingly, as if by accident, there was something cold and full of demonstrative distaste in his look, and in a half confessional and half pleading tone, the anxiety had already flooded him and filled his chest, he said that there was something wrong with him, and the young salesman nodded his head and busied himself stubbornly with the papers on his desk, and Meir repeated that there was something wrong with him and concentrated his attention on what was happening inside him, and he felt that whatever vitality was still left in his body was dissolving and draining out of him without anyone being able to stop it, like quivering air escaping through tiny invisible holes, and that everything was emptying out of him, and at the bottom of his dazed, panic-stricken mind he suddenly knew that he was going to die from a stroke, which he had suffered when he bent down to the bottom shelf, he knew this with an absolute certainty, unsoftened by any shadow of a doubt, and he said to himself that he should never have bent down like that, and at the same time he felt his breath growing cold, he felt the cold in his nostrils and on his upper lip, and the tips of his fingers too, and he turned to the salesman and said, "I am dying," and the young salesman, who was doing everything in his power to ignore Meir and everything that was happening, and thus to obliterate or at least obscure the event that was causing so much embarrassment to himself and his customers, said, "No, no. You're okay," stubbornly refusing to look at him and rummaging through the papers in front of him with an appearance of calm indifference, and Meir said, "I am dying, really," his cold breath and the coldness at the tips of his fingers left no room for doubt in his heart, and the young salesman said, "No, no," and hurried over to the floor manager. Meir sat without moving like a porous statue, the book dangling limply from his fingers, and felt how, as the cold spread through him, everything was fading and growing white—his face, his body, his breath, the air surrounding him —and at the same time he watched the salesman and the floor manager with a frozen look and saw them whispering to each other while the customers clustered here and there looked at him furtively and a movement of subdued panic stirred around him, and he said to himself that he should never have bent down to the bottom shelf, and then the young salesman came back, and hardly looking at him, he said that an ambulance would be arriving directly, and busied himself with his papers again and Meir said, "It's not necessary. It won't help. I am dying," the words coming out of his mouth slowly and clumsily and as if they were wrapped in fog, and for some reason he stood up with the book still somehow clasped weakly in his hand, as if it had been forgotten there. The young salesman raised his eyes from his papers and stared at him for a moment in anger and alarm, and then, after a distraught look at the other customers, he turned to him, still without looking at him directly, and asked him curtly, with barely suppressed hostility, to sit down and wait for the ambulance, but Meir, an inexplicable spirit of rebellion stirring within him, went on standing and said, "No. I want to stand," and he repeated this even after the young salesman, keeping his eyes on his papers, asked him again, in the same lowered voice, full of hostility, to sit down, and in his clumsy, uninflected voice he said, "I am dying. It's finished. I know. The blood pipes in my head have been splitted. I am becoming cold. In few minutes I'll be dead," and the salesman said, "Please sit down. They'll be here in a few minutes," and Meir said, "It's finished," and after a minute he said, "I should not bend my head so low. I know it. It was a mistake," and he fell silent and attended to what was happening inside his body and sensed quite clearly how death was overpowering him—the lighted area inside him was diminishing from minute to minute and everything was growing gray and black, and in the midst of his terrifying, nightmarish helplessness, with the strange surroundings making everything worse, he knew that he had only a few more minutes to live. Somewhere deep down, as if at the bottom of a big pile of earth and stones, he felt piteous, childish tears welling up unrestrainedly, his tears but at the same time already detached from him, and he turned to the young salesman, and in a voice that seemed to him like a cloud of dry smoke he said, "I have two children and I love them," and then he added, "I love my wife," and the young salesman, still without looking at him but with a somewhat gentler note in his voice, said, "Sit down, please. Everything will be all right," and Meir said, "It's finished. It's too late," and the young salesman gave him a pleading look and said, "The ambulance will be here in a minute, please sit down," but Meir shook his head, or at least that is what he intended to do, the panic had filled up every inch of his soul and frozen there, as if something inside him had resigned itself to the end, and he said, "It will not help," and then he said, "I am an engineer," and tried to look around him, and with the dread congealing in his numb, bloated body he felt as if he were imprisoned in a bubble closing him off and separating him from the world and the movement of life stirring around him, and he repeated, "I am an engineer," as if he hoped that this might make some difference, and then he said, "I have some projects to finish. I am from Israel," for some reason he wanted to ingratiate himself with the young salesman, but not with any ulterior motive in mind, he was beyond such things now, and he added, "I have two children and I am dying." The strangeness of the people around him, which seemed particularly impenetrable and oppressive now, and the thought that he was doomed to spend these final moments in a strange place surrounded by strangers, none of whom could possibly know him or his parents or someone who knew him or had even heard his name, made his feel desperately depressed, and the young salesman said, "Please sit down," and Meir said, "It will not help. The blood pipes in my head have been splitted. It's finished. I know it," and he heard his voice thickening and crumbling and sensed how he himself was receding into the distance and growing vague and indistinct, and suddenly for no reason at all, he sat down heavily on his chair. And while he sat there staring vaguely in front of him and hazily soaking up the sight of the people standing and looking at him, and the young salesman sitting and rummaging through his papers, and the crammed bookshelves, and waiting for death, the two ambulance men appeared, he recognized them by their uniforms and the way the people made way for them, and after exchanging a few words with the young salesman the younger one approached him and held his hand and took his pulse, while the older one got the folding wheelchair they had brought with them ready, and Meir watched them with resigned indifference, for he could see no point in these activities and he had already accepted the fact that he was going to die within a few minutes, and he said, "It's no use. My blood pipes in my head have been splitted. I am finished, I know it," but the older man, who was stocky and broad-shouldered like a wrestler, smiled with his heavy face full of human warmth and said, "You'll be all right. Don't worry," there was something about his sturdy figure and skillful, unhurried movements that inspired confidence, and a weak spark of hope flickered in Meir's heart, but it immediately died down again because the fact of his death within the next few minutes was already an unquestionable certainty as far as he was concerned, and he said, "My blood is running out of my blood pipes. I feel it. I have only a few minutes to live," and the older man, his face full of kindness and humanity, said, "You're all right, believe me," and supported him with his strong hands, and together with the younger man, who had finished making his tests and returned his instruments to his bag, he transferred him to the wheelchair and the two of them pushed him rapidly to the elevator, and with the curious crowd that had gathered in the street looking on, they lifted him into the ambulance and took him to the hospital with the siren wailing loudly.

In the hospital they put him to bed in a quiet corner of the corridor, and after the initial examination by a nurse he was examined by a young doctor, who took his blood pressure and listened to his heart and tested his reflexes and his control over his limbs, and at the end of the examination told him that apart from a slight rise in blood pressure and perhaps a certain slowness in his reactions, which would certainly pass, all of which were apparently the results of tension and tiredness, he couldn't find anything wrong with him and he could get up and leave the hospital as soon as he liked, and Meir felt how somewhere deep down, in the melting fog of his anxiety, in the place where the tears had welled up earlier, a lump of knots was coming undone and loosening with a sensation of happy, grateful sobs, as if at this moment and thanks to the doctor's words he had been saved from death, and he nodded his head and the doctor rose from the edge of his bed where he had been sitting, polite and matter-of-fact, no more than that, and before turning away he remarked ironically that London was too big a mouthful to swallow whole in three days, and he gave him a slight smile and disappeared into one of the rooms leading out of the corridor.

Meir lay in bed for a while, feeling very lethargic and still suffering from a peculiar sense of dullness, and afterward, when it seemed to him that he had calmed down a bit and recovered his strength, he tried to get out of bed, but he found it difficult to control his body, as if his will, which had dulled and disappeared into a fog of panic, had been cut off from his limbs. And thus, after lowering one foot and placing it on the floor he could not lower the other one, and it remained lying on the bed, and he sat looking at his leg as if it belonged to a stranger, and it was only after looking at it for some time in panic and bewilderment that he succeeded, by straining all his scattered resources, in commanding his hands to take hold of his leg and lower it to the floor. And then he struggled for a long time with his clothes: he experienced great difficulty in putting his feet into the right trouser legs and his hands into the right sleeves and it was only with difficulty and the help of confused maneuvers that he managed his zipper and buttons; his shoes presented a particular difficulty, and he struggled with them so long and with such an alarming lack of success that he almost burst into tears of rage and despair, for again and again, against his will, he held the shoe back to front and tried to put his toes into the heel, and again and again, against his will, he tried to put his right shoe on his left foot, and a number of times he couldn't let go of the shoe even when he wanted to, until he was afraid that his brain had been irreversibly damaged.

When Meir emerged with uncertain steps from the hospital, the busy street was already sunk in a gray-brown dusk, and he stood on the pavement plunged in profound confusion and gloom, and with the panic-stricken sensation that he was suffering from a general disorder affecting his body and brain and that this was evident in his expression and movements and also in something emanating from him and surrounding him with a thick, heavy cloud—even his clothes, so he felt, had a particularly slovenly appearance, but it was beyond his strength to pull them straight, and he looked around him and tried to decide what to do next, glancing as he did so at the strange people thronging the pavement, who all seemed to him to be looking at him suspiciously, since the disorder was stamped on his dull face and surrounded him like a leaden shell. And in order to erase this impression he, too, began to walk slowly, trying to make himself as inconspicuous as possible, and to decide what to do next and how to get from here to his friends' house, but on no account could he connect one thought to the other, and in addition to this he felt terribly tired, his legs trembled with weakness, and he raised his hand and stopped a cab and got in and sat down, and after the driver had asked him twice where he wanted to go he gave him the address and sank back comfortably into the seat and exhorted himself to relax and looked out with a frozen face at the people and the cars and the buildings, all the sights he had been so eager to see, but nothing stirred inside him, where everything had frozen and sunk into a profound apathy, like stagnant water in a pond covered with green slime and dead leaves, and thus, lifeless and empty, the sights seeped through the grayish-brown haze surrounding him and were absorbed by his hollow eyes.

After what seemed to him an amazingly short time—the motion of the car soothed him slightly and he would have been prepared to go on driving forever—the cab stopped in front of his friends' house and Meir went on sitting there even though he knew that they had arrived and he had to get out, and then, after a delay which seemed to him so long that the driver was getting impatient, he leaned slightly forward in order to get out, but he experienced difficulty in stretching his hand out to open the door since his hand refused to obey him, and in the end he reached out with the other hand and laboriously and clumsily opened the door and stepped onto the pavement and went around to the front window—it seemed to him that the driver was staring at him curiously—and pushed his hand into his pocket and took out a bill. Every action of this kind cost him a great effort and strained all his mental resources, but he did not succeed in giving the bill to the driver, for his fingers refused to open and went on stubbornly clinging to the money, like they had done before with his shoe, until he was obliged to pry it out of them with his other hand and give it to the driver, who from the beginning of the trip, or so it seemed to Meir, had been watching him suspiciously because there was something obviously and strikingly wrong with him, which he was straining every nerve to blur and hide, but in vain. And then he took the change, and without counting it, he felt that every additional action would only betray him further, he dropped it into his pocket and said, "Thank you, sir," and the driver waved his hand and drove off, but Meir remained standing on the pavement and listening to the sound of his own voice, which seemed to be still suspended in the gray twilight air, and it sounded very odd and strange to him and he said, "Thank you sir," again and listened anxiously for a moment, and then he said, "I like London," and the voice indeed was not his voice but the voice of a stranger somehow emerging from his throat, and he turned away and walked deep in anxiety toward the house, and when he was a few steps away from the door he stopped and cleared his throat and said again, "Thank you, sir. I like London," but to no avail, the voice was not his voice, just as the face was not his face but a shell of dry skin stretched over what had once been his face.

His friend welcomed him gladly, his wife had gone out to do some shopping and he was alone in the house with their small daughter, and before Meir had a chance to open his mouth he invited him into the kitchen and gave him a cup of tea and a piece of cake, which cheered him up a little because he was hungry and thirsty, and especially because it did something to dispel the sense of abandon-

ment and estrangement that had been oppressing him and draining
his strength.

And while they sat drinking their tea and chatting he continued
to be plagued by the feeling, which had sprung up in him the minute
he entered the house, that his friend had noticed the change that had
taken place in him and that there was something appraising about the
way he was looking at him, and in the end he could no longer restrain
himself, and he asked him if he had noticed that there was something
wrong with him, and his friend shrugged his shoulders and said that
he hadn't noticed anything wrong, but Meir insisted and asked him
if he really hadn't noticed any change in his voice or expression, and
his friend looked at him for a moment and repeated that he couldn't
see anything, except perhaps that he looked a little tired, and Meir,
although these words reassured him slightly, went on insisting that
something had changed in him and told him about what had happened, especially what had happened in Foyle's and the hospital,
going into great detail, and from time to time bursting into laughter,
since as he recounted his experiences most of the things that had
happened, especially his conviction that he was going to die, seemed
quite ridiculous and funny, and he felt that in spite of the traces of
panic and gloom something was melting and thawing and clearing up
inside him. His friend listened to him attentively, sometimes even, it
seemed to him, with a certain friendly envy, and from time to time
he joined in Meir's laughter and repeated that he couldn't see any
change in him except perhaps for the fact that he looked a little tired,
and Meir longed to hear this over and over because every time he
heard it it deepened the feeling of relief that was spreading through
him, and after he had finished his story his friend said that as far as
he knew most tourists suffered in one form or another from similar
symptoms, which were the results, as the doctor had said, of tension
and tiredness, which in themselves were the results of disorientation
and alienation, with all that they involved—loss of status and connections, disorientation in even the simplest situations, language difficulties, feelings of transience—and in addition to all these, the desire to
see everything and at the same time the knowledge that it was impos-

sible to do so, and in Meir's case it may even have been somehow connected with his mother's death, there were all kinds of currents flowing under the surface of our conscious minds, and he took a piece of cake and held it out to his little girl, who had come into the kitchen from the room where she was watching television, and said that he was sure the strange feeling would pass in a day or two, after he had calmed down a bit and grown accustomed to the unfamiliar surroundings, and at the same time he suggested that he should go and see a doctor the next day for a checkup and offered to phone a doctor he knew and make an appointment, but Meir, who felt an emotional gratitude to his friend for his willingness to listen and talk to him and for his reassuring words, and simply for being there, as if by these means he had saved him from death, decided to wait a day or two because he was feeling better all the time, and now that the Angel of Death had turned away and let go of him and the panic and malaise had grown fainter, the memory of his behavior and of everything that had happened made him feel uncomfortable, and even ashamed, because he felt that the whole thing was the result of a weakness in his character and a lack of self-confidence, which somehow took shape in his mind as evidence of a lack of manliness and virility, but he was so happy and so tired that he didn't feel like going into it, at least not now, and so despite the vestiges of the panic and distraction and malaise, he abandoned himself to the happy feeling of salvation and relief, and when he said good-bye to his friends—in the meantime his friend's wife had come home and they had eaten supper together and watched television—he felt restored, in spite of the weariness overwhelming him as a result of the traumatic events of the day.

In the morning, after a short respite of mild invigoration and the reassuring feeling that it was all over, the same heavy fatigue began seeping through him again, followed immediately by the same dull anxiety, which for all his efforts he was unable to dispel, and when he got up he experienced difficulty in dressing himself, for once again he could not control his limbs in obedience to his will, and his fingers again refused to loosen their grip on objects until he was obliged to pause and concentrate his thoughts and order them, in so many words, to let go, or else to use his other hand to help the seemingly paralyzed one, by which time he had already forgotten what he wanted to do. He held his trousers in his hands for an unconscionable length of time before putting them on, and in the same completely unfocused distraction, he forgot where he had put something that he had held in his hands only a moment before, and by the time he had managed to collect the necessary toilet articles to go into the bathroom to wash, he was already in the grip of the same tension and depression that only the night before, and even when he woke up in the morning, he had been confident were already behind him. He tried to encourage himself with the hope that it would soon pass, but when he sat down to eat his breakfast in his room, he found himself struggling clumsily with the eating utensils, or holding the knife and spoon or fork and cup in the same hand without managing to put the superfluous object down, and as he anxiously appraised himself and tested the sounds that came out of his mouth, he was once more vividly aware of the curious brittleness of his voice, and the hollowness of his look, and his face, which only a few moments earlier had looked perfectly normal to him in the mirror, once more gave rise in him to the sensation that it was bloated and porous and covered with a hard film of dead skin constricting it and turning its expression to stone. He put his hands up to his face to feel it, but the fact that his fingers refuted it again and again did nothing to dispel this impression, which was somehow, God knows how, joined by the feeling that there was someone else inside his loose and spongy flesh who had split off from it like an inner skin, the shadow of a man in his own image made of a kind of viscous smoke, and he stopped eating and sat and stared in front of him in utter despair, and for a moment he even wanted to lay his head on his hands and weep, for now he sensed quite clearly, after sensing it vaguely the day before and then dismissing it from his mind, that some obscure force, more powerful than himself, had somehow been freed and risen up from his depths, which he saw as a labyrinth of dark hollows in the lower half of his stomach and in his legs, and overpowered him, and that he would never recover from it, and a feeling of solitude and hopelessness such as he had never known before overwhelmed him, and all he wanted was for Pozner, and especially Aviva, to be with him at this moment, because he felt that only they could support him and save him from his catastrophe. And this desire was so intense and absolute, as if his whole life depended on it, that he decided to postpone walking in the park for a while and write each of them a postcard and send them express.

After he had finished eating his breakfast, which he hardly tasted in his dulled and distracted state, he put on his jacket and went out to buy postcards on Tottenham Court Road, but the sight of the street confused him and he felt himself stumbling as if he had just learned to walk, and he stopped a few houses away from his room and thought of going back and waiting until he felt better, but something inside him refused to give in and he went on walking in the fine rain to Tottenham Court Road, where he saw a tobacconist and stationer's on the other side of the street, but he could not cross the road because he suddenly realized that he had lost the ability to judge speed and distance, and the street itself looked mysteriously and frighteningly distorted, and the strange man inside him suddenly reappeared too, and he remained standing on the curb as if he were teetering on the brink of an abyss, feeling that he would rather go on standing there till evening than cross the road, but the thought of going back to his room without the postcards plunged him into a despair so black that he realized it would be even worse than crossing the road and so, after waiting until there was not a single car on the road as far as the eye could see, he plucked up his courage, and with a frightened dash, as if he were throwing himself from a cliff, he crossed the road and went into the shop and bought four postcards to last him the rest of his stay. In the meantime the rain had started coming down harder, and with the same grim effort he returned to his room and immediately, without taking off his coat, sat down to write to Aviva, but the letters he penned so laboriously were not only illegible, a nervous, meaningless scribble, but they also kept changing places, so that when he wanted to write a *b* for instance, he wrote a *d* or a *c* instead, and when he wanted to write an *s* he wrote an *r* or some other, random letter, and the words skipped all over the white paper in wild, plunging, crooked

lines looking like panic-stricken columns of black ants, with some of
them arbitrarily joined to the words before or after them and others
lying isolated on the paper, a few broken letters unconnected to
anything, in a way that he himself did not understand and that,
despite his desperate and stubborn efforts, he could do nothing to
prevent, as if some alien, demonic force had taken possession of his
hand and was bending it to its erratic will. And in the end, nervous
and depressed to the point of tears, he tore the postcard up and threw
it into the wastepaper basket, but he still believed that it was all due
to nerves and would pass and that all he had to do was rest a while,
and perhaps have something to drink, the thought that he might have
lost the ability to write, with all that it implied, was too horrifying to
contemplate, and he made himself a cup of coffee, and after drinking
it and lying down for a while with his eyes closed, he sat down to write
again, but within less than an hour of increasing desperation he had
spoiled all the other postcards, too, and he got up and, pausing only
to put on his coat, went out immediately to buy a new supply, impelled by the urgent need to know right away that he had not lost his
ability to write. Instead of going back to the first shop, however, since
he did not want to arouse the suspicions of the owner, he walked
straight ahead, with the wind that had come up in the meantime
blowing the rain into his face in irritating flurries, until he found
another shop, a little stationer's not far from the British Museum,
where he bought four postcards and put them into his coat pocket,
but instead of going straight back to his room, as he had intended,
he went on walking around the streets wrapped in a cloud of worry
and distraction and dropped into a few more stationers' and book-
shops and then, in an attempt to return to normality, went into the
British Museum and walked quickly through a few halls with his
hands in his pockets, unable to take anything in; the big halls stuffed
with exhibits oppressed him and made him feel uneasy, and besides,
he was afraid of bumping into something and doing damage, for there
was no longer any question in his mind that something basic in his
functioning had been impaired—every shop he entered and every
street he crossed proved it to him beyond the shadow of a doubt. At

lunchtime he went back to his room, but he put off writing the postcards until early evening, when after resting and showering and changing his clothes, doing everything very slowly and deliberately, he felt calmer and refreshed and ready for the task before him, and he sat down at the table with the same calm, slow deliberation, ignoring the mountains of anxiety and distraction inside him. Before writing anything on the postcards he decided to practice on a piece of paper, which he tore out of a tourist brochure, and although the letters came out nervous and ugly and the lines slanted obstinately downward, they could still be read and taken, perhaps, for lines written in a moving vehicle, but as soon as he began writing on the postcard his writing turned into an illegible, unrecognizable scrawl again, the letters changed places at random and the words fragmented and disintegrated and scattered in all directions despite his strenuous efforts to control them, and he stopped writing and then, after changing his position on the chair, resting and telling himself to keep calm, he tried again, concentrating on every single letter and trying to draw them in the right shape and place, but the same irresistible demonic force took control of his hand again and disrupted all his efforts, until in the end he tore up the postcard and replaced it with another, still trying to control himself and behave as if nothing was wrong, but the date and the very first words, "My dear distant wife, I'm sitting here in my room in London and thinking . . .", came out so jumbled and ugly that he immediately tore it up, too, feeling not only desperate but also disgusted by the sickly ugliness of his writing, and then he lay down on the bed, worn out by effort and anger and full of despair, and a few minutes later he got up and stood in front of the window and stared blankly into the street.

Now he no longer had any doubt that he had permanently lost the ability to write, just as he had irremediably lost the normality that had molded his personality and defined his identity, and while he stood looking out at the street, he felt everything inside him collapsing and turning into a pile of rags and tatters giving off a grayish-white dust like the dust rising from the rubble on the site of a demolished building, and a gray-white fog spread through him and he felt a dreadful exhaustion enveloping him in a miasma of dull indifference and despair. All he wanted now was to be with Aviva, he needed her so much that a cry stuck in his throat, and he had no doubt that she would save him or at least shelter him, and even the affair of the other man, which suddenly popped painfully into his head, did not detract from this certainty by one iota, and when he went out into the street —he felt that he would go mad if he stayed inside the four walls of his room—and walked with uncertain steps on the pavements, which were still wet with rain, he spoke to her in his head with a yearning tenderness, and as he covered her with endearments, observing himself anxiously as he did so, he once more became aware of another presence inside the hollow space of his body, which was still full of fog under the surface of his limp, porous flesh. The presence of this dark double made of a grayish, spongy matter inside him, identical with him but separate from him, filled him with alarm, since this time the figure seemed even more insubstantial than before, shifting and changing shape like a column of smoke but at the same time, in some incomprehensible way, separate and well-defined, radiating independence and power, with all the validity of an autonomous and permanent existence, and he stood still and wondered what to do next and then went up to the nearest bus stop and got onto the first bus that came. All he wanted was to be with Aviva because she was the only thing he could rely on in the chaos surrounding him, where everything was disintegrating and he himself had turned into a phantom figure and even his voice had turned its back on him and betrayed him in so astonishing and insulting a manner. Only with her, he felt, would he be able to recover himself and also his ability to write, which for some reason seemed to him the crux of the matter, and as he sat in the bus with a sealed face, looking dully through the window at the dark streets and thinking yearningly of Aviva, he returned unwillingly, with a terrified but compulsive curiosity, to the contemplation of his situation, and once again he concluded that above and beyond the tension and exhaustion and the mishap that had overtaken him because he had bent down to the bottom shelf in Foyle's, which he should never have done, it was all the fault of the weakness in his character and the miserable lack of self-confidence, which proved, beyond the shadow of a doubt, his puniness as a man and his lack of a talent for living. But as the bus journey progressed, he began to feel calmer and more relaxed and he sensed that his condition had improved and that he had recovered his ability to write, which filled him with happiness because he was convinced that if only he could succeed in writing properly everything else would be all right, too.

That night when he returned to his room, he sat down to write to Aviva and Pozner again, but after trying a few words on another page of the tourist brochure he decided to put it off to the next day, but the next day, too, and the day after, he did not succeed, in spite of all his grim efforts and painstaking, tortuous preparations, in getting anything down on the postcards except for the same ugly and meaningless scribbles, and he tore them up one after the other, going back twice to buy a new supply at different shops—he washed his face, showered, drank coffee and had something to eat, lay down on the bed, read the paper at his leisure, went out for a walk, encouraged himself, tried to forget what had happened and to pretend to himself that everything was all right, changed chairs, wrote quickly without paying attention to what he was doing, but it was all to no avail: his writing was terrible, the handwriting of a sick, primitive man, the words sprawled crookedly and the lines plunged downward as before, and the more he occupied himself with the business of writing the more nervous and depressed he grew, and thus, wrapped in a cloud of vague, unfocused worry and distraction, his impatience and despair increased from day to day, together with an oppressive feeling of guilt toward Aviva, who would be very worried at not having heard from him, and he went on trying to write the postcards, but without even a glimmer of hope that he would succeed and return to his previous, normal state, which now seemed to him like a delightful lost paradise. And three days later, walking with his friend in Regent's Park—it was a fine evening after several gray, rainy days, and he had joined his friend, who was taking his little girl for a walk—he plucked up his courage and after a lengthy hesitation, which had lasted from the moment they set out from the house, he asked again if he hadn't noticed anything wrong with him, and his friend stopped and looked at him and said that he couldn't see anything, and Meir said that he felt clearly that something was wrong with him and asked his friend to examine his face and eyes closely, and his friend examined him slowly and carefully and said, "You look a little tired, that's all," and Meir said, "No, there's something wrong with me," and they went on walking behind the little girl, and Meir asked if he hadn't noticed the change that had taken place in his voice either, and in order to give him the opportunity of noticing it he said, "This is the greenest lawn in the world, the lawn in Regent's Park," and his friend listened to him attentively, and went on standing and listening even after Meir had finished the sentence, as if he was still listening to the words, which went on hovering in the air for a moment, and then he shrugged his shoulders and said that he couldn't detect anything, and he went on walking, and Meir shook his head in disagreement and told his friend about the exhaustion and the panic and the distraction that never left him—they were now walking along a broad path with magnificent flower beds on either side of it—and especially about his inability to write, and also about his inability to let go of objects that he was holding, a phenomenon that was not as bad as before and was now manifesting itself at slightly longer intervals, like the appearance of his disembodied double, and he took a deep breath and said, "It's not me," and his friend, who had listened as attentively and sympathetically as on the previous occasions, said, "It's you, it's you," and ran to pick up his little girl, who had stumbled and fallen, and then he said that the shock of being abroad, like any other crisis, opened the way to all kinds of mental forces and symptoms that had been repressed and even completely out of our ken, and increased our little weaknesses, in other words weaknesses we had accepted and that in the course of the years had become dull and covered with layers of rust, and that suddenly, after having been stripped of these layers, took on huge dimensions and impetus—various fears and insecurities, self-indulgences, the need for attention, everything that had existed in more or less normal proportions, and everything that had been buried somewhere inside us under mountains of ignorance and repression—but when life returned to normal all this, too, would gradually settle down, and in the end perhaps all that would remain, apart from a few exciting memories, would be a little scratch, and Meir, who despite these reassuring words remained sunk in anxiety, said that he was afraid it would never leave him, and his friend said, "It will go away without your even sensing it, I promise you. You'll even miss it," and Meir smiled weakly, full of gratitude to his friend and hoping desperately that it would all be as he said, and his friend patted him affectionately on the shoulder and said that he was sure he was right —they were now walking over the broad lawn in the wake of the little girl, who was chasing a squirrel—and Meir said, "I could have done without it," and his friend said, "You're wrong," and then he said that now he had had the opportunity to get acquainted with "the other" inside him and come to terms with him, and that he shouldn't try to get rid of him because he was no less and perhaps even more himself than the thing he was familiar with and had grown accustomed to, and Meir buttoned up his coat, a cold wind was blowing from somewhere, and said, "Yes," and he really did feel relief, and even a faint, momentary glimmer of happiness, and his friend said, "People are afraid of who they are, and perhaps with some justice," and then he added, "If we weren't so afraid, we would be able to enjoy everything," and Meir smiled weakly and said, "Yes," and thought of Aviva with calm desire.

PART FOUR

A few days after Meir returned from abroad, he went to the Sick Fund clinic to see Dr. Reiner, who greeted him warmly as soon as he came into the room and asked him how he had enjoyed his trip, and he said, "Very much," mentioning the places he had visited and making a few noncommittal remarks about them, and when she asked him how he felt, he said, "All right," and then told her briefly about what had happened in London, without saying anything about the things that seemed to him insignificant from the medical point of view, such as the terror of death that had seized him or his conversation with the young salesman in Foyle's, but stressing the lack of coordination and loss of control over his limbs, as well as the persistent fatigue and distraction that made him feel not only as if there were still something clumsy and uncoordinated about his movements, and that he was still suffering from the same morbid weakness, but also that his face was slightly distorted and that there was a dry, shadowy shell covering it and clouding his vague, unfocused eyes; he listed all these symptoms, even though he was sure that Dr. Reiner must have noticed them the moment he came in, for he himself sensed them so vividly and palpably that it seemed to him that even the lack of focus was owing to a hazy cloud floating in front of his eyes, which anybody could easily see. Dr. Reiner, who listened gravely and attentively with a look of concentration in her alert green eyes, reassured him and said, like the doctor in London, that all these symptoms could be the result of tension and tiredness and not neces- sarily of any organic disturbance, and that his high blood pressure, which had apparently risen slightly as a result of the same tiredness and tension, may also have contributed something, and after giving him a thorough examination and writing out a prescription for medi- cation, she smiled slightly and said, "It will pass. Don't worry," and then told him triumphantly that she had completed the alterations to her flat, and Meir asked her how it looked and she said, "Fantas- tic," and invited him to come and see for himself, and Meir, who had already risen to leave, said, "I'd be glad to." He was only being polite, but Dr. Reiner said that he could come the very next day, at half past six, for instance, when she finished work, and Meir said, "Fine, I'll be there," and thanked her, and then, with his hand already on the handle of the door, he paused and said that if anything should happen to prevent him from coming he would call and let her know.

Meir toured the apartment with her and inspected the altera- tions to the rooms, which were full of a soft blue twilight, and after- ward they sat in the handsome living room and drank coffee and ate cookies and spoke about going abroad. Dr. Reiner told him that she had spent two years in America with her husband and that they had often gone there on trips and also to Europe, both on business and for pleasure, and Meir tried to follow what she was saying and take part in the conversation, which cost him a great effort, for he was still wrapped in the same anxious abstraction and vague, drowsy confusion and subject to a persistent urge to withdraw into a shell of indiffer- ence, all of which, it was quite plain to him, Dr. Reiner was well aware of, just as she was aware of his tremendous efforts to disguise his true condition as he fixed her with a hollow, absentminded look and tried to take in what she was saying and respond to her words. And suddenly, without any connection to what she was saying, he asked her brightly if she had not noticed the changes that had taken place in him, and Dr. Reiner interrupted the story she was telling him about a trip she had taken a few years before to the north of England and looked at him and said, "No," and after a short pause she added, "Perhaps you look a little tired." She said this perfectly simply, but there was something intimate in her tone, or so it seemed to him, and he passed his hand over his face as if to remove the film of dullness and vagueness covering it, and then, as if he were half asleep or asking for help—he felt like a gray bubble floating inside another, much bigger bubble—he put out his hand and laid it with yearning tenderness on Dr. Reiner's shoulder, and she looked at him in surprise and gentle wonder, and he drew her toward him with a very slight, barely perceptible movement, and as he did so he inclined his head toward hers, as if to rest it on her shoulder or to come closer to her, and the astonishment on her face was covered by a fine mist of embarrassment, and she said, "What's this?" and Meir said, "Nothing," and put his other hand around her neck and paused a moment to look at her face, blurred in the darkening light of the room, and then he laid his head yearningly on top of hers and paused again and breathed in the smell of her hair, which was like the smell of a clean garment, and very slowly stroked her cheek with his finger, and then her neck and her shoulder, and with the same swooning slowness lowered his head until he felt her cheek with his lips and he kissed her. His drowsiness seemed to have infected her, too, and encompassed them both, for there was no passion in the embrace but a kind of slow, dreamy drifting in the tender twilight and the wish to be absorbed in it, and with the same dreamy tenderness he slipped his hand into her blouse, and then raised her skirt a little and stroked her thighs, his hands moving sleepily and as if of their own accord, and afterward, with his eyes closed, he began to undo her buttons, but this practical action, or perhaps the sound of a car stopping abruptly, roused her, and very softly, as if she was afraid of tearing the tender threads of the web surrounding them, she said, "Not here. Let's go into the bedroom," and they got up and went into the bedroom and got undressed, with Meir taking great care not to look at her naked body, and lay on the bed and covered themselves with the sheet. The bed and the sheets had a strange, private smell, and he embraced her with his eyes closed and kissed her, the feel of her body enclosed in his arms and in his power filled him with satisfaction and quiet pride, although not for a moment could he free himself of the thought that she was older than he and, especially, stronger, and superior to him in some deep, primary and absolutely unquestionable sense, and without wanting to he felt a kind of distance and reverence for her, and as he stroked her shoulders and her full, warm breasts he examined, with half-shut eyes and from very close up, her ripe, heavy face, with its tired, slack pores and its pale skin on the verge of wilting, and its expression of profound and mature serenity, and afterward, without taking his eyes off her face he mentally followed the slow, lingering movement of his hand over her belly and hips to her vagina, stubbornly avoiding looking at her naked body, although he felt drawn to do so, and was flooded by a feeling of great attraction toward her and a tremendous desire to melt into her and pleasure her as no man had ever pleasured her before, and he closed his eyes again and concentrated on his desire, which grew more intense and filled his whole being like a dark, very dense, almost viscous liquid, spreading through all the hollow spaces in his body and sucking up all his willpower and thoughts into itself while at the same time awakening his dormant doubts and fears of failure—until it turned into a strenuous striving, an almost imperative need, and he embraced her and caressed her while at the same time racking his brains for all kinds of techniques that he had heard about or read about or knew from experience, and remember positions he had seen in films or in *The Joy of Sex,* especially the provocative position that rose again and again to the threshold of his consciousness, where it stopped and slipped away. The fears of failure kept returning like waves on a winter night and encompassing him with their roar, and for a moment he regretted the whole thing, until he surrendered to his body, which was charged and taut with the desire to give her pleasure and be pleasured in return, and he pressed her to him with all his strength, but gently, for now, too, he could not rid himself of the feelings of respect and reverence he felt for her, and she uttered a sound like a sigh of relief and he pressed her head to his and went on clasping her close to his body, and it seemed to him that a river of tenderness had opened up inside him and was streaming toward her, and afterward he tried to think of her face and body, but his whole being was concentrated like a tendon in the place where they were joined and on the infinite desire to give her pleasure, and as he moved toward her with his whole body concentrated on this desire, he felt himself slowly sliding into her with a movement that it was no longer possible to stop, not that he had any wish to do so in the drowsiness enveloping him like a wakeful sleep, sliding and sliding until he was swallowed up inside her, and with his eyes closed and his body still taut with effort he felt a warm, pleasant dampness and a delicate scent of dry grass encompassing him, and without moving his lips but aloud and distinctly he said, "This is the place, this is the place."

He lay there in the pleasant dampness and let his body relax and absorb the sweet languor and calm and luxuriate in them, and in the end, after a long time and as if against his will, he opened his eyes and looked at the undulating hills and the clean, dense sky above them. A terra-cotta-colored twilight, out of which the sky and the hills themselves seemed to be condensed, filled the air, together with the bitter smell of old orange peels mingled with Menora household soap, and Meir sat up slowly and gazed ahead of him toward the horizon, to the place where the mild slopes of two hills merged in a gently rounded movement, everything was pervaded by a sense of utter tranquillity, and he felt that thus, exactly thus, half awake and half asleep, cradled by the slow, continuous movement, he could go on sitting and gazing all summer long, and all autumn, and winter, too, with the winds and the rain pouring down his face, until the end of time. And indeed, he did not rise to his feet, or even turn his head, when out of the corner of his eye he saw Bill Gorman advancing toward him from the valley, and only when he was standing right in front of him did he incline his head and say, "Hello Bill," and smile faintly—now he wanted to give expression to his happiness and love, but they lay inert within him, wrapped in a profound slumber, and Bill said, "Hello, boy," and they shook hands, and Meir said, "I'm glad to see you," and asked Bill how he was, and Bill, smiling as usual, said, "I'm fine. There's no place like Miami. The U.S. Army looks after me like a mother and the *Golah* makes me as merry as a bird," and chuckled mischievously in his hoarse voice, and Meir smiled unwillingly at the sight of Bill's head in profile, which reminded him as always of a battered old rugby ball, and in his imagination he saw it rolling over a lawn or clasped in the arms of some hefty lout in a brightly colored helmet, running with it like a butting bull and trying to clear a way through the other louts in their helmets, who were chasing him as hard as they could in order to catch him and get the ball away from him, and Bill said, "I don't know how you can let a clown like Begin rule over you," and Meir said, "The majority were in favor of him," and Bill said, "The minority, too," and he laughed again and said, "Every nation gets the leader it deserves," and turned his body slightly and Meir, who despite his affection for him wanted to be alone now, asked him where he was going, and Bill patted the box of chocolates he was holding under his arm and said that he was going to Mr. Weiss, because it was his little girl's birthday, and when he turned to go, he said, "I'll drop in on your parents tomorrow evening. Give them my regards," and Meir said, "All right," and for a moment he thought of telling him about his mother's death, but at that very moment, perhaps because of the summer lassitude, the knowledge faded and dissolved inside him as if it were an illusion or a memory that had nothing to do with him—although she was dead, of course, of that there could be no doubt—and he repeated, "All right," and parted from him with a wave of his hand. And then, shortly after Bill had disappeared behind the hill—Meir sensed that he was gone without turning his head to look, because he was afraid to disrupt the delightful sensation of the calm summery flow of time enveloping him and washing his face as gently as water—he stood up and stretched himself and began to do a few exercises because he had to go on and he felt that the laxity of his limbs would make it very hard for him to do so, but to his great surprise and disappointment he found it almost impossible to perform the exercises because his body, as he suddenly realized, had lost the suppleness he imagined it still possessed, and to such an extent that he found it difficult to perform even the simplest and most ordinary exercises, which even very recently, or so at least he seemed to remember, he had performed easily and gracefully, but he refused to give in, and keeping time and giving himself commands as he heard the pleasant, husky voice of Gerda Altshuler in his head, he went on exercising with stubborn concentration.

Although the dim twilight remained constant, Meir knew that evening was falling and he turned and walked through the undulating hills and gentle valleys, which were strewn with morning flowers and wild grasses and low bushes giving off old country scents, whistling *"Malagenia"* to himself. In curtain after curtain, screen beyond screen, the hills rose around him as far as the eye could see, and he knew that when he left this hilly land and passed the green meadows, with their solitary carob trees, and the white dunes along the seashore, and reached the orange grove, with the mulberry trees and cypresses, which he called the "curly forest," the most blissful of all blissful things would happen, the very thought of which filled him with such happiness and strength that his mouth and even his heart were too fearful to give them expression. But all this did not cause him to hasten his steps; on the contrary—it was as if he wanted to postpone the wished-for moment and let it go on elating him and filling him with expectant joy as long as possible, and when he saw Gavrosh on a hill not far off, he stopped and surveyed the whole expanse of hills before him and the steady light, which looked as if it were somehow emanating from the earth and the edges of the sky, or perhaps it had been suspended here forever like cosmic dust from before the creation of the world, coloring the hills, which seemed for one moment to be rising to the sky and the next to be reaching from the sky to the earth, which was the sky, and then he started off again and crossed a little valley and began climbing Gavrosh's hill.

Gavrosh was sitting with his legs crossed like a Bedouin, leaning slightly forward, concentrating eagerly on something in front of him and occasionally raising the black field glasses that were hanging around his neck to his eyes, and when Meir came closer, he motioned to him with a slight gesture of his hand, without taking his eyes off whatever it was in front of him, to approach carefully, and Meir did so and knelt down next to him, and then Gavrosh pointed to a little bird whose appearance and rapid movements reminded Meir of a wagtail and said in a whisper, hardly moving his lips, "Look. She's the one I'm after." The bird was sitting on the thin branch of a meager bush, cease-lessly wagging its tail and turning its head restlessly from side to side, and Meir gazed at it intently for a long time, but only in order to please Gavrosh, whose presence, which he sensed even without turning his head, filled him with happiness, but in the end he could not contain himself any longer, the bird did nothing but wag its tail and turn its head perpetually from side to side, and he turned around and looked at Gavrosh and inspected his face, which was as shrunken and wrinkled as an apple long dried in the sun, and thought how much he loved this tired and austere face, which seemed to contain all the flavor of Eretz Israel, and how much he loved Gavrosh himself, with his profound closeness to nature and his flaring and fading enthusiasms and his boy-ish love, which never surrendered to logic or to time and which had lasted for so many years that it had become boring beyond words in its tortuous repetitiveness, for the same girl—or woman and mother of two children, to tell the truth—and he glanced again at the bird and thought of asking Gavrosh about his beloved, which he knew would make him very happy, but at that moment the bird suddenly hopped off its perch, as if something had startled it, and settled on another branch, where it perched for a moment wagging its tail with great rapidity, and almost immediately took off and flew very low over the ground and then settled on another bush on the other side of a shallow fold in the earth, and Gavrosh stood up and began walking slowly to-ward it, and Meir stood up, too, and followed him. They crossed the fold and climbed the gentle slope of the hill on the other side and Gavrosh said, "Isn't she marvelous?" and Meir said, "Yes, she's beauti-ful," glad that he could speak at last after the long silence, and Gavrosh said, "This is the second day that I've been chasing her. I discovered her by chance next to the fish pond. The whole thing is very strange because according to all the signs this is a bird that never comes to our country. Even a beginner in ornithology could tell you that," and he raised the field glasses to his eyes for a moment and surveyed the land, and then he took them down and said, "Maybe I'm mistaken? Perhaps there's something I haven't noticed and I'm mixing her up with some other bird?" and he raised his eyebrows and passed his finger over one of them in a characteristic gesture, his forehead creased with lines, and said, "If it's the bird I think it is, it's a great discovery," and he went on walking, carefully and silently now, with his eyes on the bird, which had settled on another little bush, but before he could kneel down she spread her wings and flew to the top of the hill and disappeared from view, and Meir said, "We seem to have frightened her away," hoping that this would put an end to the affair, but Gavrosh said, "I have to identify this bird. She's driving me crazy," and went on climbing the hill.

After circling the hill close to its summit they stood still, with the hilly landscape spread out before them as far as the eye could see, and Gavrosh raised the field glasses to his eyes again and searched for the bird and asked, "Can you feel the breeze in your face?" and Meir said, "Yes, it's very pleasant," and then, after a silence that seemed to him very long, he said, "Can you see her?" but Gavrosh was too absorbed in his search to reply, until at last he stretched out his hand and pointed and said, "There she is," and they began slowly descending the hill between the flowers and short grass, with a smell of dill and thistles filling the air, and Gavrosh said, "I'd really like to know what's going on," and Meir said, "What can be going on, already?" and Gavrosh said, "How do I know? It's already a week since I had any contact with her. Maybe she's decided to end it. Maybe she's decided to go back to her husband." And Meir who could sense the irritation and disgust he was so reluctant to feel rising somewhere in the distance and beginning to spread through him like a delicate fog on the horizon, said, "Let her go back to him, then, what do you care? The whole thing's as dead as a doornail by now, anyway," and Gavrosh said, "Yes, maybe you're right," and an unexpected smile appeared on his shrunken face, full of embarrassment and awkwardness,

and he picked a stalk of grass and bit it and said, "But I love her,"
and Meir said, "So what?" and suddenly, for a split second, he remembered Aviva's unfaithfulness and wondered whether he should tell
Gavrosh about it, and after a moment Gavrosh, with an irritatingly
naive stubbornness, repeated, "I love her, and that's all there is to it.
I feel it," and Meir said, "In that case there's no problem. Phone her
up," and Gavrosh, without even noticing Meir's irritation, said, "I
miss her, and I want to know if she misses me, too, that's all," and
he pulled up another stalk of grass and said that he was sure that when
people were in love their feelings operated in complete synchroniza-
tion, like interconnected vessels, in other words when one of them felt
love the other one did, too, and when one felt longing the other felt
the same, and it was the same when the love of one of them faded
or he became indifferent. Meir had heard this theory, which Gavrosh
called "the theory of the connected vessels," on innumerable previous
occasions, and he nodded his head and said, "In that case why bother
to phone at all? You know how she feels, anyway," and Gavrosh said,
"Yes, but there's always the fear that you may be mistaken," and he
said this with such profound innocence that Meir, who felt something
softening inside him with a sudden flow of warmth, was ashamed of
himself for the impatience and resistance that had interfered with his
love for Gavrosh, which he now felt in all its depth and density like
a whale filling the depths of the sea, and after a moment Gavrosh said,
"I'm afraid she'll forget me," and set out again, and after walking a
while in silence—they were now walking down the other side of the
hill—he said, "After a few months they could start living together
quite happily again. It wouldn't be the first time it's happened. Family
life has enormous power; it can overcome all kinds of things. What
do you say?" and he stopped, and Meir said, "I've already said everything I've got to say on the subject," and stopped right behind
Gavrosh, who signaled him to be quiet so as not to frighten the bird,
which was sitting on a thorny bush farther down the hill. They stood
and looked at her for a moment in silence, with Meir noticing her
unusual coloring for the first time, as if a veil of dust had been lifted
from her body, and then, very carefully, Gavrosh squatted down, and

as they were watching her, Meir saw the furniture mover from Turkey advancing toward them out of the corner of his eye, and when he reached them he stopped and looked curiously at them and at the bird and suddenly, as if in fun, he stamped his foot and waved his arms and frightened the bird, who flew away and disappeared into the broad valley spreading out before them. An expression of anger appeared on Gavrosh's face, while Meir smiled mischievously, there was something liberating about the act, and he waved gaily at the furniture mover from Turkey, who started walking away, waving back at Meir as he did so, and after a few moments disappeared from view, and Gavrosh got to his feet and turned away and started striding down the hill with big, angry steps, but Meir stayed where he was because he was sick and tired of chasing the bird—when all was said and done he was not in the least interested in birds, and but for his love for Gavrosh it was doubtful if he would have paused for more than a moment to glance at this or any other bird, however splendid its colors. But besides the boredom and irritation, which he could have borne for Gavrosh's sake, he felt once more the solemn urge, which had seemed to subside for a while, to advance toward the blissful thing that for the moment he could not clearly remember but that was still there, definite and distinct beyond the delicate, almost transparent veil of memory. And when Gavrosh paused and looked at him questioningly, he said, "I think I've already done my bit for nature for today," and smiled sheepishly, he knew that he was disappointing Gavrosh, and Gavrosh said, "Already?" and Meir said, "I have to go. I'm expected," and Gavrosh resigned himself and said, "Too bad. When will I see you again?" and Meir said, "Tomorrow or the next day," and Gavrosh waved slightly in farewell and Meir returned his wave, they knew that they would meet again in another day or two, and Gavrosh turned away and went on walking down the slope· in order to cross the valley and reach the other side, where a slightly steeper hill loomed, while Meir began walking across the slope in a southerly direction until he came to a faint, narrow path that looked like an old goats' trail.

The hills rose all around, with their low vegetation, grass and thistles and sparse bushes, a faint but vivid smell of dry earth and summer grass pervaded the twilight in the profound and utter stillness, and Meir walked with unhesitant confidence along the goats' trail, which wound gradually down toward the valley, as if he had passed this way countless times before and it was all perfectly familiar to him, and as he walked he felt the freedom he had gained since parting from Gavrosh stirring in every pore of his body, together with the alertness spreading through him and lifting the shadow of drowsiness that had infected him earlier, and he abandoned himself to the delight of these sensations, which he had not known for so long, and suddenly, almost unconsciously, as if on the impulse of this felicity, he left the path and began walking straight down the hill to the valley, which was traversed by a broader path.

Small stones and clods of earth got into his sandals as he strode down the uneven slope with its fissures and hummocks, and thorns scratched his legs, but none of this spoiled his mood, quite the contrary. It seemed to him that the stillness here was even more profound and translucent than the stillness higher up on the slopes, and as he tried, for the most part unsuccessfully, to avoid the thorns, he recalled Gavrosh's discreet but tireless efforts to awaken in him that love of nature that, buried though it might be under a mountain of ignorance and fear, he claimed was innate and inherent in everyone, and he thought that perhaps he should have told him about Aviva's unfaithfulness, and at the very moment of uttering the word *unfaithfulness* in his head, he felt, actually felt, in his mouth and in his whole body, how absurd it all was, and how it struck not a single chord of pain or insult or jealousy in him, nothing at all, as if it were a scab that had dried up and died of its own accord and dropped off his life and no longer had anything to do with him, and had never had anything to do with him, either, and for a moment, albeit only a moment, he felt an acute pang of regret and even sorrow at the thought that he had lost something important, perhaps even crucial, that had been profoundly rooted in his life and had defined it, precisely in terms of pain and injury, as a separate entity with a separate and independent fate of its own, but after a moment, and perhaps even in the midst of this sorrow and regret, a dizzy feeling of relief surged through him: after much suffering and many struggles he had succeeded in overcoming a heavy and superfluous obstacle that had poisoned his life with resentment and hostility and made him feel wretched and miserable —not because of what had actually happened but because of the lack of courage and the false pride with which he had related to it—and he was flooded by a wave of thanksgiving. And as he walked on with a broad smile on his face, he began to declaim from the bottom of his heart *"Per me si va nella città dolente, perme siva nell . . . ,"* here there were a few words missing which he had forgotten, and he filled in the gap with combinations of sounds that came into his head as he walked: *"dolore ciaiuto,"* and then continued as best he remembered, *"perme siva nella perdiuta gente, giustizia mosse mio alto fattore."* There was not a single word of those he remembered and declaimed that he was sure he had not corrupted and distorted in one way or another—on the contrary, he was sure he had distorted every single one of them, and nevertheless he immediately repeated them again, even more boldly, making the silence thunder and wondering in amusement why on earth the history teacher, the history teacher of all people, with his enormous head and mighty chin jutting out of his heavy, furious face, had decided to write these lines on the blackboard after reading them aloud in his hoarse voice, and commanded them to copy them down and learn them by heart, and a warm feeling of reverence and admiration for the man filled him, and he recited the lines, whose meaning he could no longer remember except in the most general way, aloud again, and the words rose into the air and were lost somewhere among the hills, which were growing steeper and rockier, and were swallowed up in the silence, and he repeated them again and again with the same gleeful exhilaration as he strode through the valley, which suddenly, almost from one moment to the next, turned into a ravine winding between steep, rocky walls, and suddenly, with a feeling of release, he shouted, "To be an Italian!" and with a smile full of satisfaction he stood and listened to the echoes rolling back and forth between the steep wadi walls, as if the words were being hurled from wall to wall in the winding creek until they smashed to smithereens, and then he made his hands into a trumpet around his mouth and shouted, "To be a poet!" and again he stood listening until absolute silence reigned again, the mysterious and majestic silence of the wadi.

A cool shade steeped in the smells of stone and ancient moisture filled the creek, and Meir, who had begun walking again under the dark blue strip of sky at an inconceivable height somewhere far above him, was so overwhelmed by the sense of majesty and mystery and by the feeling of loneliness, which was so different from the loneliness among the bare hills, that he stopped shouting and declaiming, even the smile had vanished from his lips, and concentrated on walking along the winding path in the middle of the wadi bed, and as he walked, he scanned the high, scarred walls, with their cracks and little orifices, which enclosed the wadi on all sides, and a sense of adventure drew him to go into one of the dim, narrow clefts in the rock and explore it. At first he was deterred, not only by a sense of hidden danger, but mainly by the fear that he would not find his way back to his path, or at any rate that he would be delayed much longer than he was prepared to be, but in the end he surrendered to his curiosity, and after deciding that he would not go far, he turned into one of the narrow creeks cleaving the rock and walked along it with an uneasy heart, trying not to lose the direction of the wadi bed. From one minute to the next the cleft between the rocks grew narrower and the shade heavier until it was almost dark, but although Meir had decided in advance only to go in a little way and then return, he did not retreat but went on advancing along the ground strewn with stones and lumps of rock, and even when the narrow creek began to wind so steeply upward that his walk turned to a strenuous climb he was not deterred, but rather spurred onward precisely by the obscure fear and especially by the physical effort that suddenly, after years, gave him a sense of his body and a feeling of pride and ambition, and after a while the creek came to an end and he found himself on the open plain of the plateau above the wadi.

He sat down on a large stone and let the faint currents of air cool his face, enjoying the sense of his sweating and tired-out body, and then he stood up and began walking along the plateau, looking for a way back down into the wadi, and not long afterward he found a creek and began walking along the edge of the towering stone walls, trying from time to time to calm his fear of heights by standing still and turning his head to look at the open plain. He kept thinking of retreating from the precipice and walking far away from it and of the danger of falling, but some stubborn force impelled him to go on placing himself in this danger, which had something exhilarating about it, and as he made his way along the edge of the cliff, casting unwilling glances every now and then into the dark depths at his feet, he thought with a smile how nice it would have been to be born an Italian or a Frenchman, or perhaps a Swede living peacefully on the shores of a blue fjord, but more than anything he wished he was an Italian and a poet, and the more he thought about it the more he wished it, and the wish turned into a bitter yearning and a conviction that this and only this would have been the appropriate destiny for him, and he went on brooding about it with longing and an increasing feeling of loss for everything that his life was truly destined to be until he came to see the thwarting of this wish not only as an act of deliberate malice against him, but also as an expression of the illogicality and inhumanity of nature and existence as a whole, since it wouldn't have made the least difference to them if he had been born an Italian and a poet, and this made him even more bitter, and he stood and looked down into the depths of the creek, where far below he saw the wadi bed to which he had to return, and he went on walking and searching for a convenient place to descend, reflecting as he did so on freedom and free will, and their total worthlessness and insignificance in light of the fact that a man had no choice in the matter of his parents or nationality, never mind the actual fact of his birth, and he brooded on this with bitterness, but especially despair, and then, in an attempt to cheer himself up and return to his previous, happier mood, he smiled to himself and said, "Freedom is the recognition of necessity, freedom is the recognition of necessity," and he wondered if this useful sentence had been coined by Marx or Lenin, it was one of them, anyway, and repeated to himself, "Freedom is the recognition of necessity," but his heart, under the skin of his smile, did not lift, for it refused to accept necessity, and even if he had recognized it, this recognition would only have added to his gloom, since the only freedom he recognized in his heart was the absolute liberty to fulfill every wish and desire. And the hopeless longings seethed inside him and gnawed at him mercilessly until he was filled with anger at having been born at all and wished that he could wipe his existence out from start to finish, but at the same moment he said to himself that it was impossible for a man to be drawn to something with such anguished yearning and with feelings of such profound intimacy and affinity unless it was somehow inherent in the source of his being, and this thought gave rise in him to a vague feeling that perhaps he really was an Italian and a poet but that things had somehow gone wrong and the truth had been forgotten in the rough and tumble of life—for otherwise where did they all come from, the longing, the feeling of intimacy and affinity, the vaguely remembered images?—and as he continued walking, after standing for a few moments and scanning the walls for a convenient way down into the wadi, which was growing broader and shallower as the walls grew gradually lower, he said to himself that although he might not be able to assert that he had definitely been born an Italian, there was no doubt in his mind that it was within the bounds of possibility, and as he climbed down to the wadi—the descent was much harder than he had imagined—he said to himself that he was an Italian and a poet, there was no doubt about it, and a Frenchman and a Swede living in the green tranquillity of the banks of a fjord—he had no desire to be an American—and a poet and an architect and an explorer and an important political leader, but also a philosopher and spiritual teacher standing at the center of the attention and hopes of multitudes for generations to come, and maybe even for all eternity, and thus, saved from the despair of meaninglessness and anonymity, he would live his exciting life and by the power of his personality and deeds change the face of poetry and architecture and the whole history of mankind. And a joyful smile expanded inside him, sending a tremor through his skin and seeping through his flesh and suffusing his whole body from top to bottom as a light breeze saturated with the cool, fresh smell of plants brushed his face and a faint radiance appeared on the stone walls as the deep shade of the wadi lightened, and he repeated jubilantly, almost singing, "Freedom is the recognition of necessity."

After a few minutes the wadi came abruptly to an end, giving way to a green plain, which spread out in front of him as far as the eye could see, and he came to a halt, elated and moved, for this was exactly the landscape he had been expecting to see, and gazed at the expanse of vivid green and the blue sky, which seemed to have been colored with ink. Here and there, rather far apart, stood lowish trees with thick, leafy branches spreading out like sunshades and casting a circle of dark shade around them, and he named them to himself, "carobs," and for a moment he felt a pang of regret that Gavrosh had not accompanied him here. After drinking in the view, he began walking through the soft wild grasses, which caressed his legs and gave off a damp steam covering the entire plain as suffocatingly as a thick, warm blanket, and bathing his face and throat and chest in streams of sweat that gave off a pungent smell, different from the smell of his previous sweat, mingling with the smell of the earth and the various plants, wild orache and dill and wild radishes and invisible oleanders, and the smell of the sea hiding somewhere at the edge of the plain, and it was the height of summer filling the wide open spaces from the roots of the earth to the ends of the sky, and it surrounded him as he walked through the dense, warm haze and trembled intoxicatingly at the tips of his nostrils, it was the sensation of summer and it grew more intense as he walked on, dripping with sweat, in the heavy, steamy, scent-laden air, and from the heart of the whirlpool of scents, like disembodied essences materializing in special fragrances, rose time without limit and bronzed youth and suppleness of body and mind, and unquestioning health, and natural confidence and the freedom of choice and action, and above all the exhilarating sense, relating mainly to sex, that all possibilities were open and everything was attainable. He sniffed at all these scents like an animal, contemplating with wonder and heartfelt excitement everything that was happening inside him, especially the vigorous sexuality that flowed through all the rest like a colder stream in the broad current of a river, and he walked toward one of the trees, whose foliage seemed to him particularly dense, and said to himself that the moment he lay down on the earth in its shade he would feel again the old sensations of pleasure that no longer existed in him except as memories empty of feeling, and as he walked, strolling at a leisurely pace and keeping time with the rhythm of the boundless summer, he stopped two or three times and bent down and dug in the moist, warm earth and took a little rotted humus and squashed it between his fingers and lifted it to his nose and said without moving his lips, "The smell of the Jezreel Valley." And when he reached the tree, he lay down in its shade with his hands crossed under his head, and he looked up at its leafy crest and abandoned himself to the inexpressible felicity of lying idly on the earth with the delicate, subtle scents rising from it and from the dry leaves enveloping him and mingling with the smells of the warm plain, and as he watched the motes of light filtering through the foliage and dissolving on the dark leaves, honeyed webs of sleep, tender as a baby's, veiled his eyes, and in the calm dissolution of time in the steamy summer air it seemed to him that he heard himself saying, half awake and half asleep, "This is the dreamed-of delay," how delicious the words tasted on his tongue, "This is the dreamed-of delay," and in the stillness of the moment after these words the whole poem by Ozer Rabin rose up at once from the depths of his body, or perhaps from the depths of the earth he was lying on, without his remembering a word of it, as if the poem existed as a pure entity, separate from its specific words, even though all of the words, with their stresses and accents and allusions were contained in it, as if it were an olive lying in his mouth or the shade of a cypress tree. And he smiled to himself and turned onto his side and thought about the world of the future that would come into being by the force of historical laws that no one could stop, after the state had withered away, together with all the forms of coercion and authority—he saw it diminishing and melting away like a candle with the same quiet inevitability that would reign in a world that was all good, bathed in sunshine and full of lawns and green fields and little woods with running brooks, and here and there a band playing and birds warbling, and everything bursting with freshness and joy, because of course all the people would be contented and happy since they would do only the things that interested them and gave them pleasure, most of them he saw walking in parks and fields or playing sports and reading and listening to music and making love, which would always be fresh and exciting because it would be dominated only by the true impulse of the moment and the instincts, which would dominate everything— within the framework of some sort of discipline, of course, whose source and purpose he could not, however, envisage at all—and they would sustain a world of absolute freedom, ridding human life of pettiness and boredom and routine and transforming it into an endless adventure full of intoxication and inspiration on behalf of society and for its sake. A feeling of pleasant languor encompassed him as if his thoughts had drained his strength, and the earth exuded warmth and drowsy vapors, which seeped into him and wrapped around him like the silken threads of a cocoon, and he turned on his side and unthinkingly took the newspaper out of his pocket and spread it out in front of him, and with the same enjoyable trancelike sensation, he browsed through it and read an item about a society whose center was located in the town of Hebron in America, which claimed that the earth was hollow and that we, the sons of the earth, lived inside it, stuck to the inner side of its crust, and they expounded this theory fanatically in propaganda pamphlets full of detailed logical and scientific proofs in order to convert people to their point of view, and he smiled and browsed through other articles, and as he did so, he wondered what the point of espousing such a view as this could be, and what it meant to those who held it, and he moved the newspaper slightly away from his eyes and looked at the edges of the sky, which were visible under the branches of the tree, and tried to imagine the world as the members of this society described it, and he saw a hollow globe with himself and the tree he was lying under stuck to the inside of its crust, and an infinite sea of blue air outside it, and he said, "The land of Pellucidar, the land of Pellucidar!" and on the same impulse of thought he saw the hollow globe inside another hollow globe, and this other hollow globe inside another one, like a Russian babushka doll, and still looking at the edges of the sky, which were undisturbed by any movement of air or cloud or bird, he tried to imagine himself lying on the inner circumference of the hollow globe with the sky underneath him, and although all his senses revolted against the idea, he refused to give up, and in the twilight of his waking thoughts he went on stubbornly trying to controvert the evidence of his senses with the power of his imagination, until in the end he felt that he was indeed lying on top of the world as in an upside-down hammock with the sky underneath him, and he delighted in his triumph and in the sense of floating and space, but these feelings gave way immediately to uneasiness followed by an anxiety that was not only the fear of heights and falling but the fear of upsetting the entire natural order of things, until all he wanted was to revert to his former feeling that he was below and the sky was above, but the opposite feeling persisted stubbornly until in the end he covered his face with the newspaper and surrendered to the sleepiness that had already invaded all his limbs, and he fell asleep and slept as blissfully as if he were in a cradle.

While he was still asleep, he felt someone standing over him, so close that her foot was touching his arm, and he knew at once that it was Raya because in his sleep he had known that she would come, and without opening his eyes, in the shadowy area between waking and sleeping, he put out his hand and slowly stroked her leg, and the stimulating pleasure flowed from his fingers along his arm and spread through his body and merged into the pleasure of the last moments of sleep and he could sense the smooth tan of her skin even with his eyes closed, and afterward he opened them a crack and looked at her for a moment through a fog of sleep and saw that she was wearing short pants and a white tee shirt and closed his eyes again and, perfectly naturally, without any hesitation, went on stroking her leg from the ankle to the thigh, he liked the back of her knee and the inside of her thigh best, and Raya stood without moving, abandoning herself to his caresses, and from one moment to the next he could feel the last vestiges of doubt and reserve dropping away and his body opening up and filling with desire like a ripe summer fruit full of sap,

and in absolute freedom and simplicity—the fear of being rejected or
making a fool of himself did not even occur to him—he slipped his
hand into her trousers, feeling as if he were about to melt with the
intensity of the pleasure and suspense, and caressed her there, nothing
existed now in the world but for his body dense with desire and her
body standing over him in the intoxicating heat of the summer, and
Raya, too, had abandoned herself entirely to delight, he could sense
this quite clearly from the way she was standing without moving and
also from something invisible emanating from her, and afterward he
told her to get undressed, or perhaps he only indicated with a gesture
that he wished her to do so, and she obeyed him and went on standing
over him, her legs slightly apart, while he stroked her legs slowly and
gently and gazed dreamily up at the slit of her vagina and her pubic
hair. Above her head the dark canopy of leaves was touched with
silvery motes of light, time flowed with the slow, suspended motion
of thick honey, and he held back the lust crammed so tightly into his
body that it seemed about to burst, and conscious as if for the first
time of its strength and suppleness and confident in the knowledge
that nothing was beyond its powers, he said "Come," and she lay
down next to him and the heat of the summer in the wide open spaces
encompassed them both, and he embraced her and tried to remember
that special position in *The Joy of Sex,* and realized how ridiculous
and superfluous it was and forgot about it, and lay with her in the
smell of the grass and the invisible oleanders and the smell of the earth
and the humus mingling with the smell of her skin, and afterward he
sunk into utter peacefulness and looked past her face at the green
plain and the dark foliage with the flecks of silvery light dissolving and
fading until he fell asleep again.

   He woke up little by little, as if he were floating to the surface
of a lake of pudding, with the feeling that something good and
enjoyable had happened to him, and was flooded by the remembered
freshness of the mornings of the spring holidays when he was a boy,
with the yellow sun at the window and patches of sunlight on the wall
and the thin woolen blanket and all the time in the world awaiting
his pleasure as he lay there cozily between the sheets, and in the end

he opened his eyes and looked dreamily at the sun-flecked leaves, it seemed to him at one and the same time that only a few moments had passed since he fell asleep and also that many hours and even days had passed, and afterward, without raising his head, he looked at the grass and dry leaves and broken twigs and clods of earth next to his face and watched an ant dragging a crumb without any feelings of guilt or regret for anything or even any vague, bittersweet yearnings, but only pleasure in the present moment and pleasure in his own existence. He had never before, except in his school days, known a feeling like it, and at the same time, without in any way detracting from this sensation of well-being, he felt the renewed stirring of the gentle but stubborn urge to go on toward the blissful thing that was waiting for him somewhere along the road, and he stretched and sat up and paused a moment and rose to his feet and stretched again, scanning the green plain merging with the sky into one vast and empty expanse as he did so, and he wondered what direction to take in order to reach the sand dunes and the sea, for there was no clear landmark on the plain, which stretched in all directions toward the blue horizon, and the few trees scattered here and there only added to his confusion because it seemed to him that on his way from the wadi he had already passed this tree or that, and he stood looking around him for a while without knowing what to do, although when he had emerged from the wadi and walked toward the tree he had known exactly which direction to take, and he lifted his head and closed his eyes to clear them of the sights in front of them, and when he opened them again he began walking, guided by an inner knowledge that brooked no doubt, in the direction of the dunes and the sea.

And indeed, after some time, at first almost imperceptibly, the steamy heat covering the plain lifted a little, and light, cool breezes stirred the air like the flapping of wet sheets and soaked into his flushed face, and the smell of the sea and the seaweed grew stronger, and in the distance, along the horizon, he saw a white stripe like a strip of foam, which spread and broadened as he drew nearer, and suddenly he stopped and surveyed the vast plain he had left behind him for a moment and then he began walking again, and when he reached the dunes of spotless sand rolling silently toward the sea, which was visible only in the grayish-brown mist hanging motionless above it like the faint vestiges of the frozen steam from the chimney of a ship, he was seized by a desire to run and leap and roll, especially roll, and he restrained himself because he did not want to spoil the unblemished virginal smoothness that made them look as if they had been created by the brush of an angel's wing, but in the end, after walking a little farther, he could no longer contain himself in the face of the happiness beckoning from these splendid slopes merging softly into one another all over the bright, sunlit expanse of sand, and he took off his shirt and sandals and trousers and bundled them up and ran leaping up one of the dunes and when he reached the top he lay down and rolled to the bottom and stood up radiant with happiness and ran up the opposite hill and rolled down the other side and did it again and again until the sea appeared before him in all its breadth, and then he stood up and shook off the sand and walked in his underpants, abandoning his body to the moist sea breeze and the rays of the sun, which he could feel penetrating his pores and awakening the pigments and tanning his skin until the healthy glow of the tan became one with the sense of strength and suppleness that increased with every step he took, and as he delighted in this feeling he heard the gentle murmur of the rippling waves, as muffled and monotonous as the movement of a distant pendulum, seeping through the transparent curtain of air, which grew purer and clearer the closer he came to the sea. And he quickened his step a little, aroused by the proximity of the sea, and dragged his feet through the sand of the dunes still separating him from the strip of cool shore until he reached it and crossed it and stood at water's edge with his face to the open sea, and he gazed hungrily at the infinite expanse of blue with a tiny white sail like the tip of a motionless feather far away in the distance, which seemed to dissolve the limits of his body and absorb it into itself until he was one with the water and the air, although at the same time he also existed as a distinct and separate entity within his body, perhaps more than ever before, because of the glow of the tan and the feeling of suppleness and strength.

He let the rippling little waves caress his feet, and as he did so a feeling of natural, self-evident closeness that had faded, as it were, and been buried under piles of estrangement and fear, stirred within him and drew him into the sea, which looked like the sea in a painting or a tapestry, a sea that would never rage and storm and in which it was impossible to drown, and he threw his bundle of clothes on the sand, and with a gay, splashing charge he ran into it, and then he threw himself into the water and swam toward the horizon until he could scarcely see the shore and the dunes, and there, in that great calm, he abandoned himself to the touch of the sun and the air and the gentle rocking of the water, which in its ceaseless motion gave rise to the sensation that it was the fathomless ocean bed itself and the sky above that were rocking to and fro. And as he lay on his back with his eyes closed, he became very conscious of the dark depths below him, as if the sea was something dense and flexible carrying him on its surface like a little chip of wood, and when he turned over onto his stomach to swim back to the shore, suddenly impatient with this passive floating, he saw a big, dark shadow somewhere in the fathomless depths beneath him, which gave rise in him to a mysterious fear, and he said to himself that it was only a rock, but at the same moment it crossed his mind that it was the mouth of a tunnel leading from this seabed to the Sargasso Sea somewhere below it, and when he got back to the shore where evening was beginning to fall, he told this to Pozner, who was crouching on the sand with the rackets and *The Book of Games, owned by Yitzhak Pozner, Grade 9b,* and building something with moats and a dam.

Pozner laughed and said that in that case perhaps there was another sea above this one too, and Meir said, "Maybe," and Pozner said, "So why doesn't it drip onto our heads?" and Meir said, "I don't know. Maybe its bed is made of quartz," and this word *quartz,* which had suddenly popped into his head, seemed to clinch the argument as far as he was concerned, but Pozner only smiled and said that quartz was quite incapable of bearing pressure of that kind, not to mention the fact that it would immediately be compounded with the nitrates in the water to form acids—coming out on top again, as usual

—and Meir said, "I'm not an expert on science," and took the racket Pozner offered him, and as they walked to the water's edge to begin their game, Pozner smiled at him and said, "Who knows, you may be right. A lot of scientific hypotheses began as a joke," and they moved apart from one another and hit the ball back and forth smoothly and enjoyably for a long time until Meir stopped playing and said that he had to go, and Pozner said, "What's the hurry? It's still early," and Meir said, "No, I'm expected," and returned the racket to Pozner and went to get dressed, glad that Pozner was sorry that he was going, and Pozner threw the rackets down on the sand and said, "When will you stop being a good little boy?" and Meir, his cheeks burning, repeated, "I'm expected," and asked Pozner if he could use his towel, and Pozner said, "What a question!" and threw it at him, they were now standing side by side on the deserted beach, and wiped his pilot's sunglasses and said that the world would soon come to an end, and Meir, who was standing and drying himself, said, "Nonsense," because Pozner's words aroused his resistance even before he took them in, and Pozner said that he had read about it in an American scientific magazine, and a smile appeared on his face, and to Meir it seemed that he could detect traces of a sneer in it, and he repeated, "That's just nonsense. They're always thinking up something new. It's probably an advertising stunt for some movie," trying with all his might to preserve an air of indifference, but Pozner went on to say that a number of famous scientists had developed a theory that one of the "white stars" would flare up as a result of various chemical reactions that would take place inside it and grow to such dimensions that in the end it would swallow up the earth and the rest of the planets of the solar system together with the sun itself, and Meir repeated, "Nonsense, it's probably an advertisement for something"—for what else could he say?—and it seemed to him that he could detect an air of anxiety under the expression of confidence and even arrogance on Pozner's face, and he added, "I don't believe it," but Pozner went on to say that before it all happened the atmosphere would heat up to such an extent that the vegetation and the oceans and the earth and everything on it would evaporate and turn into gas, the heat would be so terrible that even the sun itself would evaporate and disappear, and then, after the sun disappeared, utter darkness would descend, pitch-black darkness—he repeated this a number of times as if he was afraid that Meir was not taking it in properly—and an endless rain, a torrent of red-hot rocks and melted lead and tar, would fall on the earth for days on end in a whirlwind of burning dust, and only then would it be swallowed up in the seething darkness of the disintegrating star.

Meir looked at the calm blue sea, at the pure sky and the white sand dunes, which seemed so calm and eternal, as if he was looking at them for the last time and returned the towel to Pozner and asked, "When is all this supposed to happen?" and Pozner said, "Soon." There was something infuriating in his insistence, and Meir said, "It's never going to happen," expecting Pozner to go back on his words or at least soften them as a sign of friendship, but Pozner showed no signs of retreat or hesitation, on the contrary, there was now something dramatic and vehement in his air as he said that a lot of people, including very clever people, had said a lot of things would never happen—and they did happen, and Meir said, "That doesn't prove anything," and feeling very put out and disappointed, he added, "It's a lot of nonsense," and began to put on his trousers, and Pozner said, "I understand that it's not a very comfortable thought. Okay. Have it your way. There's no nature, there's nothing. Everything's nonsense," and he laughed, and Meir, embarrassed by his theatrical laugh, controlled himself and put on his trousers in silence, feeling that he had somehow been defeated, and after a moment, in a tone of mingled curiosity and indifference, he asked Pozner if he believed in the resurrection of the dead, he himself was surprised and embarrassed by the question, and Pozner said, "What kind of resurrection of the dead can there be if there's no world?" and Meir said, "But supposing that it doesn't happen and the world goes on existing?" and Pozner said, "In nature there's no such thing as supposing," and kicked a mound of sand, and Meir said, "There are other worlds besides ours," and Pozner, who seemed momentarily put out by this unexpected remark, said that if he meant reincarnation, he believed in it, since the law of the conservation of energy applied to nature as a whole and all natural phenomena, but as for the idea of the dead rising from their graves and coming back to life in the same shape as before they had died, that was something he didn't believe at all because it contradicted all the laws, and Meir said, "What laws?" and Pozner said, "The laws of nature, I don't know any other laws," and Meir said, "But if it's the will of God?" and Pozner said, "Do you believe in God?" and Meir, who felt an intense desire to make a crack in the wall of Pozner's cleverness and knowledge, said, "No, but still—if it's the will of God?" and Pozner said, "God can't will anything that contradicts the laws of nature." And Meir, who suddenly felt helpless and hopeless, said, "So then you don't believe in the actual resurrection of the body?" feeling that this question touched on something that was more important to him than life itself, and Pozner said, "No," as if he hadn't even noticed how important the question was to Meir, who smiled in embarrassment and said, "But you yourself said that you believed in the power of mind over matter," and Pozner said, "I understand that you want me to tell a little lie to please you, but I don't want to," and Meir said, "I don't want anything. I just want you to be a friend, that's all," and immediately added, "How do you know what's a lie and what isn't, anyway?" and Pozner, now speaking frankly and without a hint of superciliousness or irony, said that the resurrection of the dead in that form was completely incompatible with the view of modern physics, according to which the entire distinction between past, present, and future was groundless and had no application whatsoever beyond the narrow field of everyday life, and Meir, in whom these words provoked gloom and inexplicable anger, said, "I don't understand what you're talking about," and tried to push his feet into his sandals, and Pozner suddenly grew grave, as if a cloud had shadowed his face, and said, "I don't want to come back to life. That's it. I don't want to meet my father again. Once was enough for me." There was an unexpected note of painful confession in these words, and Meir said, "I understand," and bent down to fasten his sandals, and with a sudden illumination, like spring sunshine breaking through clouds, he realized how strong and endur-

ing their friendship was and knew that it would survive any vicissi-
tudes, just like his friendship with Gavrosh. And Pozner said, "Why
don't you stay a bit longer? Nothing's going to run away," his voice
as cheerful as before, and Meir said, "No, I'm expected," for a moment he thought of giving in to him, but at the same time he felt,
perhaps for the first time in their friendship, how free he was to say
no, and Pozner said, "Too bad. We could have gone on playing a little
longer," and Meir said, "That's the way it is," and filled with a feeling
of springlike freshness, he playfully threw a handful of sand at Pozner
and hurried away with a wave of his hand, and afterward he walked
southward along the shore, still steeped in a feeling of sparkling,
springlike happiness, which merged with the solemn suspense, restrained at first, which surrounded him from the moment he turned
away from the sea and started walking along the narrow path between
the fields of loam and sand sparsely covered with thistles and grass.

After walking for a while, he suddenly came upon the dark grove
with the mulberry trees and cypresses that he called the "curly forest,"
looking like a square patch of shade on the surrounding fields. Seeing
it immediately increased the suspense and excitement from which he
had been trying as hard as he could to distract himself, and when he
drew closer and felt its green shade and smell, the smell of citrus trees
and irrigated soil, he stood still for a moment and looked around him.
The acacia hedge was broken down and full of gaps, and he stepped
through it and slowly entered the grove, walking with his head bowed
under the low, motionless trees, a mixture of orange trees and *hush-
hash* and lemons, with a few mulberry trees and cypresses, jumping
for fun over the abandoned irrigation canals and stepping aside here
and there to avoid a thorny bramble bush, sending involuntary glances
of restrained expectation from side to side as he did so, and when he
reached the little clearing next to the spreading mulberry tree—this
was the place, he knew it—his grandmother appeared in her flowered
Sabbath dress with her knitted bag and her kidskin Sabbath shoes
with the bumps where the big toes were, and he hurried toward her
and embraced her with all his might and kissed her broad, wrinkled
face, the shining, clever face that he loved more than any other face

in the world, and then he raised her hands, which were as thick as a carpenter's, to his lips and kissed them and smelled them, and it was all exactly as he had expected it to be. And afterward, in the twilight of the Italian bombardment, the two of them sat next to the square brown table, his grandmother with her back to the sea and her face to the uncultivated fields and the Arab village, and Meir with his back to the brown wardrobe, which was later sold and replaced with a formica table, and the famous picture of his grandmother hanging on the wall above it, and they waited for his mother to come, and in the meantime they spoke about the rising prices and the political situation and various family affairs, with him doing his best in his broken Yiddish in order to make her happy, and even putting his hand on hers so that she would feel the love that filled him to overflowing, and as they chatted he told her about the relative from Houston, Texas, and the investigations into the family tree, and his grandmother smiled tolerantly, smoothing the velvet tablecloth repeatedly with the palm of her hand with the gesture he knew so well, as if she was trying to smooth away an invisible crease, and said, "I don't need all that. I always have the ones I want right here beside me," and she glanced into the thickets of the citrus grove, and Meir, who caught the direction of her glance, wanted to ask her when his mother would come, but he was careful not to move or speak, and she looked at him and said that his mother would come soon, and he nodded his head, full of gratitude, because he was afraid that any movement or spoken word would disrupt the happiness of that wonderful hour, which he wanted to go on forever, with all its nuances of light and shade and threads of scent stirring faintly in the summer twilight air.

His mother emerged from the trees in the white skirt divided down the middle like trousers in which she had been photographed next to the hut against the background of the big sycamore tree, and approached them panting slightly, her pure, rather pale face flushed from her haste and with a dewy freshness on it as if it had absorbed the chill of the twilight air, and she said, "The man in the bakery shop held me up," and sat down opposite him on the sofa with the wooden frame and the springs, and Meir, who could not take his eyes off her, wanted to go up to her and hug her and kiss her, but his anxiety and desire to hold her tight were so intense that he stayed where he was, barely breathing, and in the meantime a curtain of rain as soft as honey began falling on them and on the trees, and the tiny drops clung to their hair like splinters of golden light caught in the last rays of the sun filtering through the branches of the trees. And his mother took two bars of chocolate and two packages of chewing gum out of her wicker shopping basket and put them on the table and said that she had bought them for Weiss's children, and afterward she took out a brightly colored silk handkerchief, which she had bought for the little girl, it was her birthday after all, and later on, still rummaging in the depths of her basket, she brought out *Past Continuous* and put it on the table and said, "I'm going to take it with me to Gibraltar so that I'll have something to read," and in the end she brought out a set of pencils, which caught Meir's fancy and which he would very much have liked for himself, but he didn't even hint at it, and his grandmother took the set and felt the pencils with her thick fingers and said, "What lovely pencils. Where did you get them?" and his mother started putting everything back in her basket and said, "On Main Road behind the post office, but you can get them not far from King's Yard Lane too," and she cast a look full of love at Meir and said, "When you go to the Technion we'll buy some for you too," and he said, "It's quite all right, I don't need any pencils"—in his end-of-term essay he had written that he was going to be a leader and an inventor and a writer and a sportsman and an explorer, and he was certain that he would be, too, but he didn't mind learning something at the Technion as well if it would please his mother. And his grand-mother, partly to ward off the Evil Eye, but mainly to change the subject and avoid arguments that were not only pointless but might lead to the expression of ideas at variance with her own, said, "The main thing is that he should be healthy," and his mother said, "Yes, of course," but she went on nevertheless to say that in our day and age a man had to have some kind of education, otherwise he was lost, and she looked at him affectionately and said that time flew—school, high school, the army—and before you knew where you were the best years of your life were gone and what you didn't manage to get done then you would never succeed in doing later, and when a man grew older it was too late to mend matters, and Meir said, "Yes," and in his heart of hearts he tended to agree with her, but at the same time something inside him rebelled and rejected her words, because he felt in the marrow of his bones that he was young and would stay young forever, he did not doubt it for a moment because the truth of the matter was that the world was divided in two—the young and the old, those sentenced to live and those sentenced to die—and, luckily for him, he had been born young and therefore all this had nothing to do with him, and the time of which his mother spoke so anxiously seemed to him abundant and infinite, and as replete with desirable possibilities as the boundless air was replete with warmth and freshness and the light of the sun. His mother put everything back into her shopping basket and said, "I'm just going to drop in on Weiss for a moment and do a few chores in town and I'll be back before you know it," and his grandmother said, "You take too much on yourself. In the end you'll drop off your feet with exhaustion," and his mother said, "Don't worry, I'm fine," and took him by the hand and began walking through the trees toward the road that traversed the citrus grove and led out of it, and his grandmother said, "Wait, I'm coming with you," and his mother said, "What for? I'll be back soon," but his grandmother insisted and came hurrying to join them, which made Meir very happy, and when they reached the broad, red, unpaved road she held his other hand, and thus they walked down the road that led through the citrus grove, his mother on his right and his grandmother on his left with him in the middle, and he was filled with an inexpressible feeling of happiness and security because he knew, with the same mysterious, secret knowledge, that nothing would ever break their joyful unity.

And when they emerged from the grove, with the clean twilight sky above them, they went on walking down the dusty road, which crossed the uncultivated fields and continued along the straggly little vineyard and the melon patch with the mysterious hut, and after the big tamarisk tree, in the place where the dust road turned into the field and the straggly vineyard beyond it, they saw Gerda Altshuler coming toward them with a towel over her shoulder, looking as if she had just come from the sea, with a smile full of life on her face, and his mother and grandmother stopped to talk to her because they both liked her and she liked them, and they asked her how she was and she asked them how they were, especially his grandmother, and as she talked to them she stroked Meir's head as he stood there without moving, soaking up the affectionate caresses and smiling looks of this big-boned, sturdy woman with her open, lively face, who was as different from his parents as if she belonged to another world, and when they were about to part, she took a tennis ball out of her big leather bag and offered it to Meir, but his mother interfered and said, "No, no, that's quite unnecessary," and tried to take the ball away from him and give it back to Mrs. Altshuler, but she looked at him with a smile on her face and said, "It's quite all right, I love him and I've been wanting to give him a ball for a long time now." His mother was embarrassed and she thanked Mrs. Altshuler again and again, she felt uncomfortable because they belonged to different social strata, and she turned to him and told him to thank her, too, and he did so gladly because the gift of the ball made him so happy, and Mrs. Altshuler, a little overwhelmed by the flood of thanks, stroked his head again and said, "It's perfectly all right, as long as he doesn't climb into my studio through the shelter window," and his mother said, "No, no, he's a good boy," and they said good-bye to her and continued on their way.

As they started walking, his mother said, "See what you've been given! You must keep it for your birthday. Don't play with it here— it's a shame, it'll get dirty. Give it to me, or put it in your pocket before you lose it," and he stroked the ball and said, "I'll look after it," and suppressed his longing to throw it in the air and catch it because he was afraid it might get lost or dirty, too, and his mother said, "Counting the windmill and the train, you've got a lot of things already," and he said, "I don't like the windmill"—this was because of the cockroach that had suddenly fallen out of it, but he didn't tell his mother this, and she said, "You'll grow to like it," but all he could think about was the ball, surrounded by an aura of happiness, and his overwhelming desire to throw it up in the air and catch it, and his mother repeated, "Put it away in your pocket. You'll only lose it here," and Meir threw the ball in the air and caught it, and his mother said, "Don't play with it here, it would be a shame if it got lost or dirty," but he threw it up into the air again, and when he tried to catch it it slipped out of his hands and bounced away and rolled to the side of the road and his mother said, "I told you so," with a worried and disapproving expression on her face, and he ran and quickly picked it up and blew on it to remove the dust, and his mother said again, "This is no place to play with a ball," and his grandmother said, "Put it in your pocket," and he said, "In a minute," his happiness spoiled, and rubbed the ball to make it as white and shiny as before, but all in vain, a faint barely perceptible mark still clung to the ball, and his mother said, "Put it in your pocket," and urged him to walk faster, and thinking that he would wash it with soap and water as soon as he got home and that he would give the world for it to be as clean and white as it was before, he did as he was told and quickened his step. But soon afterward he couldn't control himself anymore and in spite of himself he took the ball out of his pocket and threw it in the air and caught it and immediately threw it up again, and his mother told him again to put the ball away and hurry up because he was lagging behind and holding them up, and he said, "I'm coming, I'm coming," and went on throwing the ball in the air and catching it, and from time to time it slipped out of his hands and rolled along the road or into the field, but he no longer cared, and he didn't stop even when he realized that they were receding into the distance, after telling him again to hurry up and threatening, especially his mother, to leave him there alone. For a moment, when he saw that they were on the point of vanishing from view, he thought of running after them, but the urge to go on playing was irresistible, and he didn't really believe that they would leave him alone in this strange and deserted place, and he went on playing even after their figures grew blurred and merged into the soft twilight shadows, and he remained all alone among the uncultivated fields and the vineyard and the melon patch, stricken by feelings of loneliness and abandonment, which gave rise in him, together with a mysterious fear, to a wave of bittersweet self-pity and a wish that something bad would happen to him that would hurt them very much, for it was already dusk and the place was strange and deserted, and on the other side of the melon patch, out of sight from where he stood, was the Arab's hut, and the feelings of abandonment and betrayal and self-pity spread through him, and he thought of how they would soon be sorry and come back for him and how he would make them beg and beg before he gave in to their pleas. His pleasure in the game had been spoiled, and after a while he put the ball in his pocket and sat down on a stone by the side of the road in the stillness of the fields, which he had not noticed up to now and which was full of tiny sounds of buzzing and clicking and the restless movement of invisible midges and gnats, and he let a breeze so gentle he could hardly feel it dry his sweat and decided to wait until his mother and grandmother came to take him home. And as he sat there surrounded by the pungent summer smell rising from the uncultivated fields and the vineyard and the melon patch, a heavy, dusty smell that grew clearer and purer, filling the evening air charged with its minute sounds and whispers and invisible scurrying movements, he was overwhelmed by an obscure, draining sense of longing and loss, which suffused the fields and the trees and bushes and the minute blades of grass and the ground he sat on and the darkening sky and the entire universe, as if the source of all the well-being in the world was slipping away and disappearing, and this feeling combined with the worry, which was already streaked with anger, at the continued absence of his mother and grandmother, and with a dull, creeping foreboding that seemed to rise in grayish vapors from these desolate uncultivated fields, and with the sense of impending departure, whose signs he had felt for some time now and which deep in his heart he already knew was inevitable.

When he saw Uncle Shmuel approaching, he felt a great sense of relief in addition to being very glad, which he would have been anyway, since he loved him more than any of the other family friends and relatives, and he would have risen to his feet and run to meet him,

but he was so surprised at his sudden appearance that he stayed where
he was and only sat up a little straighter. Uncle Shmuel came closer
in the gray hat and heavy, Polish winter coat, in which all his loneliness seemed to be embodied, with his right hand hidden behind his
back. The skin was stretched dry and taunt over his pale yellow
tubercular face, but the faint, mischievous smile was still there, and
all the gentleness and goodness, and when he reached Meir, he bowed
to him and whistled shrilly and whipped out his hand with a conjurer's
flourish to display the ice cream cone he had been hiding behind his
back and said, "This is for you, Your Majesty. I've already been
looking for you for half an hour in order to give it to you," and Meir,
whose joy and happiness were boundless, laughed and thanked him
and took the cone and began to lick the ice cream, which had begun
to melt, and Uncle Shmuel lifted the bottom of his coat and sat down
next to him on the ground and said, "It's good for your tonsils," and
stroked his head, and Meir wanted to tell him that his mother and
grandmother had gone to the Weisses and would be back soon, but
instead he licked the ice cream quickly to stop it from trickling down
the sides of the cone and making his fingers sticky and asked Uncle
Shmuel to whistle something for him, and Uncle Shmuel asked him
what he would like to hear and he said, "It doesn't matter," and Uncle
Shmuel smiled with his gentle, natural mischievousness, so different
from his own father, and then he grew serious and pursed his lips and
began to whistle one of his Polish songs. His whistling was clear and
tender, one moment straight as a thread and the next twittering like
a bird, and it flew over the sandy lot and the broad uncultivated fields
and the vineyards and melon patches, both those that were close at
hand and those that were out of sight, all the way to the invisible
orange groves and dusty eucalyptus glades beyond the acacia borders
and the sabra hedges, in the dry scent of the blossoming and the dust
and the smell of the smoke and the dung of the invisible Arab villages,
and climbed dizzily to the summery horizon, where the sounds were
gathered up and lingered a while until they died away. And Meir, who
sat listening to the whistling while he licked his ice cream, careful not
to waste a single drop, felt how close he was to his uncle and how

much he loved him, and when he had finished licking the ice cream, he bit the point of the cone and made a little hole in it and sucked the last of the ice cream through it, and in the end he slowly ate the cone itself, and a smile that was all pleasure and gratitude illuminated his face, and only the sweet stickiness on his fingers bothered him, and he rubbed them on the ground, and afterward in the grass, and then he spat on them and rubbed them in the ground again, and they still felt disagreeably sticky, even after he had rubbed them together and wiped them on his trousers and on the spotless handkerchief Uncle Shmuel gave him, and in the end he stood up, for he could on no account overcome the disagreeable feeling of stickiness, and returned the handkerchief and said that he was going to look for a tap to wash his hands, and Uncle Shmuel said, "All right, but be careful on your way. I'll wait for you here," and Meir said, "I'll be back in a moment," and started off down the dirt road.

He remembered that there was a tap somewhere on the other side of the melon patch, but he didn't want to go past the hut where the Arab Ahmed squatted on his dirty old mattress covered with its torn, stained mosquito net, and accordingly he turned off on a path that went around the vineyard, and crossed a large empty lot and reached the place he remembered on the other side, but there was no tap there, and he stopped and looked around him, puzzled and disappointed, trying to remember: no, he had no doubt that the tap had been there, he remembered it well, with the green weeds growing around it and the patches of moss on the pipe, and in the end he turned around to start back, it was getting rather late, but then he remembered that the tap was in another empty lot, a little farther north, beyond the great sycamore tree on the way to the red hills, and he started off in that direction and crossed the broad uncultivated field. He remembered that Uncle Shmuel was waiting for him, and perhaps his mother and grandmother had come back, too, and so he stepped out briskly, saying to himself that as soon as he found the tap he would wash his hands and go back, and he crossed another field and after it a sand dune and after that a broad empty lot, and there was something attractive in this solitary striding through the desola-

tion of these empty lots and uncultivated fields, with the slight anxiety
that accompanied it, and he could already see the sycamore tree in
the distance and the group of bushes beyond it, but here, too, there
was no tap to be found, and for a moment he stood looking around
him in bewilderment and disappointment, but no more than a moment, for he immediately remembered that the tap was farther on,
beyond the pile of stones and the sabra hedge, yes, he remembered
quite clearly, and he moved off again and started walking along the
narrow path, now he could feel the gentle but insistent urge, which
had apparently been hiding somewhere deep inside him again, and he
knew that no power on earth—neither Uncle Shmuel nor his mother
and grandmother, who must be waiting for him anxiously by now—
could stop him before he had completed his task, and he crossed the
enormous sandy plain stretching before him hollowed out like an
empty, frozen lake of sand, and then he crossed another empty lot,
and not far off he saw a little wood of dusty trees, and a pleasant
breeze blew into his face, apparently from the direction of the sea,
and refreshed him, and when he reached the top of the slope, almost
without realizing that he had left the sandy plains behind him and
was walking along the ridge of the hills, he saw somewhere on the hilly
plains on the other side of the valley, against the background of the
blue sky, a black curving wall, and for a moment he stopped to look
at it. The wind was more lively here and it penetrated the pores of
his skin and sunk into it until he himself became airy, and when he
descended the slope into the valley the black wall suddenly disappeared, and he felt a dread that filled his chest and legs with heaviness,
and for a moment he thought of going back, in the last analysis the
act and its end depended on his will, but he went on walking, and
when he started up the opposite slope, the wall appeared again, still
very far away, and he walked toward it as if he was being drawn on
invisible strings of fear and unconquerable curiosity, one moment it
seemed to him that he was standing still and the next that he was even
going backward, but he kept on walking, even more vigorously than
before, his curiosity turning into a heavy joy that surrounded him like
the oyster encasing a pearl, when suddenly, all at once, the distance

narrowed between himself and the curved black wall, which grew larger and larger until it almost covered the horizon and the sky, and something tightened and trembled inside him, and he said, "This is the end of the world," and for a split second he thought of turning back, but he only slowed down a little until he reached the wall and stood before it, and he waited a moment, something very heavy like a clotted lump of air turned over in his chest and his breath was almost dislocated with the force of the exaltation and the awe, and then he raised his eyes, but there was nothing to see apart from the black wall covering the landscape and the sky like a tidal wave, and he stretched out his hand with his eyes closed and felt the wall, which was like a jelly of thin, moist cobwebs of air, and at the same time he felt himself, very gently and buoyantly, as if he were floating, being drawn into it, and something dense and at the same time as light and insubstantial as foam lapped him in a sense of immeasurable well-being, and something within him soundlessly surmised, "This is divine bliss," and he knew that it was indeed so.

Afterward he opened his eyes and saw a pristine darkness, dense and black as could be and at the same time absolutely translucent, which did not prevent him from seeing the colored circles of light appearing and disappearing in the twinkling of an eye, or the spots of light trembling somewhere in the darkness and instantly swallowed up in it, nor yet the tender radiance like the brightness of the sun before dawn that appeared whenever he opened his eyes—but he did not open them often, and most of the time he lay curled up or floated upright or perhaps upside down with his eyes closed, half awake and half asleep, steeped in a fresh, pure serenity and a pleasurable weightlessness, hearing no sounds and feeling no pain, and at the same time he saw the faces of his mother and grandmother, which were nothing but the same spots of light, staying a while and vanishing, but he felt no longing for them or sorrow at parting, as if there were vast deserts of time and distance yawning between them, and once or twice a bird flew over, too, leaving a slight crease in the darkness, which was immediately smoothed out, behind it. And afterward, or perhaps even before this, or at the same time, he felt his flesh growing soft and pure, cleansed of any jarring discord or pain or dullness, as if piles of dust and dirt were being washed out of it and all its wrinkles were being dissolved, and so, too, his spirit, which was purified of any desire or anxiety or any thoughts or memories, which all dropped away and were swallowed up in the juicy darkness, and his body and spirit became one, a warm, dense juice flowing along its invisible, pulsating courses, until there was nothing left of him at all, while he himself, the thing which had been present in his body, remained as the shadow cast on a wall when the thing that had cast the shadow was gone, and at the same time, steeped as he was in the swooning, drowsy pleasure of the loss of his corporeality, he did not cease to sense his own existence, and afterward, very slowly, as in an everlasting stream, a warm, blissful flow like the steady trickle of milk into the mouth, something soft began to grow around him like a web of feathery down, and a very delicate but very distinct smell, like the smell of a baby's milky vomit, rose from him and his heart contracted within him in a delicious yearning, and then all of a sudden he felt a cruel, wrenching pain, as if some great force was trying to tear him limb from limb, and at first he tried to protest but he was rudely and violently pushed, subjected to jolting pressures and shocks, everything was terrifying and merciless, and suddenly the pressure increased unendurably, so cruel and painful that a shriek stuck in his throat, and a strong hand gripped him and pulled him, and he felt himself slithering, and all of a sudden the pressure stopped and for a moment he felt relief, and someone said, "Here we are," but then a glaring light hit him pitilessly in the eyes, and he felt the stinging cold slap his body until he shivered and shrank and burst into bitter tears, full of fear and insult and helplessness, and he didn't stop crying even when competent hands dried him and swaddled him and tried to comfort him, until he grew tired and calmed down, and someone took him carefully and held him up a little and said, "What a beautiful child."

Afterword

During the last year of his life, when doubt as to whether he would be able to finish the book on which he had been working for three years was gnawing at his heart, Yaakov would get up after putting in long hours of work at his desk and announce, "That's it—I'm done for today!" And then he would frequently pat the pages piling up on the corner of the desk and add: "You see this, woman—this is my will!" and his smile would slightly dispel the dread gathering like a dark cloud at the edges of our lives.

It was these words of his that encouraged me to attempt the impossible—to finish the book without its author. And the book is all his. There is not one word in it that he did not write, but not all the words he wrote are in the book.

Yaakov Shabtai, who overflowed with ideas, formulations, alternative words—everyone who ever worked with him was familiar with this prodigality—and who always strove for the one, right word, the exact formulation, the height of perfection—developed in this, his last book, a method of writing that consisted of many alternatives, side by side, on every level: the word, the sentence, the paragraph, the plot. And the manuscript (which was rewritten three times, one after the other) thus included many variations and different, though approximate, possibilities. In the spring of the last year of his life, on his birthday, he began the last stage of composition, which in his eyes was the hardest of all—the stage of final editing and rewriting, in which he selected from all the possibilities the one, right, conclusive one. He managed to do this in two of the chapters, the second and the third, and what he did not manage to accomplish himself remained as his will, and my command.

In addition to the manuscript in all its different versions, there were also many comments, notes, and instructions that he was in the habit of jotting down for his own use, and to which I was able to turn for guidance when it became my task to select one of the many possibilities he had envisaged. I relied, too, of course, on the many things he had said to me about his writing methods, preferences, and inclinations—and it was mainly about the book that he spoke during that last year: "Come hell or high water"—he would say with that smile of his—"I'll do what I must."

He would often show me passages from the book and ask me to tell him which of the "alternatives," as he called them, seemed best to me. And I could say which I preferred because I knew that in the last resort the choice would be his. But now the manuscript lay before me, abandoned in the middle, and in order for it to come out, I had to take the responsibility for the choice, the responsibility for the book, on myself.

I was not alone in this task. By my side stood Professor Dan Miron, who was very close to Yaakov in his last years, and who never stopped urging him to finish the work on the book. And from the first day, still stunned and grieving, he repeated: "The book must come out. We'll bring it out." Dan Miron went over the manuscript and assisted me in the work of selection and deletion, and in the end he did the final editing. There are no words to express my gratitude to him for his extraordinary generosity and cooperation.

Thanks to the faith of many of Yaakov's friends and my own, and knowing how eagerly those who loved him and admired his work were awaiting this last book whose title *Sof Davar** he gave it a few days before he died I found the courage within myself to carry out his will and "end the matter" for him. . . .

Edna Shabtai
March 8, 1983

**Sof Davar,* the Hebrew title of the book, is a reference to Eccles. 12:13 and means "the end of the matter." It can also mean "epilogue" or "in conclusion." The English title of the two novels *Past Continuous* and *Past Perfect* were suggested by the author himself.